"Aniagolu states that this is a 'fictional novel', but for those who live with the aftermath of rape, suicide, or reproductive endangerment, the characters and events are excerpts from the real…"

Dr. Tanya Tammie Fowler
Folklorist & Bio-Medical Anthropologist
Philadephia, Pennsylvania

"Two weeks later, it was my turn to be cleansed…chilling words propel the plot…Mikela goes through a self-discovery process and maturation as she tackles the scars of female rites of passage and rape…Aniagolu reveals tradition's stronghold on a society and the triumph of the human spirit…"

Lovette Chinwah, Ph.D.
Chair, Communications & Humanities Dept.,
Central State University, Wilberforce, Ohio

MIKELA

MIKELA

❁

Memoirs of a Maasai Woman

A Fiction Novel

Jacyee Aniagolu-Johnson

iUniverse, Inc.
New York Lincoln Shanghai

MIKELA
Memoirs of a Maasai Woman

All Rights Reserved © 1998 and 2004 by Jacinta Aniagolu

No part of this book may be reproduced or transmitted in any form or by any means, graphic, electronic, or mechanical, including photocopying, recording, taping, or by any information storage retrieval system, without the written permission of the publisher.

iUniverse, Inc.

For information address:
iUniverse, Inc.
2021 Pine Lake Road, Suite 100
Lincoln, NE 68512
www.iuniverse.com

ISBN: 0-595-30677-2

Printed in the United States of America

This book is dedicated to Almighty God. Also, to all young girls who have experienced female circumcision and to the victims of rape—be of courage, strength, and have renewed hope for a brighter tomorrow.

Contents

Chapter 1	Flashback to Tradition	3
Chapter 2	Birth of Precious Jewels	17
Chapter 3	In the Name of Tradition	27
Chapter 4	Flight from Tradition	36
Chapter 5	A Guardian Light	45
Chapter 6	Fledgling Talent	54
Chapter 7	Rape of Innocence	65
Chapter 8	Gloomy Days Ahead	77
Chapter 9	Unraveling the Mystery of the White Knight	83
Chapter 10	Unveiling Talent	94
Chapter 11	A Handsome Knight Emerges	107
Chapter 12	Tragedy Strikes	115
Chapter 13	The "Bright Traveler"	126
Chapter 14	New Strides	132
Chapter 15	Aisha Mohammed—The Arabian Princess	141
Chapter 16	Another Crossroad	154
Chapter 17	A New Season	167
Chapter 18	Links to the Past	176
Chapter 19	Union of Two Souls	184
Chapter 20	Haunting Scares	187
Chapter 21	The Past Emerges in Manhattan	195
Chapter 22	A New Trail	201

Chapter 23 An Emotional Return............................214
Chapter 24 A Lasting Friendship 223
Chapter 25 Final Absolution and Triumph....................226
About the Author..235

Acknowledgements

I would like to thank my love, Lamonte Johnson, for his unconditional support; my sister, Uche Aniagolu, for believing in Mikela; my sister Chichi for her detailed review of the manuscript; my brother, Emeka, for his special assistance; and my special prayer partner, my sister, Memoo.

Writing this book would not have been possible without the support of my mom and dad, Justice Anthony and Mrs. Maria Aniagolu, and my other brothers and sisters: Tony, Chuka, Lolly, Kizi, and Nwachu. You are all such a wonderful blessing to me.

Special thanks to my editor, Stephanee Killen, for her time and devotion to this book.

"You gain strength, courage and confidence by every experience in which you really stop to look fear in the face. You are able to say to yourself, 'I have lived through this horror. I can take the next thing that comes along.' You must do the thing you think you cannot do."

Eleanor Roosevelt (1884–1962)
United Nations Diplomat, humanitarian, and wife of U.S. President Franklin D. Roosevelt

It all started in the Tanzanian Maasailand:

CHAPTER 1

❀

Flashback to Tradition

My name is Mikela Elimu-Williams. I'm a twenty-three-year-old artist—a painter of my ethnic culture, French beaux-arts, and European Renaissance history. Art is my passion. Through it, I express my memories, emotions, and visual perspectives.

My love for art started twenty years ago when I was barely two years old, and it has taken me much time to come to terms with my past and who I am. I am a Maasai, and my journey and life's experiences started in the Tanzanian Maasailand where I was born. It has been a long journey for me—a journey that I will share with you. I have finally come to accept my life, and my past no longer haunts me.

It all started with my mother's story in the Tanzanian Maasailand, where my family still lives…

First, the Dream:

She cradled her beautiful twin babies in her arms—peacefully, they sucked their fingers. She kissed them gently on their cheeks and laid them down on the padded, hide-skin cradles. Then she covered them with a warm cloth and quietly lay down beside them. A short while later, she stepped outside to feel the cool breeze of the night faintly caress her body. It was a perfect night, with pitch-dark skies lit by glittering stars.

The exotic beauty of our Maasailand is a marvel of our Creator Enkai, she thought, as she stepped back into her *boma*, a typical Maasai hut built with grass, dry sticks, and twigs, and covered with cow dung for insulation.

Inside, for a moment, she thought her eyes were playing tricks on her—one of her babies was gone. She came closer and felt the warm cover without feeling the soft touch of her baby's body.

How could this be? I was only outside for a moment, and no one could have sneaked in without my seeing them, she thought.

Instantly, she realized what had happened. She became hysterical and called out, "Where's my baby? Oh, Enkai! Where is my baby?"

Then, in a flash, she heard someone's voice.

"Halima! Halima! Which baby are you talking about? Wake up, Halima! You're having one of your nightmares again."

"It's my baby, I can't find her," Halima said, still somewhat half asleep.

"Halima, your babies are fine. You were just having a dream. Wake up! It's almost 6:30 AM, and you are to make breakfast for the family today."

Halima was still asleep and turned to face the other side of her sleeping mat.

"Halima! Halima!" Aunt Asura called out again. "It's time to get up." She knelt next to the woman, gently shaking her awake.

My mother Halima was a very young woman—an *Esiankiki*. She'd just turned twenty years old. As part of the Maasai tradition, her head, like that of other Maasai women, had been shaved bald. Hair was considered a sign of assertiveness and an undesirable female feature in the Maasailand. Still, she was a striking tall and thin lady, with nicely defined facial features, including a small, straight nose and almond-shaped eyes, though yellowed from exposure to the dust from the strong winds of the Maasai plains. She had unremarkable thin eyebrows and eyelashes and a long face that ended with a pointed chin. Her uniquely sculptured face was accentuated by her well-defined cheekbones and curved, thin lips. Overall, even with her frail look, her height gave her a very graceful look.

"Halima, you are so beautiful…your graceful gait, along with your long and elegant neck, makes you look like a gazelle at sunset," Elimu once told her while she lay in the warmth of his bosom.

The ritual of celebrating Halima's eighth-month-old pregnancy had just been performed. During this ceremony, she was made to wear a sheepskin skirt and cape, fashioned of a sheep that had been killed by Elimu that morning. As a sign of purity, the fat and blood of the sheep was smeared over her face and body. Also, she drank water from a gourd and wore a grass necklace for future blessings. The celebration continued with all women and children from her homestead eating the ribs of one side and the front leg of the sheep.

Halima was, at the time, eight months pregnant with twins and was the youngest wife of an older man—forty-five-year-old Elimu, who was my father. At the time, my father was already a Maasai *Ilpayianis* who had three older wives prior to my mother. He was also one of many Maasai *Ilpayianis* who boasted of having four beautiful wives, three of whom could be called *Intasatis* because they were already mothers.

Halima still remembered quite vividly when Elimu came with his close relatives to visit her parents at their *boma*.

"Halima! Halima, my daughter!" her mother Naponu called out jovially.

"Mama, I'm here in the kitchen," Halima answered.

"Please come quickly…someone is here to see you."

"Yes, Halima, come my dear," her father, Saitoti echoed in a high-spirited voice.

Halima ran quickly to meet her parents.

"Here she is…Halima, my child, please sit down," Saitoti said, his face beaming with an unusual and exaggerated smile.

Halima smiled and curled up on the hide-skin mat next to her father.

"All these are for you," Saitoti said, stretching to give Halima beautiful Maasai necklaces, bracelets, and anklets.

"These gifts are for you…they are all from Elimu," Naponu said, smiling and looking in the direction of the man seated next to her.

Halima stared at the gifts and then at the man bearing them, and for moment she was gripped with disbelief. It had suddenly become clear to her what was going on. Her parents had decided to give her away to an older man, and she was barely thirteen years old.

Halima remembered swallowing very hard and forcing a smile, as she said, "Welcome, sir."

Elimu responded with a nod and smiled at the same time, exposing his yellowing and crooked teeth. He was not lanky and tall like most Maasai men. Instead, he was short, standing no more than five feet five inches tall, but characteristically very thin. He had a naturally lean face, narrowly shaped eyes, and smallish facial features. At the age of forty-five, he had lost most of his hair, which made him look puckish.

Saitoti and Naponu continued their conversation with Elimu, while Halima listened and wished at the same time that she could escape the impending marriage. She had secretly hoped that her father would change his mind and send her to school, as her friend Nashilu's parents had done when they converted to Christianity and started attending the local church. But her father had refused up until now, and with the present situation, Halima knew that the dream would never materialize.

About thirty minutes later, her parents acknowledged her presence once again, jolting Halima's thoughts back to her immediate surroundings.

"Elimu has come to ask for your hand in marriage. Halima, Elimu will be back in a few weeks when he'll pay the bride price.

"Now that you have seen him, do you like him?" Saitoti asked, wearing a nervous smile, feverishly hoping that Halima would not reject Elimu.

Halima nodded, forcing a smile.

"Now, that's my lovely daughter…I know you'll like Elimu…he's a very good man and husband," Halima's father said, while extending his hand towards Elimu for a handshake.

Seeing Saitoti's obvious approval of him, Elimu seemed to put on a permanent, forced smile as a visible expression of acquiescence with his father-in-law to be. Instinctively, he stole a glance at Halima, but she looked away, wishing she could run away from the scene.

Later that evening, her mother, Naponu tried to ease Halima's obvious tense mood.

"My dear, you didn't seem happy to meet Elimu? Why?"

"Mama, isn't he too old?" Halima asked.

"No, he's not. I was your age when your father came for me. You need a husband who can take care of you."

"Yes, Mama, but does he have to be so old?"

"Halima, Elimu is a well respected man. He is also a good man who loves his three wives dearly. He told your father and me that you'll be his favorite wife because you are so young and beautiful," Naponu said, expressing her approval of Elimu.

Naponu was right because my mother, Halima, soon became Elimu's favorite wife. My mother's name, Halima, depicted her gentle, humane, and kind nature—traits that she possessed in abundance. Her heritage was predominantly nomadic cattle herdsman from southern Sudan—a mixed race of Rashaida nomads and Dinka Sudanese. The Rashaida nomads were believed to have migrated from Saudi Arabia and intermarried with the Dinkas. Her ancestors were a mixed blend of racial heritage and had, over a period of four hundred years, wandered to various places in search of greener pastures for their cattle. Her great-grandparents finally settled in the open plains of the Maasailand in the Arusha region of Tanzania. They were well received by the native Maasai, who lived in *enkangs* or a collection of huts that they called *bomas.* Over the years, with resettlement by the Tanzanian government, Maasai *bomas* were later scattered around the Kiteto, Simanjiro, and Ngorongoro districts.

My mother Halima was born on May 20, 1946. She was raised as a typical Maasai woman and spoke the lingua Maa fluently. At twenty years of age, she'd already been married to my father Elimu for seven years. She still remembered, very vividly, the day she became Elimu's youngest wife—just before her thirteenth birthday. Her childless state seven years later made it seem like she'd been married to Elimu for an eternity. Finally, eight months ago, Mama Asura, the only midwife in the *enkang,* gave my mother the good news about her pregnancy.

"You are expecting twin baby girls," she said to Halima, with joy.

"Oh! Mama Asura, I'm overwhelmed with happiness," Halima responded, as she hugged her and started to dance in circles.

"I'll name them Mikela and Nadia when they are born," Halima said excitedly.

"But these are not Maasai names…why do you want to give your twins such names?" Mama Asura asked curiously.

"Mama Asura, these names mean a lot to me…Mama Nashilu's twin daughters were named Mikela and Nadia; they were born two years after her first child Nashilu was born, whom she named after herself."

"Who is Mama Nashilu?" Mama Asura asked.

"She was a very close friend of my mother, who lived in a neighboring *enkang* to my parents, and her daughter Nashilu was my best friend before I was married off and came to live here. After my father died and my mother became very ill, Mama Nashilu took care of her until she died."

"So, what will Elimu say about all this…he has always given his babies Maasai names," Mama Asura asked thoughtfully.

"He'll have no choice because I've waited for a long time for my babies, and he also knows how much I suffered when my mother was ill."

"Well, I'm sure he'll go along with it. Everyone says that you are his favorite wife…I believe that, too," Mama Asura said and shrugged.

Mama Asura was the first and oldest wife of my father and was forty years old at the time Elimu married Halima. She was a petite woman, barely five feet four inches tall, and weighed roughly ninety pounds. Like all other Maasai women, she was bald. She had a smooth, round face with smallish features and sparkling white, round-shaped eyes. Her lips were much fuller than usual for a

Maasai, and she had long eyelashes and slightly heavy eyebrows that always looked bushy.

Mama Asura was a highly energetic woman and her sparkling eyes often expressed her positive drive. She was very proud of being a Maasai and almost always dressed in Maasai clothing, adorned with their classic jewelry, most of which she'd inherited from her mother. According to her family history, she'd come from a lineage of pure Maasai who had not intermarried with other ethnic groups for seventy-five years.

Mama Asura was also an experienced midwife, who had been trained by her own mother in their traditional Maasai way. Her record for successful deliveries was rather impressive; in the past twenty years, out of the hundreds of babies that she had delivered, she had only lost five babies and two mothers. Some women from the neighboring *enkangs* made it a point to seek out Asura just to have her deliver their babies. They said she had the ancestral touch and knew how to get even a breached baby to turn head down just before delivery.

Everyone in the *enkang* believed that Mama Asura had a magical gift; they believed that she could predict whether a pregnant woman would have a girl or boy. The rumor was that she had a sixth sense and could see through walls and a woman's womb. Many tried and failed to get Mama Asura to divulge the secret that she'd learned from her own mother. The closest answer they got from her was a promise that she would pass on the information to her oldest daughter, who planned to be a midwife.

As the oldest wife, Mama Asura was also responsible for monitoring the housekeeping roster. This morning, kneeling at Halima's matside, Mama Asura raised her voice again, calling out Halima's name as she tried to wake her. Finally, Halima opened her eyes, looked around, and saw Mama Asura next to her.

"Good morning, Asura. How long have you been up?" she asked, letting out a yawn.

"I woke up half an hour ago; one of my children was calling out for me in her sleep, and I went to calm her. It seems like you, too, were having one of your nightmares again," Mama Asura said.

"Yes, I was, and it was a very bad one. This time, someone stole one of my twin baby girls. It's such a relief to wake up."

"Why do you keep having these awful dreams, Halima? You know your babies are well and kicking, and nothing is going to happen to them."

"Yes, I know that," Halima said, touching her protruding stomach gently. "Maybe my mind worries when I am asleep."

"Perhaps you think too much about your pregnancy when you are awake. You are worrying unnecessarily because your babies are fine. I've delivered enough babies to know when to anticipate a problem," Mama Asura said confidently.

"Yes, I believe you—I trust your experience Mama Asura," Halima replied. She yawned again. "I must get up and start preparing breakfast."

"Yes, Halima, we'll all be waiting for your delicious meal this morning. We won't excuse you from doing your wifely duties, at least not yet—your pregnancy is still a month away from full term," Asura replied, teasing Halima with her eyes.

Halima nodded. "Okay, I'm up now."

Ten minutes later, Halima emerged from her *boma*.

"Good morning, Halima," Mama Túlélèi shouted from where she stood in front of her own *boma*, which was located a few yards away from Halima's.

"Good morning, Mama Túlélèi. How are you today?" Halima replied.

"I'm very well, Halima. I should be asking you how you are feeling today."

"Mama Túlélèi, the babies can't seem to stop kicking. But I'm lucky to have Mama Asura, who's been taking good care of me," Halima said, rubbing her belly protectively.

"Isn't Mama Asura such a blessing to us all?" Túlélèi said, smiling.

When Halima nodded, Túlélèi added, "Well, today is another beautiful day in our *enkang;* we're blessed here in the Tanzanian Maasai region."

"Yes, we are. I've just been watching the brilliant rays of the sunrise that have already filled the skies over there, east of our Maasaiplains—look over there!" Halima exclaimed.

"Yes, I see it—it's beautiful, and the air is so fresh and crisp today," Túlélèi added.

"Yes, I'm enjoying the cool winds moving over to the eastern plains from the west," Halima said.

Mama Túlélèi smiled. "I feel it, too…that's why I came outside. I love to hear the birds." Túlélèi's face shined with feelings of contentment.

Halima nodded and smiled.

Mama Túlélèi was the second wife of my father. She was a tall and slender Maasai woman who was about six feet tall. She looked more Somalian than Maasai, although she'd always insisted that she was of pure Maasai ancestry. She had clear and slanted eyes with thinly lined eyebrows and long eyelashes; a small, pointed nose; and a long face that narrowed into a somewhat oval chin.

Her high cheekbones along with her lighter-brown complexion gave her an uncharacteristic Maasai appearance.

"Halima, I must leave you now, so you can get on with the kitchen duties today," Túlélèi said, watching Halima stretch and let out a loud yawn.

"Yes, Mama Túlélèi, you're right, before I forget that I'm responsible for the family's revolving kitchen duties today. I'm off now," Halima replied.

Equipped with a calabash and a beaded, animal skin-covered gourd that had been cleaned with burning embers, she headed for the barn to milk some cows. The breakfast menu was fresh milk, wild honey, *ghee,* or cow milkfat, and cornmeal for their husband, Elimu, his three wives, and their collective eight children.

I hope the lady cows are in the mood to give me good milk today, Halima thought, as she walked over to the family barn.

For a moment, she stared at the lean and tall cows.

"I think I'll start with her; she seems to be in a good mood," she said out loud, moving toward a lady cow with a black and white skin pattern. It stood by the edge of the barn munching dried elephant grass.

When Halima got closer, the lady cow turned its expressionless gaze towards her.

"Okay! I'm not so sure you are in a good mood today after all. Sometimes, it's hard to read the mood of a lady cow," Halima muttered under her breath.

"Is it okay for me to get some of your milk?" she asked, gently patting the lady cow that once again turned to the other direction and stared mindlessly into open space. Halima caressed its back for a few minutes before starting to clean and massage its huge nipples.

For the next ten minutes, watery white milk drained in spurts from its large breasts into the calabash before dwindling into trickles.

"That's enough from you today. It's time for me to move on to another lady cow," Halima said.

She went in turns to five other lady cows, and when her calabash was heavy with nature's finest milk, she headed back to the kitchen area.

An hour later, breakfast was ready and served outside in the centrally located atrium.

"Mama Halima, thank you for the meal," the children echoed, as everyone gathered in their common eating area situated in the middle of the collective *bomas.*

"You'd better wait to thank me until after you've had the meal," Halima replied, laughing and trying to mask the pain that she was feeling in the lower part of her belly. She was finding household chores harder to do, as her due date got closer.

So far, for my mother, Halima, it had already been a very difficult pregnancy, even with all of Mama Asura's coaching and advice. During the first month of her first trimester, she could barely eat, except for a mostly watery mixture of corn meal, milk, and green extracts from a Maasai age-long recipe of vitamin-rich, mixed herbs. She vomited often, and by the end of her first trimester, she had already lost well over ten pounds, making her look even skinnier than usual. Her long legs were straight and trim, and even with her pregnancy, she still had a narrow waistline that had barely expanded. In fact, it was hard to tell from her physique that she was already eight months pregnant.

Looking at the beautiful woman she had turned into would certainly not have come as a surprise to those who knew her growing up, because even as a little child she had caused the quickening of many men's hearts. Yet, no one begrudged her beauty because she was such a gentle spirit and always seemed to exude a sense of serenity and peace from within her.

After breakfast with the entire family—one husband, four wives, and eight children—Halima settled down alone on a hide-skin mat spread in front of her *boma* to rest her tired legs and quietly dozed off.

A Tradition of Cleansing a Woman:

Half an hour later, she woke up. Now rested, she was eager to complete the beading work that she'd started weeks ago on a hide wrap skirt. The skirt was for her little second cousin, Aunt Mara's youngest daughter Leela, who had just turned thirteen. Aunt Mara was Halima's mother's first cousin, who lived with her own family in a neighboring *enkang* that was about thirty minutes away.

"I need to sew all these brightly colored glass beads around the hem of this skirt in the next hour," Halima muttered to herself as she tried to quicken the pace of her sewing, not wishing to shorten her stay with her aunt to avoid walking back home in the dark.

As she sewed, she thought of her Aunt Mara who had been a powerhouse of strength for her since her own mother died. She was not a flashy looking woman, but Aunt Mara had the mark of a leader and an authority that everyone seemed to respect despite her petite and unassuming physique and boyish looks. She commanded the respect of most women in her *enkang*, as well as that of her husband's other wives, because she was a highly organized and dependable person who knew a lot about the Maasai history and tradition.

Halima relied on her for explanations that she'd never gotten from her own mother about the Maasai culture.

Aunt Mara had been married to her husband for twenty years and had two children. Her nineteen-year-old son had left two years previously for Nairobi and vowed never to return to the Maasailand. On this day, Leela, her thirteen-year-old daughter, was being "cleansed" and prepared for marriage and womanhood.

Halima remembered all too well her own initiation. She had been the same age as Leela when she'd gone through the painful experience. It was an ordeal that she and other Maasai women could relate to that would cling to her own memory forever. She remembered the day that her mother had called her to a meeting with a group of older Maasai women.

"Halima, today will be a beautiful day for you," she said.

As Halima thought about what her mother said, another woman grabbed her from behind and started to strip her naked. Then, the woman placed her on a hide-skin mat that had been softened with animal fat.

"Now, spread her legs apart," one woman said, as others pinned her firmly on the ground before putting a blindfold on her. At the same time, two other women held down her arms, spreading her legs as wide apart as possible and virtually immobilized her to the ground. What happened next, Halima remembered, had crippled her body for months and lingered forever on her mind.

She also recalled one of the women saying, "Stay still, Halima; it's not so painful," as she grabbed the middle part of her sacred self. A split second later, Halima felt excruciating pain, and her body erupted into spasms.

"Oh! Enkai, help me," she screamed out loud, her legs trembling from the pain. Blood oozed out and trickled down between her legs.

As her body struggled to handle the pain, she felt another sharp jab in the same area. Her body went into spasms, and she passed out before the women started to stitch her together. A tiny opening was left for her to pass urine, but most of her sacred self was stitched together. The stitches were not removed until after she was married to Elimu. It was Mama Asura who unstitched her; female circumcision was one of her other specialties, in addition to midwifery.

Halima still remembered very vividly when she'd regained consciousness—it had been in her mother's *boma*. She'd opened her eyes and seen her mother sitting next to her. Her mother's gentle touch was caressing the top of her left palm, and her eyes were gazing straight into hers. Her conscious state triggered a warm smile from her mother, followed by a battery of questions.

"Halima, I'm glad you are awake now. Are you feeling better? Did you sleep well, my dear?"

Halima remembered just staring back at her mother without any words escaping from her mouth.

"You did well. I'm so proud of you, and so are the other women in our *enkang*...You were very brave...I knew you could do it...I told them that you've always been my brave little girl. You have a strong Maasai spirit."

Halima also remembered being in too much pain to respond to her mother.

"It's okay, you don't have to say anything. I know it will be a while before the pain stops...then, it will all be behind you. I have prepared a hot meal for you...here, let me help you get up so you can eat some of it."

A meal was the last thing that Halima wanted, she recalled. What she really wanted was for her mother to leave her alone. She was still feeling a thumping pain in her sacred self—it felt sore and wet, and the lower part of her stomach ached.

Her mother tried to make light of what had been done to her.

"Halima, the pain will soon turn into great joy for you. You have now been initiated into womanhood. It's an honor in our tradition."

Halima remembered turning away from her mother as tears rolled down her face. Her body was hurting, and so was her heart. She felt like her mother had let her down. She'd allowed the *enkang* women to hurt her. She felt angry and betrayed by her own mother.

My mother Halima said that at first she tried to say a few words but simply couldn't. Then she paused and tried again, and finally the words came stuttering from her mouth, as a stream of tears flooded her face.

"Ma, why do we have to do this? Why? I don't understand any of this."

"Halima, tradition is not meant for a little girl like you to understand. You're too young to ask questions or to understand our tradition. I'm here to guide you through it, and all you need to do is to follow me," was her mother's response.

My mother Halima said that she knew it was pointless to ask her mother to explain any part of the Maasai tradition to her. Her mother never believed in questioning tradition, and Halima believed that her mother probably didn't understand most of it herself anyway because her grandmother had never answered questions about the Maasai tradition. Halima often turned to her mother's first cousin, Aunt Mara, to answer any questions that she had.

A few months after Halima's circumcision, she was betrothed to my father, Elimu, a man who was old enough to be her own father. Although Elimu was a well-respected man in their *enkang,* he would not have been Halima's own choice for a husband because he already had three other wives. She did not know him, and she was not physically attracted to him. Given the choice, she would have selected one of the other *ilmurrans,* or young men, she had spotted around the *enkang.* But, typically, as a young Maasai girl, she would never have been given the choice to select her own husband. She also knew that she dared not turn Elimu down because he had already paid her parents a handsome bride price—a cow or more—that they would have to give back if she refused to marry him. For Halima, refusing Elimu was simply unthinkable, as she was not prepared to bear the wrath of her parents or to embarrass them in the *enkang.*

Soon afterwards, she married Elimu, a man who was thirty-eight years old at the time and a perfect stranger to her. Her parents were visibly happy on her wedding day. They felt quite honored to have a son-in-law who was very well respected for his wisdom and knowledge. This was actually the meaning of the name, "Elimu."

During the first year of her marriage, Halima endured extremely painful times of intimacy with her husband. Lovemaking was not something she desired because it felt as though the walls of her sacred self were coming apart. She couldn't complain to Elimu for fear that she would come across as critical of her husband. She finally summoned up the courage to ask Mama Asura for some advice. Disappointingly, Mama Asura's response was hardly encouraging.

"Halima, what happens is that the scar tissue around your sacred self sometimes breaks apart and exposes fresh skin, and you start to bleed. I felt the same way, but in time, the pain will stop," Asura explained.

"But is it normal for a woman to bleed for days after that?" Halima remembered asking.

Asura cleared her throat and then stared at Halima for moment, sensing the young woman's desperate need for an answer.

Mama Asura lowered her head before responding to Halima.

"Yes, it is. I went through it myself."

"Sometimes, Mama Asura, I have extreme soreness for weeks and just walking around the *enkang* seems like a big chore," Halima complained.

"Well, as Maasai women, we must learn to endure such pain. That is part of our Maasai tradition. I'm sure that your mother has told you that our husband appreciates us better once we are 'cleansed.' We must endure the pain for his pleasure because he is our husband," Asura responded.

Halima nodded, forcing a smile to hide her despair. "Yes, Asura, I know you're right. My mother explained that to me."

Halima remembered all too well how her mother drummed into her mind the belief that the ritual of female circumcision had cleansed her, and that her chastity was saved for marriage by stitching together the fragile walls of her sacred self.

Her mother's words still echoed in her mind.

"Halima, you must endure the pain—that is the pride of womanhood. It's an old and respected tradition of the Maasai people. When you endure the pain for your husband, you show him that you are a true and worthy woman."

At the time of her cleansing, my mother Halima said that she wished she had not gone through it because she hated what the pain did to her body.

After so many years since I left home, I still remember a conversation that my mother Halima told my sister Nadia and I that she had with Mama Asura one night shortly after she married Elimu. I believe my mother was preparing us for the future after our initiation into womanhood as she rehearsed from memory her conversation with Mama Asura.

"Mama Asura, I know I am supposed to please Elimu…you know what I mean?…but I just can't bear the pain anymore."

"Shhhhhhh…Halima, please keep your voice down, so the children won't hear you. Elimu is our husband, and he must enjoy us as he wishes."

"I can't take the pain anymore…I know he is our husband, but the circumcision has made my walls very fragile, and I bleed every time he plays with me…you know what I mean?"

"Yes, I do, because I have had the same experience…. Don't worry, the pain will go away, Halima…I promise you it will."

"So, why can't Elimu wait until I heal…why can't he?" Halima asked almost defiantly, an attitude that was completely out of character for her.

"Shhhhhhhh…please, Halima, keep your voice down. What if Elimu hears you? If he or other men in our *enkang* hear what you are saying, we'll be in trouble."

"Yes, I know, Mama Asura…I know."

"Halima! Halima!" The deep, stern voice echoed in the stillness of the night.

"Oh! Enkai, it's Elimu…I told you to keep your voice down! Do you think he heard you?"

"I don't know…I don't think so," Halima said, unnerved by Elimu's voice.

"Halima! Halima!" he called out again.

"I'm here!" Halima answered.

"I've been waiting for you. Are you coming?"

"Yes, I am, Elimu," Halima said, as she looked at Mama Asura and sighed.

"I can't take the pain anymore, Mama Asura…please, can you have him tonight?"

"But he wants you, not me."

"Please, Mama Asura," Halima said and started to cry.

"Okay, I'll try."

"Papa Elimu, this is Mama Asura…can I come instead? Halima is seeing her time…"

"When did this start? She didn't tell me that this morning," Elimu said.

"Elimu, I'm sorry I forgot to tell you…I was in pain this morning," Halima said, stuttering over her words.

A brief period of silence elapsed before Elimu called out angrily, "Mama Asura, hurry up then if you are coming."

CHAPTER 2

Birth of Precious Jewels

May 20, 1966:

Now, years after her circumcision, Halima said that she finally understood why every Maasai girl must endure that pain.

Now I know I would never have been married had I not been cleansed, Halima thought. *No man would have agreed to touch me. I'm happy that my mother did the right thing for me. If Mama Asura is right and my twin babies are girls, I must make sure that they are cleansed to be ripe and ready for marriage.*

My mother finally accepted this tradition because everyone else did. The women in the *enkang* made sure that the custom was passed on from one generation to another. They performed the ritual, while the men upheld and endorsed it—after all, it was our Maasai tradition.

An hour after Halima started her beading work, her thoughts trailed back to the hide wrap skirt.

"I love Mama Asura…she's been so good to me," Halima whispered to herself.

Moments later, she exclaimed happily, "Oh good! I'm done!"

She held up the finished skirt, turning it around to examine the intricate beading work that she'd just completed. The hide wrap skirt had been very elegantly strung with beads, which were neatly sewn in asymmetrical shapes. Halima modeled the skirt, displaying her artistic craft and sewing skills.

Mama Asura happened to walk by at that moment.

"Halima! I like it! It's so beautiful!" she exclaimed.

Across from where Halima and Mama Asura stood, a slim and tall woman emerged from her own *boma*. This was my father's third wife, Sepía. She was not a stunning beauty, but she was often referred to as an "exotic beauty" because of her unique features. Her face was somewhat oval-shaped, with perfectly sculptured facial features, and she had a naturally elegant gait. She was very light-hearted and always offered gracious compliments whenever she felt it was necessary.

"It's the best work that you've done so far," Sepía said excitedly, as she joined them.

"Mama Halima, we love the colors of the beads. Leela's skirt is more beautiful than the ones you made for us," her stepchildren echoed from afar.

"Now you know that's not true! Yours were just as beautiful as this one. Leela's is new, that's why you think it's prettier," Halima replied defensively.

"I know Leela will love it," Mama Asura interrupted.

Halima smiled. "I hope Aunt Mara likes it, too."

"Aunt Mara has good taste…I think she'll love it," Sepía said.

"Oh! I'm running late. I must prepare to leave for Aunt Mara's *enkang* if I don't want to return in the dark," Halima said abruptly, quickening her steps towards her *boma*.

She wore her wide-beaded necklace and earrings and adorned her arms and legs with the bracelets and leather amulets her mother had given to her for protection. Halima could still hear her mother's advice like it was yesterday. *"My child, these amulets make evil spirits uncomfortable and drive them away. Wear them always when you leave our* enkang."

Halima had promised her mother then that she would always wear the amulets, and she had never failed to, even for a day. Moments later, she stepped outside of her *boma* fully adorned with her treasured Maasai jewelry. She stood elegantly tall, displaying her full physique.

"Halima, you look so good!" Asura exclaimed.

"Thank you, Asura," Halima responded timidly.

"As beautiful as you look today, I hope the *ilpayianis* in Aunt Mara's *enkang* don't steal you away from Elimu," Túlélèi joked.

Before Halima could respond, Sepía chuckled and said, "Don't let our husband Elimu hear that—you know how he guards us like a mother hen does her chicks."

"Who knows what the chicks do when mother hen is away?" Halima said mischievously, chuckling even louder.

"I must go now. If Elimu asks for me, let him know I'll be back before sunset," Halima called over her shoulder as she disappeared into the bushy path.

Aunt Mara's Enkang:

By the time Halima arrived at Aunt Mara's *enkang,* Leela had been cleansed. She could still hear her thirteen-year-old niece screaming.

"Leela, it's now over. Here, have some warm milk," Halima heard Aunt Mara say to Leela as she entered the *boma,* trying to comfort her.

A few minutes later, Leela's screams turned into mere muffled sobs that were barely audible.

"I gave her a herbal mixture for the pain. It's a sedative and will put her to sleep in just a few minutes," Aunt Mara whispered to Halima.

Remembering her own experience, Halima knew that the pain by itself was enough to make the little girl lose consciousness.

"Aunt Mara, here's a little gift for Leela," Halima said, handing the woman the hide wrap skirt that she'd made.

"Oh, Halima! This is a very lovely skirt. It must have taken you some time to make this. You are so kind…so very kind," Aunt Mara said.

"It's nothing, Aunt Mara. Today is Leela's big day."

"Thank you so much. Your mother always said you had a giving heart, and your spirit and soul are tender with much love," Aunt Mara said, as she admired the skirt closely. "I know that Leela will love her skirt."

Halima smiled and nodded.

"Come, let's sit outside under the shade," Aunt Mara said, pointing to the huge tree in front of her *boma*. "Wait a minute, and I'll get the mats."

She disappeared into her *boma,* emerging seconds later to arrange the hide-skin mats very neatly under the tree. It wasn't long before she started to talk about how things were drastically changing in the Tanzanian Maasailand. It was typical of Aunt Mara to reminisce about the past.

"Halima, we are losing our young people."

"How is that, Aunt Mara?"

"Well, our young Maasai men are now going to different cities in Tanzania and Kenya. Most of them don't want to return to the Maasaiplains; my son is one of them. Some work as *askaris,* or security guards, and others attend government schools where they are learning to speak English and Kiswahili. You know, the government is trying to force our Maasai children to start attending school," Aunt Mara said.

Halima nodded, feeling a bit guilty herself, since she planned to have her baby girls, once they were old enough, attend the government school and get just a little education.

"Sometimes, I see why some of our young men are leaving the Maasailand—because everything is going from bad to worse. The government has been taking more of our land and steadily reducing our cattle-grazing pasture. Our young people no longer want to herd cattle because we don't have enough pasture for our cattle to graze on," Aunt Mara explained.

"Aunt Mara, it's a pity that all this is happening because we've always been known to be great cattlemen," Halima expressed with deep regret.

"Yes, Halima, I agree with you. Our ancestors have always been herdsmen and have passed on this skill from one generation to the other. They were also known to be great warriors, always defending our land from intruders or raiding nearby settlements for more cattle. Our livestock is our sign of wealth," Aunt Mara explained, shaking her head.

"In fact, you are too young to remember how things were before. I tell you, Halima, things are so different now. It's heartbreaking to see what is happening now in our *enkangs*."

At this point, Halima knew that her aunt was about to start another lesson on the historical trials of the Maasai, and so she got herself some warm milk and laid back to hear one of her aunt's great stories.

"The Maasai emigrated from the northeastern parts of Africa," Aunt Mara said, adjusting herself more comfortably on the mat. "As nomadic people, during droughts and famine, we moved from place to place in search of fresh grazing land for our cattle. This is how we came to live in the East African savanna. Now, an artificial border separates the Tanzanian and Kenyan Maasai, and yet we are one people. Over many years of our migration from one land to another, it's a shame that the Tanzanian Maasai now live in separate communities in Tanzania and neighboring Kenya. Since we were moved out of our land in the Serengeti, Manyara, and the Ngorongoro Crater, our *enkangs* are now spread all around the Ngorongoro Crater." Aunt Mara paused and shook her head, forming a frown that clearly showed her disapproval.

"Our ancestral Maasailand is still beautiful," Halima said, attempting to lighten the conversation. "Today, our land boasts of the great Kilimanjaro Mountain, which as you know, we call the 'White Mountain' because it snows at the peak of the mountain."

"So was the Ngorongoro before it collapsed," Aunt Mara added.

"Yes, you are right," Halima responded. "Tell me, Aunt Mara, how did Enkai create the Ngorongoro Crater?"

"Well, this is what I was told. The Ngorongoro used to be volcanic mountain, but it collapsed and formed a crater. We moved into the crater until the Government of Tanzania turned it into a place for travelers to visit. They moved us out of the crater and into the neighboring areas, which they called 'Conservation areas,'" Aunt Mara explained.

"But these travelers don't understand the Maasai traditions; they don't like that our men are the chief heads of the Maasai family," Halima said, interrupting Aunt Mara.

"You are right, Halima. They don't understand that it's our tradition, and we must preserve it. They don't understand how one man like your husband Elimu and mine could have many wives. They don't know that our husbands respect us because Maasai women are very strong. We build our own *bomas* and take care of our children."

"We also take care of the children of the other wives when they are not around," Halima added. "You know what I mean, Aunt Mara—Mama Asura's children are mine, too."

Aunt Mara nodded in acquiescence.

"I cannot understand how the foreigners have no respect for what belongs to us. It's funny that they don't understand how we can share our environment with nature's wildlife—we like it, although it's not always a happy union. Lions are always a threat to our cattle, but lion hunting has always been a sign of expressing manhood, or *emorata,* for our young men. Now, the government forbids us from killing lions as part of any Maasai ritual," Aunt Mara said, shaking her head.

"Tell me, Aunt Mara, I have often wondered about the culture of these foreigners. Why do they seem to care more about the lions than us?"

Aunt Mara smiled. "I don't know, Halima—I really don't know."

As Aunt Mara seemed to go into deep thought, a group of young Maasai chanting an old warrior song became visible in the distance.

"They are training on how to spot the footsteps of lions and other animals that can kill our cattle. Each has a spear, pretending to scare off a lion. They are mimicking an echo, attempting to call for help as though they'd seen a lion," Aunt Mara explained to no one in particular, as Halima was well aware of the ritual the young men were performing. Yet, because it seemed so important to Aunt Mara to tell everything, Halima chose not to interrupt her.

As their echo got louder, Halima and Aunt Mara watched the young boys, who suddenly took to their heels and ran a short distance to a *boma* close by.

"This is the practice of the speed of flight to get help from any neighboring *enkang* in case of a real threat from a lion," Aunt Mara said.

"I love when they do that—it so nicely shows the remarkable, brave spirit of the Maasai warriors," Halima said proudly.

"Yes, I agree with you, Halima," Aunt Mara said, nodding.

"Asura tells me that our Maasai rituals for our young people are a mystery to foreigners—they always want to know what we are doing. She says that they don't like our Maasai tradition of female cleansing, but we know what we are doing—we are protecting our young women; we are keeping their chastity for their future husbands."

"What do the foreigners know? Tell me, what do they know?" was Aunt Mara's response.

Halima smiled, stretched her legs, and changed her sitting position to stare in the opposite direction. The echoes of Maasai children heard from a short distance momentarily distracted her from Aunt Mara's talk.

"These are the younger boys or *ilayioks* going through the Maasai tradition of their passage into manhood. First, these young boys are circumcised between the ages of six and eight years old. Now, at age fourteen, they are being initiated as new warriors, or *ilmurrans*. The young males are adorned with headgear made from dried birds stuffed with ashes and dried grass, which are then attached to a crown made from sticks. Their faces are masked with red ocher, and they are dressed in black robes or togas made from hide-skin. Around their waste, they are wearing beaded belts, and on their fingers, they have multiple rings," Aunt Mara continued to explain unnecessarily.

"These young boys have eagerly awaited this initiation. Elimu, your husband, is now an older man—he, too, went through it. Today, he is one of the most respected *ilpayianis* in your *enkang*. Now, these young boys are going away to a far away camp for four weeks where they will be taught the ways of the Maasai warriors. From then on, for another fourteen years, these young warriors will continue to mature to become great warriors," Aunt Mara said, visibly proud of the achievement of the young boys.

"Yes, Elimu told me all about his own experience. He said that if either of the twins turned out to be a boy, he, too, would go through the Maasai initiation for young men," Halima responded.

Aunt Mara paused for a second, fiddled with the beads on Leela's new hide wrap skirt, and smiled.

"He's wishing for boys like all men, but Mama Asura has already said we'll have two girls, right?" Aunt Mara said, laughing.

"Yes, I know."

"This is a beautiful skirt that you made for Leela. I know she'll love it. Thank you, Halima, you've done well," Aunt Mara said, changing the subject.

Halima nodded and relaxed her face with a gentle smile.

"Well, let me tell you more about our young boys. As I watch them, I think about how Enkai has blessed our beautiful Maasailand—our savanna and wildlife—all of this has always been part of our Maasai life.

"And, we've become quite accustomed to the dangers of the wild that we must always be ready for. As you know, every Maasai mother must know how to treat snakebite. If a snake bites someone, the area must be cut open immediately, and blood containing the snake poison must be sucked out from the wound. Then, you must clean the wound with medicinal herbs to neutralize the poison. We must know how to do this because we share our land with deadly snakes. The foreigners don't know this, and many of them have died from the bites of poisonous snakes—what a shame because this should not be so."

"You're right, Aunt Mara. The other day we saw a white man that was bit by a snake, and his skin turned green. He almost died, but his wife had white man's medicine that saved his life."

"That's good. I didn't know that the foreigners had good medicine for a deadly snakebite. What do they call the white man's medicine?"

"I do not know, Aunt Mara, but I don't think that it's better than our Maasai medicine. We have the best snakebite medicine," Halima said, feeling proud.

Aunt Mara nodded in agreement.

"We have the best of many things, and that's why it's a shame that our tradition is fast disappearing—yes, things have really changed around here. Halima, we don't have enough food because we have so few cattle. Now we must look outside the Maasailand to sustain our lives."

Aunt Mara paused for a brief moment, her face expressing her sadness before she continued.

"The foreigners come here to watch us; they say that we are different from other people and that our tradition is ancient. And yet, they don't mind us charging them money to show them our dances or to pose for photographs with them. We don't even know where they take our photos to—perhaps to strange lands that we don't know about."

"I hear that they make lots of money with our photographs," Halima said, "even though they pay us just a few shillings for them. They sell our photos to people in far away places."

"Well, that's good—those in far away places will also learn about our beautiful Maasai tradition," Aunt Mara said.

"But Halima, still I think it's a shame that the government is taking our land—the land of our ancestors—the land that our cattle have always grazed on. You see, because of this, many of our cattle have died, and we are now forced to find money to buy grains. In the past, there was no need for this because we could get anything that we wanted by selling our cattle," Aunt Mara said adamantly, bringing back the issue of the Maasailand. "Halima, you know what that means?" she asked, having misinterpreted Halima's perplexed look.

"Aunt Mara, you mean trading our cattle for other things that we need?"

Aunt Mara nodded.

"Yes, I do," Halima responded quietly.

Halima was accustomed to Aunt Mara's love for the Maasai tradition. She was known in her *enkang* as a historian because she knew every detail. Aunt Mara helped her understand much about the Maasai tradition that had puzzled her when she was a child, for her mother had often evaded her questions, saying, "You ask too many questions, Halima. Tradition is not for a child to understand but to follow. You'll learn these things when you grow up."

Unfortunately, Halima's mother had died before she was considered grown up.

As Aunt Mara continued, Halima started to feel pain around her waist. Initially, when she felt a sharp spasm, she thought nothing of it because in the past six weeks, she'd had a few of them. But a few minutes later, she felt wet in between her legs from fluid trickling down in between her thighs. She decided to stand up and stretch her legs. As she dragged herself up from the hide-skin mat, she noticed bloody mucus mixed with fluid on the inner side of her calves.

The mucus must be from the plug that seals the womb during pregnancy, she thought.

She'd heard many women talk about a woman's water that protected the child in the womb. She knew that it was this fluid in which a baby was suspended. When a woman's water broke, she knew that it meant the baby was ready to come out. Halima had seen this happen to the other wives in her *enkang*.

When Halima stood up, it suddenly became apparent to Aunt Mara that she was not quite listening to her anymore.

"What is it, Halima? You seem absent-minded," her aunt asked gently.

"Aunt Mara, I'm not sure. I think my water just broke. I think I am in labor...I think the babies are coming," she said, feeling slightly panicked.

Almost immediately, her aunt's eyes traveled down to the pool of liquid on the hide-skin mat.

"Oh! Halima, you are right! Your water just broke. Quick, let's get back to your *enkang!*" Aunt Mara immediately jumped up and rushed inside her *boma*. She emerged seconds later with two oval-patterned, hide-skin mats in her hand.

"Mama Moi! Mama Moi! I'm off to Halima's *enkang*. Please take care of Leela for me," Asura shouted.

"Don't you worry, Mama Mara, she'll be okay," Mama Moi called back from her *boma*.

"Here Halima, let's go," Asura said and instantly grabbed Halima's hand.

Together, they returned to Halima's *boma* in the neighboring *enkang*.

"Mama Asura! Mama Asura! Please come quickly. Halima is in labor."

Asura saw them and immediately rushed to Halima's *boma*.

"Halima, lie down and spread your legs open for me," Asura ordered, while she washed her hands with warm water and then dipped them in a bowl of warm, mixed herbs—a traditional mixture of antiseptic herbs.

Inserting her fingers into Halima, Asura checked her readiness for delivery.

"Halima, it will be a while before the babies come. Be calm so that you can bear the pain when more contractions come," Asura said gently.

Hours later, the contractions had become more frequent, and the pain had intensified. Halima was now screaming, tossing and thrashing uncontrollably.

"Asura, I can't bare the pain anymore."

"Yes you can, Halima—yes you can. You've waited for these babies for seven years. Now is the time to receive them. Yes, you can bear the pain. It's mother nature's gift to you, and it's your pride and full proof of womanhood. Just a little while longer, my dear, and the pain will turn into your joy." Asura spoke with the knowledge and experience of being a midwife and a mother of three children herself.

By sun down, the pain had become explosive, and Halima was now wailing and moaning, tossing and turning even more.

"Oh! Asura, the pain seems worse than being cleansed—this pain is going to kill me," she screamed.

"Halima, you'll be fine. The pain won't kill you," Asura replied, with firm reassurance.

She checked Halima again, this time with her five fingers. A few minutes later, she asked for another bowl of warm water and a cloth. Then she re-positioned herself between Halima's legs.

"Push, Halima! Push with all your strength!"

A loud scream came through from Halima, her arteries pulsating through her forehead and neck as beads of sweats trickled down her face.

"Push harder, Halima! Push with all your strength!" Mama Asura instructed again.

Halima's first push sent a load of waste out. The *boma* was now filled with a lingering odor. Aunt Mara started to clean the waste—the sight and odor didn't perturb her because she was used to it. She, too, had delivered quite a few babies. As Halima pushed again, the head of the first baby could be seen coming through the birth canal.

CHAPTER 3

❁

In the Name of Tradition

The Arrival of Nature's Miracles:

"Oh Halima, here she comes! She's so beautiful. What do you want to name her?" Asura asked.

"Her name is Nadia. Yes, Nadia," Halima said breathlessly, her body completely drenched in perspiration.

Momentarily, Nadia was welcomed into the Maasailand with a gentle slap on her buttocks.

"The second one is on her way out. Here she comes, Halima. She's just as beautiful as Nadia. What's her name going to be?" Asura asked again.

"This one is Mikela!" Halima exclaimed.

A few minutes later, Mikela, the second baby girl, fully arrived, and all of a sudden, Halima's pain was gone. Hearing the cries of her precious jewels lit her face with smiles.

"It has been a long wait for both of you, Nadia and Mikela—a wait worthwhile for the two most precious things, Marahaba Enkai!" Asura exclaimed, the only Kiswahili words she had learned from Halima.

"Welcome, my precious jewels," Halima whispered softly to herself, at the same time.

As they took the babies away to clean them, an exhausted Halima said a prayer of thanksgiving in her mother's adopted lingo, Kiswahili.

"Marahaba Enkai!" Asura exclaimed, the only Kiswahili words she too had learned from Halima. "Thank you, God! Thank you, God!" she meant in those words.

Then, she drifted off to sleep with a smile of complete contentment still lingering on her face.

One year later, Nadia and Mikela's naming ceremony was held, and this was a very special occasion, especially because of how long Halima had waited to have them. Early in the morning of the ritual day, she chose a cow, which was led to the forest for slaughter by men picked by Elimu. The women and the children bathed thoroughly and adorned themselves with traditional Maasai regalia. Halima was the star of the day, and she was dressed in exquisite beaded work. Nadia and Mikela were shaved bald, signifying their first haircut, and Halima's already baldhead was smoothed and oiled until it shone under the sun.

Halima and her babies had been made to stay mostly in her *boma*, where the entrance to the hut had been closed off with shrubs and branches until the day of the ceremony. When the men returned from the forest with the cow meat, Halima was made to clear the entrance to her *boma*, which signified the beginning of the ceremony. A colorful ceremony it was, Halima recalled; one that had remained vivid in her memory for years.

October 1978—My First Dream:

Ever since I could remember, I'd always had intricate dreams. It took me many years to begin to understand them, but I had my first dream when I was twelve years old.

It was pitch dark everywhere around the hilly, wet, and slippery road in what seemed the heart of our Maasailand. I was crawling on my knees and groping desperately in the dark for something to hold onto. Gasping, I tried to catch my breath. Then, I felt a mass of sturdy shrub and quickly held onto it.

"Where am I?

"Where is Ma?

"Why am I here alone—where is Nadia?"

My questions echoed with no answers.

Then, suddenly I felt a gush of powerful wind blowing over me. My grip started to weaken, and in a flash, a piercing beam of light flooded my eyes, blinding me. In my confusion, I let go of the shrub and started to slip down the hilly and wet road, my skin bruising from the roughness of the ground as I fell rapidly. Fear overtook my body, and I started to scream again.

"Ma…Ma! Nadia! Please help me!

"Oh Enkai, help me!"

Then I saw Nadia at a distance being whisked away by a man with golden hair wearing a white robe. There was a glow of light all around him, and rays of light radiated from his hands.

"Nadia, who's that, and where is he taking you to?" I screamed.

Without warning, I felt gentle hands lift me off the ground and shortly, I was afloat in the air looking down on the road—then, I was soaring like an eagle into the skies.

"Oh no! Where's my sister?...I must wait for Nadia," I said.

"Nadia is fine now," a soothing voice whispered to me.

Suddenly, a feeling of peace and tranquility overtook me, and I was no longer afraid. Then I felt someone touching me, and I also heard a faint voice calling my name.

"Mikela! Mikela! Ma is here now. It's okay!"

When I opened my eyes, my mother was cradling me in her arms. Then I realized that it had just been a dream, and I sighed.

"Mikela, you were having a bad dream again. It's fine now—it was just a dream. Don't worry, it's nothing—I have them sometimes."

I nodded and snuggled closer to my mother's bosom.

"You have to get up now," my mother said very gently.

"Ma, where's Nadia?" I asked, still feeling sluggish from my sleep but wanting immediate reassurance that Nadia had not gone away.

"Nadia is already outside working—so you must get ready now and join her," she replied.

"Okay Ma," I said, nodding.

Nadia and I were now twelve years old. We were being raised as Maasai girls, or *entitos*. As young girls gradually entering into puberty, we were also learning to perform our daily house chores in the *bomas* as other women in our *enkang*. We learned to build *bomas*, layer their roofs with wet cow dung, prepare fireplaces with dry cow dung, and stretch out animal skin to make dried hide-skin mats. Daily, we sewed beads on hide-skin mats, gathered firewood, cooked, milked cattle, collected wild honey, and made ghee from the milk.

A few times during the week, Ma allowed us to sneak out and attend a government school nearby because our father didn't like the idea of young girls attending school. He would never encourage the education of girls and was certain to throw a fit if he found out that Nadia and I were attending the government school. Like most other Maasai, our father considered education to be a threat to our culture.

On school days, Ma made up different stories for Papa about where Nadia and I were going. Then, we would trek twenty minutes to the local school. Ma knew that she was taking a huge risk by allowing Nadia and I to attend the government school. She told Nadia and I that deep in her heart, she was convinced that a little education wouldn't hurt us. She couldn't dare to admit this in public for fear of retribution from Papa and others in our *enkang*.

As a child, I was very curious about nature and life in general. I often asked my mother questions, like why the Maasai didn't want their children to be educated and to travel to other places to see and learn new things. I wanted to know why the Maasai seemed to live isolated from other cultures. There were many aspects of the Maasai tradition that I loved, but there were others that I questioned and would not accept. Often, some of my questions got me in trouble, and Ma felt that I was too young to be challenging a tradition that I should simply accept and abide by.

Nadia and I loved school and appreciated Ma's effort in getting us to school whenever she could. School was something different from the monotonous daily routine in our *enkang*. We made friends with Maasai kids from neighboring *enkangs* and started learning to speak and write English, the language of the white man, and Kiswahili, a dominant language in Tanzania and neighboring Kenya.

We would spend hours practicing the new words and sentences that we learned in school. This was the only time that we could do this because Ma didn't allow us to practice at home for fear that Papa would find out our secret. Usually, on our way back from school, we practiced English and Kiswahili words.

"I see the trees."

"*Naiona miti.*"

"The birds are flying."

"*Ndege wanaruka.*"

"Reading is very useful."

"*Kusoma kwafaa sana.*"

"The children are reading and writing."

"*Watoto wanaandika na kusoma.*"

Nadia and I were best friends, and everyone said we looked identical. Also, Ma told us that we were emerging into extraordinary beauties. To her, we were the most beautiful girls in our *enkang*. She said that we looked just like she did when she was ten years old—tall, with a graceful elegance that earned us the nickname "Maasai Queens" among our peers. I remembered that on school days, some of the *ilmurrans* sought our attention, whispering to us that they hoped someday to be the lucky bridegroom of both Nadia and I.

Nadia and I had different talents. While Nadia was doing exceptionally well in math and natural sciences, I was gifted in drawing and painting. From the age of five, Ma said it was obvious that I had a special artistic gift. She said I would spend many hours painting unique blends of colors on hide-skin mats, beads, and amulets with locally made Maasai color-paints and brushes. At the age of ten, I painted what Ma described as two spectacular and intricate scenes: Nadia playing the circling game by herself in the Maasaiplains and a collection of *bomas* in our *enkang*.

Ma also said that amazingly, one of my stepmothers, Mama Túlélèi, had somehow seen the artistic talent in me when I was a two-year-old baby. Mama Túlélèi was known for her cheerful and high-spirited nature, although she was often very quiet. My mother said that Mama Túlélèi also had a deep psychic spirit, and had once whispered to her, "Halima, I see a great artist in your child, Mikela—I see her traveling to far away places and showing her work. She'll not be here in the Maasailand—she'll be known all over the world."

"How can you tell, Mama Túlélèi? Mikela is only a baby. Besides, the Maasailand is good for Mikela and Nadia. It's better than other places. If you say that Mikela will be a great artist, then let her paint right here in our *enkang*."

This was my mother's immediate response because she couldn't bear the thought that either Nadia or I would ever leave the Maasailand.

"But who will know her, Halima? How will she become great here in the Maasailand? How will the world get to know her or see her work?" Túlélèi asked in a low and almost inaudible voice.

"I don't know, Mama Túlélèi. All I know is that my precious jewels will grow up like I did—yes, they will grow up right here in the Maasailand."

Twelve years later, Mama Túlélèi didn't need to remind Ma about her prediction of my artistic talent because my drawings and paintings had become the talk of our school and *enkang*.

Our journey back from school was our cherished time. We would talk about the changes that were occurring in our bodies as nature gradually initiated us into the early stages of womanhood. We were both entering the age of puberty. We would giggle as we talked about our small breasts, which were beginning to sprout. Not too long after our twelfth birthday, Ma hinted to us that the time had come for us to be initiated into womanhood.

"Before the next *Nkokua*, or long rains," she said, "both of you will be cleansed and ripe, ready for marriage."

"But Ma, what does it mean to be cleansed and ripe for marriage?" Nadia and I asked her.

"You'll know when the time comes. I know that both of you will make me proud then."

Ma never really explained to us what she meant by our "initiation to womanhood," but we'd seen other girls in our *enkang* go through the initiation and suddenly become withdrawn and depressed. For unexplained reasons, these girls isolated themselves from other children and cried most of the time. Some of the children who had gone through the initiation seemed to have simply vanished, and we were never told what happened to them. Some of their playmates whispered that the girls had gone to be with Enkai forever.

Just before the next rains arrived, Nadia and I started to menstruate. Our monthly cycle started a little earlier than Ma had anticipated, so she secretly hurried up preparations for our initiation ceremony. The date was now set—the ceremony was to take place in three weeks. Nadia, who was the first daughter, was scheduled for the ritual two weeks before mine would take place.

The Day of "Cleansing":

The women and men in the *enkang* all knew about the passage into puberty ceremony, which had been arranged for Nadia and me. A typical Maasai celebration showcasing the women adorned in carefully handcrafted beaded work was now in the final stages of preparation.

It was just another school day for Nadia and me, except that the weather was uncharacteristically harsh for this time of month. The air was very crisp and dry, the dead brown leaves and grass scattered all over reflecting the dryness around.

The patched and hard grounds of the Maasaiplains could do with more rains sooner than anticipated in the months ahead, I thought, as we hurried to finish our chores of milking the cows, preparing a drink of milk mixed with cow's blood, and storing ghee in a cow's horn. The days were now cooler than usual, and the cold winds had a chilling effect on the skin, making early morning chores more difficult to accomplish. I pulled my softened hide-skin mat closer to myself to keep the chill away, thankful for its warmth and protection from the cold. Stretching to relieve my weight of the strain of bending over, I heard my ma and our stepmothers calling Nadia and asking her to return to our mother's *boma*. Nadia ran to answer their call and never returned to where we'd been sitting together. A few minutes later, Ma urged me to run off to school.

"Ma, what about Nadia?" I inquired.

"Nadia will be home today, and for the next few weeks—now, run off, before your father comes out," Ma responded, without further explanation.

When I returned from school, Nadia was lying down on a hide-skin mat that was spread on the ground inside the *boma*—she was sobbing.

"Nadia! Nadia! What happened?" I asked her frantically, but she ignored me.

"Nadia! Please tell me what happened. I am your sister, and I love you," I pleaded desperately, but she still didn't respond.

Nadia, my sister, had recoiled into a world where no one could reach her. She wouldn't eat unless Ma spoon-fed her and practically forced the food into her mouth. It was obvious that Nadia was rapidly losing weight—in just a few days she'd become leaner than I'd ever seen her before. All I remembered was that Nadia was either crying or sleeping, and all of her youthful exuberance was gone.

Nadia was my only full sister, playmate, and best friend, and her withdrawal had greatly affected my own world. Although she was physically there with me, I could feel that her spirit was no longer with us. Somehow, I knew that something more than just the cleansing experience had also occurred within Nadia—something was terribly wrong. I didn't know what it was, and she wouldn't tell me.

Two weeks later, Nadia still had not spoken a word to anyone. It had been a very lonely time for me, and Ma would not explain to me what had happened; she merely told me to prepare for my own initiation.

A fortnight later, it was my turn to be cleansed.

"Your day has come, Mikela," Ma said, as I was preparing for school.

"But Ma, today is another school day."

"There'll be no school for some time, my child. Today is a big day for you. After today, your womanhood will begin to blossom, like Nadia's.

"But Ma, Nadia has not spoken a word since—"

"Shhhh…shhhh…enough of that, Mikela. Here, take my hand and let's go. Mama Asura is waiting."

A Repeat of Tradition:

An hour later, I sniffed quiet tears of anguish as I lay down next to Nadia. I no longer needed to ask Nadia what had happened to her two weeks earlier. Now I understood why she'd not spoken a word to any of us. The pain was too great to be explained to anyone. Nadia turned around and put her comforting arms around me. Now, for the first time since her ordeal, she spoke to me.

"Mikela, did they hurt you, too?"

I nodded as I tried to snuggle closer to my sister trying to find a more comfortable position to ease my maddening pain. This was yet another Maasai tradition that I certainly didn't agree with, and if I'd had the choice, I would have opted not to experience it. What my mother often referred to as my radical mind was again rekindled with fiery defiance against the tradition of female cleansing that Nadia and I had just experienced.

"Nadia, what did we do to deserve this? Why would Ma allow them to hurt us?" I asked.

"I don't know. I really don't understand why," Nadia responded.

Still in each other's embrace, we wept as I tried to say a few more words.

"We have to leave this *enkang*, Nadia. We can't live here anymore. We could never get over what they've done to us. Please, we must leave."

"But, we have no place to go, Mikela," Nadia reminded me.

"I don't care anymore. I want to be away from this *enkang*. Nadia, see what they've done to us? Don't you see that they've violated our most sacred self? It's been such a painful experience for us, and I can't see a future for us—I feel like our lives have been shattered forever," I responded.

Nadia said nothing more. We both sobbed until we drifted to sleep, which was a transient but welcomed solace for both of us.

Many years later, Ma told me that she'd come by to watch over Nadia and me as we slept. Watching us, she said she remembered her own cleansing experience when she was about our age and that she understood our physical and emotional pain. She said she watched us entangled in each other's warm and comforting embrace, just as nature's miracle of conception had placed us in her womb.

Ma said she whispered before leaving our room, "In time, they'll heal."

Emerging Saga and the Price of Tradition:

Nadia's trembling feet woke me up later that night. She was completely drenched in sweat, and her body was smoldering hot. Nadia was running a very high fever and soon began to vomit. I was terrified and didn't know what to do, so I started screaming out for my mother.

"Ma! Ma! Please come! It's Nadia…Ma! Ma! It's Nadia, please come quick."

Ma rushed in immediately. She felt Nadia's body and quickly started to dab her with a cold, wet cloth. By dawn, Nadia's body temperature was so high that she'd started to convulse. Her body was seized by violent spasms, and she was foaming at the mouth. Ma placed Nadia belly down, with her head turned to the side. Then, she quickly forced Nadia's mouth open and inserted a small, smooth wooden spoon in between her upper and lower teeth to prevent her from biting her tongue and to maintain air passage. I could see that Ma was as frightened for Nadia's life as I was. She sent me to fetch Mama Asura from her *boma*.

Mama Asura arrived almost immediately and started to administer a Maasai herbal liquid mixture to Nadia. Nadia swallowed gulps of it and threw up the remainder, but within twenty minutes, her fever started to subside. She stopped convulsing and eventually went to sleep.

Ma said that neither she nor Mama Asura had been aware that Nadia had been bleeding for the past two weeks, had become anemic, and had developed a serious infection, which then spread to her vagina, pelvic area, urethra, and bladder. She'd been retaining urine due to the infection, and this had damaged her urethra. She also suffered shock and trauma from her cleansing.

The following night, Nadia woke up in the middle of the night screaming for Ma, who was lying next to her. She had been delirious all evening so Ma thought it was just another bout of delirious talk, but what she said this time sent chills of fear down my spine.

"Ma, it's time—Enkai is here with me. It's time, Ma," Nadia repeated very softly.

"Nadia, what do you mean? What is it time for?" Ma asked in panic, as she picked Nadia up in her arms.

"Ma, Enkai is taking me with Him. I see everywhere, and it's so beautiful," Nadia said. With great effort, she wrapped her arms around Ma one last time. Slowly, the life ebbed out of her, and her whole body went limp.

CHAPTER 4

Flight from Tradition

Ma said she felt Nadia take her last breath, and she knew she was gone. Nadia passed away in Ma's arms, and minutes later, Ma started to wail.

"Nadia, my child, has paid the ultimate price for womanhood. Oh, Enkai! Help me! What shall I do now?

"I have lost one of my precious jewels, which I waited for, for seven long years. Nadia's life has ebbed away like a flower that has wilted and died before it blossomed," she cried.

I held on to my mother as she wailed and could not be comforted. No one had enough words or warmth to console me either. I felt like my spirit had descended into a deep sea of darkness and was sinking lower every hour into frightening depths of despair. The pain of Nadia's death was beyond any words for me. I could not believe that my twin sister and best friend had died. The pain I felt was like a sharp knife piercing through my innermost heart—a heartache that I thought would consume me. Nadia's death had happened so suddenly, and I could never have had enough time to expect or to prepare for it.

Her burial was equally agonizing, and my heart wrenched with excruciating pain as I watched her body—wrapped in the colorful, beaded, hide wrap skirt that Ma had made for her to celebrate the ritual of her circumcision—being lowered into the ground, never to be seen again. Numbed and motionless, I could not believe what was happening. I looked over to where Ma was standing and saw my father and another man holding her. She seemed like she was near collapsing.

As we all stood and watched my only sister and best friend Nadia being laid to rest forever in the traditional Maasai way, I let out an agonizing scream that sent spasms through my body and felt myself fall to the ground into blissful unconsciousness.

End of November 1978:

The shock of Nadia's death had forced me to ignore the horror and pain of my own circumcision, which had occurred barely forty-eight hours earlier. I felt completely numbed by my emotional pain. I couldn't eat or speak, and I cried for hours until my eyes were blood shot and there was no more water to make tears. I felt an incredible void inside of me that threatened to burn up my innocent soul. When I was alone, I cried out Nadia's name, hoping that she would come back to be with me again. I never thought that I'd ever be able to survive a day without Nadia. I could not believe that I would never see her again. I started to resent my mother because I blamed her for Nadia's death.

I could think of nothing else except that *Ma had allowed the women in the* enkang *to hurt Nadia and me, and now Nadia was gone.*

I didn't fully understand what had happened to Nadia, but I knew that Nadia had died from the ritual of cutting off flesh from her sacred self. I also knew that Nadia couldn't stop bleeding. I bled for an entire day myself, and even now, one month later, I was still sore and could barely pass water.

As I lay curled up on a hide-skin mat inside our *boma,* Ma came by and sat next to me. I could tell that she, too, was in anguish. I believe that at the time, Ma also blamed herself for Nadia's death, but she was consoled by her belief that it was our tradition, and so the cleansing ritual of womanhood had to be done.

Ma reached out to hold my hand, and I quickly snatched it from her. At the moment, I despised her and didn't want her touching me. I felt that I could no longer trust my mother to protect me.

"Mikela, I know you are hurting because of Nadia's death. I am, too. But, we must both learn to live without her. She is now with Enkai," my mother said.

I ignored her—I couldn't get myself to speak to her. I really had no words for her. I just wanted to be left alone.

My mother reached out to embrace me, but I quickly shrugged away, and she started to cry through her words.

"Here's the beautiful beaded hide wrap skirt that I made for you. I know you are still upset about the cleansing ritual that both you and Nadia experienced. It's the Maasai tradition—I went through it, Mikela, and so did my mother and grandmother. I am also heartbroken by Nadia's death, but that is how Enkai wanted it. Please! Mikela, try to understand."

I remained silent, with my face turned away from her, and a few moments later, I heard her quietly leave my room.

Four weeks after Nadia's death and after my own circumcision, I had still not spoken a word to either my mother or anyone else in our *enkang*. Daily, my mother tried, unsuccessfully, to engage me in conversation. Many years later, she would tell me that she had feared that my silent treatment would send her to the mad house, but she'd hoped and prayed ceaselessly that I would get over my grief and understand that the ritual of cleansing had been done in my interest.

I barely ate and wouldn't talk or play with other children in our *enkang*. I was completely withdrawn into my world where no one could reach me. Every opportunity that I had, I sneaked out to school, which had become my only solace. Staying in our *enkang* had become too painful.

On my way back from school, I would sit by myself in the open Maasaiplains and weep. I missed Nadia very much and didn't want to continue living without her. One day, I lay on the bare ground in the open plains and cried myself to sleep. That day, I dreamt of my sister Nadia for the first time since she'd passed away.

She was laughing and playing with other children who stood a short distance away from me. Initially, it seemed as if Nadia hadn't seen me, but suddenly she was by my side, hugging and kissing me.

"Mikela, you must learn to live again without me. I am now very happy with Enkai," she said.

Later in the dream, just before she disappeared, I heard her whispering gently, "Remember when you told me that we must leave the Maasailand? You must run now, Mikela—you must leave the *enkang* before they come for you. Don't waste any time, Mikela—run! I'll always be your guardian light."

"But why must I run, Nadia—why! Where would I run? Who is coming for me?"

The vision of Nadia in my dream seemed to fade before she could answer me.

I woke up a few minutes later only to see that I was alone in the open fields and that Nadia was gone. Somehow, I felt close to her again—I felt like she was right there with me, even though I couldn't see her. I ran back to the *enkang* happy that Nadia had visited me in my dream. I was convinced that she was happy and safe with Enkai.

Weeks later, my physical wounds were gradually healing and urination had become much less painful, but I was still torn inside from emotional anguish. As I pondered how quickly my life had changed in such a short time, my mother came by and sat next to me, watching me as I cleaned the insides of fresh calabashes and gourds, getting them ready to be washed and dried. I had still not spoken to her since the day of my circumcision.

"Mikela, your father's friend is coming to see you. He's happy that you are now cleansed and ripe," she finally said.

I looked up at my mother, anger seething in my eyes, as I momentarily stopped scraping the insides of the calabash that I had in my hands.

For the first time in weeks, I finally broke my silence.

"Ma, why is he coming to see me at sunset?" I asked defiantly.

"Ahaaa…Mikela, I'm happy that you are now speaking again. I'll tell you why when he arrives. Just know that he's coming for something good for you—something good for the whole family."

"I do not wish to see him—I don't ever want to see him," I snapped at my mother.

"Mikela, you cannot reject someone you don't know. You don't even know why he's coming to see you."

"Ma, I know why he's coming—he's coming for the same reason Naivasha's father's friend came to see her. Now she's pregnant and hasn't come to school since then."

"Who told you about Naivasha?"

"Ma, I live in this *enkang*, and I know what's going on."

"Mikela, you are too young to be listening to gossip—too young, my child," she said admonishingly.

"What your father's friend is coming for is our tradition, Mikela. I was the same age as you when I met your—"

"Ma, I don't want to hear that anymore. That was your life, but this is my life now," I interrupted rebelliously.

"Mikela, I'm your mother, and you must listen to me. The ritual of circumcision has cleansed you, and that's the pride of womanhood in our *enkang*. Now, you must be ready for the next stage of your life," my mother responded angrily.

"Ma, the next stage of my life can wait until I finish school. I am barely thirteen years old."

"It's our tradition, and it cannot wait, Mikela."

"Ma, for you everything must be done according to tradition. It's the same tradition that killed Nadia. Now, she's gone forever, and what do you have to say about that? I'm tired of a tradition that brings so much misery."

"Hush, now! That's enough, Mikela! I won't have you saying crazy things like that anymore. Please be back at our *boma* by sunset," Ma said angrily. She turned her back to me and walked away.

The Dusty Trails to Freedom:

As my mother walked away, suddenly a thought hit me—I remembered the dream that I'd had in the open plains. Nadia had warned me about this in my dream. Again, Nadia's words flashed back in my mind.

"You must run now, Mikela—you must leave the enkang *before they come for you. Don't waste any time, Mikela—run! I'll always be your guardian light."*

As Nadia's words echoed in my mind, I jumped up, sending the calabashes and gourds that were on my lap to their fate as they hit the ground. I ran toward my mother's *boma* and hid by the side. When she stepped outside the *boma* with Mama Asura, I quietly sneaked inside. I tied a few of my ragged clothes, a blanket, and a hide-skin mat into a neat bundle. Then, I took a gourd of milk, water, and cornmeal for the road. I opened my mother's clay-pot money safe and took whatever I could find in there—a mix of Tanzanian and Kenyan shillings. Then, I put on a bracelet and amulet that my grandmother had given her and slipped on my mother's pair of hide-skin slippers. I put on my school uniform—being the only western clothes I had—and wrapped my traditional Maasai toga around it to protect my legs from the mosquitoes.

In a flash, I left our *boma* and started to run towards the open plains. I didn't look back, even though I had no idea where I was going. I didn't care about where I was going. For now, I was simply determined to leave our *enkang* and never return.

I decided to go to our school with the hope that I would see someone who could tell me how to get to Dar es Salaam or Nairobi. On arrival, I was disappointed to see that there was no one there. I started to walk along the dusty road with no idea where it was leading. As I walked, I prayed.

"Please Enkai, protect me, and get me to somewhere safe."

After walking what seemed to be about ten miles, my feet started to ache, and I sat down by a tree to eat. I drank some water and milk mixed with cornmeal, felt revived, and started trekking again. I hoped to reach a safe place before sunset.

Trucks loaded with people passed by, but I had no idea where they were going, and they didn't stop anywhere near where I was walking. Finally, I reached a group of Maasai standing by the roadside that said they were going to Mombassa. I joined them and told them that I was going to visit my aunt there.

Soon, an empty truck came by and stopped. Everyone started to get on it, and I did the same. My heart was pounding from fear and anxiety, but I had to continue with my journey. Only one thing was certain, I was not going back to our *enkang*. I hoped that Enkai and Nadia would stay close by me through my flight.

Minutes later, the truck was loaded and ready to go. A man came back to ask for the fare. I had no idea if I had enough money to pay him, so I first watched to see what others were giving him. Then, I searched inside my money holder until I found what looked like what the man was asking for. I handed it over to him, and he took it and went on to the next person. I assumed that I'd given him the right coin, and I expressed a sigh of relief. Soon, the truck restarted, making a loud noise and belching smoke.

As we drove off, I looked back to where I had come from, and for a moment, I wondered what my mother was doing. Tears swirled in my eyes. I was angry with her for what had happened to Nadia and me, but I still loved her dearly and was going to miss her. I looked away, hoping to leave the memories behind.

The truck drove away, still making blasting noises and belching thick smoke. It was also raising dust that blurred the sight of the grassland in the rear. As we passed an *enkang* that was located on either side of the road, I saw *entitos* and *olayonis*, or little boys, playing the circling game. They were holding hands and skipping in circles. I remembered the many years that I had played the circling game with Nadia in the open Maasaiplains around our *enkang*. Suddenly, I felt a gush of emotion and a thick sob rise up in my throat, and I looked away from them.

Moments later, we drove by another *enkang* further down the road, and I could see an *olayoni* tending to his herd of cattle. He had the familiar Maasai stick, which he slapped against the ground, causing a cracking sound. This was to keep his cattle from straying too far. As the truck climbed a hilltop, I saw a group of *ilmurrans* holding long silver spears, their faces painted with red ocher. They were going through their warrior male initiation rites into manhood. This reminded me of the female ritual, and I quickly looked away to the opposite side of the road.

I hope the Maasai life is now behind me, I thought.

But at the same time, I was afraid because I was traveling to a place completely unknown to me. My thoughts were filled with anxiety and fearful anticipation. Drained by my emotional exhaustion, I dozed off.

The voice of a talkative old man seated next to me woke me up. I must have been asleep for at least an hour before we crossed into Kenya.

"You have been asleep for a while now. What is a young girl like you doing traveling all alone?" he asked me.

"I'm going to see my relatives in Mombassa, and they will be waiting for me at the bus station," I lied.

"I see," he said, nodding at the same time.

"Have you been to Kenya before?" he asked.

"Once before," I lied again.

"So tell me, what do you know about Kenya?"

"Mmm…well…mmm…not much," I stuttered.

"Well, would you like to know?" he asked.

I nodded.

"Okay, here—put this on, these headphones," he instructed, handing me over what he was wearing over his ears.

I started to listen to a voice:

"*The word Kenya is from the Kikuyu word Kere Nyaga, or 'Mountain of Mystery' or 'Mountain of Whiteness.' This East African country borders the Indian Ocean to the southeast and also shares its boundaries with Uganda, Sudan, Somalia, and Ethiopia.*" These were names of places that I had never heard of before, and I wondered how they were compared to the Maasailand.

"*The mixed regions of the coastal and brush plains, scrubland, and highlands show the natural geographical beauty and diversity of Kenya's landscape. The intricate mix of its arid plains, lush grasslands, magnificent mountains, and valleys are one of many gifts of nature to this country.*" Now, as I listened to him describe Kenya, I was eased of my anxiety momentarily because his description made me imagine a beautiful land, one that I would love to see someday.

"*The majestic Mount Kenya, the second highest in Africa next to the Tanzanian Mount Kilimanjaro, and Mounts Elgon and Aberdare are some of its magnificent and impressive peaks. In the Rift Valley are Kenya's most beautiful lakes—Turkana, Rudolf, Victoria, Nakuru, Naivasha, Magadi, and many others. These are luscious bodies of water that further beautify Kenya's geographical terrain.*" The mountains and lakes of Kenya I had heard of at the government school, where a few times Nadia and I were able to attend a class that talked about nature.

"The splendor of Kenya's exotic wildlife is a marvel of nature's meticulous detail in creating diversity—from the wildebeests standing on the hillside and munching grass, to the Cheetahs tearing up the remains of their game and the long-necked giraffes quietly eating leaves from trees. More herds of animals roam about in their natural habitat here than perhaps in any other region. The Kenyan safari is also the home of crocodiles, zebras, antelopes, gazelles, lions, buffaloes, and elephants."

Kenya must be a beautiful place with all of the extravagance of nature that it so richly displays, I thought.

As I listened to the voice, I dozed off again, slipping into a dream world where I saw Nadia smiling and waving at me. It was a strange dream because Nadia didn't speak to me, as she had done before; she simply came by where I was and cuddled next to me. After this dream, it would be a long time before I would see Nadia in my dreams again.

A Guiding Light:

When I woke up, I realized that the man had taken back his headphones, and when he saw that I was awake, he smiled and said, "You must be very tired, my child."

I simply nodded and tried to smile back.

"Did you learn something about Kenya?" he asked.

"Yes, I did."

"Nature is so beautiful. It is really spectacular, and you can learn a lot about life and the Creator of all life by observing nature."

I didn't know if he expected a response from me, but I said nothing.

"Did you know that nature also has soothing and healing powers from our Creator? Every disease has a cure secretly locked away in a shrub, tree, or flower. The answers are all there, it's just that we are all too busy chasing after other things and hardly spend any time with nature. She'll only educate you if you spend time with her," he said.

"So, why is a little girl like you going to Mombassa all alone?" he asked again, suddenly changing the topic.

I stared at him for a brief moment, thinking of what to say to him.

"You don't have to tell me if you don't want to. But I can read your troubled spirit, and the road ahead of your life will have some rocky spots. However, in the end, you will be fine. I can sense your future life's journey in my spirit," he said.

I thought it was really strange that a man I didn't know had suddenly taken an interest in me and was telling me about my future. At that point, I really could not think beyond the moment, but his words were both frightening and encouraging.

I smiled at him and said, "Marahaba…Thank you."

Suddenly, I heard someone shout, "Mombassa! Mombassa!"

It seemed we were getting ready to stop. I assumed that we had arrived. I could see a crowded motor park to our right, which our truck was now driving into.

Mombassa was dark, but the roads were nicely lit. This was my first time seeing streetlights, and they were a marvel to my eyes. We alighted from the truck, and I followed the flock of people, who all seemed to be moving in the same direction. But soon they began to disperse in scattered directions, and I began to panic. I had no idea what to do next.

"Please Enkai, help me!" I prayed silently.

At this point, I suddenly heard a crackling noise from under a thick, shrubby area next to where I stood, which startled me.

Could that be a snake? I thought, quickening my steps away from the direction of the noise.

CHAPTER 5

❦

A Guardian Light

"I have been watching you for a few minutes, and you look somewhat confused."

The voice came from behind me. When I turned around, I saw a short, heavy-set lady, perhaps near sixty years of age. She wore a flowery, textile wrap that matched her long sleeve blouse and complimented her light, chocolate-brown complexion. She had a kind and cheerful look, and her eyes seemed to sparkle with energy and a zest for life.

"*Jina lako nani? Kwenu ni mbali?*"

The lady spoke Swahili, which I could understand but could not speak fluently. She had asked me my name and whether my home was far.

"*Jina langu, Mikela*—my name is Mikela. *Ninatafuta mahali*—I am looking for a place. I don't have a home. My parents are dead and that is why—*Ndiyo sababu,*" I lied in my badly spoken Swahili and English. "I'm Mama Eshe," she said, introducing herself in English.

"*Unatafutiwa mahali pa kulala?*"

I realized that she was asking me if I was looking for a place to sleep.

"Yes," I responded.

"Come with me," the woman said in Swahili. "I'm going home now. I have a house for you to sleep in."

"*Kwenu ni mbali?* Is your home far," I asked nervously, even though it wouldn't have made a difference to me how far away her home was.

"*Siyo! Twendeni zetu! Twende zetuni!*"

"Yes! Let's go! Let's go!" the lady was saying.

"*Marahaba Mama! Marahaba Mama!* Thank you, Mama! Thank you, Mama!"

I followed Mama Eshe closely as we trekked to her home. Even though I was nervous and a bid afraid of following a complete stranger to her home, I knew I had no other choices, and so I prayed for Enkai's protection and hoped that the lady would not turn out to be a witch doctor who would turn me into a potion in no time. It was a twenty-five-minute walk before we arrived at her small bungalow.

Her home looks like the government school back in the Maasaiplains, I thought.

Inside were separate rooms; some rooms had chairs and tables and others had only beds. Although we sat on chairs in school, at home in the Maasailand, we always sat on hide-skin mats placed on the floor.

That night, before I went to sleep, Mama Eshe gave me a warm bath and new clothes to wear. The clothes, she said, belonged to her granddaughters, who lived with their parents in Nairobi. For the first time, I lay on a comfortable and relaxing foam bed that was placed on a box spring. A few minutes later, I drifted to sleep peacefully. This night, I had no dreams. My mind and body were at rest, and I believed that Nadia's spirit and Enkai had guided me to Mama Eshe.

The Next Day at Mama Eshe's Home:

"*Mikela Kumekucha*—the sun is up! Wake up! Did you sleep well?" Mama Eshe asked in Swahili laced with English.

"*Siyo*—yes," I responded.

"We're going into the modern center of Mombassa today. You must get ready now. Here, come with me, let's go to the bathroom!"

Mama Eshe had prepared another warm and soothing bath for me. The warm water ran over my body and pampered my skin. I closed my eyes for a moment and thought of what a wonderful lady Mama Eshe was. From there, my thoughts trailed back to the Maasailand, and I wondered what my mother was doing at that moment. Perhaps she was milking the cows or cooking breakfast for the family.

"I love you, Ma. I'm sorry I had to leave. I just had to," I whispered under my breath.

My mind must have been in my day dreaming world for at least fifteen minutes when I heard Mama Eshe's voice again.

"Mikela! Mikela! Have you not spent enough time in that bathtub, my child? Make sure that you brush your teeth. There's a toothbrush and toothpaste for you on the sink table," she shouted again from the kitchen.

My eyes scanned the sink area and rested on the items that were neatly laid on a small table to the left side. I had no idea how to use a toothbrush and toothpaste. In the Maasailand, we used special chewing sticks that had a slightly bitter taste to scrape our teeth and tongue several times in a day.

"Mama Eshe, I don't know how to use a toothbrush," I said. "Please, could you show me how?" I asked.

"Mikela! Your mama never showed you how to brush your teeth, my dear?" Mama Eshe inquired.

"Yes, she did, but at home we used chewing sticks," I responded.

At that instant, I was glad that she wasn't in the bathroom with me because I was quite embarrassed.

"I have some chewing sticks if you'd prefer those," Mama Eshe said.

"Oh no! I would like to learn how to use a toothbrush," I quickly responded.

I could see that this was the beginning of a whole new world for me. I was gradually being introduced to a new way of life that was quite different from the one I had been used to.

Half an hour later, as I admired my new clothes in the mirror, Mama Eshe called out for me again.

"Mikela, it's time for breakfast, and the table is set," she said.

I could smell her cooking in the room and had been waiting eagerly for this moment.

"Yes, Mama Eshe," I responded and quickly hurried over to her kitchen.

The breakfast table was very nicely laid out.

"You can sit over there, my child," Mama Eshe said, pointing at a chair on the other side of the breakfast table.

"We're going to have scrambled eggs and sliced, homemade bread," she said, pointing at the nicely laid out plates on the table.

"We also have some freshly squeezed orange juice to drink," she said, just before she poured out some hot cocoa-milk for both of us.

"Now, let's say the grace," she finally said and started to thank God for the meal.

The delicious breakfast was definitely a different kind of breakfast menu for me. Mama Eshe didn't have to ask me whether I enjoyed it because my plate was licked dry.

My New World:

Shortly after breakfast, we boarded a crowded bus that Mama Eshe called a *matatu* and headed for the heart of the island of Mombassa, a trip that took roughly thirty minutes.

"My child, stay close to me so you don't get lost! Also, listen to me while I tell you about this beautiful island. This is the heart of Mombassa, which is the second largest city in Kenya. Nairobi, where my daughter Bela and her family lives, is the largest city in Kenya."

From where we stood, I could see an adjacent mainland that Mama Eshe explained was connected to the island by a causeway, bridge, and ferries.

"Mombassa used to be a city where everyone came or wished they could visit—it had the largest seaport in Kenya. It also had a mixed population of indigenous Africans, Arabs, Asians, Portuguese, and Indians that was a reflection of its rich history. Foreign merchants started to arrive on this island as early as the eighth century from the Arab and Portuguese world. In the later centuries, white men from Britain came and took over the area. Later, from the Arab world, Muslims also came to live here. That's why streets and buildings of the Old Mombassa town have designs that were patterned from the Muslim culture. These old buildings on narrow streets and alleyways have now become tourist attractions, so people still come from all over the world to the city of Mombassa. The Arabs traded gold, ivory, beads, silks, porcelain, and metal products with the Bantu-speaking African natives who were here before everyone else. The language Swahili came from a mixture of Omni Arab and Bantu words."

From where we were, Mama Eshe pointed towards the Fort Jesus Museum that stood on a coral ridge at the entrance of the harbor that overlooked the Old Mombassa town.

"The Portuguese built Fort Jesus when they first conquered Mombassa. They said they built it to protect themselves from the attacks of the natives who wanted the Portuguese to leave their ancestral land. Later, the Swahili-speaking natives of Mombassa defeated the Omni Arabs who had conquered the Portuguese. Unfortunately, we lost the land again back to the Portuguese; this was before the British defeated them once again," Mama Eshe explained.

She paused of a moment, as though to collect her thoughts before she continued.

"In addition to Mombassa's historic sites, there are many modern resorts and hotels, shops, restaurants, and a huge oil refinery at Kilindini, which is also an industrial zone of sugar and oil refineries. Although the city itself lacks beaches, it provides a gateway to Makupa Causeway and to the mainland beaches," she explained.

Our tour of Mombassa aroused a child-like curiosity in me as I observed its roads, terraces, alleyways, shops, and cultural displays. I asked Mama Eshe questions about every historical building or monument that we passed.

"You ask very intelligent questions, my child; it's unusual for a child at your age to ask such questions," Mama Eshe remarked.

I quickly observed that Mombassa was a sharp deviation from the Maasai countryside. The unique cultural flavor in Mombassa was my first, real life lesson about the diversity of the world outside of the Maasailand. The tour of the city of Mombassa ended nicely with a meal at a fine restaurant that served Kenyan and Tanzanian cuisine.

The Day After:

The following day, as we had breakfast, Mama Eshe inquired about my future plans.

"Mikela, where do you plan to go from here, my child?"

"Ma, I don't know. I'm an orphan, and I have no place to go," I lied again.

"Yes, I remember you said that at the motor park yesterday. Okay, we'll think of something, my child," Mama Eshe said.

Then she paused for a brief moment and appeared to be in deep thought. Finally, she said, "Don't you worry; I think I can help you. My daughter Bela, who lives in Nairobi, asked me to find a young nanny to live with her family. Would you like to live in Nairobi?" Mama Eshe inquired.

I smiled and nodded. I think my eyes must have sparkled, showing my excitement.

"But you seem too young to do that job," she said almost immediately.

"No, Mama Eshe, I am not. Yes, I mean I'm only thirteen, but I work very hard. Already at my age I have learned to build *bomas* in the Maasailand," I added quickly, hoping that she would not change her mind about sending me to Nairobi.

I could see Mama Eshe raise her eyebrow when I mentioned that I could build a Maasai *boma*, but she said nothing about that.

"Bela lives in Nairobi with her husband Chege Mathani and two children, ten-year-old Johari and seven-year-old Jamila. Bela and Chege are looking for a nanny to care for their two daughters. So, I'll tell them about you and see if they would like to have you," she explained.

Again, after a brief moment of silence, she said, "I would have to ask them first."

I nodded with hopeful excitement. I was transparently thrilled at the possibility of having a new home.

Perhaps Johari and Jamila will become my friends. Maybe they will love me like Nadia did, I thought.

The Next Two Weeks:

During the next two weeks, I remained at Mama Eshe's home. She treated me very nicely and loved me like her own grandchild. On the day I left for Nairobi, she took me to a rowdy Mombassa bus station where I boarded a big bus and not the usual *matatu*. Before I left, I hugged her for what seemed like eternity because at that instant, I didn't want to let go of the woman that I'd come to believe was my guardian light. Just for a short while, she'd become like a mother to me, and I'd grown to love her very much.

"Mikela, although you've only been with me for a short while, I've come to love you like my own grandchild," Mama Eshe said, almost as if she'd read my mind.

"Something about your soul drew me to you the very first time I set eyes on you," she added.

"My daughter Bela is a good woman. She'll take care of you in Nairobi, and I'll come and visit you soon," Mama Eshe promised.

I could see a well of tears in her eyes when I started sobbing.

"I love you, too, Mama Eshe. Thank you for everything. Thank you for being my guardian light," I said. I hugged her tightly once more before I climbed onto the bus.

A New Home:

The bus arrived in Nairobi late that night, and Bela and Chege Mathani were at the station to receive me.

"Hello! You must be Mikela. We are Mr. and Mrs. Mathani—Bela and Chege Mathani," Bela said, with a warm and welcoming smile.

"*Siyo*—yes! *Jina langu, Mikela*—my name is Mikela," I responded in Swahili.

"Do you speak English?" Bela asked.

"A little," I said apologetically.

"Well, don't worry, you will learn in no time," she said, in her badly spoken Swahili. "And you can call me Aunt Bela."

I later learned that Mr. Chege Mathani was a career diplomat who had lived in many countries around the world. He was currently stationed at the Kenyan foreign affairs office in Nairobi. Sometime in the future, he hoped to take up a diplomatic position in New York as the next Kenyan Ambassador to the United Nations. He'd been married to Bela, who was a freelance journalist, for twelve years. They'd met while they were in college at the University of Nairobi. At the time, Chege was studying political science and international relations, while Bela was in the school of journalism.

Chege's career sprouted very quickly soon after he joined the Kenyan diplomatic core. This was partly because he was of Kikuyu decent—one of the largest and most influential ethnic groups in Kenya. Chege was a typical Kikuyu—hardworking and quickly adaptable to any changes in the society. He was also a natural politician and polished by his excellent education. His impressive qualifications, family background, and network, coupled with his hard work and good work ethic, channeled him into a prolific diplomatic career.

Ironically, Aunt Bela was of Luo decent who were a rival ethnic group of the Kikuyus. Her father came from a Luo lineage while her mother was of Bantu ancestry. Next to the Kikuyus, the Luos were the second wealthiest and most influential group in Kenya. In recent years, the Luos had become very educated and an intricate part of Kenya's workforce. For decades, the Luos and the Kikuyus had fought over political and economic dominance.

It was not surprising that Bela's parents vehemently opposed her marriage to Chege, the son of a traditional Kikuyu. Kikuyus were in many ways archrivals of the Luos—they competed for higher education, jobs, leadership, and economic dominance. At the same time, Chege's parents were not particularly happy about having a daughter-in-law that was a Luo. Nonetheless, knowing the stubborn nature of their son Chege, their disapproval didn't last too long. Bela's parents also conceded when she threatened to sever all ties with her family. Bela's father died exactly one year after her wedding, and her mother moved back to Mombassa where her own family had originally come from.

While at the University of Nairobi, Chege excelled in academics and in leadership. He started to plan his diplomatic career while he was still in college. He organized student groups and workshops on ethnic problems on campus. He presented himself with a regal air, and in many subtle ways, he emphasized that he was the heir of an aristocratic family. He was a flashy, tall, campus stud—one of the young men who seemed to be quite popular on campus and greatly sought after by many of the beautiful college women. It was no surprise to anyone who knew Chege that he'd had his share of girlfriends, or that his relationships usually lasted only two semesters on the average. He seemed unable to find the woman with whom he wanted to settle down.

Chege was also a devoted sprinter, with a strong, athletic build, broad shoulders, firm and muscular arms, a rippling chest, and tight stomach muscles. He had the body of an ancestral warrior laced with a smooth, dark-amber complexion, a chiseled bone structure, and high cheekbones. His almond-shaped eyes, and his curvy and voluptuous lips, graced his looks with the air of an African prince. Many knew him to be a playboy on campus. Oddly, many also perceived him to be a perfect gentleman.

Chege first caught a glimpse of Bela at his country club's Olympic-size swimming pool. He'd just completed twenty-four laps and was leaning against the pool edge when his eyes caught Bela's trim and elegant figure making a head-dive into the deep end of the water. He liked what he saw and waited for an opportunity to speak to her. This never came because she swam continuously for almost twenty minutes, and when she finally emerged from underneath the water, she disappeared towards the women's showers. When he saw her again, she was playing lawn tennis with an older gentleman who Chege assumed was her father because of their striking resemblance.

One evening three weeks later, Chege saw Bela again at the university campus library. She caught his attention when she got up from a study cubicle to visit the book stacks. Bela had well proportioned facial features that seemed to align in a perfect symmetry. She had Nefertiti elegance and a serene air about her, even though she was not a stunning or exotic beauty. Her nicely shaped, and slightly voluptuous lips undoubtedly added to her attractive air.

Bela was oblivious of her admirer as she went back to her study cubicle and resumed reading. She had no idea that she'd mesmerized Chege Mathani, the popular campus stud. On that day, for some inexplicable reason, Chege lacked the confidence to walk up to Bela and introduce himself. This was a problem that he'd never had with other women in the past.

The next time that he saw Bela was three months later, at a mutual friend's house during a party. Chege knelt and pleaded with his friend to introduce him to Bela. Finally, he got to meet the woman that had left him spellbound at the swimming pool and breathless at the library months earlier. Still, it took him a month to ask Bela out on a date. Twice Bela turned him down because of his reputation as a playboy on campus, but Chege kept the pressure on her for weeks, promising a drastic change in his ways. Six weeks later, Bela finally agreed to go out on a date with him. She became the last girlfriend that Chege had on campus—at least that's what he said to her. Campus rumors still had it that he had an occasional fling. Bela never found out about the other women that Chege dated after their relationship started. Quite frankly, she really didn't care to know because she'd fallen in love with the campus playboy. They were married one year after their graduation.

Mr. Chege Mathani took my few belongings—essentially my Maasai clothes and the new clothes that Mama Eshe had given to me in Mombassa—and loaded them in the trunk as Aunt Bela and I got seated in their car, which I later learned was a German-made, 700 series convertible BMW. I had never seen a car as beautiful as the Mathani's. While I was in the Maasailand, I never imagined that such a car existed because all I had ever seen back home were old trucks traveling on the only road that led from the open plains—a dusty, unpaved road. This was the same road where I'd boarded the old, rusty truck that took me to Mombassa.

As we drove along the nicely paved roads of Nairobi, I admired the beauty of the city. It was now late at night, but everything was brightly lit by the same type of tall streetlights that I'd seen in Mombassa. There were also tall buildings that seemed to be reaching the skies. On the highway were cars of all shapes and sizes, and many were moving even faster than we were. I was thrilled to be in such a beautiful city and could not wait to see it in the daytime.

Could this really be the beginning of a new life for me? I wondered.

"Let it be, Enkai…please, let it be," I mouthed in prayer.

CHAPTER 6

Fledgling Talent

A while later we arrived at the Mathani residence, which looked like a castle straight from a fairytale. Two little girls, whom I suspected were Johari and Jamila, emerged from behind the front door. They were beautiful! They both ran to greet their parents with glaring excitement.

"Mom! Dad! Welcome back!"

"Here are my lovely princesses!" Aunt Bela exclaimed, spreading her arms to engulf them in an embrace.

"Johari is ten years, and Jamila is three years younger," Aunt Bela said to me, as she held them close to her.

Johari and Jamila looked very much alike, and more like Aunt Bela than their father.

"Where is Eba?" Aunt Bela asked.

Almost immediately, a young, chubby, and very dark-complexioned lady with sparkling white eyes and teeth emerged from behind the front door. She looked a little like Aunt Bela, but she appeared to be in her early twenties.

"Oh! Here she comes!" Aunt Bela said. "Eba is my youngest sister; she's in her last year at the University of Nairobi, and is getting married soon," Aunt Bela explained to me.

"Sister Bela and Uncle Chege, welcome back," Eba said.

"Eba, I was just asking about you—did you hear us drive in?"

"Yes, Sister Bela, I did," Eba said in a soft voice. "I was just taking the last dinner dish from the oven—dinner is ready now."

"Here, meet Mikela—she'll be staying with us now that you are going back to college. She'll help take care of Johari and Jamila.

"Johari and Jamila, meet Mikela," Aunt Bela said.

Their faces relaxed into warm and gentle smiles as they hugged and welcomed me to their home. Their warmth gave me an instant feeling of bonding with them.

"Welcome, Mikela," Eba then said, her face breaking into a warm smile as she reached to help me carry one of my bundles. She motioned for me to follow her as she walked towards the font entrance, with Johari and Jamila trailing behind her. "We'll take you to your room."

I instantly felt at home with the whole family. Meeting them was like a breath of fresh air—I felt like I'd known them for years.

"Marahaba Nadia! Thank you, Enkai!" I whispered to myself.

If only my mother was here with me, I thought. *Only the future and its promises would tell, Ma, and I hope that your face is in my future. I love you, Ma, and I miss you—but for now I'm glad the Maasailand is behind me.*

The Mathani Residence—Fire in my Dream:

A week after I arrived at the Mathani home, I had an unusual dream. First, I felt the intensity of the heat in a room, and beads of sweat trickled down my face and body. I could see flames within a short distance from where I was. The smell of smoke filled my nostrils with the awful stench of mixed burning wood and cattle dung. As the flames moved closer to me, threatening to engulf me, an intense fear overtook me, and I started to scream.

"Fire! Fire! Someone please help me."

My voice echoed back through the thick cloud of smoke that had formed, and I started to choke and cough. My breathing becoming labored.

"Oh Enkai! Please help me! Please save me, Enkai!"

Suddenly, I felt a gush of wind, and a double door swung open, letting in a thick cloud of smoke that followed the direction of the wind. My coughing subsided, and my breathing became easier.

I heard the sound of an alarm going off—and I opened my eyes. I looked around and then it suddenly dawned on me that I had been dreaming.

"Marahaba Enkai!" I whispered, as I realized that I was in the safe and comfortable home of the Mathani family.

November 1979—The Mathani Home:

It had been a year since I'd arrived at the home of Chege and Bela Mathani, and I was now fourteen years old. The Mathani home was a beautiful, 3,000 square-foot mansion nestled in a valley of small mountains in an exclusive, suburban Nairobi neighborhood. It had eight bedrooms with full baths and two additional guest restrooms. The unique features of the kitchen in the main wing of their home included a custom Italian-designed turret and a butler's pantry that had a rounded nook with a glass enclosure. In the basement of their home was a party room with an ultramodern entertainment center. To the back corner of this room was a well stocked bar. Adjacent to the entertainment room was an exercise room that had workout machines, treadmills, cross trainers, dumb bells, and weight lifting equipment. Every other day, Mr. Mathani spent one to two hours exercising in this room.

There were two other floors upstairs—the first floor had four bedrooms that included a study room with a computer and a lounging area that housed a television and beautiful white piano for Jamila and Johari.

Aunt Bela and Mr. Mathani's bedroom and three other rooms were on the last level. On this same level was Mr. Mathani's home office. Sometimes, Aunt Bela used this room as her office where she edited interview tapes that she made during her freelance trips as a journalist.

Outside, there was an adjoining four-car garage and a courtyard juxtaposed to a flower garden that housed pink, red, white, and yellow roses, sunflowers, Blue Bells of Scotland, hibiscus, African bougainvillea, and lilies. To the left of the courtyard and flower garden was an oval-shaped, three-lane junior lap pool for Jamila and Johari. This pool tapered where it joined a 1,000 square-foot swimming lagoon, where Aunt Bela and Mr. Mathani had many of their extravagant cocktail parties. Next to the swimming pool was a Jacuzzi that was elegantly finished with hand-designed, Italian tiles.

The Mathani residence was clearly the fantastic outcome of careful, intelligent design and the craftsmanship of skilled architects and masons. It was a home that typified an aristocratic Kenyan family with a lifestyle of affluence—its artistry and design flaunted seasoned wealth.

The house also included the luxury of a complete staff consisting of one cook-steward, three professional house cleaners, two drivers, two gardeners, and eight security guards.

During my spare time, I immersed myself in my drawings and paintings. I would curl up on a hand-made Persian rug on the marble floor of Jamila and

Johari's study-room and express my feelings and thoughts on paper. Aunt Bela complimented my artistic drawings and paintings after seeing some of what she described as impressive artwork of their home, Jamila and Johari, the city center of Nairobi, and the island of Mombassa. To my utmost surprise and delight, on my fourteenth birthday, her gift was an artist's box that contained color guides, brushes, canvas backgrounds, watercolors, and oil paints of professional quality.

"Aunt Bela, this is beautiful—what a pleasant surprise!" I said, when I opened the package.

"You have incredible talent, Mikela, and this is my little way of encouraging you," she said, rubbing my shoulders affectionately.

"Also, I have asked the gardener to arrange the small room next to the garage for you to use as a studio. After school, you can draw and paint there whenever you feel like—after you're done with your house chores," she added.

"Marahaba, Aunt Bela!"

I spent the rest of the evening of my fourteenth birthday painting with my new artist's box until it appeared that everyone had retired for the night.

An Emerging Soft Beauty:

That night, just before I went to bed at 10 PM, I came downstairs to get some drinking water. When I thought I heard a sound in the living room, I tiptoed over to the side of the sliding door behind the drapes and saw Mr. Mathani; he was on the phone and I heard him mention my name. I knew he could not have been speaking with Aunt Bela because she was fast asleep in Johari and Jamila's room. I decided to listen for a few more seconds because I was curious about what he was saying about me.

"The young Maasai girl that lives with us is sprouting into an astonishing beauty. Every day, she appears to be visibly maturing into a stunningly gorgeous young woman…"

The rest of what he was saying I could barely hear, and his words soon turned into intermittent chuckles. A few minutes later, he resumed talking.

"Her new friend and schoolmate, Tulia, often braids her long hair into single, dangling braids, accentuating her neatly developing sensuous beauty with subtle innocence. Like the African purple bougainvillea, I see her body emerging and blossoming into a new freshness."

"*Why is he saying such things,*" I thought, as I heard him chuckle even louder.

"She's becoming like an opiate that constantly draws me to her. Her beguiling beauty is as potent to me as a powerful fragrance from a mixture of scents. She's just like a sweet smelling flower that has a strong seductiveness, drawing my body to her." Chills ran down my spine as I listened to what Mr. Mathani was saying.

"*Why would he have such unholy thoughts about me,*" I wondered.

"I know she's just a young and free-spirited soul, but I can't seem to keep her off my mind. I hope Bela has not noticed how I feel about that Maasai girl because I think I've been quite conscious about masking the unholy eruptions that seem to be occurring more frequently inside of me."

I was stunned by what I was hearing. I could not believe that Mr. Mathani would speak of me in such a manner. I decided not to listen to him anymore because I was too embarrassed to hear more of his descriptions. I had no idea that he looked at me in that manner. I quietly tiptoed away from the living room door and sneaked back to my room upstairs, hoping that he hadn't heard me.

In the ensuing days, I started to notice Mr. Mathani's embarrassing glances at me, but I would immediately look away, having been taught in the Maasailand not to stare back at elders. I didn't really know what to do about his new attitude, and I simply stayed clear of his path as much as possible.

My Love Affair with Nairobi:

The next morning being a Saturday, Aunt Bela gave me some money for a day out in town with Tulia. The city of Nairobi was a delightful and intriguing new world with lots of attractions. The Maasai meaning of "Nairobi" is "a place of cool waters" or "a place of sweet waters." Nairobi was once a small village inhabited by Maasai tribesmen and only later became a British trade center. In addition to the city of Nairobi, the country called Kenya today originally belonged to pastoral Maasai before the British took the land from them in the late 1890s. For little or no wages, the British also brought over thirty thousand East Indian laborers to build the Mombassa-to-Uganda railway and a railroad camp. Between 1900 and 1907, many buildings began to sprout in that area, which became the British East Africa Protectorate later called the "Kenya Colony."

In history class, we were told that the City of Nairobi, sometimes called the "City in the Sun," is a distinct tropical city located south of the equator. This city sits on a high altitude of between 5,000 and 6,000 feet, with a more tropical climate at lower levels and temperate weather at the higher peaks. It's quite usual for the sun to rise between 6:30 and 7:30 AM from the eastern part of the city. The powerful beams of the sun, tempered by nature; after sunset temperatures could be anywhere from 76°F to a little above 86°F during the dry season. Following the sunrise, and later after the western sunset between 6:30 and 7:30 in the evening, there were usually refreshing and cool evenings, with temperatures as low as 49°F. The Nairobi rains came in two seasons—short rains between early November and December and longer rains between early April and mid-June.

As we walked through the city eating ice cream and sipping sodas, I observed the natural beauty of the city of Nairobi, with its magnificent topography elegantly displayed at its high and low peaks in the midst of the technological interplay of towering skyscrapers and high-rises. The high peaks seemed to rise like a phantasm from the flat edges of the Embakasi and Athi plains. The size of the bustling city of Nairobi, which housed over 1.5 million people, was believed to be almost 700 square kilometers and encompassed about 120 square kilometers of the Nairobi Game Park and the Jomo Kenyatta Airport.

At the Nairobi City Center, the planned clusters of ultra modern skyscrapers and high-rises showcased the now tallest building—the Kenyatta International Conference Center. (The Hilton International Hotel used to be the tallest building.) The commercial quadrangle girdled a central block where University Way, Koinange Street, Haile Selassie Avenue, and Tom Mboya Street could be located. As the financial and governmental capital of Kenya, the Nairobi City Center also housed the National Assembly, Law Courts, Offices of the President, and the City Hall. The embassies of other nations, including offices of the United Nations and the World Health Organization, also converged, with their sprawling offices of diplomatic missions and trade centers.

For the delight of Kenyans, its permanent Asian immigrants, and local and foreign tourists, the Nairobi City Center had a variety of restaurants that served anything from delicious Kenyan cuisine to Indian, Chinese, Arab, Pakistani, and European dishes.

Around the city of Nairobi were loose boundaries, with the Nairobi River in the north part, the Nairobi Hill and Uhuru Highway to the west, and the railways in the southern part. To the south of the railways was the industrial area packed with factories, manufacturing warehouses, and small enterprises of craftsmen called "Jua Kali" or "Hot Sun." The Jua Kalis made items like buckets, charcoal-burning stoves, and cooking spoons from scrap metal.

To the north of the city of Nairobi was the agricultural sector—the home of pineapple, sisal, and maize farms. At Limuru, tea farms flourished, while coffee bean farms marked the earth at Thika all around the loose boundaries of the city limits.

The homes of some of the finest Nairobi intellectuals, and the University of Nairobi, were situated north of the city, and to the south of the city was the Kenya Polytechnic. Other tourist attractions in the north included the National Museum of Kenya, the Sorsbie Art Gallery, the International Casino, and the Norfolk hotel.

Historically, Asians, especially Indians, who settled in Nairobi functioned as middle-servants for the colonial masters and were rewarded with economic dominance over the Kenyans, the natives and owners of the land. The Asians have since assimilated into the society and started thriving businesses, and today many of them now live in secluded and up-scale suburbs like the Parklands in the north of the city of Nairobi. The western boundaries of the city housed the middle and lower class Kenyans, who lived in areas like the Ngong and Hurlingham. Others lived in areas like Eastleigh and Pangani, called "African suburbs" by foreigners and the local Asians. Some other upper-scale suburbs, such as where the Mathanis lived, were lavish and boasted the expensive homes of aristocratic Kenyan families, government officials, and a few of the nouveau-rich.

While exploring Kenya's landmarks, monuments, historic districts, and wildlife, my natural love for art drew me to the museums—the national archives of both professional and amateur art and a collection of marvelous ethnic relics of Kenya's heritage. The Nairobi National Museum flaunted the regal stylishness and richness of the exquisite cultural exhibits of the Kenyan peoples with an impressive display of historic vestiges. Within the national park were astonishing recreations of pre-historic rock sites, with amazing casts on the ground of the footprints of human ancestry dating back to over four million years ago.

Nairobi was a city that I simply cherished, and I had undoubtedly fallen in love with the fascinating historical portraits and paintings in the Railway Museum—a collection of relics of old steam engines and trains.

I convinced Tulia to visit the museum with me that day as part of my birthday treat, and although she was not particularly interested in museums and art she agreed to go to make me happy. We caught a crowded *matatu* to Haile Selassie road and then trekked to Ngair Avenue, which led to Station Road, the location of the Railway Museum. I also wanted to go to the National Archives, but it would have entailed catching a *matatu* to Moi Avenue and Tom Mboya Street in the Old Bank of India building across from the Hilton Hotel, the location of the National Archives, and it was getting late. I had promised Aunt Bela that I would be back before dark.

My Daily Routine:

During my first year in Nairobi, I had a very busy daily schedule. It was an exciting year of learning new things and adapting to a new culture. I'd started attending a nearby public school while Johari and Jamila attended an expensive private school. Every morning, when Johari and Jamila were being driven to their private school, I trekked a mile to the nearest bus stop to take a *matatu* to my own school. I rode with other schoolchildren, as well as with people carrying sacks of vegetables, live chickens or goats, bundles of personal belongings, and a variety of luggage, but I didn't mind any of that. I was quite happy to have the opportunity to attend school and live in a lovely home where I was treated well. In school, I learned to speak fluent English while still polishing my Swahili.

At home, Aunt Bela was good to me and treated me like a close relative instead of the maid I was. Her kids, Johari and Jamila, loved me like an older sister. Occasionally, Mama Eshe came down from Mombassa to visit. I shared a special bond with her. To me, she was Enkai's special gift to me. So, for now, life was great—except for the times that I missed my mother, whom I still loved very much and wished I could see again. But I had no immediate plans of going back to the Maasailand, as I was content living in the Mathani home. Daily, I prayed for my mother and for my entire family, and I simply trusted that Enkai would keep them safe until such a time in the future when I would be able to see them again.

This is a safe haven for me now. The Mathanis are a perfect and loving family, was my thinking.

My artwork remained my deep passion, where I made my illusionary escapes into past and present destinations, some of which I captured with the hopeful anticipation of a brighter future. Vividly I tried to capture the beauty of nature intermeshed with the highlights of Nairobi and Mombassa. Sometimes, traces of my young mind wrapped in the pain of my past could be seen in my paintings. I knew this because people sometimes commented that my paintings seemed to capture the not so savory reality of life. Although they didn't know my past experience, they captured glimpses of it in my paintings.

Occasionally, I painted the beauty of my traditional Maasai culture, depicting the youthful exuberance of *entitos* and showing their young and fledgling bodies. At the same time, I would capture their wounded souls after their experience of female circumcision. My memories of the *ilmurrans* helped me to recreate visual images of them vividly expressing in their eyes, a mix of excitement and yet fearful anticipation of the very moment of their initiation into manhood. I would paint the *ilmurrans* exhibiting confident postures and flaunting bold courage as they watched over their cattle on the Maasaiplains.

Aunt Bela once remarked, "Mikela, I am amazed at how well you capture the daring spirits of the *ilmurrans*."

At another time, while looking through my work, she said, "Your artistic taste and impressions somehow brings life out of still paintings. You have a unique and exotic flair that clearly stands out as an impressive original and young talent."

At school, it seemed that my paintings and drawings had begun to draw attention. My art teacher, a short and heavy-set man in his mid-forties, who we respectfully called Mr. Gathi Njora, was so impressed with my work that he decided to show them to the school principal, Mr. Wakesa Mbui. Mr. Njora had great love for art and artistic talent. He was very dedicated to his job, although he was poorly paid, like all the other teachers—including the school principal.

"Mikela, this is extraordinary work. Where did you learn to do this?" the principal asked.

"Sir, no one taught me—I've been painting since I was a child in the Maasailand."

Our school principal, Mr. Mbui was a stern man who hardly ever smiled. He had a demeanor that was quite different from Mr. Njora, who was a very jovial and light-hearted man and a teacher with a mentoring touch. Mr. Mbui was a tall and slender, dark-complexioned man with all gray hair and a receding hairline. He had an unusually long face that narrowed into a square chin, and his protruding Adam's apple was well centered in his neck. His lips were very thick, with turned up sides, and he had a big, flat, and flared nose that showed his big and wide nostrils. At first glance, you would notice that he had a slight hump and walked limply. He also had very prominent tobacco and coffee-stained teeth that drew curious attention when he smiled. He looked like he was already in his early sixties, but my classmates said he was fifty-five.

"I had been meaning to suggest that we have an art show here in the school. This way we can show off talents like Mikela," Mr. Njora said to Mr. Mbui in my presence, once I was invited to the school principal's office to discuss my artwork.

"Not a bad idea! I like that. The only problem I see is that we don't have the money for that. It's not in this year's school budget, and as you know, our budget is already very tight," Mr. Mbui explained, clearly disappointed.

"I might have an idea, sir. Please give me a little time, and I'll get back to you," my teacher suggested.

"Okay! I'm eager to hear what it is whenever you're ready," Mr. Mbui replied hopefully, politely dismissing both Mr. Njora and me.

A month later, Mr. Njora informed me that he had met with the principal again and that the school had decided to have the art show.

"Most of your work will be exhibited in the art show—bring all of your paintings tomorrow to be framed," he instructed me.

"Sir, that's wonderful news, but how's the school going to pay for it?"

"An artist who owns a gallery and art school at the Nairobi City Center agreed to help us raise some money. This morning I received a call from him, and he informed me that the French Embassy and the Nairobi National Museum will donate enough money to host the art show."

"Great! That's really great, sir!" I exclaimed, as I skipped out of the classroom.

My Debut:

In preparation for the art show, the paintings and drawings of talented students, including mine, were nicely framed with mahogany wood, polished wood finishing, gold-color trims, or simple glass frames. Mr. Njora described the oil-on-canvas paintings as being elegantly bare and vividly expressing the artistic talents of our young minds. He said that our work was a lovely blend of flaming and mild colors that displayed our emotions and thoughts.

Aunt Bela, Johari, and Jamila accompanied me to the art show at the French Embassy. Aunt Bela made me a new, long wrap skirt and tee-top made from African textiles, which I wore to the occasion.

As soon as we arrived, Mr. Njora quickly whisked me away to be introduced to the captive audience that he said had been waiting to see the young, Maasai talent whose paintings had stolen their hearts. As I explained my paintings and drawings, and the source of my inspiration, I could feel someone glaring at me from a dark corner of the French Embassy's makeshift gallery. Moments later, when I looked in that direction, I thought I saw a shadow move, but the person seemed to have disappeared into the crowd.

I shifted my attention back to my audience when someone walked up to me and whispered, "What an incredible talent you have, Mikela. No doubt you're going to be a star."

He was a middle-aged white man with a long face, pointed chin, jet-black hair, and a pronounced nose, accentuated by a slight hump on his nose bridge.

Mr. Njora interrupted the white man and said, "Hello, Jacques. I'm glad you've met our star." He turned to me. "Mikela, this has been a fantastic turn-out. The collective and elegant simplicity of your artwork flaunts your artistic genius." He patted me gently on the back.

I nodded shyly and thanked Mr. Njora for his kind words. Then I noticed that the white man had quietly slipped away.

"The number of wealthy people that have come and seemed to love our display equally amazes me," I said to Mr. Njora.

He nodded and smiled. "Keep up your good works, my child."

The rest of the evening turned out to be a smashing success. My school raised enough money to cover most of our next year's budget for the art class, and I was awarded a full art scholarship for that year.

June 1980—Loss of Innocence:

A few weeks later, I had yet another dream that played out in the Maasailand. This time I was under the rain, completely drenched—my skirt and top clung to my body as I tried to run across a small bridge. I was almost at the end of the bridge when I saw a lion coming across the bridge in my direction.

"Please help me! Someone, please help me!" I screamed.

I started to run faster, but my strides were nothing compared to that of the lion. I panicked, and again I started to scream as loud as I could.

"Please help me! Someone, please help me!"

No one seemed to have heard me. I only heard the sound of the raindrops as they landed on the wooden surface of the bridge. When I looked back again, the lion was only a stone's throw away from me.

"Oh Enkai! Please save me!" I said. Then I heard someone calling my name.

CHAPTER 7

Rape of Innocence

A Revolving Glass of Misery:

"Mikela! Mikela!"

I opened my eyes and for a brief moment wondered where I was. Then I realized that I was in my room and not on a bridge running from a lion—a sigh of relief escaped my mouth. I whispered, "Marahaba Enkai!"

"Mikela, I'm off to Mombassa with Jamila and Johari. We'll be back in three days." It was Aunt Bela's voice.

"Okay, Aunt Bela. I'll be right there." I replied.

"Don't bother…we're in a hurry to leave," Aunt Bela immediately responded, the tone of her voice clearly expressing her eagerness to leave.

"Okay, Aunt Bela, have a safe trip…bye-bye Jamila…bye Johari," I finally said, raising my voice slightly to mask my disappointment that they were leaving me behind.

It was a public holiday on this Friday, and it was a few minutes after noon. I stretched lazily on my bed and after about five minutes of daydreaming, I dragged myself up.

I would have loved to go with Aunt Bela to visit Mama Eshe, but I had housework to do. It was also the cook-steward's day off, and I needed to prepare meals for Mr. Mathani.

Hours later, I'd completed my house chores. It was now a little after 9 PM, and I'd just finished serving Mr. Mathani his dinner. I was busy cleaning the dirty dishes in the kitchen when I heard him calling my name.

"Mikela! Mikela!"

"Sir?" I immediately answered.

"Where are you?"

Quickly, I wiped my hands and ran to the living room.

"What are you doing, Mikela?"

"Sir, I'm washing the dishes."

"Get me some tea," he snapped.

"Yes, sir."

Half an hour later, I served him his favorite Kenyan-highlands tea, went upstairs, and collected a book to take with me into the children's study room to read.

About another hour later, the squeaking sound of the door swinging open interrupted my reading. I looked up and saw Mr. Mathani in his house robe, his chest visibly exposed. I was too embarrassed to look at his bare chest, so I looked away and stared down at my open book.

Mikela, are you done cleaning up?" he asked rather sternly.

"Yes, sir—I was done more than an hour ago," I replied nervously.

"What are you doing now?"

"Sir, I'm reading a book," I said, without looking up.

"I can see that," he said and paused for a brief moment before he asked, "Are you afraid of me?"

"No, sir," I quickly responded, without lifting my head.

"Then look at me when you're talking to me," Mr. Mathani said, raising his voice.

"I am sorry, sir," I said in a shaky voice, and then I raised my head to look at him. I hoped my eyes didn't express my utter fear and anxiety.

Mr. Mathani sometimes wore a grin that seemed part smile and part smirk. I could see that same expression on his face as he started to move towards me.

"Do you know that you are like a beautiful flower?" he asked.

I froze with fear when I heard his words, as I remembered the things that I'd heard him say about me in his phone conversation some time ago.

"You've been like opium to me, and I want to have a taste of your innocence," he added, his face only a few inches away from mine.

I instinctively jumped up from my chair—my legs visibly trembling. My abrupt jump coupled with my trembling legs made me unsteady and slower paced, giving him an edge over me. Before I had a chance to move backwards again, he pulled me towards his chest, holding me firmly with his left hand. Then, he started to fondle my tender breasts, massaging them in circles with the flatness of his right palm. I panicked and started to scream, pleading with him to stop.

"Please, sir! Please! Please, Mr. Mathani!" I said in a shrill and desperate voice. "Please leave me alone. I don't like what you are doing! Please stop it, sir! I don't want this—please leave me alone!"

Mr. Mathani ignored my plea and started to twirl my nipples between his fingers.

"You have beautiful young breasts. I love them," he said, breathing heavily on my neck.

"Please leave me alone, sir! I am going to scream…please leave me alone! If you don't leave me, I'll scream louder," I threatened, struggling to push him away.

My threat seemed to have infuriated him, and he shouted at me angrily.

"Shut up! I say shut up, you little brat, or I will send you back to the ugly Maasaiplains."

The ugly memories of my circumcision and Nadia's death flashed in my mind. I started to cry.

"Oh please don't, sir! Please, sir, don't! I don't want to go back to the Maasailand."

I was confused and afraid, and silently, I started to pray to Enkai to save me, but everything was happening too fast. I suddenly felt my body being jolted forward as Mr. Mathani grabbed me, and in a flash, he threw me down on the couch. He started to undress me while planting wet kisses all over my lips, ears, neck, hair, and eyelids.

I was now weeping, screaming, and kicking at the same time. My plea to Mr. Mathani went unheard even as I kicked harder with both of my legs and pushed against his heavy and muscular chest with my hands, desperately trying to use my elbows as a wedge. Suddenly, I felt one of his hands between my legs—the same area where the women in my *enkang* had hurt me and caused me unforgettable pain. At this point, I started to scream and kick even harder in utter panic—I was determined not to let him hurt me.

To keep me still, Mr. Mathani sent a firm and painful slap across my face, convulsing my whole body from the force of it. I was now in a state of utter fear and confusion—I felt like this was a flashback of my experience in the Maasailand.

Was I reliving my past? I asked myself. Then I felt Mr. Mathani's hand parting the outer lips of my sacred self and touching the smoothness and valleys of my inner rim. Momentarily he climbed on top of me and started to rub himself against me. I was now in a desperate state—I was tossing and turning with my hands in the air. I was screaming frantically, but no one outside of the Mathani Mansion seemed to hear my cry for help. My face was drenched with tears and sweat as my body shifted against him. His fingers roughly touched the inner walls of my sacred self, and I suddenly felt excruciating pain, as if my insides were tearing apart.

"Oh! No! Please, someone help me!" I started to scream louder as the rough movements of his fingers continued.

I felt wetness between my legs; I think I must have started to bleed then. Mr. Mathani didn't seem to care about my bleeding, distress, or screaming fury. He held me down firmly as I kicked and wriggled my body. Then he pulled his hands out from inside of me and, reaching into his pocket, removed a small sachet, tore it open with his teeth, and pulled out a white tube that I'd never seen before. As he started to put on the plastic tube, I tried to get up, since he seemed distracted, but he slapped me again, momentarily stunning me. I let out a loud scream as the force threw me back onto the couch.

As I struggled to deal with the pain that swept across my face, he knelt over my body, his knees pinning my waist down firmly. He fondled himself for a few seconds and then leaned forward and mounted me again. In one powerful thrust, he forced himself into me, sending an indescribable, excruciating pain down my spine. Numbed by the pain, I could no longer scream or move. I just lay there in a daze as he continued to move in and out of me at a pace that was tearing up my sacred self.

The pain was so great that my thigh muscles started to twitch, and I bled even more. Mr. Mathani's thrusting motion seemed to go on forever until suddenly, he started to groan, moan, and then pant, before his body went into a vibrating motion. Seconds later, his thrusting movement stopped, and he let his full, dead-weight fall upon me. His face and body were drenched in sweat. I simply lay there, motionless and disgusted. Moments later, he slowly lifted himself off me and left the room.

I lay on the couch in a fetal position with my hands placed in between my thighs, close to my knees. I wanted to die—I hated myself. I felt dirty and unworthy.

"Nadia! Nadia! You're supposed to be my guardian light. Where are you? Enkai, why have you left me?" I wailed.

"Where is Enkai? Why didn't you rescue me? Why did you leave Mr. Mathani to violate my body? What did I do?" I cried out a string of unanswered questions.

Perhaps, I should have stayed in the Maasailand after all, I thought. *Now, I'm all alone and frightened again with no one to help me—no one to comfort me.*

I was more confused than ever and didn't know what to do. My mind was in desperate turmoil. I was still bleeding, and the wetness was soaking the sofa, but I didn't care. At that very moment, I didn't care anymore about my life. I wanted to die.

I sobbed for hours until I was exhausted, and finally, I drifted off to sleep. That night, I dreamed of Nadia. She was lying next to me, not speaking, and I was very angry with her.

"Nadia, you're meant to be my guardian light. Where were you, Nadia? Where were you?" I asked her.

Nadia didn't respond—she didn't speak a word—she simply cried and prayed with me.

I suddenly woke up, crying from my dream. I was startled by Mr. Mathani's loud voice. He was standing over my head and screaming, "Where's my morning tea and breakfast?"

I got up from the couch, still bleeding slightly. I noticed that the couch was stained badly. I ran to the bathroom and cleaned myself before I served Mr. Mathani some tea and breakfast. He seemed calm and normal, like nothing had happened.

I fetched a bowl of warm, soapy water with some bleach in it and returned to the children's study room to clean the couch. Later that Saturday afternoon, after I'd served Mr. Mathani his lunch, he left for the country club. I locked myself in my room and cried all day, dozing off to sleep when the tears would come no more.

The following day in the afternoon, a knock on my bedroom door finally woke me up. It was Johari and Jamila, who had just returned from Mombassa with Aunt Bela. I dragged myself from my bed, hugged them, and forced a smile in an attempt to mask my deep pain.

"Your eyes are red and swollen, Mikela," Jamila pointed out.

"That's because I've been sleeping," I said, as I went down with them to welcome Aunt Bela.

"Hello Mikela—are you okay?" Aunt Bela asked. "You look awfully tired and drained," she remarked, as I emerged from behind the doors.

I nodded and said, "Aunt Bela, I'm fine. Can I help you take some things into the house?" I tried to act as normal as I could.

"Yes, thank you…here, take these," Aunt Bela said, handing over some shopping bags and still staring at me with a curious look.

I had decided that I was not going to tell Aunt Bela about the incident. I was convinced that somehow she would blame me for what had happened.

During the ensuing two weeks, my pain remained rooted in more fear and anxiety, and my youthful exuberance seemed to have vanished in an instant. I blamed myself for the violation. Somehow, I believed that I must have done something wrong to deserve all that had happened to me. The void that the horror of circumcision had created in me had suddenly re-emerged and merged with my recent rape experience, and together both had turned into a huge demon that threatened to consume my soul.

A Fog of Misery:

Four weeks had gone by, yet it seemed as if my pain and hurt had completely engulfed me. My inner world was in shambles. Daily I tried to conceal the smoldering fire that was burning inside of me and wrenching my soul. I had mixed emotions of shock, anger, fear, and self-blame. I felt nothing but hostility for the world around me, where I no longer felt safe.

Perhaps it never happened, I thought. *Perhaps it was just a dream, a nightmare that will eventually go away.*

In the meantime, as I tried to hide my torment from everyone, my body was also showing signs of my psychological trauma.

"Mikela, you seem to be losing weight. Are you okay? Are you eating well? You ought to take time from your schoolwork and painting sessions to rest, you know," Aunt Bela said a few times, visibly concerned for me.

"Yes, Aunt Bela, I'm fine, and I am getting enough rest...I'm not sure why I look tired and worn out," I often lied, although I felt nauseated by most things and was having recurrent headaches, loss of appetite, and stomach cramps.

Still, I decided not to see a doctor because then I would have to admit to Aunt Bela that I was really sick. The other alternative was to quietly visit the Mathani family physician. That was certainly risky because if I went to see her without telling Aunt Bela, she was sure to inform the Mathanis. So, I opted to buy medications from the nearby pharmacy.

Surprisingly, people still remarked that I was a beautiful girl that was blossoming into an even more beguiling woman. I guess the fact that I'd lost some weight didn't seem to raise much attention. No one knew that I was also losing my self-esteem and self-confidence and daily losing my sense of worth.

I went through many days virtually in a zombie-like state. In the house, I avoided Chege Mathani—everything about him repulsed me. I didn't understand how he could live with himself after what he'd done to me. To my utter wonder, he seemed totally at ease with himself and family, and many times, as I observed him, I wondered if I had not indeed imagined the whole thing. Of course, the least of his concerns was the physical and emotional trauma that he had caused me. Never once did he ask how I was doing or feeling.

Aunt Bela, on the other hand, had noticed a change in my behavior and demeanor. She insisted that I had become unusually quiet and withdrawn, without the boisterous, youthful zest that I'd exhibited in the past, but I continued to deny that there were any changes in me as I struggled to act as normally as possible. She would ask me on occasion if there was a problem, but I would force a smile and quietly respond, "I'm fine, Aunt Bela. I've just been very busy trying to catch up with my schoolwork."

Aunt Bela was not the only person who was concerned about me. My close friend Tulia tried desperately to find out why I had become sad and withdrawn from the world, but I insisted that I was fine.

I'd met Tulia at the City Center two weeks after I'd arrived in Nairobi. I was in a craft shop when I accidentally bumped into her, knocking over the items that she had in her hands. Luckily, none of them broke.

"Oh my God!" she exclaimed. "Please watch where you are going."

"Forgive me…I'm really sorry…I was focused on the crafts to my right and didn't see you coming down the aisle."

Something about my response must have tempered her reaction because she said, "That's okay; these things happen.

"By the way, I'm Tulia. And what's your name?" she asked.

"My name is Mikela."

From that point, we started making conversation, and soon we were walking together to other shops. That day, we spent well over two hours together and continued to see each other afterwards. In no time, Tulia had become like a sister to me. She was my best friend.

Tulia was a very pretty, dark-complexioned girl of average height, although she never believed it herself. She often overlooked the fact that she had very exquisite, dainty facial features that almost seemed perfectly aligned and an elegant look that earned her the nickname of the "Nubian Princess." Instead, she'd always tell me that she was too dark and wanted to have a light brown complexion like me, which really surprised me because I envied her smooth, velvety skin and wished my skin were as flawless as hers.

Still, as the months went by, the pain inside of me intensified, and in my dreams, Nadia started to visit me almost nightly. In my dreams, Nadia would cry and pray with me. Just seeing Nadia in dreams had become a source of comfort for me. I became convinced that she was there to share my pain and help me endure the terrors of the moment, while reassuring me that all of the anguish and misery would eventually pass.

In the meantime, Mama Eshe became sick. Aunt Bela could not go to Mombassa to stay with her because of her own job, so I opted to go instead. It was a welcome escape from Chege Mathani. My hate for Chege Mathani had become like a smoldering fire that was scorching my spirit, and the soot from its smoke was darkening my soul. What frustrated me the most was that there was nothing that I felt I could do to make him pay for what he'd done. All I could do was hate him and bear my anguish alone. But even at my young age, I knew that such a mixture of hate and deep hurt was a lethal toxin for my soul. Still, I felt trapped in a sea of negative emotions that were destroying my inner world and yet achieving nothing for me on the outside.

A Breath of Fresh Air:

During the cooler afternoons on the Island of Mombassa, I would take walks with Mama Eshe to a nearby park, where I would listen to her stories about foreign invasions of the Old Town and its relics. I tried not to think about my rape ordeal or the rapist, even as the weight of the emotional and physical trauma remained alive inside me. I tried to enjoy every minute with Mama Eshe before I returned to what was now a "House of Terror" to me.

From the day I arrived, I believed that Mama Eshe sensed that I had a huge burden on me. Mama Eshe was a wise old woman that could see through the masquerading of a fourteen-year-old child. I believed that she could feel the very depth of my soul because she was a very spiritual woman and often sensed things in her spirit before they manifested in the natural realm. Somehow, I felt that I couldn't succeed in masking my pain, although I still tried.

One evening, as we watched television in the living room, with an inquisitive look on her face, she asked me, "My child, how have you been in Nairobi?"

"Oh! Mama, everything has been wonderful. I love Aunt Bela, Johari, and Jamila," I responded, exaggerating a smile.

Mama Eshe looked into my eyes as though she was attempting to unmask the turmoil that was devouring my soul. I think that when she asked me that question, she could feel the invisible flames that were smoldering inside me.

My untruthful response, it seemed, disappointed her. I am sure she hoped that I could confide in her even though she respected my privacy and didn't prod me any further. Instead, she told me a story about a baby sparrow.

"My child, come and sit next to me and listen to this tale."

I cuddled up next to her.

"Once there was a baby sparrow that lived with his mother in the open savanna fields. He loved his mother but didn't trust her. His mother loved him, too, and as a sign of her love and trust, she gave him a precious stone. This was a rare, precious stone that had been in the family for many generations. Then, one day, his mother hurt him unintentionally. The baby sparrow cried for many days but never told his mother that she had hurt him. Nonetheless, deep inside the baby sparrow's heart, he still loved his mother.

"In the weeks ahead, the baby sparrow lost the precious stone that his mother had given him—a gift that he deeply cherished. He was flying across the savannah plains when he accidentally dropped the stone. He searched frantically for it but never found it. He was still angry with his mother and never told her that he had lost the stone.

"One day, his mother was foraging in the grasslands and found the stone. She thought that her baby sparrow had deliberately thrown the precious stone away because he was angry with her. She kept the precious stone and never told him that she'd found it.

"As time went on, the baby sparrow could not get himself to forgive his mother for what she'd done to him; his pain was so great that he decided to leave home. He left without telling his mother, and he never came back to see her. Many years went by, and his mother's health started to fail. Eventually, she died. The baby sparrow got word of his mother's death and flew back home. He was heartbroken and devastated because he had never gotten a chance to tell his mother that he loved her more than anything in the world. Before his mother was buried, the baby sparrow found the precious stone that he had lost in the open savannah plains. His mother had kept it for him under her wings. He had no idea that his mother had found the precious stone and saved it for him.

"All these past years he had cried about losing his precious jewel when it had been safe with his mother. If only he had confided in her and told her that he had lost the precious stone, she would have saved him many years of emotional pain. He had kept all his pain to himself because he'd trusted no one but himself. Yet, if he had opened up his heart to someone that loved him, they would have helped him through his pain. Now he realized how much he'd lost over the past years by staying away from his mother, whom he'd loved very much."

As I listened to Mama Eshe's story, it dawned on me that she could see through the mask that I'd placed over my inner pain. Mama Eshe had unveiled my soul, and the story about the baby sparrow was really about me. Still, I made the decision not to offload the heaviness in my heart by telling her about the horror that I'd experienced in the Mathani home.

She'll never believe me, I thought.

So, I felt that I had to deal with my pain in my own way, stupidly, like the baby sparrow.

Maybe someday I'll be able to tell her, but not now, I said to myself.

Mama Eshe never asked me again if there was anything wrong. I could tell that her hope was that when I was ready and could trust her, I would let her into my closed world, where the heaviness in my soul was noticeably drowning me.

A Strange White Knight Reappears:

The day before I left Mombassa to return to Nairobi, I visited the Old Town. It was nice to return to this preserved relic of the medieval-like times, with its narrow alleyways and ancient buildings. On my way to the open market, I wandered through the island's intersecting major streets—the Digo, Nkrumah, Moi Avenue, and Nyerere roads. Finally, I arrived at the Mwenbe Tayari open-air market—the name of this market I later learned was "Ready Mangoes." In a short while, I found what I wanted and started to bargain with the merchants. As I bargained hard on the price of souvenirs that I was eager to buy for Aunt Bela, Johari, and Jamila, I was initially unaware of a middle-aged white man with a camera watching me from under a nearby tree. Then, from the corner of my eye, he caught my attention.

When he noticed me watching him, he approached me and introduced himself. "*He looked familiar,*" I thought for a moment.

"Je suis François Jacques Paquet—I am a French artist and photographer," he said. "Elle belle—you are beautiful!" he added. "What's your name?"

I ignored him as I continued to bargain with the merchants.

"Can I take your photograph?" he asked.

Before I could turn away from him, a flash of light blinded my eyes for a brief moment.

A few moments later, the merchant finally agreed on a price, and I handed some shillings to him, stocked my purchase in my bag, and started to leave.

"You are Mykaa-la, aren't you? Your paintings were exhibited at the French Embassy in Nairobi. You have incredible talent," the French photographer said, still following me.

I quickened my steps to get away from him, but I could still hear his voice from behind me.

"I run a private art and photo gallery at the City Center in Nairobi and Paris. I also run a school for amateur artists like you. With a little bit of polishing, I think your work will be superb."

I still didn't say a word back to him, but the French man didn't seem discouraged. He brought out a little card from his pocket and handed it over to me.

"Here's my business card. Please call or come to my office. I know you'll make a great international artist someday—I can see it so clearly. You are also absolutely beautiful! Any school of beaux-arts in Paris would love to polish the works of an exotic looking woman like you."

I had no idea what the French man was talking about, but I politely took his card, still not saying a word to him, and quickened my steps even faster. I reached the bus station and boarded the next *matatu* that was going to Mama Eshe's place. As the bus started to drive away, it suddenly dawned on me that I might have seen the white man before. He looked very much like the middle-aged white man that I'd seen at my school's art exhibition at the French Embassy in Nairobi.

The next day, I cried as I left Mama Eshe's home to go back to Nairobi. I dreaded seeing Chege Mathani again.

Back at the "House of Terror":

Two weeks after I returned to the Mathani residence, Chege began making lustful advances toward me again. He did this when no one was around, and my fear was once again manifesting into reality. Sometimes when I passed by him in the short hallway that connected the living room area with the dining room, he would attempt to grab me. I tried as hard as I could to avoid him by leaving the house if we were alone.

Still, I could not tell Aunt Bela what her husband was doing to me for fear that she would blame me. I felt trapped in the Mathani home, as Chege's harassment got worse. Unable to cope with it all, I plunged into a deep depression—I felt like I had no escape from the mental and physical torture that I was going through. My loss of appetite got worse, as I sometimes went for days without food and was rapidly dropping in weight. I was also having difficulty sleeping and sometimes would wake up from nightmares in the middle of the night totally drenched in my own sweat.

My feelings of worthlessness had worsened, and I still blamed myself for the rape and the cleansing ritual. I had crying spells several times in one day, and this was frustrating because I felt like I had no control over what was happening to me. I was easily agitated, anxious, and nervous, and in time, the anger and guilt inside of me began to grow, threatening to erupt into a volcanic and explosive rage. Soon, I started having thoughts about killing myself. It seemed as if that was the only way out of my misery.

If I killed myself, I would join Nadia and Enkai, I thought and was surprised at how the continuous resolve to kill myself began to lift my spirit.

Finally, on one particular rainy Saturday night, I swallowed an entire bottle of cough syrup and collapsed.

CHAPTER 8

Gloomy Days Ahead

Aunt Bela found me lying lifeless on the kitchen floor, and two hours later, I woke up on a hospital bed. I had been purged and revived.

"I'm sorry, Aunt Bela. I had no idea that I had taken too much of the cough syrup," I said, once we had returned home.

"Mikela, I accept your apology, but please don't do such a stupid thing again," Aunt Bela said sternly.

Mr. Mathani must have overheard our conversation because he nonchalantly added, "Bela, what do you expect from an ignorant and confused Maasai girl—a silly teenage girl yearning for attention."

Hearing this, I quietly slipped away to my room and burst into tears.

Living Each Day from the Past:

A few weeks later, Tulia asked me to go shopping with her at the Nairobi City Center.

"Let's explore some of the arts and crafts shops in the open markets," she suggested.

"Great idea, Tulia! I would love to buy a gift for Mama Eshe."

I gladly accepted to go. I badly needed an excuse to leave the Mathani home for a few hours.

As usual, we took one of the crowded *matatus*, and in an hour, we arrived at a teeming open market at the Nairobi City Center. As we admired the stone carvings, sisal baskets, Maasai beadwork, ebony carvings, and tie-dyed fabrics,

I heard someone shout, "Hello! Beautiful girl, here we meet again. How are you?"

I turned to see who it was and noticed the French photographer that I'd met in Mombassa. Before I had a chance to turn, he took a snapshot of me holding a Maasai calabash covered with hide-skin and decorated with colorful glass beads. Then, he walked closer to Tulia and me.

"You never called me. Why? I would really love to work with you. Here, please take my business card again. This time, please call me—and come to my office on Moi Avenue if you want to get your pictures," he said with a smile.

Without uttering a response, I took his card and continued admiring the calabash that I had in my hands. When the white man left, Tulia looked at me, curious.

"Who was that white man? Why did he take your photo?"

"I have no idea. He is a crazy man. I have no intention of calling him."

Tulia shrugged.

"But he has your photo."

"Does it matter? I don't think I'll ever see him again," I responded.

Tulia shrugged again and went on to the next stall to price the hide-skin sandals, and I trailed behind her.

In the weeks ahead, I gave no real thought to the French man. For now, my life seemed to be a continuous struggle to keep my sanity. My mind was always in a depressed state, and I felt like my life was in daily combat with demonic forces that were torturing my mind and crippling my young body. For now, all that I could see ahead of me were more gloomy days in the Mathani home.

Another Dream—The Ocean:

My dreams had become a regular occurrence. However, this particular dream left me puzzled for weeks. I could see Nadia swimming across the ocean. She looked up in the direction where I stood and waved at me to join her. Next thing I saw, I was swimming with her, enjoying the feel of the gentle waves of the ocean. Then, for a moment, I thought I heard someone calling my name.

"Mikela! Mikela!" the voice rang out again. I immediately turned in the direction the voice was coming from but saw no one, and so I turned back to continue my swim with Nadia. Then, I noticed that Nadia had disappeared from beside me, and I was now swimming alone.

"Nadia! Nadia! Where are you?" I called out, but all I could hear was the tremulous sound of the waves.

"Nadia! Nadia!" I called out a second time, and still she didn't answer.

At this instant, I saw a huge wave from afar, and it seemed to be coming in my direction. I started to swim back in the opposite direction, but I was not fast enough as soon the waves were right behind me. In a flash, they carried me right into its center. I started to drown, as I could no longer swim inside the powerful waves.

Oh Enkai! Please help me. I'm drowning, I thought.

Then, I felt someone grab my hand.

"Soon, you'll be okay, Mikela," a voice said.

I thought it was Nadia, but I could not see clearly inside the waves.

All of a sudden, this person who had held my hand let go of me, and I started to stumble inside the waves, going downwards into the deep waters. I was gulping water faster than I could swallow it, and I was struggling to breathe. At the very moment that I was convinced I was going to die, I woke up and realized that I had been dreaming.

April 1982—Unending Assault of Innocence:

I was now approaching my sixteenth birthday. I was six feet tall, and although I didn't feel like I looked any different, Tulia said many people still saw me as a very striking and elegant young woman. She often teased me about heads that spun just to watch me as I walked with her anywhere in the streets of Nairobi. Oddly, I was never aware of any such attention.

At this time, it had been almost two years since my rape ordeal, and luckily, Chege Mathani had not tried to rape me again, although he'd continued to harass me with his offensive approaches. He would grab me or whisper vulgar and obscene words into my ears when no one was watching. I had learned to endure his torment while hoping that someday I would have the courage to leave the Mathani residence.

One month after my sixteenth birthday, on a Sunday afternoon that the house chef was off-duty, Aunt Bela was making lunch when she received a call from her sister Eba.

Eba had since graduated from the university. She'd been married for a year and was already in her third trimester of pregnancy. She was calling because she had gone into labor one month early and needed Aunt Bela's assistance. Her husband was attending a meeting in South Africa, and she was alone. Since the cook was off duty, Aunt Bela asked me to finish cooking lunch while she drove off with Johari and Jamila to Eba's home.

Now for the first time in two years, after all my hard work and careful planning to avoid such a situation, I was left alone in the house with Mr. Mathani, frightened in anticipation of what could happen to me, I literally trembled as I prepared the lunch Aunt Bela had cooked halfway. About twenty minutes later, he came into the kitchen and stood by the door. He stared at me for what seemed like forever, and finally, he spoke.

"Mikela, what time is Bela coming back?"

I stuttered as I quickly thought of a response that would discourage him from lingering around me.

"Sir, I think she'll be back in just a few minutes. She went to the nearby pharmacy—she'll be back any moment now," I lied.

For a minute, he left the kitchen, and I exhaled with relief only to hear him bolting the front door. My heart started to pound in fear as I listened intently for his footsteps. About ten minutes later, he returned to the kitchen and stood by the door, staring at me lustfully. Moments later, he walked up to me, grabbed me by the neck, and pushed me against the wall, firmly pinning me against the cold concrete. I was forced to turn my face to the side to relieve the strain from the pressure of his hands.

"Not again! Please leave me alone!" I yelled. "This time, I swear I'll tell Aunt Bela."

Mr. Mathani didn't seem to be listening to me as he tore my wrap skirt from around my waist, leaving me clad only in my underwear. Without warning, he started to kiss my neck while fondling my breasts and nipples with his hands. As I felt his wet tongue licking my neck, my stomach began to nauseate from disgust. I started screaming as loud as my voice could carry and tried to kick him within the limited space I had to maneuver my body—I was determined that Mr. Mathani would not hurt me again. I pushed and wriggled my six-foot body, which was almost a foot taller than his own, but his massive and muscular frame was pressed against me on the wall, and my strength was no match for his muscular arms.

With his left arm pressed across my neck, he undid his trouser zipper with his right hand. When I heard the sound of his zipper, I panicked and bit his ear. He let out a loud yelp and slapped me hard across my face.

"How dare you, you little brat! For your sake, I hope I am not hurt!"

I tried to bite him again, but he held my head in a position that made it impossible for me to reach him, even though our bodies were pressed so close together. My mind was completely clouded by fear and hysteria, but I kept trying desperately to think of what to do to save myself. Nothing rational was coming up. From the jarred recesses of my bewildered mind, I felt his right hand roughly tearing my panties off. From the corner of my eyes, I saw him tear open another perfumed bag with his teeth.

"Someone, please help me. Please! Please! Help me," I screamed as loud as I could, hoping that someone would hear me. To stop me from screaming, he pressed his left hand over my mouth, and in what seemed like a flash, he started to force himself on me. I felt helpless as I tried to push his heavy and strong body away from me, to no avail. His powerful thrusts were now tearing up my fragile walls, and the lacerating pain caused me to spasm continuously. My legs were trembling, and sweat streamed down my body like water from a leaking pipe, drenching my blouse and forming a puddle on the floor directly beneath us.

A few minutes later, the sweat on the floor was mingled with my blood as I started to bleed, feeling the wetness trickle down from between my legs. He didn't seem to notice or care—he simply kept thrusting himself in and out of me. The pain was excruciating, and I could no longer move from its intensity.

"Oh! Enkai, help me! Help me, Nadia! Where are you? Why are you not helping me? Why are you letting this happen to me again?" I whispered gently to myself, unable to muster the strength to cry out loud to my God.

In my hysteria, I didn't notice his body start to vibrate and tremble. I was too preoccupied by the destruction taking place in my body and soul with his every violent thrust. Suddenly, he let out a loud moan, and his legs started to tremble. In a few seconds, it was all over. He pulled away from me and left the kitchen as quickly as he had arrived.

I slumped to the kitchen floor, unable to do anything else but whimper like a puppy. I held my lower stomach, somehow hoping that my hands would bring relief to the aching emanating from there. I had no remedy for the pain except to hope for blissful unconsciousness or death—neither of which came. "Someone, anyone out there, please help me! Please help me!" I called out limply, as the pain threatened to overwhelm me. I knew no one would come.

In reply, I could only hear the whistling sounds of the kettle on the gas cooker and the crackling sounds of the burning pot of rice getting louder. Then, suddenly, I started to smell smoke.

"Oh my God, the food is burning," I muttered, as I dragged myself up from the floor and half crawled towards the gas cooker.

Gradually, more smoke began to fill the kitchen. I turned the cooker off and slowly made my way out of the kitchen into my bedroom.

Escape in a Tropical Storm:

Mustering all the strength I could, I started to dump my few belongings and books inside my suitcase. I'd finally decided that I was leaving the Mathani residence. I was no longer going to stay and endure the violation and torture from Chege Mathani. I'd had enough of the physical and emotional pain.

Within fifteen minutes, I was packed. I walked as fast as my pain would let me down the emergency stairs, towards the back entrance through the kitchen, and within minutes, I was out of the house. I started to run towards the main street, looking back to make sure that no one was following me.

It had started to rain, but I didn't care. I wanted to be as far away as possible from Mr. Mathani's House of Terror. I was crying as I half ran on the paved road, drenched under the rain while my thoughts spun, the pain shooting through my body with every step.

Finally, I reached Tulia's home. She answered the door and looked shocked to see me standing by the door, shivering, completely drenched by the rain, and crying.

"Oh my God! Mikela, what happened to you?" she asked in a shaky and panicked voice.

I stared at her blankly, unsure of whether she had spoken and what she had said, although I had seen her lips move. As she continued to move her lips, I started to feel dizzy and my vision turned blurry. I reached for her hands and tried to speak, but I was rapidly losing consciousness. Then, my vision turned completely black, and I collapsed.

CHAPTER 9

Unraveling the Mystery of the White Knight

Tulia must have dragged me into their house because when I regained consciousness, I was lying on the living room floor with a blanket over me.

"What happened?" I heard her ask.

Initially, I couldn't respond because I had started to sob heavily again.

"It's okay. Let's go upstairs," Tulia said soothingly, although visibly disturbed by my appearance and emotional state.

Together we went up to her room where she towel-dried me in her bathroom and then wrapped me in a warm blanket. While I was still crying hysterically, she ran downstairs to the kitchen and quickly prepared a mug of hot cocoa drink for me. For a long time, she held me in her arms trying to comfort me. It must have taken at least twenty minutes for her to calm me down, and when she finally did, for the first time, I narrated my ordeal. First, I started with my journey from the Maasailand.

Without any interruptions, Tulia listened attentively to my vivid recollection of what had happened to me on the day that I was circumcised. From the look in her eyes, I felt that in her innocent and naïve mind, she could barely comprehend the details of my horrific experience.

Tulia was still holding me in a warm and comforting embrace. She reassured me that my nightmare was now over after she heard what Mr. Mathani had done to me.

"I'm shocked and disgusted that Mr. Mathani could do such an awful thing to a young girl like you. I respected him as a father and elder myself, but I had no idea that he was such a monster," Tulia said.

"Mikela, God will make him pay one day. Believe me, God will make him pay dearly, no matter how many years it takes," Tulia swore, as she cradled me in her warm embrace.

"You can stay here with me for a few weeks. My parents are away, and I'm here with my grandmother. She won't mind your staying here for a while. Before my parents get back, I'm sure that we'll think of something to do," she said.

"We'll find a place for you to stay where Mr. Mathani will never hurt you again," she promised.

I nodded in agreement, as I sipped the soothing, warm, chocolate drink. Then later, I crawled under the sheets of the soft, warm bed in the guestroom and went to sleep. I was mentally and emotionally exhausted, and sleep was a very welcome escape.

During the next week, with Tulia's help, I started to respond to newspaper advertisements that were seeking live-in nannies. I went for a number of interviews, but all the mothers asked for personal references from persons that knew me well. I really had no such references. All my friends were almost as young as I was, and I could not use Aunt Bela as a reference. I had left her house without telling her with food burning on the gas stove.

Aunt Bela probably doesn't think much of me anymore, I thought.

I had decided that someday I would write her and Mama Eshe and explain to them why I had run away, but now my focus was on finding a means of livelihood and a roof over my head.

After two weeks of trying unsuccessfully to get a job, I started to think about the French photographer that I had met in Mombassa and at the craft shop in downtown Nairobi. I remembered him saying that he would like to work with me.

I decided to share my thoughts with Tulia and see what she thought of it.

"Tulia, do you remember the white man who took my photograph at the craft shop in the downtown area some time ago? He said his name is François Jacques Paquet."

"Yes I do. The white man you said was crazy. Why do you ask?" Tulia asked.

"Well, actually I met him before. When I went to visit Mama Eshe in Mombassa, I went to the Old Town to buy gifts for Aunt Bela, Johari, and Jamila when he saw me and started to follow me. He said that he was a French artist and photographer and that he would like to work with me. I ignored him, but he gave me his business card. I was surprised when I saw him again at the Nairobi City Center. Remember? He took a picture of me and asked me to come by his office on Moi Avenue to get it. Maybe he can help me get a job," I said.

"I don't know, Mikela. Many of these foreign men here in Nairobi make prostitutes out of young, desperate girls that need money. I have heard of strange stories about foreign photographers that force young girls to perform dirty sexual acts and then take photographs of the girls and pay them just a few shillings. Many of the girls eventually become prostitutes because they develop very low self-esteem and sleeping with men becomes the only way that they believe they can make a living. My mother told me that in the big tourist hotels and Safari resorts, you see many young girls prostituting for foreign men," Tulia responded, expressing her disapproval.

"I would never let anyone violate me again like Mr. Mathani did. I just want to find out what kind of business he runs. If it's anything like you say, then of course I wouldn't want to do that," I responded.

After a brief period of silence, Tulia shrugged, seeming persuaded.

"Okay, we'll make time and go to Moi Avenue and find his office," Tulia said grudgingly. "I guess we have nothing to lose by checking out François Jacques Paquet," she added.

"Thanks, Tulia—you are a great friend!"

Les Galeries des Beaux-arts de François Jacques Paquet:

The next day, we took one of the crowded *matatus* to Moi Avenue. We trekked a few blocks from the rowdy bus stop before we found François Jacques Paquet's office—a sign read "Les Galeries des Beaux-arts de François Jacques Paquet." First, we peeked in through the glass windows and saw a few young women seated in the lounge. They all seemed relaxed. I pressed the doorbell and someone opened the door. It was a middle-aged white man of average height, with long, reddish hair in a ponytail.

"Hello. Je suis Monsieur Pierre Duboef. How can I help you?" he asked, a warm smile showing a set of badly stained teeth.

"We are here to see Mr. François Jacques Paquet. My name is Mikela."

"Come in and have a seat," Mr. Pierre Duboef said, stepping away from the door and motioning for us to come inside.

Tulia and I stepped inside the office. The walls were beautifully decorated with flowery-designed wallpaper, while the marble tiles on the floor were immaculately clean. It felt cool and refreshing, with a couple of air-conditioning units in the wall blowing out cold air—a radical change from the hot and humid air outside in the streets of Nairobi.

The walls of an adjacent room were adorned with exquisite African carvings, paintings, and photographs that were beautifully framed in all shapes and sizes. As we surveyed François Jacques Paquet's office, a tall and elegant young lady wearing a pleasant smile and dressed in a sleeveless, peach top over a long, white fish skirt walked up to us. Although she was not a dashing beauty, she had a natural charm that could easily win anyone's heart.

"She has a striking resemblance to Aunt Bela," I whispered to Tulia.

"It's strange that you say that, because I also had the same thought…She's probably his secretary," Tulia whispered to me as the lady approached us.

"Welcome to Les Galeries des Beaux-arts de François Jacques Paquet," she said pleasantly and handed us application forms.

"Thank you, but we only need one for her," Tulia said, pointing toward me as she handed her own form back to the lady.

"I'm sorry…I just assumed that both of you would be applying," she said and took back Tulia's forms before walking back to her desk.

I quickly completed the form and returned it to the lady. Tulia said that as I walked gracefully across the room, she felt the eyes of the other ladies trailing me. She said that some of the girls appeared to be whispering to each other as they stared at me.

The lady took the form from me and checked it over.

"Thanks. Please have a seat, and I'll let Monsieur François know that you are here."

She got up and walked into another room. A few minutes later, she returned and informed me that Monsieur François Jacques Paquet would see me shortly. As she was done speaking to me, François Jacques Paquet came out of his office and said something to the lady, and she immediately motioned for Tulia and me to come forward. We followed her through a narrow and short hallway into François Jacques Paquet's office.

"Hello! Mykala—I am glad that you decided to collect your picture. Please, have a seat," François Jacques Paquet said, gesturing with his hand to a nearby chair.

"Now tell me, how do you say your name? Is it Mykala?" he asked.

"Mee-kay-la…we pronounce it just as it is spelled."

"It's a beautiful name—it sounds exotic. I've never heard of that name before. Where's your name from? It sounds Russian."

"It's a Maasai name. I'm a Tanzanian Maasai. Actually, it's not really a Maasai name…mmmm…my ancestors migrated from southern Sudan. They were descendants of a mixed heritage of Rashaida nomads and Dinka Sudanese. Quite frankly, I'm not sure what my name means," I explained.

"Well, it doesn't really matter what the ancestral origins of your name are. You're a Maasai—I should have guessed. You have the elegant gait of a Maasai Queen. Mee-kay-la is a beautiful name."

I was shocked to hear him use the expression "Maasai Queen." The only time anyone had ever called me that was at the government school back in the Maasailand.

"Thank you, sir. It's nice of you to say such kind words," I responded politely.

"So, who's the lovely young lady with you?"

"She's my best friend, Tulia."

"How are you, Tulia?"

"I'm fine, Mr. Jacques Paquet."

"Tulia, you don't have to call me Mr. Jacques Paquet. It's fine to call me François—just François is fine.

"Now, Mee-kay-la, here's your picture. It's absolutely breathtaking. So far, I think that it's one of my best shots in Africa," he said.

I took the picture and stared at it for a moment, and then nodded in agreement.

"Yes, I think it looks very nice," I said politely.

In the picture, I was holding a hide-skin-covered calabash that was decorated with colorful glass beads. It was a Maasai beaded work that I'd bought for Mama Eshe.

"Lovely! This was the photo he took at the open market? It's absolutely beautiful, Mikela. You look gorgeous," Tulia said, as she admired the photo.

I started to hand the photo back to François when he said, "It's yours to keep."

"Thank you," I graciously responded.

"Now tell me, where did you learn to paint so well?" he asked.

"I never really learned how to paint—I started painting when I was just a few years old, and I painted my first real work when I was ten."

"Well, I must say that for a young lady your age, your talent is of rare quality."

"Thank you, sir, for your kind words," I replied timidly.

"So, are you interested in polishing your talent?"

"Yes, sir, I am."

Then, there was silence. No one said anything for a brief moment as François simply stared at me. His direct gaze made me a bit uncomfortable, and I looked away and started to fiddle with my bag.

Finally, he said, "Mee-kay-la, tell me, what do you really want to do?"

"François, I want to be an artist, a painter, and a photographer all in one. I want to paint my traditional Maasai culture, our history, our wildlife, and the Maasaiplains. I want to paint the historical buildings and relics of Mombassa and Nairobi. I just want to paint Africa's most cherished mountains, valleys, and waters—I want to paint nature. I love nature because it's simply spectacular."

Tulia later told me that my eyes sparkled with enthusiasm and excitement when I said this.

"Then you have come to the right place. François Jacques Paquet Galeries des Beaux-arts has been seeking you for a while now. Welcome Mee-kay-la."

He smiled.

"So, when can I meet your parents—your family?" he said seconds later.

I looked at Tulia and then back at François. I couldn't find the right words to speak, so I lowered my eyes again, focusing on my trembling hands. Tulia seemed to realize that I was too nervous to speak, and she interrupted the brief silence.

"She lost her parents—that's why she's looking for a job and a place to stay," Tulia lied.

François glanced at Tulia, and then his eyes trailed back to me. At that moment, I really could not tell if he believed Tulia or not.

"Then you have come to the right place," he finally repeated calmly.

I was surprised that François didn't ask me any more questions. I expected him to ask me what had happened to my parents, but he didn't. He simply picked up his phone.

"Ayan, do you have a moment please?" he said.

In seconds, the lady who'd received us came into François's office.

"Ayan, meet Mikela and her friend, Tulia. Mikela will start working for us tomorrow, but she needs a place to stay for a while before she gets a place of her own. Do you think that you can help?"

"Oh yes! That's not a problem. I live alone, and I have a two-bedroom flat. She can stay with me for as long as she needs to," Ayan said.

When I heard this, my eyes widened with surprise, and I couldn't conceal the smile that spread across my entire jaw. Tulia looked at me and smiled, too—we were both visibly excited. Before Ayan left François Jacques Paquet's office, she gave me her home address and started to tell me how to get there when Tulia said excitedly, "I know where it is—it's only a few streets down from Moi Avenue."

"That's great then. I'll be home after 6 PM—see you sometime after then," Ayan said with a smile before she excused herself from François's office.

"Well then, everything is set. Welcome to our agency. I can see your talent, and I know that you'll be a spectacular international artist. It's my prediction—and I'm pretty good at this. Not once have I been wrong in the past," François boasted.

Tulia and I thanked him and left his office. As soon as we stepped outside, we both started to scream.

"Marahaba Enkai!"

We held hands and skipped along the road as we headed toward the rowdy *matatu* station for a hectic bus ride back to Tulia's house.

The Beginning of Another Priceless Friendship:

Later that evening, Tulia escorted me to Ayan's apartment. She received us very warmly and gladly showed me the room where I'd be staying. Ayan appeared to be very kind and gentle.

"Her apartment is nice and cozy," Tulia whispered to me.

It was a tastefully decorated and expensive-looking flat that was kept very neat. After I settled into my new room, Tulia said she had to leave because she had promised her grandmother that she'd be back shortly after sunset.

An hour later, Ayan announced that dinner was ready—baked Tilapia fish, fried rice, peas, and spinach was on the menu.

"Would you like some wine?" she offered.

"Oh, no thanks. I think I'm too young to drink alcohol—orange juice will be fine," I graciously responded.

We both ate in silence for about five minutes until Ayan decided to break the silence.

"So, you are a Maasai?"

"Well, I guess, but my ancestors were not. My grandparents settled in the Maasailand and assimilated into the culture, but I consider myself a Maasai."

Ayan nodded.

"Well, let me tell you a little about myself," she said.

"I was born on the island of Zanzibar in Tanzania, but I ran away from home a few years ago and have never been home since then. I met François by accident when I was working as a prostitute on the streets of Nairobi. Then I was sleeping with mostly foreign men who paid me for the services that I provided them. When François walked up to me, I thought that he was a customer and started to quote my price to him. He quietly told me that he was not interested in my body but wanted me to work in his modeling agency."

"Does he have a modeling school as well?" I asked.

"Yes, I'm a beaux-arts model. We model for still art, without nudity. On that day, he gave me his business card and asked me to call him the next day. He told me something else that changed my life at that instant. Till this day, what he said to me still echoes in my mind.

"'You are a lovely girl,' he said. 'You don't have to live like this anymore. You are worth so much more. Don't let men or anyone downgrade your worth. You are a beautiful creation of God. Don't you see that your worth is priceless?' At the time, I definitely could not see myself as priceless. I was in a profession where I sold my most scared self for money. So, you can imagine what Jacques Paquet's words did to me—they pierced through my heart with a touch of love.

"No one had ever said such kind words to me. No one had ever told me that I was worth anything good, let alone priceless. I was hearing it for the very first time in my life. At this period, my self-esteem was at its all-time low, and I didn't think much of myself. All the men that I'd ever met before François only wanted to use my body, and sometimes they would even refuse to pay me. I felt worthless and useless. Actually, at the time, prostitution didn't mean anything to me; I couldn't see how degrading it was. I hated my life and didn't care one bit what I did with it.

"The next day, after I met François, I called him and he asked me to come by his office. That same day, he enrolled me as one of his still art models and since he didn't have a secretary at the time, I opted to help with administrative work in his office. He paid me two months salary in advance for the extra secretarial duties that I was going to be doing for him, and later that day, he called a friend of his, who is now my landlord, and asked him to rent this place to me. He did all this and never once tried to touch me or ask me for a sexual favor. I've been modeling for two years, and now I have saved enough money to attend college if I decide to."

Ayan paused for a moment to stop the well of tears that had accumulated in her eyes.

"I must tell you, Mikela, François changed my whole life forever. You should consider yourself lucky to have met him. He has been a human angel to so many young women who have lost all hope."

I listened to Ayan without interrupting. I, too, was struggling to hold back my tears. Ayan's story was a powerful story of how one person, by extending a kind gesture, could change the life of another person who may be drowning in the sea called life. This reminded me of the way that Mama Eshe had reached out and saved me from the streets.

Ayan paused again to hold back her tears.

"Ayan, why did you run away from home?" I asked.

"Well, it's a long story. I went through an awful ordeal in my village. When I was sixteen years old and just graduating from high school, my mother, who was a staunch Muslim woman, took me to a place to be circumcised."

She paused before she asked, "Do you know what female circumcision is?"

"Yes, I have heard of it," I said, trying to sound familiar but distant about it. I was not ready to unmask my past so soon.

Ayan nodded and continued.

"It was meant to be a rite of womanhood and a religious obligation. I will never forget that experience in my life. It was the most cruel and humiliating experience that I have ever had. After so many years, I still remember the women pinning me to the ground with my legs so widely spread apart that my pelvic bones were hurting. Using a sharp razor blade, they started to cut off some of my female parts. Of course, at the time, I didn't really understand what they were doing. It was only recently, since I started working for François, that I was able to afford to see a female doctor, a gynecologist, who explained to me what had been done to me during the circumcision.

"Anyway, while they were cutting off my most sacred parts, I was screaming and crying, and my body was trembling from the intensity of the pain. Blood was trickling down between my legs as I struggled desperately, attempting to free myself from their hold. My struggling was in vain because there were too many of them, including my mother, and they had me firmly pinned to the ground. The razorblade slicing through my flesh seemed to last for a lifetime. Later, using a needle and a special type of locally made thread, they started to inflict more pain on me—they sewed the two sides of my fragile walls together. Can you imagine how excruciating the pain was? Can you imagine a needle going in and out of your flesh countless times without being under anesthesia? Finally, I think I must have collapsed, because my body could no longer take the pain.

"When I woke up a few hours later, my mother was by my side asking me how I was feeling. She tried to explain to me that this was a necessary passage to womanhood and a religious ritual. I was too hurt to listen to what she was saying. Besides, I had decided that I was going to leave my village.

"As soon as my wounds started to heal and I felt better, I hitched rides to many stops and finally ended up in Nairobi. I had no money, no food, and no place to stay. I ran into a white man who offered me money, but first he told me that I had to sleep with him. I felt like I had no other option, and I went ahead with him. The experience with the white man was very painful. I felt my insides tearing, maybe it was the stitches that I'd received during the circumcision that were coming apart—my flesh was literally tearing. I bled the whole night after I slept with the white man. He gave me a few shillings that I used to buy some food.

"The next day, when my money was gone, I went back to him and slept with him again. I had to endure more pain because prostituting myself was my only means of livelihood; at least that's what I thought at that time. Gradually, prostitution became a way of life for me."

At this point, Ayan paused and stared into her plate. I fought back tears, still trying to mask the emotional turmoil that had started to swirl up inside of me. A few minutes later, Ayan seemed to have regained her composure and resumed her story.

"Although I felt both physical and emotional pain and no joy from sleeping with strange and oftentimes disgusting men, I felt trapped in it with no place else to go. It took meeting a man like François for me to realize that there was still a beautiful world out there for me to explore."

She stopped speaking to take a sip of wine, then she looked at me. "By the way, many years later, I discovered that there is no place in the Koran where it mentions or demands that we have our female parts cut off. I felt betrayed by the women in my village, especially my mother. I don't know why they continue such a horrible tradition. Some say that it forces young girls to keep their virginity; others say that it reduces a woman's sexual drive. To me, it's an ignorant way of thinking, and they don't fully realize how circumcising young girls destroys their lives."

As I listened to Ayan, my own memories gushed back and tears filled my eyes. As the first teardrop started to run down my face, I looked away and wiped them off. Ayan's story had instantly resuscitated bitter memories inside me.

"Well, Mikela, tell me something about you—your homeland, the Maasailand? How did you meet François?" Ayan asked.

I was literally frozen with emotional pain and started to stutter as I tried to get words out of my mouth. I was not ready to share my ordeal with Ayan, although I admired her own sincerity and openness. So far, I'd been able to tell only Tulia my life's encounters. I took a deep breath, forcing back the sorrow.

"I met him at the open arts and crafts market at the Nairobi City Center. I was working as a nanny for a wealthy Kikuyu family. Things didn't work out, so I had to leave," was all that I managed to say before I quickly changed the topic.

"So, who is Pierre Duboef?" I asked. "He received Tulia and me at the door when we first arrived at François's art agency."

"Oh! We all call him Duboef-Duboef. He's a very nice person. He's François's boyfriend."

I widened my eyes as I looked up at Ayan.

"What do you mean by that?" I asked. "They are both men. The Maasai tradition frowns at such things, you know; they say that Enkai does not approve of that."

The news stunned me into silence, my tears and earlier trials temporarily forgotten, but Ayan simply smiled and shook her head at the same time, leaning back against her chair.

CHAPTER 10

❦

Unveiling Talent

My look of shock must have mirrored my perplexed mind because what I was hearing was a completely new concept to me.

"Yes, so does my tradition, but they are men who don't like women—actually, it's not that they don't like women; they are simply not attracted to women. They prefer to be with men," Ayan explained.

Seeing my puzzled expression, she added, "Well, what do you care? It's all for the better. This means that you are safe with François. At least he won't try to use you like many men would. The way I see it is that his personal life is not my business, and whatever he does with Duboef-Duboef doesn't really bother me.

"I still see François as a very kind and good person," she continued defiantly. "He helps a lot of young women to start their careers, and I'm glad that I met him. Soon you will appreciate what a really wonderful person he is. With a stunning beauty and talent such as yours, he's sure to make a star out of you. Already, you have become the talk among the other still art models. Some are even now quite jealous of your extraordinary beauty and talent. In fact, rumor has it that your paintings are exceptional."

I listened to Ayan's fierce defense of François's sexual orientation. I had never met a homosexual up until meeting François, and I was glad to have someone like Ayan to give me a new slant on the issue. I appreciated Ayan mentioning this aspect of François' life to me, or I would have made a blundering fool of myself someday with François over the matter.

Ayan spent the rest of the evening telling me about François Jacques Paquet's art gallery and updating me on all the office gossip.

The next day was my first day at work. I was looking forward to the beginning of a re-birth, which I hoped would blossom into a new career and life.

The Dream—The Throne of Success:

A week after I moved in with Ayan, I had a unique dream—the type that I'd never had before. I was sitting on what looked like a throne, and I was beautifully dressed in a typical Maasai bridal costume like the *Orkiripa* or *Imankek* and adorned with exotic ornaments, *Imasaa,* which were embellished with a blend of the Maasai colors of white, red, green, blue, and orange. Seated next to me was Nadia, and she was beaming with smiles.

"Mikela, the world is about to see the beauty and excellence of your work," she whispered gently.

"What do you mean?" I asked.

She smiled again and answered, "Enkai has released your blessings, and they are all yours to claim."

At this point, a young girl that appeared to be my chaperone came by with more ornaments.

"Mikela, would you like to wear any of these?" she asked.

I took the ornaments from her and started to observe them closely. One of them was a bull necklace, *Enkoyiapiyap,* which some also called *Norkiteng.* The other was a medallion style necklace that my mother said was *Orkamishina* in the Maa lingua. Both ornaments were delicately made and flaunted the exquisite and regal design of traditional Maasai jewelry.

"They're beautiful!" I exclaimed. "I'll wear them tomorrow."

As the girl turned to leave, Nadia leaned closer to me and whispered, "It's time, Mikela—the guests are waiting. They're ready to receive you."

I stood up and started to walk behind Nadia. She seemed to be taking me to where she said the guests were waiting when I heard the sound of my alarm clock, which woke me from my dream. I checked the time. It was 6 AM—time for me to get up.

May 1983—The Golden Hands of the White Knight:

After I left the Mathani's home, I never went back to my former school, and every day, I prayed not to run into Aunt Bella and her kids, Mama Eshe, or Chege Mathani himself on the streets of Nairobi. I think Enkai heard my prayers because I never did.

It had been one year since I'd joined Les Galeries des Beaux-arts de François Jacques Paquet, and I was now seventeen years old. I had since moved out of Ayan's place and was now renting a place of my own—a small studio apartment close to the Nairobi City Center a few blocks from Ayan's flat. During the past year, I'd also developed a close friendship with Ayan. On some weekends when Tulia visited, we would spend time together at Ayan's place or venture into the Nairobi City Center to explore more of its beautiful and exciting enclaves.

During the first six months working at the François galleries, I went through daily rigorous training acquiring new artistic skills. I learned new color mixtures and patterns, and François said that my newly acquired skills, along with my creative talent, had emerged as a new and exquisite artistic amalgam. At the same time, I started learning about European beaux-arts and was soon creating unique mosaic-collage paintings from Safari snapshots of me that were taken by François. These had a blend of Maasai artistry. Some of my paintings were featured in Nairobi fashion magazines for Safari advertisements.

François described my paintings of the photos as having a fascinating air of unique creativity. One of my most exquisite works, he said, was a painting of my photo in which I wore a Maasai contemporary outfit designed by Duboef-Duboef, who was the official designer of African outfits for Les Galeries des Beaux-arts de François Jacques Paquet.

Another was a particular painting that I created from my own photo that was taken in a makeshift-studio of the Maasaiplains; this was also one of François's favorites. In the painting, I wore a short and sleeveless top and skirt with Kazuri beads around my waist and neck, and my hair was in thin braids. When François took the shot, I appeared to be running in a studio-made Maasai field and had my hands stretched out to my sides. François said that I looked like the traditional Maasai Ruwa, or Sun goddess, because my face, enhanced by flawless makeup, glowed under the studio lights. He also said that my long and shiny braids accentuated the air of graceful elegance around me.

"Mikela, you are another living proof that exotic beauty exists in every race and ethnic group. You've blossomed from the intricate artistry of mother nature—beauty that is meticulously molded by nature," François would often say.

Frankly, sometimes, I didn't fully grasp the meaning of his words, although his belief in my work was a source of great motivation and encouragement. It was François who started to teach me to believe in my work. One year after I started working with him, I could now look at each work of mine and admit that they uniquely captured my inner feelings and outer perspectives.

Once, I saw a finished poster from one of my Safari resort paintings, and my own talent amazed me. I remembered François Jacques Paquet showing the poster around the office and exclaiming, *"Regardez! Elle Belle! Viola."*

"Look! She's beautiful! See!"

Somehow, François believed that my paintings were on the way to the international art scene. He always said that I was a star in the making, and it was just a matter of time before I would become an internationally renowned artist. He believed so much in my talent that he was my foremost champion, mentor, and teacher. He was also very patient with me, knowing that this was a whole new world for me.

François was blatantly showing special attention to me, to the envy of the other artists that had worked longer at his agency. Once in the presence of a few models, he described my work as ravishingly beautiful and also said that his instinct for my success came from what he perceived as an alluring air around me. He was not subtle in showing that I'd become his favorite artist.

I believe that François loved me as he would his own sister, although he couldn't always explain his special feelings for me. He guarded and protected me closely, like his precious jewel. I was now juggling an emerging career as a professional artist with trying to finish high school. In addition, I started to take French classes with Ayan—François had advised us to as a step toward taking our work to Paris, the world's cosmopolitan scene of Western art.

Unknown to me, François had sent two re-prints of my original works to L'Ecole des Beaux-arts and Ecole nationale supérieure des Beaux-arts in Paris. He received letters from them showing interest in exhibiting my work. They also suggested that they would gladly accept me into their French beaux-arts circle to help me polish what they described as my natural flair for fine art. They were willing to offer me a real taste of the European renaissance beaux-arts, they said.

After six months of intensive French courses in Nairobi, Ayan spoke with a strong Tanzanian accent, and I started to speak a little bit of the language with a blended Maasai and Kenyan touch. To help us with our spoken French, François and Duboef-Duboef spoke French to us most of the time.

A year later, on my eighteenth birthday, I received my high school diploma. This was two years after I'd started working for François. He called me into his office the next morning and announced that he thought that I was ready for Paris. He said he would like for me to spend at least two years in Paris. During those years, if things went well, he said, and the Parisian art world appreciated my work, he would suggest my staying in Paris longer.

I was excited beyond description because I'd never imagined that I would ever leave Africa and explore other worlds. I remembered what Mama Túlélèi said to my mother, and I was amazed that she could have had such prophetic insight when I was just a baby.

I started to think about Mama Eshe and Aunt Bela.

Should I go and visit them or write a letter to them? Was this a good time to try and explain to them what had really happened at Aunt Bela's home?

I was afraid of what they would say to me. I was not ready to bear the pain of their not believing my story. So, I decided to postpone my meeting with them until sometime in the future—maybe I would be ready after I settled down in Paris. Then I would write them, I thought. I convinced myself that this was the best plan and buried the thoughts.

During my quiet and lonely moments, I thought about my mother and how she was going to be even further away from me.

"Ma, I love you. I really do miss you very much," I whispered to myself frequently, hoping to make her sneeze and in the sneeze know that I am thinking of her, as I had learned back home. This was old African superstition, which claimed that when you call someone's name and talk about them, they will begin to sneeze for no apparent reason. I had believed it as a child, and now I hoped with all hope that it was true. I liked the thought of Ma sneezing because I was thinking of her and calling her name. Daily, I wished that my mother would leave the Maasailand and explore the world with me—a wish that I knew was not likely to happen anytime soon.

I waited for a few weeks before I shared the news with Tulia. She was my best friend and had been like a sister to me. A part of my heart was with her and hers was with me, and I knew that it was going to be difficult for both of us to deal with my leaving Nairobi for Paris. I prayed to Enkai to give us both the courage and heart to deal with the separation.

Later, when I found out that Ayan would be traveling with me, I was even more excited about the trip.

Ayan's comforting words helped lessen my anxiety about going far away from Africa. She reminded me that she and François would be familiar faces around me.

Yet, in the midst of my excitement, there was a tiny part of me that was afraid of going so far away from Africa.

May 1984—Meeting with Tulia:

I invited Tulia to visit the Nairobi City Center with me, and as usual, we caught a *matatu*. On arrival, we found a nice café, and we both settled for a cold chocolate drink.

"Mikela, I'm so happy that things have turned around nicely for you. I thank God for everything that He has done for you. Look at you! In just two years, you have blossomed, and your career has taken off. Isn't God so wonderful!" Tulia said.

"Yes, I owe it all to Enkai. I look back to the day that I ran away from home and all that I went through at the Mathani home. Yet, Enkai has delivered me from it all. He sent François to me, and he has been so wonderful to me," I responded.

"Yes, it's been just terrific for you and for me, too. Your experience really helped me make up my mind on what to do with my life. I am going to be a doctor, Mikela."

"A doctor! Oh Tulia, that is fantastic!" I said.

"I hoped you would approve," Tulia replied, laughing. "Yes, I decided to become a doctor and specialize in gynecology in order to help women who have been circumcised and raped. After what happened to you, it dawned on me that there were probably thousands of girls going through the same thing you went through with no one to help them," she explained.

Tears welled in my eyes as I listened to Tulia and silently prayed that she would hold that dream and become a doctor indeed.

"You'll be my doctor when I return to Nairobi," I finally managed to say, unable to express all the emotions I was feeling at her decision.

"What do you mean by when you return to Nairobi? Are you going somewhere?" Tulia asked, looking confused.

"Yes, Tulia, I'm going away—just for a while," I added quickly. "François has asked Ayan and me to go to Paris with him. He would like to introduce my work to the Parisian world."

For a minute or two, there was silence, as we both tried to deal with our emotions, my tears finally escaping the confines of my eyes. Finally, Tulia reached out and held my hands.

"Mikela, I'm so happy for you," she said, her voice thick with tears. "How could I not be? I always knew that God had such great plans for your life, as He has for all of us."

She paused again, wiping away the mucus threatening to escape from her nose.

Regaining her composure, she continued. "I'm also sad that you are leaving because you have been my best friend and sister. I'll miss you very much."

The emotion and passion in her words pierced my heart.

"I love you, Tulia. I love you dearly. I'll write you from Paris. Maybe you can come and visit us soon."

She nodded and smiled.

We both stood up and embraced, sobbing softly, uncaring of the odd looks we were getting from other customers in the café. Finally, she said, "We should be celebrating, not crying, Mikela. God has done such a wonderful thing for you. Here, let's toast."

She raised her cup. "To the success of my best friend and wonderful sister, Mikela!"

"And to my most bosom friend and God's gift to me, Tulia—I love you with all my heart, and we are friends for life."

"It's a deal!" she said.

En Route to Paris—June 1984:

On June 20, 1984, François, Ayan, and I were scheduled to fly out from Nairobi International Airport. Before we boarded the Air France Boeing 747 jet, François and Ayan tried to calm my anxiety by telling me that flying had a soothing and relaxing effect on the body. I remained doubtful that a trip inside an iron bird would not be a terrifying one. This was my first time flying, and to me it was a scary event.

The flight took off on time, and as it lifted off the ground, I shut my eyes and grasped the arms of my seat very tightly. As I shuddered with fear, François and Ayan were enjoying what they said was a spectacular aerial view of Nairobi.

"Mikela, viola!" François exclaimed. "It's fantastic scenery."

"You can see the tapering buildings surrounded by nature's dazzling display of the Kenyan and Tanzanian Highlands," Ayan said, trying to lure me into taking a peak.

"François, I don't have the courage to stare out of the window," I said.

Despite François and Ayan's excitement about the aerial view over the city of Nairobi and its surrounding geographical terrain, I was terrified of the height. To me, the plane appeared to be slanted, as if it was headed straight for the heavens. As a young *entito* growing up in the Maasailand, I remembered watching many iron birds fly over the open plains while I played with Nadia. The first time we saw an iron bird, we asked our mother what it was, and she told us that it was one of the creatures of white man's magic—giant, man-made iron birds that carried people to and from far-away places within a short time. Later, at the government school, we learned that they were called airplanes. When I was still living with the Mathani family, I went to the airport on many occasions with Aunt Bela, Johari, and Jamila to see Mr. Mathani off on his travels. Never did I ever think that one day I, too, would be on board an iron bird going far away from Africa to the white man's world.

As we gradually approached the desired flying altitude announced by the pilot, the aircraft appeared less slanted and felt like it was now belly down. I became a little more comfortable, although I still had to deal with the unfamiliar engine sounds that sometimes sounded like the plane was stopping in mid-air and other times like it was re-starting and trying to rev-up speed. At one point, the plane started to shake, and I started screaming because I thought that the plane was about to fall out of the skies. François explained that we had encountered air pockets, which sometimes caused slight turbulence. It took two flight hostesses and an amused co-pilot to calm me down. Some passengers empathized with what they perceived as a naïve woman's fear of flying, while others were simply irritated by the commotion I was causing.

Eventually, François gave me a sleeping pill and shortly after, I went to sleep. I must have slept for most of the seven-and-a-half-hour flight to Roissy-Charles de Gaulle International Airport in Paris because when I finally woke up, the pilot announced that we were two hours away from Paris. A snack was being served, which I barely ate—having lost my appetite due to my anxiety.

Shortly after the pilot had announced it, the aircraft started to drop its altitude in preparation for landing. Once again, I held tightly to my chair, as air pockets slightly roughed up the plane's balance before it descended to an altitude that was low enough to see Paris at night from its aerial view—an enchanting and romantic scene, Ayan and François said. They finally convinced me to take a quick glance at the splendor and glamour of the city of Paris.

I stuck my head against an adjacent window and started to view a city of dramatic floodlights that glittered beneath the skies. Paris and its suburbs could be seen as a giant map-outlay beautified with a color-mosaic of lights. Momentarily, I forgot my fear of flying as the splendor of Paris by night captivated my attention and intensified my anticipation. The arrays of floodlights of the city of Paris seen from the skies were like the interplay of heavenly highlights, and the ambience of the city lights seemed to capture the sparkling detail of the fabulous illumination. Unique structures and monuments, some of which were brightly lit, seemed to reach for the skies, accentuating the beauty of the city.

From our bird's-eye view, François pointed out to Ayan and me the area where the Montparnasse-Bienvenüe stood—a tower that stood on the southern edge of the city halfway between the famous Eiffel Tower on Quai Branly and Gare d'Austerlitz.

"Can you see the tapering top of the monumental latticed ironwork of the Eiffel Tower itself?" he asked, as he pointed in that direction.

"The Eiffel Tower was built by Gustave Eiffel in 1889 and is Paris's most famous landmark and attraction. Its complex and clever engineering has been tested by some of the most powerful winds, which only caused the tower to sway but a few inches. From its one-thousand-foot height, its spectacular view of Paris is a marvel made possible by architectural wizardry.

"When you are on the ground, a southeast view of the Eiffel Tower can be seen from the Parc du Champ de Mars. This is a rectangular park that is located between the Eiffel Tower and the École Militaire—another one of Paris's best-known monuments and a site with a classic touch of French architecture that was used in the past for military parades. The École Militaire terminated Champ de Mars, a vast formal garden on one end," François explained.

Then he pointed in another direction, where he said the Tower of Notre-Dame would be located—one of the oldest and most romantic views of the city between medieval chimeras. François stressed that the Notre-Dame was more impressive when the floodlights of the riverboats accentuated its exquisite and sculpted façade. He also explained that other monuments, like the dome De Panthéon, the bell-tower of the Church of St-Etienne-du-Mont, Beauborg, and the sequence of bridges also marked the location over the Seine.

The history lesson on Paris went on to the Arc de Triomphe, Cour Napoléon, Pei's Pyramid, Centre Georges-Pompidou, and Dome of the Sacré-Coeur. There was so much to learn about the city of Paris, Ayan and I realized. The bird's-eye view was merely a glimpse of a spectacular city built on a series of hills, with characteristic undulating streets.

The sound of the landing gear flaps being deployed by the pilot distracted my view of Paris, as one of the flight stewardesses announced our final approach to Roissy-Charles de Gaulle International Airport, which François said was one of the busiest airports in the world.

Twenty minutes later, the aircraft touched down on the runway. Now, once it landed and sped-away on the runway, did I fully appreciate its unimaginable speed. Earlier onboard, there were times that I could have sworn the aircraft was not moving at all.

Throughout the landing exercise, I clutched tightly to my seat while I muffled prayers to Enkai. The aircraft came to a final halt at the arrival gate, a welcomed end to both an arduous and memorable flight.

Soon after the immigration and customs check, we boarded a taxi and headed to François's place on Rue de Marbeuf in Champs-Élysées, somewhere along the banks of the Seine. On our way, he gave Ayan and me a second history lesson and a first night tour of Paris by road.

"This is the Bastille, the location of the Opéra de Paris-Bastille and the exciting Rue de Lappe with its series of dance halls, produce shops, and art galleries. Here's the Le Louvre, a former royal palace, which is now the home of the richest collections of art and antiquities in the world. Around the Le Louvre are the Tuileries gardens, an intricate part of the architecture that offers beauty and serenity to its spectators. Over there is the Place Vendôme, the hub of theatre land. It brings to light the richness and beauty of seventeenth century French architecture—a central square ringed by continuous arches that are supported by huge pilasters up to steep and pitched-top windows. The buildings on the square exhibit unique projecting pedimented façades. From Vendôme, we will drive past the district Opéra, location of the Garnier's Opera House, down to the Palais-Royal and Avenue de l'Opéra."

As we listened intensely and excitedly to François, we admired the fancy shops, especially the fashion boutiques of Paris. Finally, we heard him say, "Here we are! We've arrived at the famous Champs-Élysées—an avenue that is two kilometers long and seventy meters wide. From the Arch of Triumph to Concorde Square is a grand perspective of Avenue des Champs-Élysées. It's recognized worldwide as an avenue with a spectacular view, and it offers a variety of exclusive and expensive shops and entertainment. As you can see, over there are endless stretches of shops, restaurants, cinemas, offices, banks, and cafés—an insatiable stretch for tourists and even the local Parisians."

Finally, we arrived at François's three-bedroom apartment on Rue de Marbeuf. Ayan and I were both exhausted from the trip and gladly succumbed to a hot bath before we retired for the night.

Our First Work Day in Paris:

It was a typical cool, early summer day in Paris, and the sun was still very mild. The rainy days had become less frequent than two to three months earlier in April and May, François said. It was our first Monday, which was as also our first workday in Paris, and it started as a very busy day. Ayan and I went with François to his Paris gallery on Rue Lincoln, a few streets away from Rue de Marbeuf. We met his older sister, Chantal Jacques Paquet-Duval, for the first time. She, too, was an artist and had been trained at the Ecole des Beaux-arts where she studied sculpture and drawing. Her works were well respected and acclaimed both in Paris and in other parts of Europe. She'd been divorced for many years, and her work had since become her first love. She'd lived in Paris all her life and had been managing the Paris galleries for more than ten years.

Everyone at the office called her Madame Duval. She was a very petite brunette, no taller than five feet three inches and about ninety pounds. Madame Duval was probably close to sixty years old, although her official age was forty-eight, and to her credit, she didn't look a day older than forty-eight. She received Ayan and me rather shabbily the first time. Later, François apologized on her behalf, explaining that she knew very little about foreigners, especially Africans. It didn't take Ayan and me long to realize that working with Madame Duval was going to be a challenge.

The same day, I started off on new projects for my first Paris exhibitions already scheduled: one at the L'Ecole des Beaux-arts and the other at the Ecole nationale supérieure des Beaux-arts. François had arranged for my original Maasai works to be shipped from Nairobi to Paris. For the first painting work I did in Paris, Ayan was my still life model. This was also my first official work that had a European touch; I named it the "Renoir," and it depicted Ayan emerging from the city of Zanzibar into the city of Paris—Zanzibar was in the far background while Paris dominated the front end of the painting. In "Renoir," I tried to capture Ayan rather vividly as taking a pleasant stroll in the romantic city of Zanzibar that transitioned into the enchanting city of Paris. I remember François saying that painting this kind of work on canvas required a touch of artistic illusion.

My second work in Paris was the "Enk-áló." Here I captured Ayan in an elegant Dubeof-Duboef Maasai outfit sitting in the heart of the Champs-Élysées, with its blend of aristocratic, cosmopolitan, and regal surroundings. The "Enk-áló" was meant to capture a new direction in Paris. In my next painting, I switched back to expressing my thoughts of the Maasailand in the "*Mpólosi–*

Enkang." This was a painting of my mother Halima seated on a hide-skin mat in an atrium bordered by a cloister of *bomas*. The *"Mpólosi"* was my personal memoir of my mother, whom I painted solely from my treasured memory.

For Ayan and me, our daily schedule was very hectic. Usually, we would barely have an hour to rush home and get prepared for our night French classes. This routine was so chaotic for us both that by the end of our first month in Paris, we had each lost close to six pounds.

In between our daily schedules, while I was on the train or grabbing lunch, I studied books on European beaux-arts. I studied the history of beaux-arts, which I first came to know in Nairobi to mean "fine arts." This type of art was based on ideas that were taught and flourished at L'Ecole des Beaux-arts in Paris between 1825 and 1920. I understood that the origins of beaux-arts had a touch of Greek and Roman art forms, with great renaissance ideas that emerged with versatile neoclassical styles and beauty. I now began to understand the history of the gigantic masonry patterns of Paris buildings—adorned with shields, garlands, and corsages on the lavishness of window balconies, pillars, pilasters, and balustrades. Paris was a tribute to the beaux-arts tradition in its museums, government and office buildings, homes, gardens, and shops. It seemed like a huge collage of Renaissance beaux-arts masonry and artistry, with patches of modern-day work that still emphasized the historical origins of the city with all of its ostentatious and landed gentry.

Six months after we arrived in Paris, I was ready for my first gallery exhibitions at the L'Ecole des Beaux-arts and Ecole nationale supérieure des Beaux-arts, which were scheduled two weeks apart. François was enraptured—his instincts for my success, he said, were rapidly manifesting. A Parisian magazine did a major story on me as the newly discovered Parisian-Maasai beaux-arts artist and painter with a unique blend of Maasai artistry and French Renaissance Beaux-arts. My exhibition was advertised as "Paris-Maasai des Beaux-arts de Paris," and the bulk of my paintings were oil on canvas.

As François predicted, and to my utter amazement, the week-long exhibition turned out to be a huge success, with over five hundred wealthy art lovers who wanted to see the unique blend of my artwork. Not a single painting was left, except *"Mpólosi–Enkang"* that meant "The beginning in the village," which I politely declined to sell. My first exhibition in Paris earned over two million French francs. Three weeks later, my exhibit at the Ecole nationale supérieure des Beaux-arts attracted as many art lovers as the first, and collectively my paintings raised over three million francs.

My artwork had become an instant success, as François had predicted. The Parisian art world had accepted my work and placed it in a unique class of mosaic blend of artistry that depicted European Renaissance and Tanzanian Maasai art. This was a new style of art that François said no one had ever thought of capturing and expressing so vividly and exquisitely in oil and canvas paintings. This would become my exclusive specialty in the Paris art world.

A month after the French magazine issue featured me on their front cover, François said that many in the beaux-arts world had started to ask about me and wanted to know more about the young Maasai woman that had hit the Parisian world. In the subway, people asked for my autograph, and it was hard for me to grasp the reality that I, a local Maasai *entito,* was being recognized in the Parisian beaux-arts circle. Then, I remembered my dream where I was dressed in Maasai bridal costume and adorned with *Imasaa.*

Could my success in Paris be what Nadia was trying to show me when she said that the guests were waiting to receive me? I wondered.

In the weeks ahead, I was booked for future exhibitions in the most prestigious museums and galleries in Paris. François said that he was impressed that even with my newly found fame and fortune, I remained down-to-earth, humble, clear-headed, and handled Parisian high life very cautiously. François also remarked that he was very proud of how I was handling my newly evolving success and urged me to stay away from drugs and alcohol. He said that these were some of the many evils that he'd observed to be intricately woven into the world of fame and glamour.

I trusted François and loved him dearly—he was my beautiful knight with golden hands. He was a new and loving father to me, not like my biological father, who had always been a stranger. François had taken a gamble on my career and believed in my work, and now Paris had embraced me.

Deep down inside of me, I was a simple Maasai *entito* who was still amazed to see that what my stepmother Mama Túlélèi had predicted had indeed come to pass. Yet, despite my success, I battled depression daily, and my mangled emotions about my past experiences seemed to dominate the depths of my soul. Where could I turn? Who could really understand what was going on inside of my mind? Not even François could understand, even if I bared my soul to him.

CHAPTER 11

❦

A Handsome Knight Emerges

End of June 1984—A Piercing Light in a Dark Tunnel:

The summer weather was still gradually picking up in June of 1984, and I had just finished my latest exhibition at the L'Ecole des Beaux-arts and Ecole nationale supérieure des Beaux-arts, which had been a success. A week after the exhibition, I had another inexplicable dream. Ayan was wearing a flowing and shimmering white gown. She appeared like a silhouette of her real self and seemed to be gliding in the direction of a powerful wind that blew open my bedroom door. I could see her stretch her hands toward me. Then, I heard her say, "Come quickly, François is waiting for us at the entrance of the tunnel." As she said this, I felt the forces of the powerful wind gently lift me from my bed, and I began to float in the air. For a brief moment, Ayan seemed to have disappeared, and when I saw her again, she was with François about a quarter of a mile away.

"François! Ayan! Wait for me," I shouted, hoping that the wind would carry my body a little faster towards them.

Momentarily, a very bright and piercing light appeared and blinded me. Then, the light twirled with the forces of the wind and formed what seemed like a brightly lit, hollow channel inside the dark tunnel. I saw François and Ayan holding hands and smiling, as the wind seemed to swiftly take them through the hollow channel, where they were fast disappearing.

"Oh no! Where are you going?" I screamed. "François! Ayan! Where are you going? Please come back!" I yelled out, panic engulfing me, as the distance between us got wider.

The next thing I heard was someone calling my name.

"Mikela! Mikela! Are you okay?"

I opened my eyes and saw Ayan sitting by my bed, gently shaking me.

"Are you all right?" she asked again.

Still very frightened by what I had seen in my dream, I simply nodded.

"I was having a very bad dream about François and you. Like birds, it seemed like both of you were flying away, and I was left behind," I said.

"It's just a dream—we have no plans of leaving you behind, even if we plan to go anywhere," Ayan said with a gentle smile.

"Ayan, please hold me, just for a moment," I requested.

I held onto her tightly, the warmth of her body comforting and reassuring me that she was there with me and that she was not going anywhere.

"I love you, Ayan."

"And I love you, too," she said.

Now, a Handsome Knight Emerges:

By this time, it had been two years since we'd arrived in Paris. I'd already grown to love it and its exotic surroundings, and I was excited about my new career. Yet, in the midst of all the huge success that was unraveling in my life, a deep and dark cloud of pain and hurt still loomed inside me. In my quiet moments, I would still remember with pain what Chege Mathani had done to me, and my circumcision, and Nadia's senseless death. Lately my mother was always in my thoughts, my love and longing for her sometimes threatening to choke me.

During these moments, which I preferred to spend alone, I would explore the endless stretches of Paris parks and theatres. I would also spend hours in Paris museums, like the Musée des Arts d'Afrique et d'Océabie on Avenue Daumesnil, admiring Aborigine bark painting, masks from Papua New Guinea, Banda and Molo masks, Kota wood and copper figures from Gabon, and ceremonial and pendant masks from West Africa. At the Musée Jacquemart-Andre on Boulevard Haussmann, I would immerse my mind in the intricacies of European and Italian Renaissance Art—the paintings and drawings by the likes of Chardin and Boucher and the sculptures of Pigalle. At the Musée National d'Art Moderne, I learned about the evolution of the contemporary art scene from color impressionism and silhouetted forms to pastel tones. The sheer diversity of the exhibits in Paris museums and galleries was a marvel to my eyes.

To me, Paris parks and gardens were cherished hectares of flowers, fountains, ponds, and man-made waterfalls. The most exquisite to me was the elegant Palais-Royal Gardens—a haven of peace in the heart of Paris. Others, like the Bagatelle, filled with irises and roses, and the sprawling landscapes of the Buttes-Chaumont and the Luxemburg Gardens, were also spectacular scenes of nature's blossoming colors.

When Ayan would notice that I had gone into one of my depressions, she would insist that we hit the Parisian night scene and indulge in heart pumping pleasure till we dropped. On these occasions, we would visit Café-Théatres, Chansonniers, and Cabarets—usually ending up in the ethnic enclaves of Paris, like the Afro-Caribbean Jazz, Calypso, and Zouk nightclubs. These outings never failed to lift my spirit, and I grew to look forward to them more often.

It was on one of these outings that I met the man that was to change my life forever. It was in early July, and Ayan and I were seated inside the Zouk-La Cinquiéme at the Montreuil-sous-Bois Shopping center, the weekend place for Zouk music, when two tall men walked in. Shortly after, they came around to our table. One of them, a dark-complexioned man who looked African-American and had a uniquely shaped, thin moustache, seemed instantly attracted to me, and so was I to him.

"Hello! It's always nice to see beautiful black sisters in Paris. I'm Alex Williams," he said, with a piercing gaze that seemed to be penetrating my soul.

"Hello! I'm Mikela, and this is my friend, Ayan."

"You look like someone I've seen before. Could this be déjà vu?" he said jokingly, stretching out his hand for a handshake.

"Maybe we knew each other in a past life," I responded, chuckling. Strangely, I felt nervous tickles in my stomach, something I'd heard Ayan describe as "butterflies in the belly."

"Yeah! That must be it," he replied, catching on to my joke and chuckling. "Do you mind if my friend Brian and I join you two?" he asked.

I looked at Ayan, seeking her approval. She smiled and nodded.

"Sure, it's no problem," I responded casually, trying not to sound too eager.

Alex and Brian Edwards gladly joined us at our table, sending hot flushes up my face. "Would you like another drink?" Alex asked.

"Actually, Mikela and I were about to order a bottle of champagne," Ayan responded.

"Well, that sounds great—we'll join you and the bottle is on Brian and me."

Waving at the waiter, Brian smiled and said, "Certainly, it's our pleasure. Please, Garçon!"

"I like this place because of the variety of Zouk they play. I'd never heard of Zouk until I came to Paris—I think it's real cool music," Alex said.

"I understand that it's a blend of Afro-Caribbean rhythms and French music," Ayan explained.

"Yeah! It's the music of the French Islands of Martinique and Guadeloupe. I think it's got a lot of soul in it. I'm not sure why it's never quite made it into the American music scene," Brian added.

"Interesting point—I don't know either," Alex said.

"Do you know that Zouk means 'party' in the native Creole language? When it has a driving tempo, it stirs everyone to their feet, but it can also have a seductive feel, 'Zouk love,' as they call it—the beat that makes you fall in love with a stranger," Ayan explained.

Momentarily, Alex's gaze traveled to me.

"I've been practicing my Zouk steps, but unfortunately, I don't think I've made much progress. I think I need a few more lessons," Alex said, still looking at me.

"Actually, it's quite easy to dance to because it's a uniquely rhythmic music. Just watch the dancers on the floor, and you'll catch on in no time," I said.

"I'm a much better learner when I get private lessons. Would you care to dance with me, my sister?" he asked, with a charming smile, sending hot flushes up my face.

"Well, I'll gladly offer you your first private lesson in Zouk," I said, loosening my face into a warm smile and hoping that the somersaults going on in my belly were not reflecting in my voice.

As Alex's well-sculptured body pressed closer to mine, I could not help but notice how ravishingly handsome he was. At over six feet, he had the body of a practiced athlete, firm and muscular but without the exaggerated biceps. His skin was the color and feel of polished mahogany, smooth and clear. He had a face that reminded me of the African sunset; it was so beautiful that it took my breath away every time he looked at me. I could not believe that a mere mortal could have such an impact on me in such a short time.

Alex and I ended up dancing all night, while Ayan and Brian paired up. In the midst of a variety of rhythmic body movements that rocked the Zouk-La Cinquiéme, Alex looked at me, his lovely hazel colored, almond shaped eyes twinkling, and said, "Mikela, I hope you don't mind my saying this, but I'm enchanted by your elegance, grace, and beauty. You're the most beautiful woman I've ever met."

"You are not so bad yourself," I replied, making him laugh.

Why was I giving Alex green lights? I wondered, as I enjoyed the slow, monotonous dance steps that we synchronized to the Calypso-Reggae beats of Mighty Sparrow. Quickly, I shook the thought out of my head, deciding that I was going to enjoy myself for once without guilt or any theorizing.

As we danced to the sizzling brass and melodic mix of the music, I asked Alex about himself, and as he began to tell me, I laid my head on his shoulders, breathing in his strong masculine perfume and feeling caressed by his deep, velvety voice.

"I just turned twenty-six, and I have completed my third year at Columbia University in New York. I am an Electrical Engineering major, and this is my second degree; my first degree was in business and finance. Now, I work part-time and attend college at the same time. Luckily, my father allowed me to cash some of the investments that he has slated for me to start my own engineering firm after I graduate and gain some work experience.

"I'm of mixed heritage—African, Cherokee Indian, and white. My parents are originally from Charlotte, North Carolina; they are now divorced—my father left my mother for a white woman. Initially, I was very upset with my father, as most of our relatives were. However, as I grew older, I started to realize that my father really loves his present wife, not because she's a white woman but simply because he fell in love with her. I've spent time with them, and they seem to have a very peaceful relationship, unlike when he was living at home with my mother and me.

"My parents always had fights and that used to sadden me. At one point, I used to pray for their separation and divorce for the sake of peace. But then when they finally agreed to divorce, I became very upset because I could see our once cohesive family splitting apart. I can tell you from experiencing my parents' divorce that it can be a terrible and painful ordeal—it tears the entire extended family apart."

There was a brief silence and an expression of transient sadness in Alex's eyes, as his mind seemed to wander momentarily to a sadder time and place.

As I sensed Alex's discomfort, I quickened my steps, forcing him to do the same, and this appeared to help jolt his mind back.

"Wow! I can't believe that I've spent almost thirty minutes telling a perfect stranger about my family. Do you mind if I ask you about yours? What do you do here? Where are you from? Where do your parents live?" Alex asked, redirecting the conversation.

"I'm a Tanzanian Maasai, and my parents live in the open plains of the Maasai Steppe," I said.

"I feel embarrassed to admit that I have no idea where that is. I know that Tanzania is somewhere in North Africa right?" Alex said.

"Oh no! Tanzania is actually in East Africa," I quickly corrected him.

"Do you go home often?" Alex inquired, trying to mask his embarrassment about his obvious lack of knowledge of the African continent.

"No. It's been a long time since I've been home," I said, my eyes suddenly saddening and my voice dropping to a whisper.

"If you don't mind my asking, why is that? You seem to be doing quite well here in Paris."

At this point, I was lost for words. Talking about my family was still a very difficult ordeal. Up till that point, not even Ayan or François knew anything about my family, and I was not going to tell a perfect stranger, no matter how comfortable he might have felt telling me about his. "I've just not been able to go home, that's all," I finally said.

It was obvious to Alex that I didn't want to discuss the reasons why I'd not seen my parents, and he didn't pry any further.

We spent the rest of the evening dancing and talking about Paris. We were obviously attracted to each other, but I was not ready to open up the floodgates of my inner soul to any man. Since my experience with Mr. Mathani, I'd avoided men like the plague. The only man that I'd ever trusted was François, and this was because he was more like a father and guardian to me.

Before Alex and I parted that night, we exchanged telephone numbers. Days later, he called me and left a couple of messages on my answering machine. I listened to each message repeatedly to hear his gentle and deep voice. His words seemed to ignite the kind of passion that I'd never felt for any man before. At the same time, I was afraid that the same passion would make me vulnerable to Alex, and I was not ready to open the door to my heart to him or any other man. I did not want to bare my life's experiences to anyone or to dig up the memories that I struggled every day to keep buried.

"No, I won't return his calls," I finally decided. I had convinced myself that I was not ready for Alex.

Ayan:

Three months later, Ayan fell sick. First, she had rashes all over her body, then she felt nauseous every morning, and on some days, she was too sick to get out of bed. I suspected that she was pregnant, but Ayan later told me that she'd seen a doctor who told her that she was fatigued. I advised her to take a break from her very busy schedule. François was very understanding, and he gave her a few weeks off.

Ayan was losing weight rapidly and looking emaciated. Still, she maintained her usual high-spirited moods. She tried not to dwell on her illness and often suggested that we go out and have fun. One day, she invited me to go with her to a Black Cinema, the Images d'ailleurs on Rue de la Clef.

"They are showing a documentary film on Africa, which I think would be interesting to watch," she said.

I didn't bother asking her what the movie was about—I trusted her judgment. Together, we left for the Images d'ailleurs. It was not until I got there that I realized that the documentary was on female circumcision. I tried to stay calm about it because I didn't want Ayan to suspect that I, too, had been a victim of circumcision.

The documentary was about a Kenyan Maasai girl who had been circumcised when she was just eight years old. The images that were shown on the screen during her circumcision were quite vivid. I could clearly see the fleshy part and inner walls of the little girl's sacred self when her legs were spread apart. The Maasai woman circumciser then picked up a filthy, locally made razorblade with her right hand, and using her left hand, she grabbed the little girl's sacred self and started to cut through the fleshy part.

For the very first time, I saw what had been done to me, and I started to tremble. My palms were now sweaty, and I felt bile coming up my throat. As the razorblade started cutting the little girl's flesh, she started screaming, and her tiny legs trembled. I was now almost passing out as flashes of my own experience and Nadia's death swirled through my mind. I closed my eyes and placed my palms over my ears to drown out the little girl's screams.

I didn't know that Ayan had observed my obvious discomfort.

"Mikela, are you okay?" she asked.

I barely heard her question, and I didn't respond.

Then, suddenly, I felt like I could no longer continue to watch what was being done to the little girl. I jumped up from my chair and ran out of the Cinema Theater into the bathroom, where I began to throw up. I was now sobbing helplessly, and my entire body was shivering. I wished that Ayan had told me what the movie was about—I would have opted not to see it. As I cried in the bathroom, Ayan came rushing in.

"Mikela! Mikela! Are you all right?" she asked frantically.

"I can't go in there again. I can't see any more of that stuff. Why didn't you tell me the movie was about female circumcision?" I asked, as I cried through my words.

"Because I want you to start facing what happened to you with strength and courage. All these past years, you never fooled me, Mikela. From the very first day I told you about my own experience, the look in your eyes told me that you, too, had gone through it."

I turned away from her, unable to hide the tears streaming down my face.

"Mikela, look at me!" Ayan exclaimed, raising her voice. "It's not the end of your world. You have a terrific career ahead of you—you should be thankful for that and not wallow in self-pity every day of your life. Mikela, confront the past, deal with it, but don't let it consume your soul. There are many ways you can heal from the horrible things that happened to you. If you stay strong and become an international artist, then you'll become the voice of other Maasai children that have gone unheard. Be strong for me, too. I had to deal with the circumcision, my days of prostitution, and now I have AIDS," Ayan said.

The word AIDS hits me like a bolt of lightening, and I immediately turned around and stared blankly at Ayan.

"Oh no! Oh God! No! This can't be—Ayan. No, Ayan, it can't be true! Why! Why!" I asked. Suddenly, it seemed that too many wounds were ripping at my soul.

CHAPTER 12

❋

Tragedy Strikes

"What did you say? How can it be, Ayan?" I finally asked, when I regained my composure.

"Yes, Mikela, it's true. I said that I have AIDS. A few months ago, when I told you that the doctor thought that I was fatigued, that's when I found out. I didn't want to tell you because I felt that you could not handle it at that time. Now, my life is steadily ebbing away, and I feel like I must tell you. François knows—he was the only one that I told about my condition," Ayan explained.

I threw my hands around Ayan, holding her tightly as I started to sob again.

"Oh no!" I exclaimed again in desperation.

"It's okay, Mikela. Stop crying! Remember, you have to be strong for me. I'm paying the price for my days of prostitution on the streets of Nairobi," Ayan said, with admirable courage.

"No! Ayan, it was not entirely your fault. If you had not been circumcised at home in Zanzibar, you would not have run away and ended up on the mean streets of Nairobi. See! It's ruined our lives," I said, still sobbing.

"Hush! It's okay now. You know me, Mikela—I take challenges as they come. If you love me, just ask Enkai to give me the courage to hang on."

Later, after I had calmed down, Ayan and I held hands as we left the Images d'ailleurs. We arrived home at 12:45 AM on Sunday only to receive a shocking telephone voice message from Madame Duval.

"Just wanted to let you know that François has been hospitalized at the Sainte Antoine Hospital. He is very ill…Monsieur Duboef should be arriving tomorrow from Nairobi," she said.

Ayan and I panicked, wondering what was wrong with François. We'd just seen him on Friday, and he had appeared fine then. Later that morning, we left for Sainte Antoine hospital to see him.

End of July 1985—A Step Backward toward a New Future:

"The patient is in a private room in the Infectious Disease Unit. I'll walk you over there—it's to your right at the end of this hallway," the nurse said, as she guided Ayan and me to François's room.

François appeared lifeless on the bed—his whole body was literally wired with tubes. His breathing was labored, and he looked rather emaciated. Ayan and I sat on either side of his bed holding his hand. I kissed his hand, then bowed my head and started to pray silently.

Please Enkai, don't let François die, please!

As I lifted my head, I looked at Ayan hoping for some answers, bewilderment written all over my face because I could not understand what was happening. I believe that my eyes must have revealed the burning questions on my mind because Ayan looked away as though she had no answers for me, or perhaps she was not ready to discuss François's condition.

With no hope of any answers coming from Ayan or anyone else, I leaned back against my chair, closed my eyes, and resumed praying. When I opened my eyes again, a medical chart that was hanging at the foot of François's bed caught my attention. I started reading the information that was scribbled on it.

"Patient name: François Jacques Paquet; Diagnosis: Pneumocystis Carnii Pneumonia (PCP); History: HIV Positive; Recent Diagnosis: AIDS."

For a few seconds, I suddenly froze with shock. "Oh my God!"

Instantly, Ayan turned toward me.

"What is it, Mikela?"

"Did you read François's medical chart?" I asked.

"No. Why?" Ayan responded calmly.

"Ayan, François has AIDS, too," I said, my voice trembling.

Ayan said nothing; instead, she looked away.

"Did you know about this?" I asked.

"Why do you ask?" Ayan said.

"Because you don't seem surprised."

"Okay, François told me a few months ago when I went to inform him that I had been diagnosed with AIDS. He told me that he and Duboef-Duboef had been living with AIDS for ten years. It was his way of telling me that I could have this disease and still live a full life. I couldn't share his information with you because it wasn't my place to tell you."

I didn't know what to say or do. I couldn't believe that the two most important people in my life, Ayan and François, had AIDS, and there was nothing that I could do to help them. In just a few hours, this was all too much for me to take in. Once again, I felt like I was faced with a different set of complex challenges, and I had no control. It dawned on me that the piercing light that I had seen inside the dark tunnel in my dream had started to unfold.

In the days ahead, Ayan remained an inspiration to me because she was filled with optimism about life. Ayan was fighting her illness with great courage and never once did she shed a tear for François or herself. During our daily visits to the hospital, Ayan would talk to François in his unconscious state, telling him that there was still so much to do at his agency and that Madame Duval was swamped with work. She would crack jokes about our photo-sessions or heavily accented French, which sometimes had to be re-interpreted back to Parisian French by François.

During the times that Ayan talked to François, I could have sworn that many times I saw his face relax into a smile. It seemed as if wherever his unconscious mind was, he could hear Ayan and was enjoying her jokes. Ayan's positive attitude helped me deal with François's condition. Gradually, I, too, started to emulate Ayan's optimism for François's recovery, although daily it appeared that his condition was slowly and steadily deteriorating. Painfully, two months later, François passed away quietly in his sleep. He was buried two days after.

Mr. Duboef who returned to Paris once he heard of François's illness had gone back to Nairobi for a few days to attend to urgent office matters. Unfortunately, he was still in Nairobi when François passed away. He flew back to Paris a day before François was buried. Ayan and I spent most of the day with him trying to console him—he was emotionally devastated. François's burial attracted much of the Parisian art world—everyone who knew him had something good to say about him. Too distraught, I had only a few words to say to François.

"Thank you for letting God use you in my life. You have been a human angel to so many like me. I love you, François, and may your soul rest in perfect peace."

Ayan's words were also brief and captured her experience with François.

"Some used me, others violated me, and even others walked past me and judged me. But you did none of these. You simply stretched out your hands and helped pull me back on my feet. You taught me how to live and value my life once again. How could anyone except God understand how much you truly mean to me? I, too, love you, François, with all my heart."

Mr. Duboef said nothing. He simply sobbed. The week following François's burial, he flew back to Nairobi.

A Brief Moment for Ayan:

A day after Mr. Duboef left for Nairobi, Ayan and her new boyfriend, a French physician, Édouard Monet, left for Sweden. She had met him at the hospital where François died—he was one of François's physicians. Édouard was a typical Swedish blonde of about five feet eleven inches. Ayan described his looks as a blonde-wigged Richard Burton. He had beautiful blue eyes that often caught people's attention and a very quiet and humble demeanor. He was instantly drawn to Ayan when he first met her.

Édouard also had a tasteful sense of humor, which he told Ayan that he had gotten from his late grandmother. After they had started seeing each other more regularly, Ayan asked him why he had been so nice and attentive when they first met, and he told her that when he was eight years old, his grandmother had told him to be nice to black people wherever and whenever he saw them. When he'd asked her why, she told him that black people were God's chosen people but didn't know it themselves. He also said that up until his grandmother died, twenty years later, she'd still never met a black person herself. Her grandmother told him before she died that his great-grandmother, who also had never met a black person in her life, passed on the belief to her. Nonetheless, the belief that black people are God's chosen people had become accepted in his family over generations.

Being one of her physicians, Édouard knew that Ayan had AIDS, but he still vowed to love her, regardless of her ill health. Ayan said that he told her that for as long as she had to live, he would love and support her as she fought the disease. He was a unique soul because he reached out to Ayan with a love and compassion that seemed more fiction than reality. From watching how Édouard Monet loved Ayan, I learned that true love comes in unique shades, molds, and blends, and one would be a fool to reject such love just because of the color in which it was presented.

August 1985—The Solace of Another Knight:

After François's death, and with Ayan's health rapidly deteriorating, I decided to drown my sorrow by escaping into the Paris art world. In addition to my own work, I delved into the seemingly inexhaustible museums of Paris. First, I visited the Musée Jacquemart-Andre on Boulevard Haussmann—an elegant nineteenth century house of European and Italian Renaissance Art display. Deliberately, I immersed my mind and thoughts in the drawings and paintings of the likes of Watteau, Chardin, and Grueze, and the sculptures of Pigalle and Lemoyne. I relished in the remarkable Italian collections of Donatello and Boticelli and the Venetian Renaissance Art by the likes of Titian and Tintoretto. Next, I visited the Musée Rodin on Rue de Varenne, where Rodin's sculptures in bronze, white marble, and terracotta were beautifully displayed. Rodin's masterpieces, "The man with the Broken Nose," "Hand of God," "St. John the Baptist," "The Cathedral," and "The Kiss" vividly expressed his unique passion and talent for art.

One day, I was so completely engrossed in the spectacular beauty of this nineteenth century artist's work that I barely noticed the young man that stood next to me. He was waiting patiently for me to finish reading the history on each piece of art before approaching me. Finally, when he felt that it was time to make his presence felt, he faked a cough that startled me and made me turn in his direction.

"Alex! What a surprise! What are you doing here?"

"I happen to be a lover of European and Italian Renaissance Art as well," he said. "How are you, Mikela? You never returned any of my calls. Why?"

"I'm sorry. I guess I don't have a good enough reason," I replied.

For a moment, we were silent, and Alex's piercing look seemed to be penetrating my innermost soul, making my heart skip a beat. Suddenly, all the emotions and attraction I felt for him that first night started to flood back. I immediately lowered my eyes, trying to avoid his piercing gaze.

"I thought you'd gone back to the United States. How's Brian?" I finally said.

"Brian has gone back to the States, but I'm still here. I elected to do an engineering internship with a company here in Paris. It's a pretty big company—some of their engineers played a critical role in the design of the French-English Channel. The practical training that I am receiving would count as an elective course credit for me, and I'll get to learn to speak French a little better," Alex explained.

"How's your career progressing in the Paris art scene?" he asked.

"Very well, except that I just lost my agent. He was like a father and friend to me. He was my White Knight."

"Your White Knight!" Alex exclaimed, surprised.

"Yes, Alex, that's exactly what he was. I've known him since I was sixteen years old. He was the person that rekindled my hopes at a time when I felt like my whole world had collapsed."

"I am truly sorry—I didn't mean to act that surprised when you referred to him as your White Knight."

"That's fine. I can understand that people don't understand the kind of close relationship that I had with him. He and Ayan were my best friends. His death has been a big loss to me," I responded calmly.

"I'm really sorry to hear that, Mikela. So, what do you intend to do now?"

"Well, I plan to continue working for his agency. His sister runs it now," I added.

"You seem to really like Paris a lot. Have you thought about moving to the United States, somewhere like New York? I think you'd do quite well in New York, with your new touch of European Renaissance-Maasai art," Alex said.

"To be quite frank, I've never given that a thought. I'm quite content with my agency here in Paris. Besides, I don't really know anybody in the United States," I said.

Alex smiled.

"You do now. I think you should come visit the States sometime and check out the New York art galleries."

"Maybe I will," I said in a quiet voice, which I hoped indicated that it was an unlikely possibility.

At this point, Alex said, "I'm dying of thirst. Would you care to join me for a drink?"

"Sure, I'd love that."

In a café that was situated a few blocks from where we were on Rue de Varenne, we settled down and ordered some drinks. As I sipped my margarita, which Alex had recommended, he seemed to be satisfied just watching me for the first few minutes. I felt his eyes tracing the contours of my face before he finally said, "I don't mean to make you uncomfortable by my stare, Mikela, but I must say that you're absolutely beautiful! The subtle curve of your supple lips, the elegance of your high cheekbones, and the dainty curve of your eyes—I've never seen a woman so exquisitely designed by nature."

As he spoke, I could see his eyes tracing the contours of my face and neck.

"I love your braids—they are such neatly woven braids, and I love how they rest on your shoulders," he said, as he continued to ravage me with his eyes.

"Thank you," I said, completely awed by his flood of compliments.

Alex's rather intense gaze made me slightly uncomfortable because it was setting off my own hidden passion. To control the surge of emotions that were erupting inside me, I quickly changed the topic and started to talk about the city of Paris.

"Alex, do you know that despite the beauty and sheer elegance of Paris, it has its ugly sides that tourists don't get to see? Have you been to the slums of Paris, where some of the new immigrants from North Africa, French West-Central Africa, and the Arab world live, and which the average French citizen abhors? The French police are brutal in these ethnic enclaves. Often, they physically brutalize many innocent men and women whose only crime happens to be their race or ethnicity. I once witnessed a herd of five French policemen beat an Arab man to pulp. Apparently, he was in the wrong neighborhood, a rich aristocratic suburban residential area, at the 'wrong time' and fit the profile of a potential criminal. Mind you, this profile to an average French policeman could simply mean being Arab.

"When I first came to Paris, its beauty dazzled me. I thought it was just a city of love, passion, and romance, with all of its exquisite galleries, musée and gardens. However, it didn't take a long time for me to discover that Parisians were like any ethnic group of people—some were good and kind, others were cruel and racist, and some simply didn't care. I have had some Parisians call me 'Blackie' and others 'Beautiful.' What bothers me is the hate and animosity that is growing between the Arabs and French. It gets worse daily and might explode into a bloody riot one day."

Alex nodded.

"We have race problems in the United States as well. Paris is not unique when it comes to racial divisions. It seems to be a problem that is endemic in the world—it's not just a Parisian problem."

"So, what do you think the solution to the world's race problem is?" I asked.

"Well, that's a tough question. I think there's no one answer to it. Perhaps we need more cultural mixing—people of different races and ethnic groups should blend more, become friends, and get to know one another on a personal level. Usually, once you get to know someone, you find that your preconceived prejudices diminish and sometimes, disappear entirely—as they say, love conquerors all," Alex answered.

"Alex, I think you're right. I guess we all need to start reaching out to others, regardless of race or ethnicity. Personally, I really don't understand why some people seem so eccentric about their own race. After all, we are all human beings and belong to the one big race—the human race."

A Hidden Touch of Nature's Priceless Gift—Love:

We talked for hours, oblivious of time. As we discussed the many facets of Parisian life, we had both become fully aware of the growing attraction between us. Alex seemed to be completely immersed in what he described as my inner and outward beauty and virgin simplicity. As we talked about the darker sides of Paris and the world in general, his eyes continued to pierce through mine as though he was trying to decipher my hidden thoughts and release my wounded spirit.

Months later, he told me that he had perceived a certain sadness that seemed to linger around me, and that no matter how hard I tried to conceal it, he still felt it strongly within him. He said that when we first met, he couldn't decipher what the sadness was about, but he felt that in time, if I let him into my world, he could help me release it from my soul.

Alex said that as these thoughts swirled through his mind, he suddenly felt the urge to take me in his arms, hug me, and reassure me that everything would be fine. I remembered seeing his hands reach for mine and his fingers caress the top of my palm. Initially, I froze and tried to move away.

Looking warmly into my eyes, he said, "It's okay, Mikela, I'm not going to hurt you."

His words suddenly brought an air of calmness within and around me, and I relaxed again, letting him gently caress my palm. Inside, I was trembling with an explosion of desire for him. I could feel my nipples harden and my heartbeat intensify as my stomach quivered. This was the very first time that I'd had such strong passion for any man, and I was getting very confused reading what was happening to me. After my encounter with Chege Mathani, I'd kept away from any man other than François. François was different because he protected me from the claws of ruthless men. He was like a shield that protected me from wolf packs in the guise of men. Now, for the first time, my soul was responding to a man, Alex, who was nearly a stranger to me.

My thoughts were interrupted when, on the spur of the moment, Alex suggested that we visit one more museum, the musée du Louvre situated on Paris Cedex-01. I graciously accepted his invitation as a temporary escape from the fire of passion smoldering inside me.

"Thanks for accepting my offer," he said, delighted. "I just want to spend a little more time with you."

From the café, we walked a few blocks to where we took the Métro to Palais-Royal, and then we walked through the shopping mall entrance to the musée du Louvre—an impressive collection of marvelous architecture. As we started our tour of the largest royal palace, the home of the world's richest art and antiquities, Alex's right hand reached out for mine. I hesitated for a moment, but looking at his reassuring eyes, I smiled and took his hand. I felt him gently squeeze my hand, and suddenly, something about his touch made me feel at ease and safe with him.

Our exploration of the musée du Louvre was like a love affair with exquisite art from as far back as the eighteenth century. The Louvre was originally the royal château, a palace of French kings and princes. Philippe Augusta built it in the thirteenth century. It was renovated a century later by Charles V, and continued to undergo renovation and was eventually rebuilt from the time of François I to the 19th century. The Louvre had been known for its rich collection of diverse history collection, which ranges from Egyptian art of 5000 BC to nineteenth-century work. Inside, it showcased seven major sections: Graphic arts, Sculpture and Decorative Arts, Egyptian Antiques, Oriental and Islamic Antiquities, Greek, Roman and Etruscan Antiques, and Painting.

The original collections of the musée du Louvre—the likes of La Belle Jardinière by Raphael and Mona Lisa by Leonardo da Vinci—were displayed in three separate areas.

Later, we went around the Escalier Daru to the Sully wing that displayed the medieval Louvre on the Entresol and the Egyptian and Beistegui collections on the first and second floors. On the Entresol level of the Sully wing was a rotunda, with a round opening at its center that overlooked the Egyptian pink granite sphinx in the crypt on the first floor. We also explored the spectacular recreations of Egyptian antiquities inspired by the legacy of Jean-François Champollion, who helped to unravel some of the mysteries of hieroglyphics in Egyptology in the nineteenth century. The artistic recreation of the sphinx was exquisite—a semblance to the original gigantic monument in pink granite found at the Tanis in the Nile Delta in Egypt.

Other recreations were equally a sensation—the Tomb of Chancellor Nakhti from the year 2000 BC, a beautiful statue in acacia wood that depicted the Chancellor in loincloth. The Bust of Amenophis IV, a sculpture of Akhenaton from the fourteenth century BC, was among many Egyptian antiquities that we admired. Later, at the Richelieu wing, we saw Oriental, Islamic, and French sculptures and antiquities. The diversity of collections at the Louvre could never be explored in fine detail in one day.

After what was an exhausting historical trip, we both opted to reserve our exploration of more art and antiquities for another day. Together, we rode on the Métro to the Avenue Montaigne at the Rond Point des Champs Élysées, and from there we walked to my apartment.

I invited Alex in. Even though this was the first time since my two years of living in Paris that I'd ever invited a man to my place, I felt very comfortable. We talked until the wee hours of the morning and laughed about our funny encounters in Paris. His company helped take my mind off François's death and Ayan's illness. It was almost 3 AM when he decided to leave, but instead I offered him the couch, since his place at the Bastille was quite a distance from mine and would have cost him quite a tidy sum to get back to at that hour of the morning.

Before I retreated into my bedroom, Alex held my hands and drew me close to him.

"Mikela, thank you for a great day—you're truly a wonderful person. I have enjoyed every minute we spent together."

"Same here, Alex—I enjoyed our time together," I gladly admitted.

"I'm glad you did as well because I find you absolutely fascinating and would love to see you again and again and again," he replied, making me laugh. As my laughter died down, Alex reached up to touch my face and in a sudden serious voice said, "I'm somewhat embarrassed to admit it, but I am falling in love with you, Mikela."

Alex's disclosure of his feelings caused tears to swirl up in my own eyes, and my hand started to tremble. I had not been expecting to hear him say those words. I was speechless and confused.

There was a moment of silence as I tried to regain my composure. Alex's last statement had surprised me. I had no idea that in such a short time of knowing him, he felt that deeply for me. I knew that I, too, was drawn to him in a very special way, but I was not sure if it was love. I still had physical and strong feelings of sorrow that I needed to clear up inside me.

For a moment, I looked away from him, trying unsuccessfully to hide my pain.

"What is it, Mikela?" Alex inquired.

"What's this pain inside you that you can't seem to share with anyone? I'm a good listener, and I want to help you deal with your pain, if you let me," he pleaded.

"There's nothing that anyone can do for me. It's my pain, Alex—mine. No one can understand it. It can't be undone, and it can't be wiped away because it has hardened inside me like plaque on a decaying tooth," I responded.

"Then let me be your dentist, Mikela and chisel away your plaque and save your tooth. Remember that there is no pain that cannot be healed, but you have to let go and let love. I'll be here to listen, whenever you are ready," he said, kissing me gently on my cheeks and caressing my long braids.

I allowed myself to be lost in his calming caress for a fleeting moment, enjoying the soft touch of his palm on my face, but when he cupped his palms around my face and leaned closer to kiss my lips, I was jerked back into reality. I turned away, and his kiss landed at the edge of my lips.

"I'm sorry, Alex—I'm not ready," I whispered.

"It's okay, I understand. I'm not rushing you—and I never will."

At this point, he gently released me and said, "Goodnight, Mikela."

"Goodnight Alex," I responded softly. "Have sweet dreams." As I started to walk away from the living room towards my bedroom, I glanced back to look at him again, hoping to see a reason to let go and let love.

He left later that morning but not before he told me again that he loved me and was willing to be patient. He said he'd wait until I was ready to release my soul and body to him with trust and without hesitation.

His eyes trailed mine as he walked away, leaving me with kindling flames of passion burning in my heart.

"What next, Enkai?" I whispered.

CHAPTER 13

❀

The "Bright Traveler"

Early September 1985—An End to a New Beginning:

It was now early September in 1985, and Paris weather was gradually tapering into fall-like temperatures, although there were still hot days that seemed to be the last residue of the summer. Alex had started a new chapter of life for me, but at the same time, I was still facing the aftermath of François's death.

Ayan and I had started having problems with Madame Duval. She had become even more impatient, irritable, and abrupt with us than she had been in the past. To make matters worse, she was hardly scheduling us for art exhibitions. Duboef-Duboef, who had returned to the Nairobi Les Galeries des Beaux-arts de François Jacques Paquet, didn't seem to have much influence anymore in running the Paris location.

In the ensuing months, Madame Duval was gradually getting rid of the non-European artists that François had hired. The talk among the artists was that Madame Duval did not know the ethnic market and preferred to stay out of it.

"It was François's idea in the first place to start recruiting non-white artists," was the statement that Madame Duval was said to have made to a black Egyptian still art model that François had hired just before he went into the hospital.

As our relationship with Madame Duval continued to deteriorate, Ayan and I requested to dissolve our contract with the agency. Madame Duval delightfully accepted our offer, and we made our graceful exit.

In the meantime, Ayan's health continued to deteriorate, and I advised her to take more time off of her work schedule. With the income that my artwork was generating, I was able to take care of all of our expenses. In the meantime, I started a search for a new agent.

A few weeks later, I made an appointment to meet Maurice Lenoir, a famous agent who had an office on Galerie Élysées near the Rond Point des Champs Élysées.

The decor of Lenoir's office was impressive with a simple but elegant layout of marble floors, chandeliers, and beautifully tailored window draperies. A petite and pleasant French lady welcomed me and led me into a medium-sized salon adorned with African art—Maghreb jewelry, embroidered belts, Tunisian giant pottery, East African Maasai beaded work, and West African Masks and statues beautifully exhibited behind glass cases projecting from the wall. Lenoir's office reminded me of François's office in downtown Nairobi.

"Monsieur Lenoir will be with you shortly," the petite lady said, interrupting my thoughts on the elegance of the salon.

"*Merci*," I replied, as I took a fashion magazine from a side table and started to look through it.

Ten minutes later, Monsieur Lenoir stepped out of his office.

"*Ca va, Mikela?*" he asked.

"*Ca va bien et vous?*" I responded, as I started to walk toward him.

I could see his eyes scanning over my body like a laser beam. He extended his hand for a handshake and whispered, "You are beautiful."

"*Merci*," I replied.

"This way please. Come with me," Monsieur Lenoir said, gesturing with his hands.

I stepped into his office, which was a spacious room with exquisite paintings from the French Renaissance age.

"Please, have a seat," Monsieur Lenoir offered.

"Those are exquisite portraits of Jean Clouet and his son François," I said, pointing at the display of sixteenth century talent on the wall as I perched on the chair, trying to mask my nervous tension.

"I'm impressed with your knowledge of French art. How did a Maasai woman learn so much about art and paintings from the French Renaissance age?" Lenoir asked, arching his eyebrows in surprise.

"I taught myself—the musée de Paris have done a good job of educating me on your exquisite artists and their work. Also, I received some informal training at L'Ecole des Beaux-arts and Ecole nationale supérieure des Beaux-arts." I handed over my portfolio to Monsieur Lenoir, who reached for it eagerly and immediately started looking over it.

"I've seen your work—your paintings are in a class of their own. I'm sorry about what happened to…"

"François?"

"Yes, François—it's a shame," Lenoir echoed. "Did you know him well?"

"Yes, he was a close friend of mine—he was like a father to me."

"I see," Monsieur Lenoir said, nodding at the same time.

He continued to flip through my work as he said, "Unlike François, I like women, beautiful women like you. We, the agents, make lots of money and our artists do, too. However, everyone has to pay a price. We do, and so do our models and artists. You're a beautiful lady, and I can take your work worldwide, beyond Paris, and make you an international artist. The world will really get to know who you are."

"What exactly is the price that the models have to pay?" I asked.

"You're a grown woman, and you should know what I mean. A little of themselves here and there," Lenoir said, smiling.

"Monsieur Lenoir, already I've paid a huge price—none of which I deserved. It's clear to me that I've come to the wrong place," I said, rising.

"But I thought François was your—"

"What I've just said has nothing to do with François. Please leave him out of this conversation, and let him rest in perfect peace," I said, making for the door.

"Well, think about what I said, and let me know when you're ready. This is how the real world is, Mikela—so welcome to the real Paris beaux-arts world," Lenoir responded, holding my portfolio out to me.

I snatched it and fled the building rudely awakened. François's nurturing and protective shield had disappeared, exposing me to the ruthless men—men like Monsieur Lenoir—that controlled the industry.

He was right about one thing, I thought. *I am now in the real world.*

In the meantime, Ayan was in and out of the hospital. The viral load in her blood stream had increased dramatically, and the disease-fighting white blood cells in her blood were now very low. Ayan had become prone to recurrent bacterial, viral, skin, and yeast infections. A few days earlier, she'd come down with a bout of pneumonia and was re-admitted to the hospital. It was rather painful to watch her life gradually ebbing away. Often, she experienced high fevers and night sweats that threatened to dry up her entire body. Many nights, her bed sheets and covers were literally drenched with her own body fluid, which oozed out in the form of sweat. Ayan would complain of chronic and persistent diarrhea, a dry and painful cough, and constricting chest pains and headaches, as well as persistent yeast infections. Her doctors had put her on some anti-HIV drugs—different cocktails of mixed drugs that seemed to slow down the progression of the disease in other individuals. Strangely, she didn't respond to the drugs and was suffering from their serious side effects.

Still, amazingly, despite Ayan's failing therapies, her spirit remained strong and high through her battle with AIDS. Her high and strong spirit reflected the true meaning of her name, Ayan Ghedi—her first name signified "brightness," while her last meant the "traveler." Many nights I sat by Ayan's bedside bringing down her temperature with a cold cloth and even then she would be cracking jokes about our Nairobi experiences and François's creative new dialect of French-Swahili. Ayan seemed to waste no time on self-pity and simply dwelt on the happier times of her life, cherishing the fun moments of her life, both past and present.

When I was with her, I tried desperately to fake a courageous exterior, while inside, I was experiencing turbulent and painful emotional tides. When I was alone in our apartment, I would sometimes cry all night. The thought of losing Ayan was too distressing and scary. I'd grown to love Ayan like my own sister—I loved her as I had loved Nadia, and watching her precious life ebb away was awful. It was then that the stark awfulness of AIDS became apparent to me. It's gradual but steady ravaging of the body and mind of its victims was an intimidating wonder to behold. Still, I was proud of Ayan's courage and strength in battling this disease. She did so with so much dignity and grace. Somehow, her strength and courage kept me going.

Ayan's boyfriend Édouard was also absolutely splendid. He loved Ayan unconditionally, kept her company, made her laugh, and always pretended as if nothing was wrong with her. I was convinced that he was Ayan's guardian light, sent to be with her through her ordeal and final moments. He was a blessing to Ayan, and his presence made her days so much easier to live.

September End 1985—A Bright Journey to Eternity:

On a quiet Sunday morning as Édouard and I sat by Ayan, she woke up from her sleep, smiled, looked at both of us, and then closed her eyes again. Her journey through life seemed to have ended within a twinkle of an eye. Ayan Ghedi, our "Bright Traveler" born on August 30, 1964, quietly passed on to eternity.

I could still feel the warmth of her hand in mine, and the smile on her face made it even more difficult to believe that she was dead and not just having a nap.

"She's going to wake up any time from now. She can't be gone forever," I kept whispering. Édouard Monet gently released my hold from Ayan's hand and said, "She's fine now, Mikela; she really is fine."

At this point, I started to weep. It finally dawned on me that I'd indeed lost another friend and sister. As he watched me weep and tried to console me, Édouard Monet could no longer contain himself and also started weeping. As he wept, he spoke the words in his heart. He had lost his beautiful African queen, he said. He'd lost his love—a woman that had brought so much happiness to his world during every minute he'd spent with her. He'd hoped that they would one day get married, but now all that hope was lost, he wailed.

As he quieted down, he started to share their many happy moments together. He talked about the parks, museums, galleries, and cabarets they had visited and how they'd both cherished the times they simply cuddled up together in front of the fireplace and listened to a blend of music—Zouk, Calypso, Rock n' Roll, Jazz, and Classical. He smiled as he recalled her great sense of humor and the charming laugh that seemed to drown all sorrows.

"She was like a bright and shining star that lit darkness and ignited everyone's soul to cherish the beauty of every moment and the breath of life while we still have it in us, wasn't she, Mikela?" he asked, without really expecting an answer. But I replied and said, "The brightest, Édouard, the brightest."

Ayan Ghedi may have passed on, but she had touched many lives in special ways.

"Perhaps that was the mission of her spirit—to experience grief and sorrow and yet at the same time, to bring smiles and joy to many still burdened with pain and sorrow," Édouard said, sharing his thoughts as he sobbed over the loss of Ayan, his lovely African queen.

A few minutes after Ayan passed on, a gust of wind started to shake the horizontal blinds in her hospital room, although the windows were firmly shut. Édouard was not a superstitious man, but when this happened, he stared at me and his eyes seemed to express unuttered questions. The Maasai in me was convinced that Ayan's spirit was making its final exit. She, Ayan, was now in the spirit world and free of AIDS.

She's probably already having fun on the side of eternity, I thought.

Then I said, "Édouard, Ayan has now reached higher levels of peace, serenity, and happiness far beyond our mortal understanding."

He nodded and placed his trembling hands gently over mine, forcing a smile through the painful expression that lingered on his face.

CHAPTER 14

New Strides

End September 1985—A Wakekeeping of Strength and Courage:

Ayan had asked that her wakekeeping be a happy occasion with lots of jokes, and I remember saying to her during the earlier days of her final hospital admission, "You're asking me to do what is impossible, Ayan. I do not think I can bear to laugh if such a time ever came, but please don't talk like this. You will pull through this illness and be around until your old age."

Ayan laughed her crackling laughter and said, "Old age, my dear, I will never see, and I begrudge no one that.

"Mikela, seriously, what I have asked you is exactly what I want. My life has not been in vain. Despite all of my unpalatable experiences, Enkai still fulfilled His purpose in my life. He has given me love, joy, and happiness while my spirit is still in my mortal body, and finally, when my death comes, it would only be a transition into everlasting eternity with Enkai."

Ayan always had a powerful and spiritual way of explaining things that made no sense, and finally, I grudgingly agreed.

"Okay, I'll do what you ask."

"One more thing, Mikela—please tell my mom that I have forgiven her for everything that she allowed to happen to me years back when I was a little girl…and don't forget to tell her how much I love her. Let her know that I've never stopped loving her for even one day."

"Okay, I will…I will, Ayan," I promised, holding back tears. "If need be, but I tell you, you will live to tell her these things yourself."

As I watched the soft smile on Ayan's face as she lay in her coffin, I began to reminisce about the past. Her body may have succumbed to the scourging and ravaging disease, but she'd made sure that she was cleansed of the emotional scar of female circumcision and the guilt of acquiring the deadly virus, HIV. This was what she told me a few weeks before she died, when she urged me to absolve myself from the emotional torture of the horror of my experience of female circumcision and live my life to its fullest.

I remember her saying, "Mikela, that's precisely what I did. Despite the physical scars and emotional burdens of my past experiences, I let Édouard Monet love me as much as he could. I have not allowed guilt or sorrow to consume my life. I have tried to enjoy my life as much as I possibly could. I have dwelt more on the beauty of life than on the disease that is ravaging my body."

I could not agree more because she had confronted her illness with courage and not self-pity. With her high spirited and happy disposition, she'd fought AIDS with the bravery of God's grace, and when mortality finally knocked at her door, she peacefully answered it with courage and without bitterness or anger. In a rather diabolical manner, I felt she had defeated the disease because she'd never allowed it to rob her of her joy and happiness.

The angelic smile on her face was Ayan's way of telling Édouard and me that she'd returned happily to Enkai.

My thoughts were interrupted as I was called up to honor her request and celebrate the life she had. I had promised Ayan that I would not cry and ruin honoring her joy-filled life the way that she had wanted. I had promised her that I would celebrate rather than mourn her life. So, I walked up to the podium smiling, shaking hands with the guests I recognized. As I reached Édouard, I pulled him up and we both stood on the altar facing the guests.

"Monsieur Édouard, do you remember the joke that Ayan told us when—"

"Here, let me mimic her. I think I can do it better than anyone here," Édouard said, laughing as he interrupted me.

Shortly after, we were all cracking jokes and laughing, just as Ayan wanted.

First Week in November 1985—Meeting Ayan's Family:

Still, the days following the reality of Ayan's illness, death, and funeral arrangements left me completely devastated and exhausted. I was a wreck, and physically my body seemed to be breaking down. On the last day of September 1985, Monsieur Édouard and I flew to Zanzibar, Tanzania, taking Ayan's body with us.

The natives who were mostly Muslim called Zanzibar, Unguja. The name Zanzibar came from the Persian Zendji-Bar, which means "land of blacks." The city was located about 22 miles off the coast of Tanzania and occupied approximately 600 square miles. Among fifty others, its main neighboring island was "Pemba," which is located about 32 miles north of Unguja, and the natives are well known for deep-sea fishing and scuba diving. It was easy for me to communicate with the natives because Kiswahili was the main language.

Zanzibar Town, the current national capital of Zanzibar and the seat of government, was once the trading center of present day East Africa. It attracted the ancient Sumerians, Assyrians, Phoenicians, Arabs, Chinese, and Malays and entertained many of the European explorers. Ironically, despite its mixed history of a romantic, colorful history of the riches of seafarers and explorers, blended with tragedy and the dark stain of slavery and its human cruelty and exploitation, Zanzibar was often referred to as the jewel of the Indian Ocean.

The two distinct areas of the city of Zanzibar were the Stone Town and Ngambo. We were headed for the Stone Town where Ayan's mother, Sereti lived. Approaching sun down as we drove through the town, we observed the beautiful streaks of sunset from the western horizon that typified the Stone Town. We also caught a glimpse of ornate latticework on balconies and admired the intricacy of carved doors made of sun-warmed wood. On the sides of ancient stone buildings, some with crumbling stonewalls, were narrow, winding staircases that seemed to disappear into unseen doorways and dark corners. A strong Muslim presence was obvious in Zanzibar, a city built by Arab and Indian merchants in the 19th century. Young, modestly dressed women, some with draping veils, could be seen graciously walking the streets.

Finally, we arrived at Sereti's home, a small, stone-walled bungalow shaded by surrounding trees. I still remembered watching Ayan's mother, Sereti, emerge from her house when we arrived. She was a slim and tall, gentle lady that appeared to be of mixed Tanzanian and Ethiopian descent. She was very beautiful, with a glowing, smooth looking, light brown complexion. She had light brown eyes, nicely curved lips, and well-maintained thin-lined eyebrows and eyelashes. Her hair was nicely plaited into single, thin braids and resting neatly on her shoulders.

She smiled very warmly when she saw us, and the touch of her smile instantly warmed my heart.

"Thank you, Mikela, for bringing back my daughter. Ayan wrote me some time ago and told me about you. She said she loved you very much and that you've been a sister to her," Sereti said, as I handed her a letter that Ayan had written weeks before she'd died.

"Yes, Ma Sereti. She, too, was like a sister to me. She asked me to tell you that she'd forgiven you for everything that happened to her when she was here. She asked me to tell you that she loved you very much and never stopped loving you for even one day."

When I paused, there was a brief moment of pensive silence, as I watched Sereti fight back tears.

"And who is the white man with you?" she asked, choking over some of her words.

"Ma Sereti, his name is Monsieur Édouard. He's also a friend of Ayan's. He loved her very much and was there with her through her illness."

"Welcome, my son. Welcome. Thank you for loving Ayan. Thank you for bringing her back with Mikela."

Monsieur Édouard nodded and smiled, wiping away tears as he appeared suddenly overcome by his own emotions.

Watching Ayan's mother maintain her poise and composure despite the deep pain she was obviously feeling, I began to see where Ayan had gotten her strength of character.

"Please have a seat, both of you," she gestured.

Then, she paused for a moment before saying, "You know, I had cried for so many years for Ayan. Finally, I resigned myself to accepting that I may never see her again. I had hoped that I would, but now it seems my hope would never be fulfilled."

I thought about my own mother as she spoke. I'd been away for a long time now and had not written her. I was in Zanzibar, closer to the Tanzanian Maasailand than I'd been in the past two years, but I had no plans to visit home. I was still afraid of what I might encounter there and was not ready for more pain.

"Ayan's father passed away two years ago," Sereti added, interrupting my thoughts.

"I'm sorry to hear than. Ayan did not share that with me," I said.

"She did not know herself. It was not too long ago when she first contacted me after such a long time. It was then that I told her that her father had passed on to be with His Maker."

As Sereti talked, I seemed to have so few words for her. I, too, was in such great pain from the loss of Ayan.

Monsieur Édouard was also very silent, and finally, I said, "Ma Sereti, Ayan also asked me to give this to you. It was all of her savings. I think it's about 50,000 U.S. dollars."

She stared at me for a moment, and now tears filled her eyes again. For a moment, she lost her well-guarded composure.

"What will I do with all this money when my child is dead? Tell me, Mikela, what would I do with it?"

I simply stared back at her. I had no words to console her. I didn't know what to say.

As she fought to regain her composure, we were suddenly interrupted by greetings from relatives and friends; most of whom were wailing as they approached Ma Sereti.

That evening, and the rest of the week we spent with Ma Sereti and her family, was perhaps the hardest period of my life. The sadness that hung heavily in the air was overpowering and threatened most times to consume me. At the end of the week, Ayan was buried, and I was glad to be on my way back to Paris.

Mid-November 1985—Back in Paris, True Love Persists:

Fall had arrived in full swing, and the cold weather had finally crept in. Now, I was feeling the loss of Ayan more than ever. I felt that I needed to be alone to sort through my pain. During the entire ordeal of Ayan's illness, I had kept my distance from Alex, and now, I felt no different. On occasion, he had offered to come by the apartment that I shared with Ayan to help me deal with the pain of losing my best friend. I always graciously declined his offer—I felt I was in an emotionally vulnerable state, and I did not want to do anything I would regret in the future even though it had become clear to me that I was very much attracted to Alex. Yet, I was not ready to start a relationship with him. I still had unresolved emotions and a deep distrust for men in general. Alex, on the other hand, couldn't understand why I was pushing him away. Daily, he wondered why I wasn't giving him the chance to show me how much he could love me.

On a day in mid-November 1985, after I'd just returned from Tanzania, the events of the past weeks finally overtook me emotionally. I crawled under a comforter on the living room sofa and started to wail. Suddenly, it seemed like Ayan's death had become a more vivid reality. I missed her so much; she was my best friend in Paris. As I lay on my sofa crying, all manner of thoughts swirled in my head. Suddenly, a phone ring startled me. At first, I ignored it, wanting to be left alone in my world so that I could wallow in self-pity. Whoever it was remained determined, calling back repeatedly every time the phone rang itself out, forcing me to eventually answer the call.

"Hello?" I said.

"Hi, this is Alex. How are you? You sound awful…are you okay?"

"Not too good, but I'll live," I responded.

"I'm on Rond Point des Champs Élysées, a few blocks from your apartment, and I would like to pop by and see you, if that's okay."

When I did not respond, Alex seized the opportunity and said, "I'll be on my way then."

He hung up the phone before I could say no.

I dragged myself up from the sofa to the bathroom to freshen up.

I sunk my face in cold water, feeling the instant sting of its icy coldness bring me temporary relief and a sense of renewal. Wanting to prolong the feeling for as long as possible, I scooped more water into my cupped palms, splashing it over my face in a seemingly unending, monotonous fashion, until my hands and face felt numb. Finally, I raised my head and stared into the mirror above the sink, noticing for the first time the heavy bags under my eyes and the deep age lines criss-crossing my face. *Oh no! I look like hell,* I thought.

Not wanting Alex to ask too many questions, I quickly applied make-up, hoping to hide as many lines as possible. Then, I changed into a short-sleeved, jewel-necked tee shirt with a feminine satin and elastic-trimmed neckline made of a soft blend of rayon, polyester, and cotton. For a bottom, I wore a long, wrap-around skirt with a slit on the side that went as far as the upper end of my left thigh. Then, I put on a pair of simple dangling earrings and a Maasai beaded choker around my neck.

Fifteen minutes later, the doorbell rang, and I walked over to answer it, welcoming Alex with a smile and a warm embrace.

"Hello Alex. Please come in."

"Thanks," he responded softly, in his soothing, velvety deep voice. As he stepped inside, his eyes scanned the entire length of my body with loving approval. Just seeing him had quickened my heartbeat, and he, too, was visibly excited. He held my hands for a few moments and then moved closer to me and kissed me gently on both cheeks.

"I'm sorry about Ayan."

I merely nodded. I didn't wish to discuss Ayan's illness or death because I knew that I would break down and start to cry.

"Can I get you some coffee?" I asked.

"Sure, that would be nice," he replied.

"Okay, I'll start brewing it now. What flavor would you prefer?"

"A blend of sweet Arabic coffees would be fine."

"I can see that you're already getting addicted to the Parisian's unique taste for exquisite coffee-Arrabicas."

"Yes, I finally caught the Paris fever, among other things," Alex said jokingly, giving me a flirtatious glance at the same time.

As I walked toward the kitchen counter, I could feel his eyes follow me.

He walked over to where I stood in the kitchen, and we both watched the coffee brew.

Then he wrapped his hands around my waist from the back and started to kiss my neck gently. For a brief moment, I closed my eyes as I felt his strong arms about me and the warmth of his body melt into mine.

Momentarily, his touch brought a dose of serenity to my soul. At that instant, there was no doubt in my mind that my soul was drawn to his, even as my inner fears and distrust for men remained vividly awake. I felt Alex's hands caressing my waistline and hips, and I turned around to face him. For what seemed like an eternity, we were locked in a long and passionate embrace. Slowly, his hands moved to my chest and started to cup my breasts. At that instant, my body froze. Flashes of the horrific scenes with Chege Mathani were all of a sudden awakened in my memory. As Alex tried to plant a kiss on my lips, I wrenched my body away from his.

"No, please don't," I cried, trembling.

"Why are you recoiling from me? What's the problem? Why can't you trust me? I need you? I'm in love with you, Mikela, can't you see?" Alex asked.

I was speechless as I struggled to get the right words out of my mouth. Finally, I said, "I can't help the way that I react to men. My body simply freezes when a man tries to get too close to me. I just can't help it." I looked away from him for a moment, tears in my eyes.

"Well, then tell me what the problem is," Alex pleaded desperately. "Let me into your world, Mikela…let me help you, my love." The desperation in his voice was matched only by the hurt in his eyes.

I could no longer bear the pain I was causing Alex, and even though I did not feel totally ready to share my life's story with him, I decided to nonetheless.

"Okay," I said. "I'll try. I guess I'll have to start from the very beginning, way back home in the Tanzanian Maasailand."

A few minutes later, Alex was seated on the far end of the sofa sipping his freshly brewed coffee while I drank caffeine-free herbal tea curled up on the floor next to his feet. As Alex waited patiently for me to start my narrative, I noticed that his eyes were filled with a mixed expression of concern and anxiety.

As I hesitated to start my story, he whispered, "I need to know the source of your pain, fear, and distrust of me."

Flashback to My Deep Pain:

I was deep in thought as I stared into the burning fireplace. Fumbling with my tea mug, I searched for the words to begin my story. Even though Alex would be the second person to hear my life story, it was no easier to tell. I stared into the fireplace, and to me the burning shapes of wood seemed to reflect all the pain that I felt inside.

Finally, a word stumbled out of my mouth, followed by a second, and then a string of sentences filled my narrative.

Alex listened keenly, not masking any of the burning emotions and angry feelings he experienced as I told my story.

When I was done, neither of us could say anything, the only sound between us being the crackling of the dying wood in the fireplace.

Finally, Alex said, "Mikela, I'm stunned by the tradition of female circumcision. I never knew that such a thing existed. So, now I think I better understand the strong ties that you had with François and Ayan. Why you thought of him as your 'White Knight,' and why Ayan was your 'Tanzanian Princess.' I'm sorry if I misunderstood your relationship with François. He offered you genuine and priceless love and unconditional friendship, just as Ayan did."

"Yes," I said, nodding.

"Mikela, I want to assure you that you're not alone in the world, even with François and Ayan gone. I'm here, and I'll be around for you as long as I have breath in me."

"Thank you, Alex. I really appreciate your saying that. It means a lot to me."

Impulsively, I moved closer to Alex's feet and legs and gently laid my head on his lap.

"Alex, at this instant, I feel the same emptiness that I did on the day I left the Mathani home, terrified by the present and the past, unsure of the future, and with a broken will that doesn't wish to live any longer," I said.

"Mikela, I would say a will that must continue to fight to triumph," Alex immediately stated.

"Well, this is it, Alex. Now you know it all. These are the reasons for the pain that you often said you could see in my eyes. This is my life's story. Now you know my pain."

Alex said nothing but instead toyed with his empty coffee mug, while I took the last gulps of my herbal tea. At last, Alex broke the silence.

"Your world's not empty, Mikela—I'll be with you whenever you want me to. I'm sorry that you had to go through these horrible experiences, but as Ayan said, you must put all of it behind you and start to live again. All that I ask is that you let me love you the best way that I can—you deserve so much love, Mikela."

As Alex talked, my gaze rested on the meandering flames in the fireplace.

"Please look at me, Mikela," Alex said. He gently touched my chin with his left palm to raise my head.

I turned toward him and stared back into his piercing gaze. I had mixed thoughts that were yet to be fully deciphered, even by me.

"I don't know if I can ever love any man in an intimate or romantic manner, but I'm willing to try to love you in the manner that you so richly deserve, Alex."

When I said this, I could see his face brighten up.

He stood up and took my hands, then gently pulled me from the floor. Next, he took me into a warm embrace. He started to run his fingers gently through my long braids.

"You can always count on my love, Mikela. On this day, I promise to always love you. I would never hurt you or let anyone else hurt you. I've given you my word, which is more precious than gold."

I looked into Alex's eyes and suddenly, most of my doubts were gone, and I snuggled closer into his arms. I felt completely safe in his warm embrace and silently hoped that Enkai had sent him as my true knight in glittering armor to lift my spirit from the midst of pain and despair.

"Marahaba Enkai!" I whispered, suddenly experiencing a moment of gratitude and knowing what a great source of strength Enkai had been for me. Now, I could recognize when He, Enkai, was about to open up a nicely packaged gift harboring a pleasant surprise for me.

"Marahaba Enkai!" I whispered again.

CHAPTER 15

✿

Aisha Mohammed—The Arabian Princess

March 1986—Unburdening of Pain Continues:

In the months ahead, I decided to work as a freelance artist. On my own, I was able to schedule routine exhibitions at the L'Ecole des Beaux-arts and Ecole nationale supérieure des Beaux-arts. My Paris-Maasai exhibits were topping all beaux-arts ratings.

Meanwhile, Alex and I had started to spend a lot of time together, and we were gradually developing a cozy, comfortable, and trusting relationship. On one early Saturday afternoon, I'd gone to a café near the Black Cinema, The Imagés d'ailleurs on Rue de La Clef, to meet with Alex on a lunch date. I arrived early, ordered a drink, and sat comfortably by a window seat that overlooked a major bustling intersection.

I was reading a book on female circumcision written by a relatively unknown Black African female Muslim writer, Fatu Amina Salami. In the past, I would never have been able to read a book on female circumcision, but now I actually craved for such books and longed to read about the experiences of other women like myself. For me, this was a clear sign that I was beginning to deal with my entangled and painful emotions. As Ayan had said, I needed to deal with my pain and fears and bring closure to the horrors of that fateful day in the open Maasaiplains.

The book was about Aisha Mohammed, a North African woman of mixed heritage. She was of Egyptian and Arab-Maghreb racial mix who as an adult, chose to experience female circumcision. This was shocking to me because I couldn't understand why anyone in her right mind would opt to undergo such a humiliating and horrific experience.

Fatu Amina Salami described Aisha as a tall and elegant woman with a smooth, oil-brushed looking complexion, naturally tanned skin, and long, jet-black hair. She had a round face with slightly slanted eyes, and her lips were curvy and full-bodied.

Twenty-eight years old, Aisha Mohammed was born in Cairo and raised as an Egyptian Muslim until she was fifteen years old. Her parents were very educated—her father was an engineer and her mother, a lawyer. Both worked and lived in Cairo. Her father was from Northern Cairo, and her mother was of Arab-Maghreb descent.

Shortly after Aisha's tenth birthday, her father's parents, who were illiterate and adhered strictly to all traditional and religious doctrines, started to hint that she was ready to undergo circumcision or the so-called "rites of passage to womanhood." In their opinion, female circumcision was a sacred ritual that cleansed a young girl, secured her virginity, and carried her gracefully into womanhood. Aisha remembered fiery debates between her parents, especially her mother and her grandparents. Her parents, being educated, upper class Egyptians, strongly opposed the tradition of female circumcision. Aisha recalled her mother stressing that any tradition that required parts of a young woman's external genitalia to be cut off and the birth hole stitched up to keep her virginity was absolutely absurd. Her mother would raise her voice and gesticulate with her hands and head at the same time, emphasizing that no one was ever going to lay hands on her daughter.

As I read Aisha's story, I wished that my own mother had been educated and exposed to the world outside of the Maasailand to understand that such a tradition needed to be stopped. Perhaps, if armed with an education, my mother would have had similar objections.

Once, during one of the aggravated debates, Aisha recalled that her grandmother had gotten so angry that her face had flushed, and her hands trembled as she accused Aisha's mother of having no respect for a tradition that had existed for centuries. She accused her mother of being influenced by Western ideas and opinions about a culture that she knew and understood very little about. Aisha's grandmother insisted that her mother was quick to condemn a tradition that had successfully minimized pre-marital sex and teenage pregnancy.

"Why do you concentrate on pain that lasts no more than a few weeks instead of a lifetime of benefits?" her grandmother had asked.

Eventually, as Aisha recalled, her grandmother had said, "If Aisha is not circumcised, it will bring shame to our family, and I don't think that I'll ever be able to forgive you for that. I've circumcised many young girls, and now my own grandchild will have the honor of experiencing the same tradition by my hands. If you decide that our granddaughter, Aisha, is above our tradition, then I never want to see either you or her again."

Her grandmother stormed out of the house, and that was the last time Aisha ever saw her. Her mother told her ten years later, when she was in Europe, that her grandmother had died and was buried the day after.

Aisha left Cairo when she turned eighteen, after she passed her two-year, post-high school "A-Level" exams. Her mother was afraid that some of their relatives might get desperate and try to kidnap Aisha and force her to undergo the ritual of female circumcision, so she decided to send Aisha away to college in Switzerland. Aisha hated being away in a strange country where she saw very few Arab-African people. In the dorms, the majority of the students didn't want to have anything to do with her, and most blatantly admitted that they wouldn't want to share a room with her.

As time went by, the social pressure of alienation became unbearable for her, and her parents transferred her to Oxford University in England. During short breaks or holidays and weekends, she spent time at her family residence at St. John's Wood in London. Life was certainly more bearable in England in comparison to Switzerland because she met other African and Arab students, some of whom became her good friends.

As part of college life, she joined the African student's union and was soon elected as a special subcommittee Chairwoman on "Social Rights for Africans." Her group organized seminars and mini-conferences on traditional, contemporary, and political issues that socially impacted upon Africans. One of the seminars that they organized was on "Women's Rights and the Tradition of Female Circumcision." The president of the committee was Kalima, a girl of mixed ethnic heritage—her mother was from the Middle East while her father hailed from southern Somalia. She was strongly opposed to female circumcision. She, too, had been a victim of this practice at the tender age of ten. She had since dedicated her life to speaking out against the "act of genital mutilation," as she referred to it, and tirelessly rallied students, staff, and people outside the college to raise funds for educating members of a few rural enclaves in Somali where female circumcision was still being practiced.

The seminar turned out to be a huge success and was well attended by individuals within and outside the school. Sub-Saharan Africans, North Africans, Middle Eastern-Arabs, Jews, and Europeans from many diverse regions attended the mini conference.

Kalima was a light skinned, heavy-set woman. She had wide eyes that seemed to protrude slightly and a small, straight nose and thin lips. Her fashion trademark was the badly styled wigs that she wore. She was not considered attractive but had a dynamic personality that was distinctly a leadership quality.

Kalima opened the conference with a vivid medical description of what is done to a woman during female circumcision. During the rest of the conference debate on the tradition of female circumcision, there was a wide range of opinions about the practice among individuals from the rural enclaves that still practiced it and from around the globe.

First, it started with two very well educated Muslim gentlemen—Musa, a tall Arab who lived and worked as an electrical engineer in Saudi Arabia and who strongly supported female circumcision, and Yusuf, a slender-shaped Kenyan surgeon of average height, who had married a Somalian victim of circumcision and didn't want another young girl to experience his wife's ordeal.

"As a physician, I'm stunned to see that such an act of butchery has continued in many parts of the world in the name of tradition. Even a trained surgeon such as myself could never conceive of excising a woman's external female parts."

"Anyone listening to you would think that the essence of the tradition is to brutalize young women," Musa responded. "That's simply not true. It's both a religious and cultural rite of passage that is performed for the good of these young women."

"If you really want to do these young women some good, let them keep their God-given body parts," Yusuf stated, with heated emotion. "Do you realize the physical and emotional impact that your so-called religious or cultural rites have on young women? I have a wife who has suffered her entire life because her innocence was raped at the age of ten. I challenge you to show me where it is written in the Muslim Koran or the Christian Bible that a woman's external female parts should be excised."

"As for the physical or emotional impact on women, that is news to me," Musa said, waving his index finger at Yusuf in a most unruly manner. "With all due respect, perhaps your wife is suffering from some other ailment, and as a physician, you might want to check her mind."

At this point, Yusuf became visibly agitated, leaped from his chair, and launched at the man from the Middle East, raising his voice.

"Don't you dare make such a remark about my wife! Don't you dare trivialize what she's endured—what she continues to endure! How dare you make a cynical remark about her pain and agony!"

Two men seated at Yusuf's side restrained him as the moderator interrupted the obviously heated debate, inviting the American sociologist, David Mack, on the panel to air his views. David was a white, American, dark-haired, chubby-looking sociologist who was about five feet eight inches tall. He was a seasoned, community-based sociologist who had, for many years, studied the social impact of specific traditions on individuals and the community as a whole. Some of his earlier research was on the impact of female circumcision on specific traditions, especially on the development of the minds of the children that endured the experience.

"My question to Musa is whether the social benefits of circumcision outweigh the ravaging and devastating lifelong physical and emotional consequences experienced by the circumcised women? In a modern and civilized world, should women exercise the freedom of choice—the option to be circumcised if they wish—or exercise the right to keep all of their external female parts? Are you not concerned at all about the mortality rates and the prevalence of serious medical complications that arise as a result of the crude and unsanitary surgical procedures utilized by medically non-qualified individuals?" David asked.

"First, I remain unconvinced about the so-called lifelong physical and emotional consequences. All we see are a handful of young women who sensationalize their experience as a way of getting media exposure, especially in the Western World. As for the social benefits of female circumcision, I can't overemphasize those—the record speaks for itself."

At this point, Yusuf interrupted.

"What exact records are you referring to?"

"Mr. Yusuf, please let him finish his response to David's questions," the moderator said.

"Before I was interrupted, I was about to talk about the immense social benefits from female circumcision, which include drastic reduction of promiscuity. As for their freedom of choice, that's another debate. I refuse to admit that the Western world holds the key to social morality, and if they did, why do they treat so many of their ethnic minorities like outcasts?"

"Let's stick to the subject in question. We are not here to debate the state of ethnic minorities in the Western World," David responded rather sharply.

"I was not deviating. I was merely trying to make a point, if you would let me. With regards to the mortality rates and prevalence of medical complications, there's no accurate scientific data that directly links mortality rates and serious medical conditions to female circumcision," Musa said.

"You might be somewhat in denial," David responded.

"It's pretty obvious that he is," Yusuf said, in support of David.

"I'm not in denial at all. Can you show me a well-controlled and unbiased study that directly links deaths and medical complications to female circumcision? If you can, I promise to review it objectively. The fact remains that what we are talking about here are rural enclaves that ordinarily have limited access to medical care, so how can one tell what ailment they might have had before they went through circumcision?" Musa said, in vehement defense of his viewpoint.

"You are right, we may not be able to tell, but it sure doesn't help them any more to cut through their skin with dirty and septic razors, knives, pieces of glass, spears, and other metal objects, exposing children directly to infectious bacterial agents such as tetanus. This seems to me to be a rather primitive and outdated tradition that needs to be abolished," David responded.

"Of course, from the white man's perspective, anything that is non-Western is either bad or primitive," Musa responded angrily.

"That's your interpretation. I didn't exactly say that," David said defensively.

"I can give you my data," Yusuf added. "I have practiced as a physician for over fifteen years in Nairobi, and I have operated on many young women, re-opening their birth canals. These women come from Sudan, Maasailand, Somali, Kenya, and other parts of Africa. Many have already had recurrent pelvic and urinary tract infections spread to their reproductive organs, causing permanent sterility. I once treated a young Kenyan Maasai girl that had complete excision of all of her external female parts and had her birth cavity stitched together. For many years, she accumulated menstrual fluid in her uterus, which had only a tiny hole left in her vulva to exit. Her body could only let out the fluid in trickles, and she would go for months bleeding, one menstrual cycle running into another. Sometimes clots of blood persisted in her uterus, causing all forms of uterine infections.

"I can tell you that today, even after many years of specialized medical attention, this young lady still suffers immense menstrual cramps, persistent pelvic and urinary tract infections, and after ten years of marriage, she is still unable to conceive a child. It is highly unlikely that this young lady will ever be able to have a child. In my clinic in Nairobi, I have piles of clinical data about similar cases."

At this point, the gentleman from the Middle East seemed shocked by the information being provided by Yusuf. He appeared struck by the seriousness of the medical complications that seemed to be a direct consequence of female circumcision. This was obviously news to him.

"Your information is very important," he humbly acknowledged. "If these young women are suffering these things that you claim, then we must further investigate more cases."

The debate lasted all day, with a two-hour lunch break and intermittent short breaks. It was obvious that most who attended the seminar left more informed about the tradition of female circumcision. Many of the proponents now seemed less convinced of its value.

A year later, Musa, the gentleman from Saudi Arabia, wrote a letter of appreciation to the organizers of the seminar, thanking them for giving him the opportunity to re-evaluate the tradition of female circumcision. He had followed up with the information that Yusuf, the physician from Nairobi, had shared during the conference. Now he, Musa, had become a strong opponent of female circumcision. He started a major anti-female circumcision campaign in his own rural enclave in the Middle East. His hope was to bring female circumcision to an end in that region.

In his letter he said, "Our organization hopes to bring an end to the desperate screams of young girls and to the deaths of young, innocent victims from a senseless tradition. We hope that collectively, we can bring to an end the revolving pain and misery of young girls. We are committed to the fight against female circumcision and will not stop until every rural enclave in the Middle East abolishes this senseless practice."

As I read this book, my resolve was strengthened to join others in fighting the tradition of female circumcision through organizations such as this.

Aisha's Story:

In Aisha's own words in the book, she stated that she, too, had learned an awful lot about female circumcision from the conference. She had a better understanding of why her parents had insisted against it, now that she'd become more knowledgeable about the tradition.

Her own story seemed rather unique. She met a young man, Prince Abdul Raman, a Political Science Major in his graduating year at Oxford University.

Prince Raman was from a Middle Eastern country. He was tall, dark, and handsome, with a moderately bulky build that emphasized his firm and broad chest. Aisha met him at a house party that was held by an Ethiopian friend of hers. She literally fell in love with him at first sight. Their first date took place only a few days after they met.

Prince Raman was from a very wealthy royal family. He had come from a lineage of kings and queens whose ancestry was from Saudi Arabia. Through multiple migrations, his family came to settle in Dubai. Already, as the first son, he had been named the heir to the throne and was popularly known as "Prince Raman." Yet on campus, Prince Raman was known to be quiet and unassuming by nature, although his expensive German automobiles and elegant homes often revealed his wealthy and royal background. Those close to him were fully aware that he was a "blue blood" and already a millionaire at the age of twenty-one.

Once Aisha and Prince Raman started dating, it didn't take very long for them to be seen as a tight couple on campus. It was obvious to most observers that they were in love. On their graduation day, Prince Raman proposed to Aisha, and she accepted. A few weeks later, he initiated the lengthy protocol of family introductions. First, his family resisted because Aisha was not from the Middle East, but after much negotiation and pleading from Prince Raman, with his mother's assistance, certain conditions were laid down that had to be met before the marriage ceremony could take place. The one non-negotiable term was that everything about the wedding was to be done according to the Muslim tradition. Aisha would have to become a practicing Muslim.

Raman's family was happy that Aisha was from a staunch Muslim family, although they complained that her having been in the West for some time had soured her understanding and practice of the Holy Koran. They emphasized that she needed a refresher course on Islam, the Muslim culture, and the traditions and expectations for women.

Aisha was madly in love with Prince Raman and was willing to do anything to marry him. However, when she was first informed that she would have to undergo female circumcision, she resisted this. She explained to Prince Raman that her parents had fought all their lives to shelter her from the tradition of female circumcision, and now she was faced with a difficult decision of either leaving the man she loved or having part of her outer female parts excised.

She had many discussions with Prince Raman, who told her that he had no real powers, even though he was the heir to the family's inheritance. He still had to abide by the stipulated conditions if the marriage was to take place. He wanted to marry Aisha, who would then become the Princess of the land and the mother of his children.

Eventually, Aisha conceded to undergoing the ritual of female circumcision. However, she hid her decision to go on with it from her parents, who she knew would have preferred to stop the marriage. The date for the circumcision was set for six months after she graduated—she'd just turned twenty-one.

Aisha was flown into Dubai in the family's private jet. She was welcomed with a shower of jubilation and waited on by maids and chaperons that adorned her in expensive and exquisite regalia made from beautifully decorated, hand crafted silk material.

This was the first time that it dawned on her that she was actually a stone's throw away from becoming a princess and, in time, a queen. She had mixed emotions—fear of the responsibilities that came with being a princess, fear of losing the privacy and simplicity of her life, and the burden of adhering to traditions that seemed to keep women in perpetual bondage. She had intermittent flashes of escaping to a normal life in England, where she could simply exist freely as a young and energetic woman and not be restrained by the religious codes ironed out for women.

Somehow, she felt it was too late to withdraw from the scene. Despite her genuine love for Prince Raman, she already felt trapped in the shackles of tradition, gagged with religious doctrines, and only a few hours away from going through the rite of passage into womanhood. Technically, no one was forcing her to undergo female circumcision—she'd made the decision to experience it in order to marry the man that she loved.

Soon, it was time for the ordeal. She was taken to a quiet room that was beautifully decorated with imported Persian rugs and silk draperies. The mostly unfurnished room looked rather bare. In the center lay a thin-foam mattress covered with elegantly tailored sheets patterned with floral designs. She was asked to lie down on it and spread her legs as wide apart as possible. In this position, she felt like her hip was going to split in two halves—she felt like a female African Agama lizard basking in the sun with its belly facing up.

Two or three chaperons held each of her legs and hands. A maid brought in a bowl of warm water and a white hand cloth for the lady who was about to perform the ritual. The lady washed her hands for a few seconds, and then tore open a sterile pack of razor blades and jokingly said, "For a beautiful princess, everything we use must be brand new—never been used by anyone else. At home, we can use one razor for as many as fifty girls, or sometimes until the razor goes blunt."

Aisha cringed when she heard this, as she wondered about the possibility of disease transmission by such a practice. A few seconds later, she felt the lady grab her, and then the razorblade cut through her skin. In an instant, she saw a chunk of her flesh, nature's gift of womanhood, in the lady's hands. At this point, the other women started to chant in a typical Arabic style, each beaming with smiles.

"You are now a woman befitting of our Prince and ready to become a Princess," they echoed in Arabic.

Aisha was experiencing excruciating spasms of pain, so intense that her legs started to tremble. With her fingers, she grabbed the sides of the sheets on which she lay. Her teeth were clenched tightly, and her eyes squeezed shut. This was her way of dealing with the pain. She didn't want to scream or cry. She'd been advised that by taking the pain as a grown woman, she would show that she was truly befitting to be a princess.

"The Prince specially requested that I not stitch you up. That's the way that he wants it, so I'll leave it open," the lady said, as she applied a wad of cotton wool in the cut area, applying slight pressure in an attempt to stop the bleeding. Then, she applied some iodine and opened up a packet of sanitary napkins, which she inserted in between Aisha's legs. At this point, they helped Aisha put on her silk panties, held her up, and took her out of the room back to her private quarters.

The pain was so intense that the short walk back to her private quarters seemed to last forever. During the next few weeks, Aisha gradually healed, but she experienced daily throbbing pain in her private area. During these weeks, the wedding arrangements intensified—the wedding was only eight weeks away.

A week before the wedding, Aisha was awakened in the middle of the night by what seemed like women wailing. She jumped up from her bed and went to the adjacent room where one of her chaperons lodged. There were a group of women whispering to themselves, and when they saw Aisha they stopped, and her chaperon raced to her side.

"Do you need my assistance, young princess?"

"Not really. The wailing of women awakened me. Is everything okay?"

"Yes...sshh," the chaperon stuttered. "You can go back to sleep now."

Aisha found the chaperon's unusual nervous behavior rather suspicious. Nonetheless, she quietly went back to sleep. The next morning, they told her the news they had learned the previous night. She was utterly shocked to hear that her prince had died in a plane crash as he returned from a one-day trip to Saudi Arabia.

Aisha's body went into shock—her mind became locked in a state of total disarray. For the rest of the day, she was sedated to keep her contained. The next day, her prince was buried wrapped in a sparkling white sheet according to Muslim rites. After the period of mourning required by Muslim tradition, Aisha opted to return to Egypt. A year later, she left for the United States to pursue a post-graduate degree in Computer Management Information Systems.

Aisha's story was digging up memories of my own experience, and at the same time, anger toward her for having been a willing participant in her own case.

What was she thinking? I thought. *What kind of love would require a woman to lose any of her God-given parts?*

I was curious more than ever to meet Aisha someday, and hopefully, find out her thoughts on her experience in retrospect.

At this point, I looked at my watch. It was obvious that Alex was running late. It was already ten minutes past one, and he had not arrived at the restaurant. I decided to visit the lady's bathroom in the interim.

True Love—An Unbreakable Bond:

Five minutes later, when I emerged from the bathroom, I saw Alex standing by the reception table, his eyes hovering around the restaurant. As I walked towards him, his eyes caught mine and he smiled. In his usual manner, he swept me into his gentle and warm embrace.

"I apologize for being late. I was delayed at the office," he said.

"That's fine. I kept myself busy; I was reading a rather fascinating story and was not bored for a moment," I responded.

"What's the book about?" he inquired.

"It's about female circumcision," I answered.

At this point, a waiter came by.

"Madame…Monsieur…what would you like to drink? *Vous Parle Francais?*"

"*Oui, N'importe quel Chardonnay français suffira, si vous plais,*" I responded.

"*Et vous Monsieur?*"

"Ahhhh…*projectiles du double deux de cognac, merci.*"

"Do you think that you can handle all that yet," Alex asked, pointing at my book, which was still on the table, as the waiter walked away.

"Yes, I think so. Besides, it's about time I did. Don't you think?"

"Yes, as long as you are ready emotionally to deal with it. There's no rush; remember you have to take it one day at a time. Don't get me wrong," Alex said, in his usual supportive manner. "I'm proud of the baby steps that you are taking."

"*Viola, Madame,*" the waiter said, setting my drink down on the table.

"*...et pour votre Monsieur.*"

"*Merci.*"

"*Et ce qui vous veulent comme apetitzer?*"

"*Champignons et pain Crabe-bourrés d'ail,*" I said, asking for Crab-stuffed mushrooms and garlic bread.

"*Et je passerai dessus un aperitif...*I'll pass on an appetizer," Alex immediately responded. "Well, I'm glad that you've started dealing with the emotional scars of your past experiences. I believe that this is your first stride to facing your innermost emotional pains, and by reading about other women's stories, I hope it will help you to realize that you're not alone in the pain." He smiled at me and added, "I'd like to read the book after you are done."

I nodded in agreement, as my mind trailed back to Aisha's story, and I thought about the senseless decision that she'd made in the name of love. Sometimes, social expectations clogged the sense of logic of some women, making them yield to the whims and caprices of men. Their eagerness to please men gets prioritized above what is beneficial to them as women.

"But do you think that Aisha was simply a young woman that was caught between the expectations of the society and her love for a man that she wanted to marry?" Alex asked, as I told him some of what was on my mind.

"Yes, you have a point there. Perhaps, somewhere in the process, she seemed to have lost her sense of logical reasoning," I said.

"Maybe it's not as clear-cut as it may appear to someone reading her story. As ridiculous as her actions may seem now, she made a choice for the path that she perceived to be of least resistance. Perhaps her ultimate goal was survival in the world in which she found herself—a world where women were second-class citizens expected to conform to tradition at all costs."

"I guess you have a point, Alex. Still, I just don't get it—I really don't. I maintain that she didn't have to—she really didn't. I'm sorry if I sound a bit judgmental; I just wish I'd had the choice that she had."

The waiter returned with my steaming hors d'oeuvre, re-directing our attention.

Alex spent the rest of lunchtime talking about his engineering internship, which was coming to an end. He planned to return to the United States in eight weeks.

"Come back to the States with me, Mikela. You'll love it," he pleaded.

"I'd love to, but I have a lot of unfinished business here. Besides, I really don't know the American art world—I am afraid to venture into yet another new world at this time."

"But, Mikela, it's my world—one that I know very well. I'll be there to guide and protect you. It's not like you will be there by yourself."

"I know, Alex. It's just that I feel like I need to be in Paris for a little while longer. I need to mourn François and Ayan. This may not make sense to anyone, but it does to me. It's something that I need to do—I must do it for them and myself."

Alex nodded and smiled.

"I promise, I'll think about it more."

"Okay. Honey, please let me know when you finally make a decision."

"I will," I said, with a gentle smile.

He's simply gorgeous—and he's never pushy. I'm glad I met him, I thought, as I took a sip of my wine.

The waiter interrupted us again.

"Madame, a card for you from the gentleman in the brown tweed coat at the bar. He said to ask you to call him."

"Who's he?" Alex inquired.

I took the card from the waiter and responded, "I have no idea. The card reads La Galerie des Beaux-arts de Alan Verseck. I guess he's an agent." I smiled, thinking for a moment that perhaps Enkai had suddenly shown me the clear path once again.

CHAPTER 16

❦

Another Crossroad

End March 1986—Prelude to Alex's Departure:

The last weeks that Alex was in Paris were a memorable time for both of us. We spent every moment we could with each other, taking walks and cycling in the day and in the night going to theatres, discovering cozy little restaurants for candlelit dinners, or just staying at home listening to music and cuddling. One Saturday evening, two weeks before his departure, we had yet another excellent night out, dining and exploring the nightlife. After an exhaustive evening, we returned to my apartment and cuddled up to listen to Jazz, French-Caribbean Zouk music, and my newly acquired taste in music, Makosa. Alex moved closer and started to caress me. I let him kiss me, but as our steaming passion intensified and tried to transform into a French kiss, I quickly stopped him.

"Mikela, why do you lead me on and then stop? Why can't you trust my touch? I'll never hurt you like Che—"

"I know," I quickly said, not wanting him to say that name. Just hearing the name I knew would make me sick and foul the rest of the evening for me.

"I'm sorry if it looks like I lead you on and then withdraw. I really don't mean to do that. I want you as much as you want me. It's just that…I mean, I'm not ready to go beyond a light kiss with you. Alex, that's all I can offer you for now…. The past is still a huge burden for me, and I'm still going through my healing process. I know it seems like it's taking a while, but I need all the time I can get. Really, I know it probably sounds selfish of me, but I'm being honest about how I feel…and now that I'm getting to know more about what

Enkai expects of me, frankly, it's not such a bad idea for us to wait for the right time, anyway."

"Well, I think I understand your need to heal before you are ready to move forward with me, and I'll be the last person to rush you. But, Mikela, please, can I ask you a favor?"

"Yes, absolutely!" I said.

"Please, don't come up with another excuse…you know the Enkai stuff and all that, please…"

I could always sense Alex's frustration, and there was no way that I could explain to him that it was not a scheme on my part to make him feel that way. I just needed time.

"Remember that it's Enkai who brought me this far and no one else. Always remember that He means everything to me."

"Mikela, I'm not against your religious belief. I just think that Enkai would want us to have fun together."

"And we do have fun, Alex. Don't we? Haven't we? We don't have to have sex for all that we do to suddenly become fun. We have a great time together—at least that's what I think."

"Yes, we do, Mikela, and you know that I love spending time with you."

Alex looked at me with eyes that expressed a mixture of frustration and resignation, and then he nodded.

"Okay, let's drop the arguing. I get your point."

Reaching for my hand, he added, "Let's focus on spending quality time together during the next two weeks. I'm not looking forward to leaving you here and going back to the States."

He paused, his eyes burrowing into mine.

"I'll miss you, Mikela. I'm really in love with you."

"And, I love you, too, Alex. I'm already missing you."

Our embrace seemed to have lasted for unending minutes before he whispered, "Here, come dance with me, my Maasai Queen."

Mid-March 1986—Alex's Departure:

Two weeks later, we arrived at Roissy-Charles de Gaulle International Airport two hours before Alex's flight departure time to J.F. Kennedy airport in New York. After check-in at Air France, we retreated into the airline's club class.

"I miss you already, Mikela."

"I will miss you, too," I said, fighting back tears.

"I hope you'll soon make up your mind to join me in New York. You and I belong with each other."

I nodded in agreement.

We remained in each other's arms until his flight departure was announced. As he kissed me and then gently released me from his arms to step towards the boarding gate, a feeling of loneliness overtook me. I could no longer control the stream of tears that rolled down my face.

"Bye, my love…hope to see you soon," I whispered.

Mid-April 1986—Mystique in Regal Elegance:

Within the next three weeks, I finally met Alan Verseck, the foremost freelance Swiss photographer based in Paris. In a week, he had a contract already outlined for me to do multiple paintings of my own photos. He'd also seen many of my works in exhibitions, and he thought the paintings were sensational. Ten days later, I signed a contract with him.

Four weeks later, the oil on canvas paintings of my own photo that I'd done were elegantly displayed on the front cover of a Parisian magazine. I wore a Maasai outfit and appeared to be in a makeshift Maasaiplains merged into a background of the Swiss Alps.

My next work for Alan was a painting where I was dressed as a Shuwa Arab woman reaching out for a bottle of a newly introduced designer perfume, "Arab Mystique." I was on an illusionary desert setting that had been created in a Paris studio. This painting was scheduled to appear in a well-known Swiss fashion magazine.

I was elated by the progress I was making on my own in Paris. All the anxiety that I had felt about the future with François's death was slowing fading, even though the ache from the pain of losing both him and Ayan was still there. Slowly but surely, my life fell into a pattern, my daily routine becoming somewhat predictable. I was working eight to ten full hours a day and returning home late everyday, usually to a pile of mail. I would kick the mail aside, too exhausted to go over it, but on this particular day in mid-April 1986, even though I was more tired than usual after the day's photo-session with Alan, I decided to go through my mail.

Relaxing on my living room sofa, I poured myself a glass of well-aged French Chardonnay and started leafing through my mail. I was just about to give up, irritated by the volume of useless junk mail I had received, when I noticed a postcard with the New York's night skyline and a letter from Alex. My exhaustion evaporated instantly as I reached for the post card and read its contents with tingling excitement. "I'm back safely—love you, Alex." Giggling to myself like a little girl, I tore open his letter.

>

My darling Maasai Queen:

I arrived safely in the Big Apple, but I miss you terribly already. New York will never be the same again without you here with me. I miss you terribly and can't wait to see you again. Perhaps I should have stayed in Paris with you a little longer. I know, I already sound like a crybaby.

How are you, my love? Do you miss me as I miss you? Have you given coming to New York some more thought? It would be great if you could bring your paintings to the New York art world.

Of course, by now, you probably think that I'm merely trying to get you to move to New York just to be with me. Well, that's true, too, but darling, I really want the best for you. Please hurry up and decide——I'd love to see you soon.

All my love,

Alex

I caressed the letter in my hands for a few moments as though I was trying to feel his warmth through the paper. His words sounded just like him—always respectfully letting me make my own decisions.

"I miss you, Alex, and I want to see you, too," I whispered.

Still, a part of me was afraid to venture out into another world. Without François and Ayan, I would never have had the courage to leave Nairobi. Now the thought of going two continents away from Africa to the United States was scary. Somehow, I'd gotten accustomed to Paris, and I wasn't ready to explore new grounds again.

I started to rummage through the rest of my mail. An envelope that fell off the table caught my attention, and I opened it.

>

Dear Mikela:

We absolutely loved your paintings in the Swiss magazine. We would like you to oil paint the New York skyline for us to showcase your work on the front cover page of our new American beaux-arts Magazine The Rapture. *Judging from your extraordinary work, we think you will do a terrific job. Please give us a call within the next few days if you are interested. We must add that if you accept this job, you would have to travel to New York within the next four weeks to start this work. We hope you will be available to take on this unique opportunity.*

Sincerely,

Joe McKinley
Paris Representative
Rapture Inc.

I almost couldn't believe my eyes as I read the letter over and over, but finally the reality of what I had read hit me. I burst out laughing and started to dance around my living room as I had with Nadia so many years earlier in the Maasaiplains. I ran to my kitchen and pulled out a bottle of champagne from the fridge. In my excitement, I popped the cork too quickly and half of the bottle spilled. I didn't care about the spill—I toasted to my reunion with Alex. Then, I reached for Salif Keita's CD, *Folon—The Past* and started to dance to its beautiful rhythm.

"Ayan, I'm making a new beginning, I promise. Thank you for your encouragement," I whispered.

More than half an hour later, the drink finally took its normal course, and I drifted to sleep on my living room couch. Shortly after, I was in my dream world.

Another Dream—The Enclosure:

I found myself in an enclosed space that was dark and stuffy. I reached out to feel for the door, but I couldn't find the knob. So, I panicked and started to bang on the walls.

"Someone please let me out! I think I am stuck in the elevator."

The door opened and light blinded my sight for a few seconds. Then I felt a tall, dark figure walk through the door into the room. I peeked into the darkness and saw a human form and frame that looked like Chege Mathani's.

"Oh no! Not you!" I screamed.

Instantly, I tried to force my way past the bulky mass of his body and the door slammed shut. Once again, it was dark in the enclosed space.

Then, I heard the sound of a phone ringing. Quickly, my brain kicked in, recapping what had happened before I'd fallen asleep.

"It was dream—it was just a dream!" I said.

Love Breaking All Boundaries:

I dragged myself up and reached for the phone on the other side of the couch.

"Hello?" I heard Alex say in his deep and masculine voice.

"*Ca va Mon Cheri,*" I responded.

"Hi honey, did I wake you up? I'm sorry."

"It's fine. How are you, my love?"

"Great!" Alex exclaimed.

"Well, I have great news for you," I said.

"Go ahead—don't keep me waiting then."

"I received a letter from an American beaux-arts agency, Rapture Inc. They would like me to paint a unique photo of the New York skyline to appear on the front cover of their new beaux-arts magazine, *The Rapture,*" I said excitedly.

"That's fantastic! Great news! When do you start the photo-sessions?" Alex asked.

"Guess what? The photo-sessions will be in New York, and I'll do my paintings there as well," I screamed.

"Yes! Yes! Yes! Honey, this is fantastic. Yes! Yes! Enkai is on our side," Alex yelled back. "I think Enkai is telling you something, Mikela—my instincts were right in the first place."

"Yes, I agree with you now. Thank you for believing in me and for seeing in me what I didn't see," I responded.

"Well, now, mi casa es su casa," Alex said.

"And what does that mean?"

"It's a Spanish expression for my house is your house," Alex said, unable to hide his excitement.

"Merci, Mon Cheri," I responded, chuckling with excitement.

During the rest of our conversation, I was thrilled by Alex's juicy stories about New York, the "Big Apple" as he called it. It was obvious to me that he loved the city very much.

The Access Pass:

Ten days after I spoke with Alex, I had secured an appointment at the U.S. embassy for my visa application. It was scheduled to take place at nine o'clock in the morning. By half past eight, I was already seated in the lounge of the visa section at the U.S. embassy. The numerical appointment number on a small paper stub that I was given was sixty-five. This meant that sixty-four other individuals would be interviewed before it was my turn to be attended to. It was a long wait of more than two hours, which I spent listening to the embassy officials seated behind bulletproof glass windows shouting out to more than fifty percent of the applicants, "Sorry, we cannot issue you a U.S. non-immigrant visa at this time. In one year, come back here or return to your home country and try the embassy there."

From my estimate, only about fifteen out of the forty-five candidates that had been interviewed were actually granted visas. Although I appeared calm where I was seated, inside, I was worried that my visa application might be denied like many of the previously interviewed candidates. In an attempt to distract my mind from the interviewing process, I started to read the complimentary copy of the Swiss-French magazine that I'd received from Alan Verseck. It featured my "Arabic Mystique" perfume oil-on-canvas painting. Alan had slipped a note inside the magazine with another offer for a one-year contract with his Swiss agency.

I will need to discuss Alan's offer with Alex. I hope I can work out something with Rapture Inc. I would like to do both jobs, I thought, as I waited for my number to show up for the interview with the embassy official.

My thoughts were suddenly interrupted when I heard my number called twice over the public announcement system. I immediately approached the window, and a middle-aged white man greeted me with a warm smile.

"Hello, and how are you today?"

"Ca va bien et vous," I responded in French.

"I know that much, but I can tell you right now, my French is pitiful," he responded, smiling and shaking his head at the same time.

"That's fine by me. Besides, this is an English speaking territory in Paris," I responded with a smile.

"Okay, I see that you are an artist here in Paris. What agency do you work for?" he asked, changing the subject.

"I'm freelancing—I recently secured this contract with a U.S. magazine company, Rapture Inc.," I responded, as I handed him a copy of the contract.

"I've seen your oil on canvas paintings. I must say that they are quite unique and impressive. Have you done any gallery exhibitions lately?" he asked.

"Yes, at the L'Ecole des Beaux-arts and Ecole nationale supérieure des Beaux-arts."

"That's what I thought—I remember seeing your paintings there. They were exquisite but rather too expensive for my budget."

"Well, authentic Parisian art tends to be expensive," I said, as I handed him the Swiss-French magazine, pointing out the page that he needed to look at.

"I also work as a freelance artist for a Swiss agent," I said, when I gave him a copy of Alan's letter proposing a one-year contract in Switzerland.

The embassy official stared at the painting in the magazine for a few seconds, then looked up at me and said, "This is an absolutely beautiful painting. Where was the setting?"

"You wouldn't believe it if I told you that the background was a make-believe desert in a Champs Élysées photo-studio. It's also an oil-on-canvas painting—most of my work now is," I explained.

"Impressive! Rather impressive!" he remarked. "How long do you intend to stay in New York, and do you plan to seek an agent while you are there?" he asked.

"A few months, but if an American agent makes me a great offer, I certainly wouldn't turn him or her down," I responded truthfully.

"I assume that you intend to leave the United States when your visa expires," he inquired, his face expressing a sudden serious and strange look.

"If you are asking me if I intend to stay out of legal immigration status while in the United States, the answer to that is no. As you can see, my passport shows that my French temporary residency status has always been renewed in chronological date sequence," I explained.

He appeared to be half listening as he scribbled some words on my forms. Finally, he raised his head and said, "Ma'am, I'll grant you a four-year visa with multiple entry to the United States. This does not mean that you are allowed to stay in the United States for four years. This simply means that you are allowed to enter or leave the country during the next four years. When you get to the John F. Kennedy International Airport in New York, the immigration's officer will stamp your passport with the specific time duration that you would be allowed to stay in the country, after which you must leave and re-enter the country. Any questions, ma'am?"

"Not at all. Thank you," I responded, trying to conceal my excitement.

"Your visa will be ready in an hour."

I left the United States embassy in jubilation. I could almost not believe that I would see Alex within the next ten days. I knew that he'd be very excited when he learned that I was on my way to the Big Apple.

After running other errands, it was almost six o'clock that evening when I finally arrived home. I dropped my bags and coat on the floor and dashed to the phone to call Alex.

"Hello," Alex said in drowsy voice. "I must have fallen asleep on my couch," he added.

"Hello, Mon Cheri. It's Mikela. I got it! I got it!"

"You got what?" Alex inquired.

"I got a four-year multiple entry visa to the United States," I screamed.

It seemed to take his brain more than a few seconds to process this information.

"Oh my God! That's great," Alex exclaimed. "I'm so excited. What's your flight itinerary? When are you arriving? When am I going to see you?"

"I don't know yet, Alex. I just got the visa issued today. I'll call the travel agency tomorrow, and I'll let you know," I replied, laughing at his almost childlike excitement.

"Okay, the day after tomorrow, I'll call you around 11 AM your time," Alex said.

"I love you, honey," he added.

"I love you, too, Mon Cheri."

Summer, Early June 1986—The Big Apple:

About six weeks later, I was on board an Air France Jumbo jet en route to the JFK airport in New York. Snuggled into a window seat in the first class section of the huge aircraft, I braced myself for a seven-hour flight ordeal. This time, I was well prepared for it—I brought some sleeping pills with me, popping a couple in my mouth as soon as I was settled and fastened securely into my seat. By the time the plane was taxiing on the runway in preparation for take off, I'd drifted off to sleep.

I woke up four hours later when breakfast was being served—I'd missed hors d'oeuvres, dinner, and in-between meal snacks that had been served after dinner, but I didn't mind and was glad that I only had to endure less than two hours of being suspended in mid-air.

Shortly after I woke up and let out a huge yawn, a guy with a strong American accent seated next to me introduced himself.

"Hi, I'm Jim Reeves. I'm glad you've finally come around."

He was a bulky looking white man who was leaning towards the heavy side. He looked like he could be in his late fifties.

"Hello, I'm Mikela. I prefer to sleep through a flight. I'm not terribly comfortable with flying." I replied, taking in his fat, cherubim face hidden under a shock of white hair.

"Did you say Mee-kay-la?"

"Yes, you've got it," I said.
"You have a beautiful name."
"Thank you."
"Well, you were out there for a while. If not for your purring, I'd have thought that you had died and gone to heaven," Jim said, laughing hard at his own joke.
"Yes, it was deliberate. I took sleeping tablets—I don't like flying," I repeated, quite surprised by his forwardness.
"It's all in the mind. I don't worry too much about what could happen when I am stuck in mid-air because there is not much that I can do, is there?" he said, laughing heartily and this time elbowing me teasingly.
"I realize that," I said, stiffening from his slightly painful nudge.
"Where are you from? I detect an accent," he asked, quickly changing the subject.
"I'm a Tanzanian Maasai."
"Is that somewhere in North Africa?" he asked.
I shook my head. "Tanzania is in East Africa."
He flushed, seemingly embarrassed.
"I know a young lady from Ethiopia—she does still art beaux-arts modeling for my agency. You remind me of her," he said. "If you don't mind my asking, are you the Paris-Maasai beaux-artist?" he asked.
"Yes, I am," I replied, surprised that this brash man would know anything about art, much less of my art.
"Something told me that you were. Somehow, I recognized your exotic look," he remarked, and then he said, "I hope I didn't embarrass you by being rather blunt."
"Oh no! I appreciate your compliment," I responded. "So, what do you do, Jim?"
"I own an American beaux-arts agency in Manhattan. I also own quite a few galleries in Manhattan, Paris, Switzerland, and London. I visit Paris quite often, where I try to recruit new faces from the still art beaux-arts modeling world. I find your paintings spectacular," he said, as he reached into his side pocket and pulled out a business card, which he handed over to me.
"Please, give me a call as soon as you get settled in New York," he added.
"Certainly," I said.
"What magazine is that?" he asked, pointing to the magazine that I had on my tray.

"It's a Parisian art magazine. You can have a look," I said, handing it over to him.

"Wow…this is fabulous! I like this!" he exclaimed after a few minutes. "Is this one of yours?"

"Yes, it's a painting of the Swiss Alps."

"Impressive. Very impressive," he remarked. "I guess I'm sold already. Let's get together in New York. Do you have a phone number where I can reach you?"

"Yes, I do," I said, quickly scribbling my name and Alex's phone number on a piece of paper.

Jim spent the next hour talking about beaux-arts business in New York and how it compared to the Paris world.

"A spectacular artist with extraordinary talent such as yours is better off in New York than in Paris," he said.

"Why do you say so?" I inquired.

"Well, there are more opportunities—a greater variety of stuff. You know what I mean?"

"Kind of," I replied, even though my expression showed that I didn't.

Jim seemed like a really pleasant person. For the remainder of the flight, he kept my ears filled. I really enjoyed listening to him and didn't mind his habitual painful nudges anymore.

Roughly two hours later, the pilot announced our initial descent towards the JFK international airport. Momentarily, the New York skyline, a cluster of the tallest skyscrapers that I'd ever seen, was in view. Jim immediately took the honor of giving me a bird's-eye tour of New York, pointing out the exquisite World Trade Center, the Empire State Building, and Lady Liberty. The New York skyline, I suddenly realized, was an intricate mesh of technological miracles that patterned buildings into unique shapes and sizes that seemed to dwarf towering Parisian points.

Painting the New York skyline is going to be fun, I was thinking, before Jim interrupted to tell me that we were almost on the ground.

I could now see the stretch of the runway in sight, and within a breath, the aircraft touched down and roared at an incredible speed as it taxied on the runway. A few minutes later, we were at our arrival gate.

Thank you, Enkai. It's over for now. I survived the flight, and I'm not looking forward to another flight soon, I thought.

Later, as we approached the immigration booths, Jim bade me goodbye.

"Make sure to ring me, Mee-kay-la," he called over his shoulder as he headed off towards the short queue that was for Americans and permanent residents only, while I joined the unbelievably long queue for all other foreign nationals.

Luckily, my encounter with the immigration officials was brief and uneventful. I was allowed to stay in the country for up to six consecutive months, after which I had to leave and renter the country.

By the time I collected my luggage and went through the custom's check, I realized that it had been more than two hours since our flight had arrived. I hoped that Alex had not been waiting for too long. As I stepped into the huge arrival lounge, my eyes scanned the crowd looking for him. A hoard of people waited patiently for the arriving passengers to emerge from behind the last barricade of the immigration and custom checking areas, but I could not see Alex anywhere. As I pondered what to do next, I suddenly heard someone shout my name.

"Mikela! Mikela!"

It sounded just like Alex. I tried to follow the sound of the voice, but I still could not see him. As I merged with the crowd, still working in the direction of the voice, I felt a hand slowly wrap itself around me from behind. I swung around instinctively and facing me with the biggest, broadest smile was Mon Cheri Alex. I threw my arms around him, almost knocking over the young man by my side with my hand bang, and melted into his strong, powerful embrace. His hands trembling, Alex reached for the arch of my neck and pulled me into a long and passionate kiss. After what seemed like a lifetime, he pulled away and led me to a quieter corner of the airport.

"Honey, do you have any idea how much I have missed you?" he whispered into my left ear as we locked hands and giggled like teenage lovers.

"If it's anything like how much I have missed you myself then I probably have an idea," I replied, pressing my body closer to his.

Oblivious of the crowd around us, he started to caress the contours of my face, tracing invisible lines with his fingers.

"I had almost forgotten how beautiful you are. Looking at you just takes my breath away," he whispered, as he kissed my eyes.

Now, I felt my body erupting into a caldron of passion—the feel of Alex's warm body and hands igniting my insides like wild fire on a virgin forest.

"I love it when you kiss me like that," I whispered.

Smiling ever so lightly, he bent to kiss my lips, and instantly, I felt the intensity of his succulent lips on mine—his tongue exploring the insides of my mouth as though journeying into my soul and his muscled arms crushing me in a warm and passionate embrace. For a moment, we seemed to have frozen the rest of the world around us and created a temporary illusion of physical separation from them. We were like two lovebirds encased in a bubble of passion.

Reluctantly, Alex lifted his lips off mine, making a smacking sound that made us both reel in with laughter. "Welcome to the Big Apple, my love. I intend to give you the best time of your life," Alex whispered into my ear.

Within the depths of my soul, I had a renewed feeling that a beautiful renaissance was nearer on the unknown horizon of the bustling city of skyscrapers.

CHAPTER 17

A New Season

June 1986—A Bustling City of Skyscrapers:

Alex led the way as we walked towards a bus stand, where a shuttle bus took us to the nearest subway station. His eyes were fixed on me, expressing a continuous twinkling of excitement.

Finally, when we were seated inside a subway coach and heading in the direction of Broadway, East New York, and Fulton Street, he pulled me into his warm embrace and gently caressed my hands.

"I'm so happy to see you, Mikela," Alex whispered again and again into my ears.

"I missed you so much, Alex," I replied, reaching up to kiss his face.

Our eyes locked for a fleeting second, our burning passion almost tangible.

"Here I am with my gorgeous Maasai Queen in the heart of the Big Apple," he said. "I've had this mental picture and visualized it for months, and now it has finally materialized."

Suddenly, I felt a surge of his euphoria and a rapture of blissful eternity as his hands started to stroke my slender shoulders. I leaned closer and gently placed my head on his chest. Closing my eyes for a brief moment, I visualized lying on his bare chest while his back rested on the hammock in the patio that he'd described as his favorite relaxing place at his home. Warmed by my increasingly naughty thoughts, I slowly opened my eyes and, peering through the window, gasped at the splendor of the perfect moon overhead, surrounded by a streak of twinkling stars that added to the already romantic ambiance created by our passion. *Even nature approves,* I thought, snuggling closer to Alex and enjoying the tingling sensation all over my body and the blissfulness of pure romance.

The announcement of our arrival at Broadway-East New York-Fulton Street jolted my mind back to the present moment, and Alex informed me that we had to change quickly to the Z line in the direction of Broad Street and Wall Street. After seven metro stops, we arrived at the Chamber Street-Center Street stop, where we took Line 5 in the direction of our final destination, Pelham Parkway, one stop after the Bronx Park East-White Plains Road subway station. From there, we took a cab to Alex's two-bedroom apartment on 665 Barker Avenue.

The Blossoming of an Unquenchable Love:

"Welcome to my humble abode, my love," Alex said with a warm smile, as he led me into his neat and very tastefully furnished apartment.

As a collector of African art, his walls, corners, and bookshelves were tastefully embellished with exquisite carvings and paintings. Some of the artwork he said he'd bought from New York African merchants and others from talented African-American artists who believed they were inspired by the heritage of their motherland. The uncarpeted wooden floors of his living room were impressively polished and nicely layered with hand-made Persian rugs.

"I like your place. It has a simple and yet elegant touch," I said.

"Your taste has rubbed off on me, my dear. Didn't you once tell me that there was grace in elegant simplicity? I'm a fast learner," Alex said rather graciously.

I responded with a flirtatious look that seemed to send his heart racing. He hurriedly took my luggage into his room.

"Can I get you something to drink?" Alex inquired, when he emerged from the room and headed toward his bar at the corner of the living room.

"For a casual drinker, you have a well stocked bar," I remarked.

"Yeah, I know. My friends, who are more than casual drinkers, make sure that I keep my bar pretty well stocked," Alex said.

"I would like a glass of spring water for now, thank you. Do you mind if I help myself?"

"How terribly polite of you, my love. Of course you can. Please feel free here and consider this your new home. Remember, mi casa es su casa," Alex responded.

I smiled as I poured myself a cold glass of water and started telling Alex about Jim, the white American that I'd met on the flight.

"He owns art galleries in Manhattan and all over the world. He said he'd like me to call him. What do you think?" I asked.

"I think that's great. Give him a call whenever you feel like it. Maybe he can get you started in the New York art world.

"Honey, I don't mean to change the subject, but are you hungry, my love? Would you like me to order some food?" Alex asked.

"Oh no! I had some food just before our flight landed. I'm not hungry at all. However, I would appreciate a hot shower or bath," I responded.

"It would be my pleasure to prepare a bath for you, my love," Alex said.

A Future Wrapped in the Past:

Half an hour later, I was soaking in a warm bubble bath with my favorite perfumed pebbles and bath grains. I closed my eyes and tried to relax my mind, not worrying about the past or the future but merely relishing the moment. I thanked Enkai and Nadia for Alex, my handsome knight with a beautiful spirit, who loved me unconditionally and was not afraid to show it. I promised myself that I'd never take him for granted. In Paris, I'd met a few men and women who had no one to love and others that were exploited by those that claimed to love them. Alex's love was like a precious pearl to me because he'd always been willing to love me without setting any conditions.

His knock on the bathroom door interrupted my thoughts.

"May I come in, Mikela?"

"Yes, you may."

From behind the transparent shower curtains, he appeared in a white towel robe, exposing his broad and hairy chest as he leaned against the wall adjacent to the door. The view of his dark silhouette ignited my body, and a tingling sensation seemed to zip through me.

"May I join you?" Alex asked, in a deep and husky voice.

For a brief moment, there was complete silence as I struggled for words. I wanted Alex, and yet a part of me was afraid of the male part of him, the product of potent testosterone that brought flashbacks of Chege Mathani. I knew that my thoughts were unfair to Alex because he didn't deserve to be viewed in the same light as the likes of Chege Mathani. But my mangled thoughts sometimes could not distinguish between the violent acts of one man and the beauty of love and passion offered by another. Before I could find the right words to say to Alex, he said, "It's all right if you're not comfortable with me joining you." He started to leave the bathroom.

At this point, I finally responded.

"It's fine, Alex. Please join me."

I could see him through the curtain removing his robe, which dropped to the floor. My heart started to pace even quicker. A mixture of fear and desire started volcanic feelings inside me. *Alex had the body of an African warrior,* I thought. He had bulging and rippling chest muscles and strong arms that I loved to have wrapped around me. As my thoughts struggled to reach some resolution with my desire and passion for Alex, he pushed the curtain slightly to the left and started to step into the water. Suddenly, absolute fear seemed to overtake me for a moment.

To steady myself, I looked down into the water bubbles, seeking a momentary escape from the intense flames of my burning passion and desire. I was still too timid to boldly admire the exquisite work of Mother Nature, which manifested itself rather handsomely on Alex's body. Noticing my unease, he slipped under the water to my side, obscuring most of his body. Gently, he lifted me slightly from under and placed my back on his chest, as he leaned against the tub. Then, he started to kiss my neck and caress my shoulders and wet braids. His touch seemed to have quenched my momentary fear. I closed my eyes, hoping that his touch would have a magic influence and cleansing effect on my thoughts about Chege Mathani and the Maasailand.

As I relished in the luscious feel of Alex's warm body, his touch ignited my soul, and my heart erupted into a hidden fire of desire for him.

"I'm glad you're here, Mikela," Alex said very softly.

"I'm so happy to be here, too," I immediately responded.

For the next few minutes, Alex held me in his arms, caressing my body gently. For the first time, I had the courage to initiate a touch and started to trace an invisible line on his thigh.

"What are you doing?" Alex asked jokingly.

"I'm tracing my uncharted journey from the Maasailand. So far, I like my current destination," I said, chuckling.

"I think that your current destination is a wise choice," Alex responded, as he started to tickle my sides.

I laughed and wriggled hopelessly, begging and pleading with Alex to spare me as I splattered water all around us. For the first time in many years, I suddenly felt like a little child again—free of worries and burdens. The last time I recalled feeling that way was in the open fields of the Maasailand where I'd played and sang with Nadia. That was more than six years ago. Now, I could feel deep within my soul that Alex's love was real, and I had no plans of letting go of it.

During the rest of the evening, we cuddled up on the sofa and listened to soft, sensuous music while Alex talked about the city of New York and life as a student at Columbia University. I listened with calm curiosity, relishing in our love; I was unperturbed by the possible uncertainties of the future. I was hopeful that the bond that connected us would only grow stronger in time.

November 1986—Two Days Before Thanksgiving:

Six months after I arrived in New York, it was Thanksgiving, a very special holiday for all Americans, Alex explained to me. It was a time of family reunion and thanksgiving for loved ones and a time to be thankful to God for our life's blessings. Alex planned to spend Thanksgiving in upstate New York with his father and his new wife. This particular Thanksgiving was going to be a very special one because, for the first time since his parents' divorce, his mother and her fiancée had agreed to join Alex's father and his new wife, Julia. Also, as the new addition to the family, I, too, was invited to their family Thanksgiving. Alex had informed his family about his "Maasai Queen." His stepmother Julia eagerly invited us to spend four days with Alex's father and her at their new residence in upstate New York.

Upstate New York in Rhode Island was very nice—certainly much quieter than the daily madness of New York City enclaves like the Bronx. Alex's father, Leroy Williams, lived in a lovely six-bedroom house that was strategically perched on elevated ground and surrounded by acres of neatly manicured lawn, which reminded me of the open plains back home.

Alex's stepmother, Julia, received us at the front entrance. I was struck by her simplicity and beauty. She was a sharp looking white woman—a petite brunette, about five feet seven inches tall and about one hundred and thirty pounds. Her hair was cut short into a trendy style that complimented her uniquely sculptured Italian facial features. With a warm smile that exposed her slightly discolored teeth, she said, "Welcome Alex. It's good to see you." She kissed him on both cheeks and then turned to me.

"This must be your lovely Mikela. She's definitely as beautiful as you said. Welcome Mikela—I'm Julia. How are you, my dear? Please, come right in."

Her warmth and charm helped me to relax a little. I had been quite tense in anticipation of the reception that I would receive from Alex's family.

"Yes, she's my Maasai Queen," Alex said.

"I can see that, Alex. Africans would say that her beauty radiates like the petals of a blossoming flower welcoming the arrival of spring," Julia remarked.

"I'm flattered. You're so kind," I said modestly.

"Now, where did you get that from, Julia?" Alex asked.

"Well, you see, I, too, happen to have some of the motherland in me," Julia responded.

"I can see that—I sure can see that, my sister," Alex joked.

While Alex and his stepmother joked around, I admired the contemporary design of their home, which had well-positioned skylights. Its massive French windows allowed the powerfully illuminating rays of the sun into the home. The eastern exposure of the atrium gave the living room natural light from the radiant sunbeams that were tempered by the shade provided by the surrounding trees. The inside walls of the house manifested a certain taste and love for European renaissance artistry—one that I was very familiar with, having been schooled by the great collections of Parisian museums.

"Isn't this an impeccable piece of art—I mean, the artist's impressive repainting of 'Mona Lisa' by the famous Leonardo da Vinci," I remarked, pointing to a painting on the wall.

"You seem to have a good eye for art. Yes, you are right, it's an exquisite repainting. Actually, it's one of my favorite paintings," Julia proudly acknowledged.

"So, you are familiar with European renaissance art? I'm impressed," Julia said, as she led us up a spiral staircase to the guestroom.

"Here we are! I hope it's enough space for both of you," she said.

"We don't need that much space," Alex said, laughing.

I smiled nervously and hoped that I didn't appear visibly embarrassed.

Later, Alex's father Leroy returned home in time to join us at the dinner table. He was a lean, tall, and handsome man with a distinct moustache. He had a well-groomed appearance, with a neatly trimmed hairline. Leroy had a creased forehead that he seemed to exaggerate whenever he made a cynical remark. He had an oval-shaped face with a distinctly- shaped flat nose and very thick lips. His complexion mirrored that of the ancient Nubians—smooth dark mahogany color, the mark of the dominant genes from his rich African ancestry. He seemed to maintain an interesting smirk on his face as a permanent expression.

"Alex, nice to see you. You look well."

"Thanks Dad, I feel very well. Meet my beautiful Maasai Queen, Mikela."

"Hello Mikela, and welcome to civilization," Leroy said.

There was a second or two of complete silence and everyone appeared uncomfortable by his comment. Alex seemed to fake a light cough as he glared at his father.

"Has New York been a major shock coming from the wild jungles of Africa?" Leroy asked.

Shocked by his immediate and obvious antagonism and blatant disrespect, I responded with carefully calculated words.

"Well, sir, we have nice cities, too, although I grew up in a more traditional setting in the Tanzanian Maasailand. New York is very nice and certainly more technologically advanced than Nairobi, where I was for a few years. But Africa is still my home, and I love it—it's my ancestral home, and I'm really not ashamed of where I come from."

"Leroy, please, not now!" Julia snapped.

"What do you mean, not now? I was merely welcoming the young lady."

"Dad, I agree with Julia. Not now, please! I invited Mikela to meet my family, and I think she deserves some respect. However, if you insist on being unpleasant, then we'll have to leave," Alex said, calmly but firmly.

Leroy simply nodded in response.

Alex was visibly upset by his father's comment, and for the rest of the evening, his mood seemed subdued. He became visibly withdrawn and hardly spoke, while I tried to be gracious, though I had been hurt by Leroy's remark.

Finally, Alex said, "Excuse me everyone. I would like to spend a brief moment with Mikela." He reached out for my hand.

"Thank you, Mr. and Mrs. Williams, for such a gracious meal," I said, as I stood up to leave.

"It's such a pleasure having you with us, Mikela," Julia responded, with a warm smile.

In the guest room, Alex took me into his arms and whispered closely into my ears, "Honey, I'm so sorry about all this. I really am. I had no idea that my father still had such deep prejudice against Africans."

"It's okay. It's really not your fault, Alex," I said.

"But this is my father's house. Leroy is my father, and I invited you to our home. He had no right to say such cruel things to you."

"Well, that's his way of letting out all the anger, bitterness, and possible distaste he has for Africans. Perhaps I represented Africa to him, and that's why he lashed out at me."

"You are being quite understanding about all this, honey, and I really appreciate it. But, I'm still quite upset and embarrassed about my father's behavior."

"No worries, my love. He'll soon come around," I replied. "Anyway, I'm curious to know why and how he developed such negative feelings about Africans."

"Well, I'm not exactly sure about the origins. But my mom once told me that my father blames Africans for their role in slavery. He believes that some Africans cooperated with the Europeans and Arabs and sold some of their own relatives in exchange for material gifts, like mirrors and guns. I mean, I know a whole bunch of wicked stuff happened during the four hundred years of the Transatlantic Slave Trade, but we must all really forgive the past and try to move beyond it all. Isn't that what Enkai has asked us to do?"

"Yes, you are right. And besides, not all Africans participated in slavery. Many Africans lost their loved ones to slavery, which devastated their families. We can't really blame the actions of a few individuals on all Africans," I replied.

"Well, honey, we only have a few days to stay here, and I promise you, I won't let my father insult you any further," Alex finally said.

The Next Day:

Alex's mother, Zena, and her fiancé, Paul Janssen, arrived the next day—the day before Thanksgiving. She was a stunning beauty, with a regal presence. Her hair was very neatly braided in thin singles that accentuated her natural elegance, and her dazzling dark and velvety skin tone made her stand out like a Nubian Princess. Her nicely sculptured facial features reminded me of the beautiful African American actress Diane Carol. Zena seemed a very high-spirited and happy person. I was instantly more comfortable with Zena than I was with Alex's father, as she embraced me like her own child.

Zena's fiancée, Paul, was a blonde and blue-eyed gynecologist and obstetrician from the Netherlands. He had an aristocratic air and regal presence, although his demeanor lacked an arrogant flair. He looked like a tall and blonde Yul Bryner who didn't have the arrogance of Pharaoh Rhamses. He had moved to the United States nearly fifteen years ago and, after passing his medical board examinations, started his own practice in Rhode Island. He politely welcomed me and jokingly told me that he would like to be my first choice for a gynecologist and obstetrician.

Thanksgiving Day went well. Everyone made every attempt to act cordial towards one another. Zena and Paul left the day after Thanksgiving, while Alex and I ended up leaving for New York City on Sunday morning. The next day was the beginning of another hectic weekly routine for Alex. Also, my photo-sessions with Rapture were also starting that week, and I could feel that this was going to be a new season in my life. The Big Apple was not just a new place; it was a new horizon with its own set of bustling attractions and entertainment.

I wondered if I had the strength to break the unsavory links to my painful past, releasing it so that my future would unfold. And was I ready to take a bold step into a blessed future of many positive possibilities? These were some of the questions that were ringing in my mind as we boarded the train back to New York City.

CHAPTER 18

❁

Links to the Past

Special Letters in the Mail:

When I returned home from Thanksgiving, a letter from Tulia was waiting for me. She informed me that she'd graduated from the University of Nairobi Medical School and was about to start her residency program. She'd also fallen in love with a Tanzanian physician—he had proposed marriage to her, and she'd accepted.

Tulia is such a wonderful person and deserving of everything good, I thought.

After dinner with Alex, I decided to reply to Tulia's letter, inviting her to visit New York with her fiancée. As I sealed my letter to her, my mind flashed back to my last day at Aunt Bela's home—the rape incident and my final escape from the house of terror…and how the rain had drenched my body by the time I appeared at Tulia's doorstep. Tears filled my eyes as my thoughts reincarnated the painful events of the past.

Now, I thought about Mama Eshe and Aunt Bela and how they must have been shocked by my sudden disappearance. I thought about how Jamila and Johari must have missed me very much, as I had missed them. My mind trailed back to the Maasailand, to my mother, and the tears that had loaded in my eyes started to trickle down my face. Soon, they became a continuous waterfall.

So much time has gone by, and yet the pain remains lodged within me. Will I ever escape this pain? I asked silently.

As these thoughts swirled in my mind, I decided to write to Mama Eshe and Aunt Bela for the first time in over six years.

My dear Mama Eshe and Aunt Bela:

It has been many years since I left Aunt Bela's home, and I know that you must have wondered all these years what happened to me. I still remember the story about the baby sparrow that Mama Eshe told me in Mombassa. So, now I'm ready to tell you why I left the kitchen with burnt rice on the gas stove—why I didn't say goodbye to both of you, Mama Eshe, Jamila, or Johari. All these past years, I have struggled with the pain of what happened to me in Aunt Bela's house and before then in the Maasailand. Now, I have finally decided to tell you the whole story.

In my letter, I recounted in detail my ordeal of female circumcision in the Maasailand and the two incidents of rape by Chege Mathani at Aunt Bela's home, as well as his continuous obnoxious harassment in between.

Mama Eshe! Aunt Bela! I love both of you dearly. You treated me so well. I loved Jamila and Johari and still do. They were like my own sisters. Before I met them, Nadia was my only sister before she died. When I met Aunt Bela's daughters, I felt like I had gained two sisters at a time. But my world turned around after what Mr. Mathani did to me. He destroyed my innocence and happiness. I had to leave! I just had to leave! Ever since then, every day has been a healing experience, and I still have a long way to go.

I met a wonderful man in Paris. His name is Alex. He is an African-American, and he lives in New York City in the United States, where I am now. I have become an artist, and I'm working in New York for a short while. One day, I hope to come back to Kenya to see you, if you don't mind. I also hope to visit my mother, whom I have not seen or heard from since I left the Maasailand almost ten years ago. I'm really sorry I lied when I told you that I was an orphan.

Mama Eshe, as for the story of the young baby sparrow that you told me when I came to visit you in Mombassa from Nairobi, you were right then—I had a lot of pain lodged inside me, but I really could not share it with you. After you read this letter, I hope you'll understand why I behaved like the young baby sparrow and hid my pain within me.

Please write when you receive this letter. I would love to hear from you. Jamila and Johari must be grown women now. Please give them my love, and tell them that their sister Mikela misses them very much.

I love you Mama Eshe! I love you Aunt Bela!

—Mikela

I must have dozed off on the couch shortly after I finished writing the letter. Faintly, I could hear Alex telling me that it was time to retire to bed as he helped me to my feet. Drowsily, I joined him in bed. He reached out to me and gently wrapped his strong and muscular arms around me. We both cuddled up and in seconds, I dozed off again. As always in his arms, I slept like a baby, safe and sound in the arms of my handsome knight and the love of my life.

Discovering New York City:

The following two weeks were dedicated to sightseeing and exploring the Big Apple.

As we stepped into a cab, Alex gently whispered to me, "Welcome to one of the most beautiful cities in the world. I promise you that it's going to be much more exciting than Paris."

"You mean that New York is far more enchanting than the romantic city of Paris?"

"But, of course, Mon Cheri. With me by your side, Paris will be no match for the splendor and beauty of the Big Apple. Welcome, once again, my love, to the radiant city of New York," Alex said.

The Big Apple was certainly as exciting as Alex had promised. Armed with maps, tour guides, and sometimes with Alex as a patient guiding light, I explored the New York City subway system. Some days, when Alex was either at school or work, I would venture by myself into the enclaves of the city of Manhattan—a technological embellishment of modernization with its impressive skyscrapers that threatened to reach the skies.

My exploration of Manhattan included a taste of famous restaurants and cafés—from The Four Seasons on 53rd Street between Park and Lexington Avenue in Midtown Manhattan to Windows on the World at the World Trade Center between Church and West streets in Lower Manhattan. In the Upper West Side, I would have a taste of New York French cuisine at Café des Aristes on West 67th Street and exquisite dessert at Café Lalo on West 83rd Street at

Amsterdam Avenue. Sometimes, on the East Side on East 55th Street, between Fifth and Madison Avenue, I enjoyed more French cuisine at the La Cote Basque in the Midtown area, which managed to fill my appetite and nostalgia for exquisite Parisian recipes.

Undoing the Physical Stitches of Tradition:

Finally, it was time to start work, and I quickly immersed myself in the busy schedule that ensued. As appreciation for my work grew in New York, for the first time, the possibility of a career in New York began to seem more real, but I knew that if I was going to make a new life in this country, I had to finally sever my destructive links with the past. So, after a straight two months of hectic work without a break, I took six weeks off to undergo surgery to remove my infibulation stitches. I had delayed this for too long now because I didn't want to deal with this aspect of my past.

With Alex's assistance, I located a well-respected obstetrician and gynecological surgeon, Dr. Susan Baker, who ran a flourishing practice in Manhattan. She was also a known certified psychotherapist that had been treating rape-traumatized patients for over a decade.

"Well, hello! Welcome, Mikela and Alex—I'm Susan Baker. Nice to meet both of you, and please have a seat and make yourselves comfortable."

Susan was a very dark-skinned, elegant, and beautiful African-American woman. She was of average height, with a well-proportioned body. Susan was forty-nine years old but didn't look a day older than thirty. She attributed her youthful appearance to a healthy diet, vitamins, a sustained exercise regimen, and the power of her faith in God. She'd been happily married for twenty years with two children—a seventeen-year-old son and a thirteen-year-old daughter.

"Mikela, if you don't mind, let's go over your experiences."

Half an hour later, Susan said, "It's going to be fine—believe me, it is. My advice to you is to take care of your physical scars first, and later, we'll attend to the psychological wounds."

Alex turned to me, seeking my approval, and I nodded in agreement.

Susan scheduled me for surgery to remove the infibulation stitches. The surgery itself was successful and uneventful, but the physical pain afterwards was excruciating. I was hospitalized for a week, after which I was sent home.

During the next three weeks, the daily pain from my surgery and the gradual healing made it seem like I was reliving my past. I could barely walk or urinate, and daily my pain reminded me of the journey away from my ancestral home: from the Maasaiplains to the Mathani house of terror.

At home, I started having crying spells and recurrent dreams about Nadia. Once, in my dream, Nadia gave me a single red rose and said, "Mikela, it's over now! It's all behind you now! Take care of him, for he is a good man from Enkai to you."

Throughout my recovery period, Alex remained my solid support and love, constantly reminding me that the surgery was the last vestige of my experience of female circumcision. My daily prayers to Enkai and Alex's words of comfort gave me strength and courage.

A week after I was discharged from the hospital, I returned to see Dr. Susan Baker. She was pleased with the rapid healing of my surgical wound.

"Mikela, whenever you're ready, we can start your psychotherapy sessions. We would like to help you close all doors to both the physical and emotional pains from the past."

"It will be a while, Susan. I'm still trying to deal with my emotional pain in my own way," I responded politely.

"Take your time, Mikela. I never rush my patients. You'll know when you are ready."

To aid my recuperation, I resumed my exploration of New York, discovering new cafés and boutiques. Once I dared American cuisine at the Ambassador Grill at the Park Hyatt Hotel on United Nations Plaza between 1st and 2nd Avenues. While I waited for grilled chicken breast and roasted mixed vegetables and wild rice, a very well dressed gentleman in a business suit walked in with a stunningly beautiful lady who looked Kenyan. She had the features of Ayan. The man had a striking resemblance to Jim, the gentleman that I'd met on board the Air France flight to JFK. As the couple got seated, the eyes of the gentleman caught mine.

He certainly looks like Jim, I thought, when I saw his full profile.

Shortly afterwards, the waiter appeared, interrupting my thoughts, and I diverted my attention from the Jim look-alike. I started to eat the tastefully prepared grilled chicken with roasted vegetables and wild rice—it was delicious.

As I enjoyed my meal, my mind went back to Nairobi and the Maasailand, and I thought about my mother. I thought about Aunt Bela and Mama Eshe, wondering whether they'd ever received my letter. I thought about Chege Mathani and wondered when he'd pay for what he had done to me. While my thoughts trailed into the abyss of my past, I'd become oblivious of my surroundings. Suddenly, a deep and husky voice startled me.

"Hello! Are you Mee-kay-la? You have a striking resemblance to a Parisian artist I met on board a flight from Paris to JFK some time ago."

"Jim?"

"Yes, Jim. Remember me?"

"Of course I do. Hello Jim. Yes, I'm Mikela. When I first saw you, I thought you looked very much like the guy that I met on the flight, but I wasn't sure," I responded with a warm smile.

"Would you care to sit with Lily and me?" Jim asked.

"Absolutely!"

A few minutes later, I was introduced to Lily, a still life model who worked for Jim's agency. She was a soft-spoken lady with a strong Kenyan accent.

"Lily is from Kenya," Jim said. "If I remember clearly, Mikela, you are a Maasai," he added.

"Yes, I am."

Reaching out her hand for a handshake, Lily said, "Nice to meet you, Mikela."

After we made small talk for a while, I turned to Lily and casually asked how she had come to live in New York. Much to my shock, she started telling me about herself. Being somewhat guarded about my own life, it never ceased to amaze me how easily some people could talk about their lives at the slightest prompting. At first, I was not sure that I wanted a peek into her life, but after a while, I began to relax and embrace Lily's casual nature and warmth.

Lily left Kenya when she was fourteen years old to attend school in Johannesburg, South Africa. Four years later, shortly after she'd graduated from high school at the age of eighteen, she met Bruce, a thirty-five-year-old Swiss Freelance photographer and artist that introduced her to the world of still art modeling. They became close friends, and later they started dating. She left Johannesburg with him and returned to Switzerland, where he owned a home. A short while later, he made contact with a big agency in Paris where she started working as a beaux-arts still art model.

When she turned twenty years old, she met Jim at a beaux-arts exhibition in Paris, and he convinced her to come to New York. She was now happily married to Bruce, and they lived in Manhattan.

I saved my own life's history for sometime in the future. I only told Jim and Lily that I was visiting my boyfriend, Alex. After lunch, Jim invited me to take a tour of his art gallery on Lexington Avenue, and I gladly accepted his offer.

New Fashion Treadmills:

By the end of our tour, Jim asked me to work as a freelance artist for his agency.

"Mikela, I love the uniqueness of your paintings. I think they are simply terrific. Since we first met on the flight from Paris, I have researched more of your work—I can tell you, it's in an exclusive class of its own."

"Thank you, Jim. Thank you for your kind words," I said.

"I've been thinking that if we can get you on board, we would like your first work for us to be an original oil-on-canvas painting of Lady Liberty. What do you think?"

"Not a bad idea, Jim. I envision a painting that encompasses my journey from the Maasaiplains to Lady Liberty with a touch of the city of Nairobi intermeshed with Parisian beaux-arts," I responded.

"Splendid! Absolutely splendid!" Jim exclaimed, visibly excited about such a future project.

"Let's get together and talk about this in more detail. We are shooting for an upscale gallery exhibition in Zurich in four month's time. We are arranging for photo-shots to be done by a Swiss photographer in Geneva. I understand that you paint from photos?"

"Yes. Do you know about a Swiss arts agency owned by Alan Verseck?" I inquired.

"Actually, I don't. We work with Peter Randell, an American entrepreneur who lives in Zurich. He owns one of the largest art galleries in Geneva and Zurich," Jim responded.

I accepted Jim's offer and went home to Alex to share the good news. A week after, I started work with Jim's agency, and within four weeks, I was flying back and forth from New York to Geneva and Zurich. Everything was happening so fast, and the future was once again looking bright. My Maasai paintings were being featured on the cover of beaux-arts magazines around the world.

"*You have a terrific career ahead of you for which you should be thankful. Confront the past, deal with it, but don't let it consume you. There are many ways you can heal. If you stay strong and become an international artist, then you can become the voice of so many other Maasai children that have gone through the same experience.*"

Ayan's words often echoed in my mind and somehow gave me the strength and courage to take on this new beaux-arts scene.

The Museum Collections of New York:

During spurts of my free time in New York, I explored the museums of New York City—including the Museum for African Art, the Bronx Museum of the Arts, the Brooklyn Museum of the Arts, the Museum of Modern Art, the Metropolitan Museum of Art, and the New Museum of Contemporary Art. I studied the vast collections of African, American, Asian, European, classical, ancient, Middle Eastern, and Pacific-Asian art.

Once I spent a full, eight-hour workday at the Brooklyn Museum of Art. In the Meyer Schapiro gallery, I studied the vast collections of ancient Egyptian art that displayed collections from the reign of Akhenaten and his wife Nefertiti to the deities of Amun and Mut of the XXV Dynasty. From the famous Brooklyn Museum Black Head of Ptolemaic Period to the galleries that displayed the relics of ancient Egyptian tombs and objects, I marveled at the rich cultural history of the ancient Black African Nubians that built the great pyramids of Egypt. The Brooklyn Museum of Art housed other African art collections, especially from Central and West Africa. I admired the elegant artistry of the likes of the famous Ashanti art of Ghana and the exquisite bronze sculptures of Edo-Benin art of Nigeria.

The paintings, sculptures, photography, and fine arts of European-American origins included the works of George Inness, Singer Sargent, Auguste Rodin, Camille Pissaro, and an unending list of other talented artists.

As I quickly found out, New York was yet another city sprawling with great museum collections that had captivated my artistic mind and focus. Already, I had fallen in love with this city—the Big Apple.

CHAPTER 19

❀

Union of Two Souls

January 1987—Rapture of our Love:

From Switzerland, I returned to New York to work with Rapture Inc. for two straight months, after which I finished my first ever oil-on-canvas painting of the New York skyline, which was featured on the front cover of *Rapture on Paper* art magazine. A week after the magazine issue was published, I received well over fifteen calls from art dealers and agencies from around the world. I was very happy that I was now gradually breaking into the New York art world. Enkai had remained faithful to me, and I thanked Him for the blessings, none of which I ever took for granted.

Still, in the midst of the success of my first works in New York, I was sad and disappointed that I had not heard back from Mama Eshe and Aunt Bela, or even Tulia.

Did they ever receive my letter? I wondered.

All these years, they had always been on my mind, and more recently in the past few months, the longing to hear from them had intensified. I had hoped that they would respond immediately to my letter. I thought I'd meant something to them, especially Mama Eshe. How could she have forgotten the spiritual bond between us? I often wondered. During my quiet moments, I prayed to Enkai and asked him to restore my relationship with Mama Eshe and Aunt Bela.

Still, I was glad to spend quality time with Alex, and he was equally glad to have me at home for a while.

On a very cold Saturday in January 1987, I had been out all day doing routine shopping for the house. I rushed in around 5:30 PM and went straight to the kitchen to start dinner. Alex came into the kitchen shortly afterwards and welcomed me with a warm embrace. He planted a soft kiss on my cheek.

"Honey! Not so fast," he said, as he took the bulb of onion from my hand and set it on the table.

"Honey, I have to start dinner now. I've been out all day. Have you had something to eat today?"

"I'm just fine. First, I would like you to do something for me," he said.

"Sure honey, anything for you, my love," I said, masking my impatience.

"Well then, can you have a shower with me now and afterwards wear my favorite dress and…mmmm." His voice trailed off as he gently pulled me away from the kitchen to the bathroom.

He started to relieve me of the burden of my clothes. In minutes, my tall and lean body stood bare.

I stepped behind the glass doors of the shower, while Alex followed seconds later. Then he captured me into his arms as the warm water from the shower massaged and soothed our bodies. As he lathered me with a soft-scented strawberry soap, my body was threatening to explode with passion. Then, he planted a kiss on my lips and blissfully, I dissolved into his warm embrace.

The bath lasted long enough for the glass door to be steamed up, allowing merely a peek of our entangled bodies to be visualized as a silhouette of two souls in perfect union.

"Oh honey! How nice of you," I started to say when I stepped into our room and saw my gift—an exquisite new dress with a card that read, "Mikela, you're my cherished queen. I love you with all my heart. You are the love of my life."

I put on the beautiful dress that turned out to be a perfect fit.

"I love it! It's absolutely exquisite!" I exclaimed. "You have incredible taste. Oh honey, this is so sweet of you. Thank very much," I said, as tears of appreciation swirled up in my eyes.

I reached out to Alex and hugged and kissed him.

With a flirtatious and mischievous smile, he said, "Honey, if you don't mind, I would like to sit here and watch you doll-up, and it would be my honor to escort you to our patio for a little rendezvous."

I responded with a nod in the affirmative; I was filled with loving warmth and excitement.

Ten minutes later, Alex said I looked even more ravishing wearing a pair of dainty pearl earrings. He said that my make-up was flawless and emphasized the beauty of my eyes and lips. With our arms linked, we both walked towards the patio. My eyes widened in surprise as I saw the meticulously laid-out table complete with a waiter.

"What would I do without my wonderful knight? You're simply marvelous, Alex!"

"Is Beaujolais wine acceptable?" the smartly dressed waiter asked.

"Exquisite!" I responded, as I sipped a taste of it.

Dinner was great. Appetizers started with lemon-spiced shrimp and garlic bread. The main course of chicken curry, Cajun-grilled catfish, baked authentic crab cakes, mixed garden salad, and grilled chicken breasts was delightfully tasty. Dessert was equally exquisite—light Irish coffee cheesecake and the French-Arrabicas coffee.

"Honey, thank you for this wonderful surprise. I loved every bit of it."

"It's not over yet, my love," Alex said, smiling as he got up from his chair, knelt on one knee, and reached inside his pocket for a black jewelry case. My heart started to throb from excitement. I could not believe what I thought was about to happen.

Alex opened the case and took out a diamond ring. I was too excited to figure out how many carats it was.

"Honey, will you be my Maasai Queen forever? Will you marry me?" he asked.

Without hesitation, I said, "Yes! Yes! Honey, I'll marry you."

Tears of joy were streaming down my face as I threw my arms around him.

"Well, Mrs. Mikela Williams to-be, this certainly calls for a celebration," Alex said in an excited voice.

The waiter perfectly timed the start of a love song as Alex swept me into his arms. Together, we celebrated the beginning of what we hoped would be a lasting union of our bodies, souls, and mortal lives.

CHAPTER 20

Haunting Scares

Spring, April 1987:

Three and half months later, Alex and I were married in a quiet ceremony in a non-denominational church near his father's residence. It was a small family affair with less than fifty guests. Alex's mother, Zena said I looked absolutely marvelous in a simple and elegant straight-cut wedding dress designed by Alfred Angelo, the third—an exquisite work of art with a simple, detachable, silky train.

I had my hair pulled back with a trailing veil knotted in a single bow attached neatly to the back of my head. Alex wore a black, double-breasted, four-button tuxedo and a white-collar shirt by Oscar de la Renta. His appearance typified aristocracy and perfectly fit my description of a handsome and dignified African prince. The wedding ceremony was followed by a small reception at Alex's father's home.

"I think we're still missing some folks—the jungle part of the family," Leroy said, as he stood to make a toast to Alex and me.

I was hurt by his comment, but as usual, I maintained my composure. I'd decided that no one was going to ruin my wedding day. Leroy seemed to be a man with so much anger within him, and this was one of his ways of letting off steam, I thought.

Alex had noticed my discomfort. He reached under the table with his left hand and gently took my hand and squeezed it. Then, he slowly leaned over to me and whispered, "I'm very proud of you, honey—always, and I love you with all my heart."

I turned to face him, nodded, and smiled.

I love you, too, my prince," I whispered.

"Leroy, not today please," Zena said, showing her irritation. "Today is a wonderful day for Alex and Mikela. Let's not ruin the day for them, please."

"That was just a joke…I didn't mean any harm," Leroy said sarcastically, smirking at me.

"Okay, I'll deliver the toast," Alex's stepmother, Julia, said, and without waiting to be approved, she immediately began.

"Congratulations to Alex and Mikela for their wonderful union. I wish them wonderful years ahead with the blessed additions of beautiful children in the future. Mikela, we're truly very blessed and happy to have you as family."

The guests applauded and rattled Polish crystal wineglasses.

"Thank you, Julia. Thank you, Mom and Dad. Thank you everyone—you've been so kind," Alex stood up to say.

"Now, I would like to ask my lovely wife for a dance," he continued, as he gestured towards me.

With a beaming smile, he reached out for my hand, and his palm cupped over mine. In an instant, I felt the union of our souls, which Enkai had blessed and sanctified. Again, the guests applauded, rattling their crystal wineglasses.

Alex swept me into his arms, and we slowly stepped to the Rhythm and Blues music. He closed his eyes as my body melted into his, and I followed suit, gently kissing his neck over and over again. For the moment, we both appeared lost in our small world where our love was safely encased in a neat, indestructible, and invisible bubble that was crystallized by our faith in Enkai—the very source of our union.

"I love you, honey," Alex whispered into my ear.

"I love you, too, with all my heart," I said, as I snuggled closer to him, hoping that my body would fuse into his through eternity.

Alex and I spent the night at his father's place in each other's arms, but I still could not bring myself to consummate our marriage. It was hurtful to both of us when I confessed to him that I was not yet ready for that. Despite his obvious disappointment, he whispered encouragingly, "Honey, I promise to wait until you're ready—I plan to wait…I hope I can wait…"

The next morning, we left for our one-week honeymoon trip to the Island of Aruba in the Caribbean Sea, north of Venezuela.

Lurking Demons from the Past Reappear:

We arrived at the Queen Beatrix Airport in Aruba Island, which was seven miles from the Aruba Marriot Resort where we checked in. This was an exquisite, five-star hotel resort that was located on the northwest coast of the island and situated on a Palm Beach which was approximately four miles from the capital of Oranjestad. The resort was elegantly built on six hundred feet of shimmering white sand beach, a perfect setting for our honeymoon vacation.

From the glass-walled elevators, Alex and I had a panoramic view of sprawling fields of cacti in low-lying hills. Once inside our room, the splendor of the ocean was in full view, and the northeastern exposure of the room ensured regular sunshine. Our first evening at the resort started with a delightful traditional three-course dinner set by the sea. A light band was playing calypso in the background, reminding me of my childhood in the Maasaiplains where as children we would gather in the village square during a full moon to eat, sing, and dance.

After dinner, we took a stroll on the beach; the full moon overhead increased the tidal waves, making the roar of the sea on the quiet night most enchanting. I pleaded with Alex that we should spend the night out there in the open, but he would not hear of it, afraid that it might get chilly in the night and that I would catch a cold. Shortly afterwards, we retired to our room and opened the bottle of champagne that was waiting for us.

I slipped into my new turquoise lingerie, a wedding gift from Zena. I'd promised her that I would wear it on the first night of our honeymoon. Alex's bulging chest was exaggerated under a Kimono made of a mixed fabric silk-rayon that he wore with matching boxer shorts. He softened the lights and turned on Barry White's "Never gonna give you up." As Barry's rich, sensuous voice filled the room, Alex slipped into bed beside me, visibly excited by the thought of our first intimate night.

Gently, he started to explore my body with his fingertips and lips. I closed my eyes, letting out little moans of pleasure as he stroked, caressed, massaged, and kissed my back, arms, chest, belly button, and legs. My body was responding to his touch and love-play in a way it had never done before. I was practically on fire with excitement. I wanted him as much as he wanted me. I fondled and caressed him back, kissing him intensely and passionately. As my moans got louder, he reached in between my legs, inserting a finger into my sacred self. I froze—all that passion dissolving in one split second. I started to cry. I thought that I had overcome my fear of sex with the passion I felt during our love play, and it was bitterly disappointing for me to realize that nothing had changed.

"I'm so sorry, honey. I don't think that I can go through with this tonight. Please forgive me. I'm sorry."

"It's me, Mikela, and there's no one else here but me. I'm now your husband; I'm not Chege Mathani or the Maasai women who hurt you when you were a little kid. Honey, can you understand that I've looked forward to this day for so long? I've waited for two years for us to get to this point. Why is it so hard for you to leave the past alone?"

I did not respond; I simply sobbed.

"Honey, it's hard to explain to you what I'm going through," he continued. "I have tried to be there for you. I have tried to be understanding and patient, but I dare say that you have not been as considerate. You are taking me for granted, and I don't know for how much longer I can stand for it." Alex was unmistakably annoyed and irritated, and for the first time, I feared that I might lose him.

When I still did not respond, he got up from the bed and went to the bathroom. I knew he was angry, frustrated, and confused. I so wanted to reach out to him and comfort him, to explain how much I loved him, loved being his wife and wanted to be intimate with him. To tell him it was insane for him to think that I took him for granted and to let him realize that I, too, was hurting from the situation, but I could not move from the bed or find the words to say the things I so deeply felt. So I lay there, afraid and hurting but unable to do anything about it.

A few minutes later, Alex emerged from the bathroom looking calmer and more resigned. He came over to my side of the bed and sat by the edge. Taking my hand in his, he gazed into my eyes for a long time, tears forming in his eyes and slowly trickling down his cheeks. I reached up to wipe the tears, but he shook my hand away, preferring to let the tears flow freely. Finally, he said, "Honey, I just want you to know that there's no pain that is encrusted that cannot be healed. It remains inside of us only if we let it. Open your heart to me and let me help you, please. I beg you."

Alex's words melted my heart. I swallowed hard to stop myself from bawling uncontrollably. There were so many things I wanted to say in response, but I knew that if I started speaking I would start bawling, and it would be hours before I would be able to calm down. So, instead of all the beautiful things that were in my head to say, I only managed to say, "I promise, I'll try."

"Okay. We'll work this out together—okay? That's my own promise," he said, smiling weakly.

I nodded, relieved that he was back to his old self but still afraid that if I did not do something quickly about my situation, I would lose the most wonderful man that had ever walked the face of the earth. I was tired of causing him and myself pain because I could not deal with my past. I silently promised myself to get help as soon as possible. I raised myself halfway on the bed and threw my arms around him, finally allowing myself to bawl loudly. We held each other for a while as he rocked me in his arms and caressed my hair, running his fingers through it.

"I think some air will do us both good," he said after a while, picking me up and carrying me to the patio overlooking the ocean. After planting me safely on the handcrafted bamboo couch, he went back into the room and re-emerged with a bottle of chilled champagne. We sat in silence, deep in thought, sipping our champagne and listening to the crickets and many other sounds of the night around us. I wondered what Alex was thinking of. Perhaps he feared that my mind and body would never be rid of my painful past. Perhaps he was considering leaving me. I shuddered from the thought and quickly erased it from my mind. I was too afraid to even contemplate the possibility of living without Alex.

Finally, Alex broke the silence.

"Honey, we have to see a therapist, psychologist, or whoever can help unchain your mind from the past."

I nodded in agreement, still too emotional to talk. I hated what the lingering effects of my past were doing to our relationship. I knew that Alex didn't deserve me rejecting him. He deserved so much more. He deserved to have all of me. And yet my mind was in chains, and so was my body.

Yes, he's right—the chains must be broken forever. Chege Mathani cannot win. The Maasai tradition of female circumcision won't steal my handsome knight from me. The chains of the past must be broken, I decided.

Still, an Island of Nature's Grace:

Alex and I tried to enjoy what was left of our honeymoon. We went swimming, snorkeling, and bicycle riding, exploring the island's rich flora and fauna. On days we were too tired to cycle, we would take the rainbow-colored Kukoo Kunuku Paranda tour bus into town, shopping for indigenous arts and craft. It was always a delight to watch the locals wave and cheer and the country dogs race us as the bus journeyed through the "Cunucu," or countryside. It reminded me of myself as a child in the Maasailand doing the exact same thing when tourist buses conveying loads of foreigner went through our little village. On the way back from town, we would stop for a swim at the Arashi Beach and a champagne toast at sunset.

Some nights, we would go dancing on the *Tatoo*, a 104-foot catamaran that sailed out from the Aruba Palm Beach Pier—sometimes staying up until four in the morning dancing to a live band that played excellent calypso, reggae, zouk, lambada, and macarena. We stayed away from the casinos because Alex was not particularly interested in the gambling extravaganza spots, but I often wondered what it would be like to play the slot machines and throw dice, so one evening when Alex slept in late, I succumbed to my urge and went. After losing a thousand dollars, my curiosity was quenched.

Even though I enjoyed every single thing we did in Aruba, my best memories were of the dinners. The cuisine, especially the seafood, was always excellent, presenting different but exciting recipes everyday, such as pineapple and coconut shrimp and eel cake and mussel in goat milk sauce. A favorite for Alex and me was the "Honeymoon sauce," a spicy aphrodisiac mixture of fermented vegetables and home grown Madame Jeanette hot peppers served with chicken, fish, or any sea food platter, sheep soup, steak n' chicken, and "Keshi Yena," or stuffed cheese.

Nighttime was, however, the most awkward. Alex consciously avoided touching me in any passionate way. He would not even indulge in foreplay. If I tried to touch him, he would recoil and make some excuse about being tired. I knew he was still hurting from the rejection of the first night, and so I did not push it, even though I longed to have him kiss and caress me. I contented myself with snuggling next to him and sleeping on his powerful chest, silently praying for a resolution to my sexual problems.

We left the beautiful island of Aruba after a fortnight. Despite the excellent time we had, neither the honeymoon sauce, believed to be an aphrodisiac, nor the romantic beaches, nor night sails succeeded in removing the invisible handcuffs that had me chained to the past. One thing was certain at this point: I was eager and ready to seek professional help.

Struggles with the Past Continue:

One week after we arrived home, I made my first appointment to see Dr. Susan Baker to start my psychotherapy sessions. Alex accompanied me to my first appointment.

"Well, hello! Welcome, Alex and Mikela. It is nice to see both of you again. Please, have a seat and make yourselves comfortable."

Once we were situated, Susan asked me how I was feeling.

"Not too good, Susan."

"Well, I'm glad that you've decided to start the therapy sessions. I told you you'd know when you were ready to start the process. Now, concerning your visit today, ordinarily I would have a thirty-minute session with you to get a summary of your history and why you are here, but we will skip this because we went through this when you first visited, and I still have my notes. So, I would suggest we go straight and begin the therapy that I am recommending. For the therapy to be successful, Mikela, I'll need to listen to every single detail of the events that happened to you. Really, I mean every single detail. Unfortunately, some of it may be too painful to bring up, but you must try to remember all of it. That's part of the therapy, to recall and confront the past events that have haunted you for years. Then you must unchain yourself from them as though you had a physical key to the chains. And believe it or not, you do have the key to unlocking your mind from every single painful event of the past that is affecting your present life. You have the power within you to do it, and my job is to help you use that power within you as the tool to free your soul forever from all the pain of the past. Alex may listen in today, but for all future sessions, I would like you to attend alone.

"At the end of the sessions, you should be able to recall the events without feeling self-pity or victimized. You'll become empowered to know that the past has no grip on your future unless you let it. You can then be able to use your inner power to move forward into the future with a positive and healthy soul, a sharp turn from the negative past."

As Alex and I listened to Susan Baker's powerful words, which she delivered with admirable confidence and conviction, something told me that I'd found the perfect person to help me unchain my mind and soul from the horrors of the past.

"Just for you to know, in addition to being a psychotherapist and surgeon, I was once a rape victim myself. So, I know how you feel. I understand the shame, anger, frustration, lack of forgiveness, self-pity, and so on. But all of these are self-defeating emotions because you cannot change what happened to you—but you can overcome the negative effects that it has or can have on you. Mikela, this journey will be between God, you, and me, and no one else. Yes, I'll take you back to Nairobi and the Maasailand and then bring you back.

As we journey together, you may cry and wail—that's fine, that's okay—that's all part of the therapy.

"The good news is that when we are all done and finished, you'll feel much better, and as every day goes by, your inner willpower will become your weapon of defeat against the negative emotions that have plagued you for so many years."

I nodded in acquiescence and forced a smile as Dr. Baker talked.

"And as the days go by, your willpower will get stronger. When we are done with all the sessions and you feel like you're ready to move on, then I'll introduce you to a support group of rape victims, and there you'll complete your healing. Mikela, you're not alone—you were never alone."

Susan stood up and walked around her elegantly designed, rich mahogany desk to the opposite side where Alex and I sat. She perched on the edge of the desk next to me and reached for my hand. Squeezing my hand gently, and staring into my eyes, she smiled and said, "Mikela, you have to trust God, then yourself, and then me—you'll be fine."

"I believe you, Susan," I responded.

To Alex she said, "Alex, thanks for bringing your wife in today. She'll need your support in the days ahead. Not many men are able to be as patient and understanding as you. Mikela is very lucky. If you wish, you may listen in for the remainder of this session or you may leave."

"If it's fine with you, I would like to stay," Alex responded without hesitation.

"Very well, Mikela. I'm ready when you are," Susan said.

Thirty minutes later, my first therapy session had left me completely emotionally exhausted. I dozed off shortly after Alex and I arrived at home, and soon, I found myself in yet another dream world.

CHAPTER 21

❊

The Past Emerges in Manhattan

The Dream:

The first two weeks of my therapy sessions with Dr. Baker had been tough for me. I'd started to have more dreams about Chege Mathani, the Maasai women, and Nadia. In my dreams, I seemed to have flashbacks from the past, as though they'd just occurred yesterday. I still recall one of those dreams vividly.

I was in a dimly lit room in an isolated beach house on a lonely island, and all of a sudden, a large and faceless figure started to attack me. I screamed out loud as I wrestled with the figure.

"No! Please no! Leave me alone! Oh Enkai, please save me," I cried.

"Why me? What have I done?"

"Mikela! Mikela! It's me, Alex. Are you okay?"

Then I woke up and realized that I had been dreaming.

"Someone was trying to hurt me in my dream. I couldn't see their face. I think it was him."

"Who are you talking about?" he asked, perplexed.

"Chege Mathani."

"It's okay—I'm here. No one is going to hurt you while I'm still here," Alex reassured me, as he took me into his comforting arms and kissed my forehead.

"I love you, Mikela," he whispered.

Ten minutes later, I was sleeping peacefully again. These were dreams that I had not had for some time now. Even though Dr. Baker had warned me that this might happen, it was still traumatizing. It was a slow and painful process, but thankfully, I was making progress in a positive direction.

With time, however, things got better, but some sessions still proved harder than others. In all this, Dr. Baker remained patient and supportive, helping me to heal at my own pace. The effectiveness of her therapy was, however, to be tested shortly.

On that particular day, I had just finished my early evening session with Dr. Baker, and to celebrate how well the session had gone that day, having cried far less than usual, I decided to go window-shopping in Manhattan instead of going home directly, as I typically did. I called Alex to inform him.

As I walked into Saks Fifth Avenue, an attendant quickly appeared, welcoming me and inquiring if I needed some help. I shook my head. "No thank you."

Making my way towards the women's suits, I heard voices, one of which had a strong Kenyan accent. I stopped to gauge the direction the voices were coming from. Suddenly, I caught a glimpse of someone from the corner of my eye—and I could have sworn that it was Chege Mathani. I turned quickly to get a better look, but the figure had disappeared into the line of clothing. I felt dizzy with nausea, and I quickly held onto a rack of clothes. The attendant that had welcomed me and had been watching me all along quickly appeared at my side when she noticed my discomfort.

"Ma'am, are you okay?"

"Yes, thank you, I'm fine," I responded, struggling to regain my composure.

Meanwhile, I heard the voices again, and this time they were louder and seemed to be coming in my direction. I became visibly terrified as the male voice became more distinct, sounding more surely like Chege Mathani's.

"Ma'am, are you sure you're fine? Do you need help?" the attendant asked again in a slightly panicked voice.

Before I could respond to her question, a man wearing a brown tweed jacket, a black pair of pants, and a cream-colored shirt appeared in full view. There was no mistaking the fact now that it was Chege Mathani, flanked by Lily, the Kenyan still art model that I'd met with Jim at a Manhattan restaurant.

"Hello Mikela, what a surprise," Lily said.

I stared at Lily, still holding the rack and unable to say a word.

Oblivious of my discomfort, Lily continued chatting. "Mikela, it's nice to see you again. Meet Chege Mathani, a friend of mine. He's just been appointed the Kenyan Ambassador to the United Nations. Chege, meet Mikela—she's a gorgeous Maasai artist that I met recently through my agent, Jim. Mikela is a freelance artist. In fact, she's doing some freelance work for Jim as well," Lily explained.

I felt the blood drain from my face, and I staggered slightly, losing my balance for a second. I must have looked like I'd seen a ghost. The attendant was puzzled by my obvious distress, but she did not want to interfere in the ensuing conversation so she quietly slipped away. I struggled for words to speak, but my lips remained shut. I was completely frozen—my mind gripped with a fear I had not known since my time in the Mathani residence.

Chege Mathani appeared unnerved by my presence. He smiled at Lily as he reached towards me, his right hand outstretched for a handshake.

"Well, nice to meet you, Mikela," he said, grinning sarcastically.

I made no effort to take his hand, unable to bear the thought of making physical contact with him, no matter how slight. Besides, I feared that if I took my hand off the rack, I would slump to the floor from shock.

Realizing that I was never going to present my hand for a handshake, Chege withdrew his hand and said, "You're right, Lily, she's a looker."

"Mikela! Are you okay?" Lily asked, ignoring Chege's remark and finally noticing that there was something wrong.

Oh God, please help me—Enkai, please help me, I prayed silently.

Bile gushed up my throat, and I swallowed hard to force it back down.

"Mikela, you've not said a word yet. Are you okay?" Lily asked again.

Finally, I managed to force some words out.

"Lily, it's nice to see you again. I'm fine, just a bit dizzy from too much shopping."

"Can we help anyone find anything?" a shop attendant said, interrupting the moment.

"Actually, yes. I'm looking for a navy blue Jaeger suit," I said, grateful for the interruption.

"I'll be glad to find one for you, ma'am—this way please," the attendant responded.

"Lily, I'll see you at Jim's office next week. Sorry, I have to run," I muttered, finally plying myself off the clothes rack and rushing after the attendant.

My Cry for Courage:

Seeing Chege Mathani had turned into a nightmarish event for me. I'd taken two bathroom breaks at Saks Fifth Avenue, and each time I'd vomited. Finally, I acknowledged to the attendant that I was not feeling very well and requested a cab. By the time I arrived at home, I was a nervous wreck. My eyes were swollen, and my hands were still trembling.

Alex was lying on the living room couch watching television when I walked in. He took one look at me and immediately jumped to my side.

"Honey! What happened?" he asked.

I slumped into his arms and started sobbing.

"Alex, I saw him—I saw him! I hate him! I absolutely hate his guts!"

"Honey, who did you see? Tell me—what are you talking about? Hate whose guts?"

"I saw Chege Mathani in Manhattan. I saw him at Saks Fifth Avenue with Lily, the Kenyan model that I met with Jim," I explained.

"Oh my God!" Alex exclaimed.

"Lily introduced him as the new Kenyan Ambassador to the United Nations. This means that he lives right here in New York. I can't believe what's happening. Alex, I can't live that nightmare again," I said, as I cried hysterically.

"Shhhhhh...it's okay for now. Honey, calm down...it's going to be fine. Chege Mathani can't hurt you again—not while I'm still alive," Alex said, as he gently caressed me.

"It was obvious that after all these years, he still has no remorse about what he did to me," I said. "He seems to have carried on with his life like nothing happened. His career has been going well...all these years I have suffered.... This is not fair! No! No! It's simply not fair," I cried.

"Honey, this is why you must fight within you to overcome the negative emotions. Chege Mathani does not deserve to have you live the rest of your life in misery. He's a damned SOB. He's simply a piece of scum...don't you see?" Alex responded. "Here, let's sit for a moment."

Alex cuddled me closer in his arms, drawing me towards the couch.

"It's not over, Mikela. One day, you'll have the courage to face Chege Mathani and tell him that he tried to destroy you but didn't succeed. Honey, that will be your triumph."

"I thought I should be able to do that now after eleven weeks of therapy," I cried, very worried that the therapy was a failure after all.

"Don't worry, my dear. I am sure your therapy is going fine. The shock of seeing Chege without any warning was just too much for you to take now, but I am sure that if you were to have a second encounter with him, you would do so much better. But you may feel better calling Dr. Baker and discussing it with her," Alex replied.

I called Dr. Baker shortly afterwards, and as Alex predicted, she was not concerned about my reaction, believing it to be a natural first response. Like

Alex, she was confident that subsequent meetings with Chege would go so much better.

Nature's Soothing Warmth:

An hour later, I lay in the bathtub with Alex, relishing the soothing effect of warm bubbles in a perfumed bath.

"Honey, you are right about what you said earlier. I simply can't allow any events of the past to keep me bound anymore. If Ayan or Nadia were alive today, they would want me to live my life as if I had only one more day. I'm now determined more than ever to let go of the past. I'm determined to purge my soul of the bad memories of the past. Honey, with the grace that I know Enkai has given me, I plan to free my soul forever!"

"Now, that's my sweetheart—that's the true spirit of my Maasai Queen," Alex responded, kissing me softly on the neck. "I love you, Mikela. I love you with all my heart."

"Alex, you are the love of my life. Everyday, I thank Enkai for you."

I went to bed somewhat relieved but still worried about Chege living so close to me.

The Daily Struggle Continued:

During the next few weeks, Susan Baker's techniques seemed to be working. Gradually, I started talking freely about what had happened to me with other members of a support group for rape victims. I had the opportunity to listen to other women who had been traumatized, and I felt free to cry and vocalize how I hated Chege Mathani for what he had done to me. Dr. Baker told me that I must learn to forgive Chege Mathani, if I wanted to heal completely, but for now, that seemed virtually impossible.

To my surprise, as the weeks went by, I also started to feel comfortable talking about my experience of female circumcision with members of my support group. Although the pain of how Nadia died was still inside me, I was now fueled with new courage and determination not to be bound by it any longer. Gradually, I felt like I was stepping away from the past and embracing the life ahead of me more wholly and boldly.

Alex was also noticing the positive changes occurring in me. At home, I had started to initiate love play, something I'd never done before. Once, I even allowed Alex to explore my most intimate body parts and willingly listened to him talk about my lovely sensuality.

But it was not until six months after I started therapy sessions with Dr. Susan Baker that Alex and I finally made love for the first time. It was a night I would never forget. It had started like any other ordinary evening. We had ordered a Mexican takeaway for dinner, both of us feeling too tired to cook. As we ate and drank wine, we told each other how our day had gone and joked about the funny things that had occurred. The effect of the wine was beginning to take its toll on me, and I started to flirt with Alex over the dinner table, making romantic overtures and talking dirty. Unable to bear my taunting anymore, Alex reached across the table and grabbed me, and in no time, we were on the floor of the dining area wrestling each other. I managed to extricate myself from the floor and ran into our bedroom, with Alex in hot pursuit. We both collapsed on the bed, giggling like two teenage lovebirds in heat. As our passion heightened, Alex reached to touch my sacred self. Then, as if suddenly remembering, he stopped. I whispered for him to continue, but he was hesitant, perhaps afraid of another rejection. So, I took his hand and slowly led him to my inner self, allowing him to continue the rest.

Alex became more confident as he saw that I was not pushing him away, and in no time, he was on top of me, thrusting gently at first but more urgently later. I began to moan loudly, my body soaked in sweat. Suddenly, I started to feel my whole body tingle with unimaginable excitement, my inner self throbbing almost violently. I started to wriggle beneath Alex, hoping to prolong this magical feeling I was having. My wriggling must have excited Alex the more because he, too, began to shudder, his whole body twitching uncontrollably. Shortly afterwards, with a loud cry, he came inside me, filling me with an exhilarating sensation that I'd never before experienced. Alex confessed that this was the best love making he had ever had, which somehow made all the waiting worthwhile. For him, it felt like heaven on earth, he had said.

Finally, we would consummate our marriage after two years and six months. Lying in each other's arms, we knew that we'd just untangled the first chains of female circumcision and rape that had wrapped up my mind and body for so many years. That night, we went to sleep like two turtledoves that had found a lost treasure. For now, we were content with the beauty of today's love and our renewed hope for a brighter tomorrow.

CHAPTER 22

A New Trail

June 1987:

As the months went by, the love that Alex and I had for each other grew even stronger. We were like two lovebirds with an insatiable appetite for one another. To make it even better, my career had also reached remarkable crescendos. It appeared that overnight I'd become the premier modern-day African artist in Europe and the United States.

It seemed that more fame and fortune had crossed my path than I'd ever dreamed possible. Looking back to where I'd come from and where I was now all seemed like a transition that was beyond reality. Who would have thought that the life of a Tanzanian Maasai *entito* would have turned around so beautifully?

Alex graduated from engineering school with honors and was now working for an engineering firm, and I decided to start taking evening and weekend classes towards getting a college degree. With all of my success so far, I still yearned for a college degree; no one in my family had ever gone to school, much less college, and I wanted to be the first educated Maasai woman from our *enkang*. This, I hoped, would one day inspire other Maasai women to pursue their life's goals, including getting educated. I planned to attend law school in the near future.

In the meantime, we decided that it was time to move out of the Bronx and buy a new home in upstate New York. We found the house of our dreams in Long Island—a luxurious and remodeled home that was nicely hidden in a cluster of trees, shrubs, and flowers and situated by a man-made lake that was the home of wild ducks and swans. It was a ten-bedroom home that had a grand travertine entry delineated by classic columns that led to an expansive living and dining room decorated with Victorian Age artistry and a dramatic and spacious fireplace. It had a four-car garage outside that was adjacent to an indoor plant and flower garden.

We decided to decorate the walls of the grand atrium and some of the rooms with exquisite works of African artists. The bathroom in the master bedroom boasted of handcrafted marble paraphernalia with a spa-tub and decorative wall mirrors, creating a romantic oasis of elegant design.

The lake was one of my favorite early evening spots. I would sit by the edge of its water and feed the hungry ducks breadcrumbs while I read a book or magazine. It was also a sanctuary of escape from the hustle and bustle of my life's daily activities. It was during my quiet moments by the lake that I would sometimes think about my mother. It had been so many years since I'd last seen her, and lately I'd started to think that it was time to forgive her for Nadia's death, our ordeal with female circumcision, and whatever wrong I felt she'd done.

A Note from my Guardian Light:

I came home one day from my usual Manhattan daily schedule and was surprised to find a letter from Mama Eshe waiting for me. I was excited and eager to read the long awaited response, although a little apprehensive, since I was not sure of what I would find inside it.

Why did it take her so long to respond to my letter? I wondered, as I picked up the letter and took it with me to the lakeside. I spread a mat beneath my favorite tree by the edge of the water and started to read Mama Eshe's letter.

My darling Mikela:

It has been so many years since I last saw you. I received your letter a while back, but I must admit, at that time, I was shocked by the content of the letter and could not get myself to believe it. I felt that I knew Chege well enough that I believed that he could never have done such an awful thing to you or anyone else. I shared the letter with Aunt Bela, and she, too, was very upset and felt betrayed by you. Anyway, we decided to ignore your letter and never asked Chege about the rape incident that you alleged.

Bela hired a new nanny shortly afterward—a fifteen-year-old Kikuyu girl that had lived in the village for most of her life. She was young and naïve but beautiful, just like you were. Nine months later, Bela discovered that she was pregnant. The girl told her that Chege had raped her repeatedly, and she had been too afraid to tell anyone. The baby boy was born seven months later, and the doctor confirmed that he was Chege's son. Bela and I were shocked and devastated. Then we realized that what you had written in your letter had been the truth.

The laws could not touch Chege because as a professional diplomat, they said he had immunity from prosecution. Also, his lawyer was able to convince the judge that the relationship between Chege and the Kikuyu girl had been concentual. He had the right connections to cover up the case, and Aunt Bela was too emotionally drained to continue to pursue the case further. Instead, she opted to file for divorce.

I finally decided to write you and apologize for not believing your story. Now, I understand why you felt the need to run away from Bela's home—no one would have believed your story then, not even I. All I can say is that I'm so sorry for everything that happened to you in Bela's home. You were a young, innocent, and beautiful girl with a great heart, and you had no one to protect you from the horrible things that Chege did to you. Bela and I would like to say that we are sorry for everything.

You might want to know that Bela and Chege are now separated and finalizing their divorce. Bela, God bless her heart, adopted the little baby boy because her young mother could not afford to take care of him. Bela and the kids spent six months with me in Mombassa, but now she lives in South Africa with the kids where she works as Chief News Correspondent with an international news agency. She's doing very well. I plan to visit them in three months time——that will be my very fourth trip to South Africa. Should you want to write her, I have included her address.

As for Chege, I hear that he is now the Kenyan Ambassador to the United States and lives in a New York suburb—I'm not sure where exactly he is. I must confess that I have spent all my time and energy in helping Bela and the kids to start a new life. I really don't know much about Chege anymore. I pray that he does not do to another woman what he did to you and the Kikuyu girl. I think that Bela is still in communication with him because of the kids. After all, she says, he's still their father, and they love him dearly.

I have said so much already. Please take care of yourself. I pray that I'll see you, my little angel, again soon. When next you are in Kenya, please come and see me in Mombassa. I miss you very much and love you dearly.

> By the way, Bela and I have forgiven you for telling us that you are an orphan——we understand how the burden must have been too much for you to bear at the time.
>
> Love,
>
> Mama Eshe

I placed the letter on my chest, close to my heart. Suddenly, I felt exonerated, relieved, and vindicated from Chege Mathani. I shouted and raised my hands to the skies at the same time, "Marahaba Enkai! Marahaba Mama Eshe! Marahaba Aunt Bela!"

Chege Mathani was paying for what he had done to the Kikuyu girl and to me in a different way—he'd lost Aunt Bela forever and the comfort of a nice family.

Now, I felt that Mama Eshe's letter had opened up a new path for me to begin exploring the possibility of a visit back home. I stayed in communication with her and Aunt Bela.

Two years later, I received my college degree in communications and passed the qualifying exam to attend St. John's University Law School. My career as an artist remained my foremost passion, and my paintings continued to sell worldwide.

Law School—Another Stepping Stone:

Attending law school at St. John's University was both tedious and exciting, and it was certainly a new world for me. I was very studious, but at the same time, I was involved in many social activities. As a freshman, I joined an international student association that promoted human civil rights worldwide. As a member of this association, I started a subcommittee that focused on educating people on the horrors of female circumcision and the violence of rape.

For our first international conference on female circumcision, I became a lead member of the regional sub-committee that reviewed papers and posters sent in by interested speakers and participants. One of the papers caught my attention. It was from an Egyptian lady that worked with an international non-governmental organization that focused on gender equality and anti-female circumcision issues. I immediately recognized her name—Aisha Mohammed, the Egyptian lady that I'd read about in Paris. She was the lady that had chosen to undergo female circumcision in order to marry an Arab Prince who had later died in a plane crash before the marriage could take place. I was eager to meet Aisha—and I did shortly afterwards.

A Memorable Meeting:

Aisha and I had a lunch date two days before the conference started. She was a petite and soft-spoken, light-skinned lady who looked more Mediterranean than Egyptian. She was well spoken and clearly very educated. When I informed her that I'd read about her story, she smiled and said, "It's quite a story, isn't it?"

I nodded. "All of our life stories are unique in some way," I responded cautiously. "We are all a manifestation of our different destinies and destinations."

I spent the next twenty minutes telling Aisha about my own experience of female circumcision in the Maasailand and the death of my sister, Nadia. She listened and nibbled at her food at the same time. When I was finished, she looked up at me and said, "Mikela, there's something about your spirit that tells me that you are going to do greater things for so many in need—I mean the poor, the heart-broken, and the down trodden. Something tells me that I'm sitting with a true Maasai Queen, and I'm not sure if you know it yourself. I'm glad that you'll be one of the speakers at the conference. Our group also invited the Kenyan Ambassador to the United Nations, Mr. Chege Mathani, to chair the conference."

I froze when I heard the name.

"We just learned yesterday that he finally accepted our invitation to attend the conference. Previously, he was unsure about attending, which is why the international committee didn't advertise his name in the conference manual, newsletter, and flyers. We are quite happy that he'll be there," Aisha explained, completely oblivious to the emotions that had erupted within me.

"Mikela, do you know him?" Aisha asked.

"Yes, sort of—I have met him," I stuttered, staring blankly into my drink to avoid any eye contact with her.

"Well, he's a very well respected diplomat who's had a very prolific career. I met him at an international conference session on 'Widows' in Zurich, Switzerland. He's an intellectual and a man who has compassion for the young, weak, and the defenseless," Aisha said. "His effort has been a banner of hope for many young women like you."

When she said this, I stared at her and swallowed hard, forcing the liquid I was drinking down my throat.

"I'm looking forward to the conference," I finally managed to say.

It was a welcome change in our conversation when Aisha started talking about the foundation that she'd started, which was now campaigning against female circumcision around the world.

"We provide money to rural enclaves for mass literacy and education about the horrific practice of female circumcision. Actually, we've made impressive inroads into many rural areas in Africa and the Middle East, and in some cases, we have helped in stopping the practice of female circumcision," she explained.

"I would like to become a member of your foundation," I said, trying to focus. "We can also raise money here to help educate the Tanzanian Maasai to stop female circumcision. It has always been my dream to start a campaign against female circumcision at home, where the tragedies of my past happened and my life's journey started."

She smiled, obviously delighted that I was interested in her organization.

"Aisha, I'm finally ready to face my past with bold courage. I'm ready to be the voice of Nadia and Ayan and every Maasai young girl that has died from female circumcision. Until I speak for them, I will feel like their voices have remained unheard and their pain has been in vain."

"Mikela, I'm glad that you've reached this point. It's a point that everyone who's carrying a painful burden must reach. It is a point of strength and courage. I reached that point a while back myself, and when I did, all I could say was, until today, I have not harnessed the power of God within me to face my challenges and gain control and victory over them.

"From that day, I made the decision to lean on God's power for my daily strength, and since then, my challenges have transformed into stepping stones of triumph, and my past has become only a reason for the present—and maybe the future," Aisha said.

"I agree with you, Aisha. I, too, have since made the decision to use God's awesome grace, might, and power as a lamp unto my feet when everywhere around me seems to be enveloped in darkness."

The Day of the Conference:

The day of the conference arrived, and I still had not told Alex that Chege Mathani was going to be there. It was not that I was hiding this from Alex; I was going through so much emotional upheaval inside. I was also afraid that he might stop me from going to the conference all together, so I decided I would tell him at some point during the conference.

As we prepared to get into the car, Alex gave me compliments that boosted my ego and confidence.

"Honey, that's an exquisite dress; I like the style. Where did you find it?" he asked, undressing me with his eyes.

"My favorite shopping place—Saks Fifth Avenue; it's made by a French designer."

He nodded. "It's really nice. I remember these, too," he said, gently caressing the fresh, water-cultured pearl necklace that I was wearing.

"Every time I wear this pearl set, I remember when you bought it for me. I love it."

"I'm glad you do, honey. It looks great on you…and with the dress…beautiful!"

"Thank you, honey. I love it when you compliment my taste, and you look very nice…I like your tux."

"Thanks," he said. "Are you ready?"

I nodded. "Yes, I am."

Shortly afterwards, we arrived at the Manhattan hotel ballroom. The ballroom was an elegantly decorated room, with hanging crystal chandeliers and walls that were richly adorned with what seemed like re-prints of classical paintings in gold-trimmed, glass frames.

We must have looked exquisite because people stopped to stare as Alex and I walked in hand in hand.

A chaperon came to ask for our names and led us to a front table directly facing the podium, where some of the guests of honor were already seated. The slight commotion to get us seated caught Aisha's attention, where she was seated next to Chege Mathani. She waved at me from where she sat at the left side of the podium. I responded with a smile and a nod and quickly looked away.

"Alex, I'd like to go to the ladies' room. I'll be right back," I said, a few minutes later.

As I walked across the hall towards the exit, I felt Chege Mathani's eyes trailing me until I disappeared behind the exit double doors.

"Excuse me, please, which way is it to the ladies' room?" I asked a uniformed hotel chaperone.

"Ma'am, this way please. Just take this elevator to the next floor and turn right once you exit the elevator. The ladies' room is the first door to your left."

As soon as I walked into the ladies' room, I slumped into a chair and buried my face in my hands.

How can I get through this night? I thought. *How can I deliver this speech looking Chege Mathani right in the eye? This was the man who raped me when I was just a child. Oh God, please help me. Enkai! I ask your help. I have to tell Alex that he is here.*

Moments later, when I regained my composure, I headed back to the lift. When the door opened, a lady stepped out, and to my shock, Chege Mathani emerged from behind her. I could not believe my eyes. Stomach fluid rushed up my throat and for a moment, I thought I was going to vomit. I held onto the doors, and it seemed like for the first few seconds, my feet were frozen and glued to the ground. I could not lift them off the floor.

"Are you going down, Mikela?" Chege asked, displaying his characteristic smirk.

After what seemed like an endless moment, I saw myself lifting my feet off the ground and stepping into the lift. As weird as it seemed, I was stepping into an enclosed space with a man that had raped me, and I could not understand why.

The doors slowly shut, and for a minute, I was locked in the small space with Chege Mathani. Flashes of my rape experience in the study room and kitchen of the Mathani home went through my mind. At that instant, I felt like running, but at the same time, my feet refused to move.

"So, I see that you've blossomed into the ravishing beauty that I always thought you would. You know that I discovered you first, before the rest of the world," he said, leaning closer to me. "Who's that gentleman next to you—is he having the taste of my leftovers?"

When his words hit my ears, anger boiled up inside me, and I suddenly felt that I needed to stand up to Chege Mathani. If I ran from him again, then I would have set myself back in my recovery process. Besides, I needed to tell Chege Mathani that he may have bullied me in the past, but that was then. A new Mikela had emerged; I was no longer afraid of him. As these thoughts went through my mind, I felt a string of words coming from me.

"You despicable scum of the earth. You piece of trash. You deceive the world with your fake charm, but one day, the world would know the evil that lives in you."

Chege smiled and started to say, "I'm not the Maasai trash—" when the elevator door opened, and I stormed out.

My brief and close encounter with Chege had, for the first time, stirred up a different kind of anger inside of me. I felt like it was the kind of anger that made one want to fight against injustice and win, not the self-destructive anger that will chew up your insides or give you a victim mentality. I felt a conquering anger—one that lets you recognize the strength of the power within you, one that can move mountains when merged with holy faith.

I walked back to my seat with renewed courage to deliver the best speech of my life and to become an active member of the world against rape in addition to female circumcision. I leaned over to Alex and said, "He's here—that dirtball is here."

"Who? What are you talking about?" Alex asked, confused.

"Chege Mathani—he's the keynote speaker of this conference. That's him, there on the podium seated next to the lady to the left—that's Aisha Mohammed, the Egyptian lady that I read about in Paris."

"My goodness!" Alex exclaimed. "Honey, this is the time to expose him. This is the time to tell the world what this man did to you…what he's really like."

"Alex, I'm not sure I can say what Chege did to me in front of all these people. Today is not only about me; it's about Nadia, Ayan, and many others. Today, I'm finally going to purge my spirit of the past, and I'll speak for Nadia, Ayan, and every Maasai *entito*. I'll speak for young girls and women all over the world. As for Chege Mathani, Enkai will take care of him at his appointed time," I said.

The conference started officially about ten minutes later. Chege Mathani delivered his speech shortly after introductions and opening speeches were made.

"I must commend the effort of everyone here for this international conference on female circumcision," he began. "This is a tradition that maims so many innocent young women and ravages their emotions forever. In Kenya, we have the rural Maasai who still practice female circumcision—it remains to date an arduous task for our government to educate and stop them from continuing the tradition of female circumcision. Personally, I come from a family of respectful and decent people and cringe at the very thought of any kind of violation of women, let alone children."

At this point, Chege turned toward Alex and me and loosened his face into a sardonic smirk. Purposely, he seemed to stare directly into my eyes.

"To end the practice of female circumcision or any other form of violence against women, we need the collective effort of people like you and many more in the world. I would like to say that it's indeed a great honor for me to be here today. Thank you."

The audience gave him a standing ovation. Once again, he turned to look at me.

Minutes later, he said, "And, we're quite glad to introduce one of our guest speakers, the famous international and renowned African artist, Mrs. Mikela Williams."

Alex, squeezed my hand and whispered, "I love you, honey."

As I took the microphone from Chege Mathani, I stared right into his eyes.

"I'm no longer afraid of you, Chege Mathani," I mouthed.

He turned away.

"Good evening ladies and gentlemen. I must say that it's quite an honor for me to be speaking with rather distinguished guests from all walks of life. I would like to thank the conference committee for their very kind invitation to me. Also, I would like to thank my husband, Alex Williams, who is here with me and who has been very supportive of me over the years."

Alex nodded in recognition and smiled.

"While I'm happy to be here as a speaker, I must also admit that some of my past experiences, which contributed to my being here today, were not happy events."

As I spoke, I alternated between gazing at the audience and at Chege Mathani. I wanted him to get the message that I was no longer scared of him.

"Over the years, traditional cultures like the Maasai have continued to practice female circumcision. They have justified this ritual despite the fact that it leaves lifetime emotional and physical scars on women. They believe that it's desirable for female hygiene and that it preserves a woman's virginity by lessening pre-marital sexual desires, thus raising the value of a woman. None of these reasons were enough justification for what happened to my twin sister, Nadia, my best friend, Ayan, so many others, and myself. Some of the young girls that I mention are not here today and will never walk the face of this earth again. This is because they died at the brutal hands of female circumcision. It is for them and many more that I'm here today. It is them that I represent.

"Due to the nature of female circumcision, some people now refer to it as 'genital mutilation.' Female circumcision is a ritual that has occurred for many centuries, not only in the Tanzanian Maasailand but also in other rural parts of Africa, Asia, South America, and the Middle East. In many of these cultures, girls ranging from infants to the age of thirteen first go through circumcision of the clitoris, and then at a later age, infibulation, when the vaginal lips are stitched together, leaving only a small opening for urination and menstruation. In the Maasai culture, as Nadia and I experienced at the age of thirteen, the girls go through both circumcision and infibulation at the beginning of the age of puberty or shortly before marriage, depending on their parents' wish.

It's quite common during the ritual of circumcision not to have anesthesia or any pain-numbing drug. Nadia and I didn't.

"The first step could be 'clitorectomy,' or complete removal of the clitoris. This usually involves cutting off the clitoral head as well as the 'prepuce' or clitoral hood, the labia minora, and part of the entrance into the vaginal opening. The clitoris has four distinct parts. The 'glans' or the head is the only visible part of the clitoris and is covered by a hood. Below the clitoris head and under the skin is the shaft or body and below this spread the crura, or two wings. The body and the wings are attached to the pubic bone. The clitoral hood may cover the clitoris completely, or the clitoris may project from the hood." I paused for a moment, glancing around the room.

"I apologize if I am being a bit too graphic for your comfort. However, I feel like I must describe the female parts in clear detail for members of this audience to fully appreciate what it must feel like to have such an intricate part of who you are cut off in the name of tradition."

I went on to deafening silence in the audience. I could see that my words were piercing their hearts. Many had teary eyes while others maintained a frown or looks of shock and disgust.

"The experience of female circumcision was the direct cause of my twin sister Nadia's death and indirectly the cause of my best friend, Ayan's death. They are by no means the only victims of female circumcision because there are many more, and there'll be even more if we don't stop this tradition.

"My own story continued after Nadia's death. I ran away from home and was picked up by a stranger—a kind woman who gave me a place to stay in Mombassa, Kenya. Later, she sent me to Nairobi to work as a nanny. There, I was raped twice by the master of the house—first when I was fourteen and again at the age of sixteen."

As I recounted my past experiences, I kept my gaze in the direction of Chege Mathani.

"Today, I'm here to speak on behalf of Nadia, Ayan, and other deceased children whose voices cannot be heard from their graves. I'm here to speak for the children who are going through female circumcision today and the unborn children who may someday go through it, if we don't stop the tradition. The saying goes that the truthful voice of the people is the voice of God. I believe that the collective voices of truth represent God's opinion. Therefore, I implore all of you to please speak up against female circumcision. Speak for Nadia, Ayan, and every child whose life has withered like a flower before its blossom. I implore every one of you to also join hands and fight against the molestation of children and women. Thank you, and may God bless you all."

The standing ovation for me seemed to last almost five minutes. It was obvious that I had delivered a speech that touched the hearts of the audience. At that moment, I felt that I had made Nadia and Ayan proud of me.

As I waited for the applause to wane, my eyes scanned through the audience like a laser beam and finally, I rested my cold gaze on Chege Mathani for what seemed like an eternity. This time, he looked away.

The applause from the audience went on as if it would never end. I turned to look in the direction where Alex was seated. He caught my glance, winked, blew a kiss at me, and mouthed, "I love you, my beautiful Maasai Queen."

I could see in Alex's eyes his utmost respect and love for me.

"Honey, you're truly a phenomenal woman," Alex said to me as I took my seat next to him again. "You're truly a Maasai Queen—a woman of solid and impeccable substance. I love you with all my heart. Your victory today is already Chege Mathani's shame. He didn't succeed in destroying you. Here you are still standing and waxing strong. I'm very proud of you, my love."

The conference was well attended, with more than three hundred participants. Over fifty women presented their horrific stories on their individual experiences of female circumcision, and others talked of how they had been sexually exploited in other circumstances. Quite a few men presented their wives' experiences after having undergone female circumcision. It was both an educational and emotional experience for most people in the audience. The proponents of female circumcision received little or no applause. The audience was largely in favor of complete eradication of female circumcision.

Alex and I got home about nine thirty that evening. I felt at peace with myself for the first time in a long time, and I knew that it was time to finally put to rest the ghost of Chege Mathani. Although I knew that the United States laws had no jurisdiction over the Nairobi suburbs where Chege Mathani raped me, I picked up the phone and dialed 9-1-1 to report the incident that happened years ago. I just felt the need to finally report the incident to a law enforcement agency.

"Good evening," I said to the voice on the other end, "my name is Mikela Williams, and I would like to report a rape…"

In the Spirit of Nadia and Ayan:

In four weeks, the international organization had raised more than $50,000 for the anti-female circumcision campaign in the Tanzanian Maasailand. Work was already underway there through Aisha's group, which had initiated massive campaigns there. I was not sure how successful the campaign was going to be, but I was glad that I'd taken the first steps toward helping to end the tradition.

I hoped that my first steps were merely the beginning of my personal crusade and campaign against female circumcision and rape. Next year, I planned to visit the Maasailand with Alex to see my mother. It would be my first trip back home since I'd run away and Alex's first trip to Africa.

"I'm coming home, Ma—I'm coming home to see you," I whispered under my breath.

The telephone ringing interrupted these thoughts. I ran to answer it, and my heart sank as I listened to the officer on the other end telling me that the police could not continue investigations or prosecutions on my rape allegations, as Mr. Mathani was a diplomat and thus had immunity from prosecution in the United States.

I dropped the phone and could not contain my anger. I started smashing things around the house. I could not believe that this man was going to get away with everything he had done to me because of a technicality. I finally calmed down and did the only thing I could do—I prayed. I asked Enkai to take control of the situation and avenge me. I poured out my heart to Him and asked him to grant me peace if He would not avenge me. After about an hour of intense praying, I felt better, and strangely, I had a feeling that everything would be fine in a short while.

CHAPTER 23

An Emotional Return

It was time for my long awaited trip back home. It was time for me to physically embrace the past, purge my spirit and soul, and return to the Tanzanian Maasailand where my journey first began. I had left my homeland powerless and in fear, but I was returning with strength, courage, and the power of Enkai richly seeded within my spirit and soul. It had been a journey of simple faith that had withstood the ups and downs of life—a journey of innocence that overcame evil in a quiet and subtle manner. My strength to pull through life's challenges was now solidly built within me, and I was standing on my faith in Enkai as I'd never before in my life. This was why I could finally embark on the trip to the Tanzanian Maasailand without anger or malice but with hopeful anticipation that the spiritual bond I had with my mother remained intact.

Yes Ma, I'm coming home to rekindle the power of your unconditional love for me; and with me is the love of my life, my handsome knight, Alex.

August 1988—The Journey Back to the Beginning:

It had been more than ten years since I'd left the Maasailand. I had no idea if my parents were still living. However, the radiant images of my mother, Halima, never left my memory during the many years that I was gone from the Tanzanian Maasailand. The hurt, pain, and confusion I'd felt after Nadia's death had been with me for too long, and my journey back to the Maasailand was meant to bring a final closure to the past.

Now, at the age of twenty-three, I'd become a very mature young woman and was in the first month of the initial trimester of my pregnancy. Also, I'd graduated from St. John's University Law School and passed the New York Bar in July of 1988. One month later, Alex and I were on board the first class cabin of a Kenyan Airline's flight to Nairobi.

Alex was as excited as a little kid—this was his very first trip to Africa. Though he had traveled widely in Europe and Asia, he'd never even thought of setting foot on the African soil that was his ancestral home. Had he not met me, he probably never would have thought about going to Africa, he admitted. He also admitted that it had taken him a while to get rid of the negative cloud that his father had reared in his mind about Africa and Africans.

As the plane glided at a very low altitude over Nairobi, we could finally see the Jomo Kenyatta International Airport in full view, and my heart started pounding. It suddenly dawned on me that I was getting closer to home. I started feeling anxious, scared, and exhilarated. At about five in the evening, Nairobi local time, Alex and I arrived at the Jomo Kenyatta International Airport, 13 kilometers southeast of the city. The plane taxied on the runway to its designated arrival gate. It had been a long flight—almost fourteen hours—and both Alex and I were glad when it was finally over.

Uneventfully and quickly, we went through the immigration services, and within an hour, we were seated in an airport cab going to the Nairobi Hilton five-star hotel. Among our choices of five-star hotels, such as The New Stanley, Inter-Continental, and Nairobi Serena, we had chosen the Hilton simply because of its international reputation and panoramic view of the city of Nairobi.

Settled in our hotel room, from the heights of the Hilton, Alex was preoccupied with taking snapshots of the city. He'd never thought that Africa had developed cities like Nairobi, with skyscrapers and paved, dual carriage roads. His lessons on Africa had always started with the animals in the jungle or safaris and ended with nude bodies that trailed the paths of what seemed like endless countryside.

After a relaxing bath and rest, we decided to visit the Le Chateau Inter-Continental Hotel roof top restaurant, where we had a very nice meal of mixed Kenyan, European, and Asian cuisine. From there, we made a quick stop at the Coffee Bar on Mama Ngina Street.

By the time we headed back to the Hilton on our first night, the refreshing coolness of a typical Nairobi evening was now quickly turning into a cold and crisp night. The beauty of the city of Nairobi pleasantly surprised Alex. The warmth, kindness, and courtesy of the Kenyans were also a marvel to him. At first, he was convinced that everyone knew him because of the warm greetings.

Jokingly, he said, "Honey, I feel like my brothers here still remember me, even though it has been a while since I left—you know, just a few centuries ago."

"Alex, I knew you would love Africa—I just knew it because we have so much love and warmth to share. I'm so glad that you came with me."

The next morning, we rented a four-wheel drive vehicle and a driver for the duration of our stay. Our first stop was Mombassa, which was a seven-hour drive from Nairobi. Mama Eshe was expecting us and had cooked enough food to feed the whole of the island. When we arrived, she was sitting on her front porch in her favorite rocking chair in anticipation of our arrival. It was close to 5 PM when the car pulled up in front of her house. Tears swirled in my eyes as my memory flashed back to my first night at Mama Eshe's home.

"Oh my God! Mikela is here!"

From the car window, we watched her spring from her chair and stride quickly towards our car. I leaped from the car and ran into her arms.

"Thank God! My child is back! Mikela, look at you—as beautiful as always. Look at you, my child—look at what God has done for you. My dear, you look beautiful! Yes, a lovely woman you are now," Mama Eshe said, as she held me tightly in a warm embrace, releasing me now and then only to look at me before clasping me back in her arms.

Alex stood by the car and watched us until Mama Eshe smiled. "My son, please come," she said, reaching toward him.

"Mikela tells me that you are her American husband and that you are a good man."

"Yes, ma'am," Alex said respectfully, though slightly embarrassed.

Before he could say more, Mama Eshe opened up her arms, gesturing for a warm embrace; her face was radiant, beaming with a smile that could only have emanated from the depths of her soul. Then, bringing me closer as well, she started to sing, crying out, "Hallelujah! Thank you, God!"

Later, when we settled in, I told Mama Eshe the story of my childhood and circumcision. Now she finally knew about my Maasai homeland. She insisted that she would accompany Alex and me to the Tanzanian Maasailand, and I was grateful for that because I needed additional moral support as well as a guide.

The rest of that evening was filled with my stories about the years since I'd left Aunt Bela's home. There were many moments of tears and laughter as I told my stories until a little after midnight.

As Alex listened and watched us, feeling pride in his culture and heritage for the first time, he said he admired the simplicity of the culture and its peoples and their genuine love for family. Sharing what we had was automatic, no matter how little it was, he observed.

"Alex, my son, I've been too selfish already. I must release your wife, my child Mikela, to spend time with you. Please feel at home—this is your home," Mama Eshe said, interrupting Alex's thoughts.

We spent the next day sightseeing in Mombassa. Mama Eshe had arranged a tour of Mombassa for Alex as a surprise. Alex seemed to have an insatiable taste for the island and for the relics of the Old Town. First, we took a ferry to Likoni, the south side of the island, and from there through the causeway, we went to Makupa. We returned to the island to visit its famous curvy alley-roads, Fort Jesus, and the Mwembe Tayari open-air market, where I'd first met François. At intervals, Alex bargained with the merchants for lower prices and stocked his purchases of arts and crafts for his friends and relatives in his Mombassa-souvenir cotton bag. He had a few gifts to purchase because back in the United States, everyone who knew that he was traveling to Africa had asked him for a souvenir—except his father. I decided to buy his father an African textile beachwear nonetheless, which read, "Made in Kenya"—my ancestral home.

"It would be fun to see him wear that," Alex said, chuckling.

I nodded, smiling mischievously.

The Final Leg back to the Tanzanian Maasailand:

The next day, Alex and I left for the Arusha region en route to the Tanzanian Maasaiplains, and Mama Eshe gladly joined us as our faithful guide. Alex was clearly enjoying his rendezvous with Kenya. Now, he was getting a real glimpse of Africa's rural enclaves for the very first time. This was not a photo from *National Geographic* but a real-life, panoramic view of nature's excellence.

As we arrived closer to the Maasailand, he saw the *ilmurrans* herding cattle and the *entitos* doing their house chores.

I, on the other hand, was in a quiet and somber mood, meditating on the journey to my homeland. The scenic view had resurrected buried childhood memories for me. Nothing seemed to have changed, I thought. As the world was moving to higher levels of technological advancement, it seemed that the Maasailand remained in its virgin state of nature, untouched by any trends of modernization.

Perhaps our coexistent state with nature is neither good nor bad but simply our way of life, I thought.

As we approached my parents' *enkang,* the surroundings became quite familiar.

"The brain is an amazing bank of memory. It has been ten years since I've been here—how is it possible that my brain still retains familiar memories of the environment?" I thought.

I was now able to direct the driver of the car to my mother's *boma.*

The Long Awaited Moment:

When we finally arrived, my body was literally shaking. Alex held me closely in his arms and whispered, "It's okay, baby—you are home now."

As we alighted from the car, we became the spectacle of the villagers that had started to gather around us. My gaze was on my mother's *boma* when suddenly someone screamed, "Mikela! Mikela is back!"

"That's Mama Asura, the oldest wife of my father, Elimu," I whispered to Alex. She had spotted me from her *boma* where she was standing and started rushing towards us. As she ran to meet us, she opened her arms wide and launched at me with a hug that almost sent me to the ground.

"Welcome home, my daughter," Mama Asura said, her face radiating with smiles.

Asura's scream had caught everyone's attention, including my mother, who was in her *boma*. Seconds later, I saw her emerge from her hut. She had not changed very much—she'd only aged a little, with a few wrinkles around her eyes and a dark and sunken patch underneath them. She was holding hands with a little boy that was probably around seven years old. At first, she simply stared at me. Her gaze appeared bemused by all that was going on. I took a few steps towards her and stopped. I suddenly froze with emotions—I could not move or speak. I simply stared at my beautiful mother.

"Mikela?" my mother asked in a soft, tender, and shaky voice.

Speechless, I nodded and looked to my side. Mama Eshe and Alex nodded almost simultaneously, and Mama Eshe whispered, "Go, my child. It's time to make peace with your mother."

Spontaneously, my mother and I started to run towards each other. She dragged the little boy along with her. Within seconds, we were in a warm embrace, each sobbing uncontrollably and muttering, "Marahaba Enkai! Marahaba Enkai!"

For what seemed like an endless moment, we stood in a warm embrace while the rest of the village, including Alex and Mama Eshe, watched. It was like a celebration of the eternal bond between a mother and child—a precious gift of unconditional love from Enkai, the Grand Architect of nature's best.

"Welcome back home, Mikela. You look so beautiful! This is your brother, Malik. He's now nine years old. He has been my consolation. Your father is away and will be back by sunset," Mother finally said.

"Who's your company?" she asked.

"Mama, please come and meet my husband, Alex, and Mama Eshe. Mama Eshe was the guardian light that gave me a place to stay when I ran away," I responded, as I picked up my brother and held him close to my heart. He wrapped his arms around me and held me tightly, muttering, "Welcome home, sister."

My mother hugged Alex and Mama Eshe and welcomed them to the Maasailand. She invited us into her *boma*. Soon, what seemed like a barrage of people started arriving at her *boma* with gifts and warm greetings. The *enkang* had started a celebration to welcome me.

By sunset, my father returned and came to see me at my mother's *boma*. He was polite but distant. His attitude had not changed in all these years, I thought. He still appeared hard, aloof, and unexpressive of any emotions. He left shortly after he arrived, returning to his *boma* and informing my mother that he would be leaving early the next morning for a meeting in the neighboring *enkang*.

"Mikela, don't worry about your father—he'll eventually come around. He was deeply hurt when you left—he felt betrayed by you," my mother said, sensing my disappointment.

I simply smiled and nodded.

"Ma, it's fine with me—I'm not here to fight anymore. I'm very happy to see you, and I praise Enkai that you've been well all these past years. Now I know that I have a brother. Look at Malik; he's so handsome."

Malik smiled shyly, hiding his face behind my mother. My mother later told me that inside my father's *boma* he wept because for so many years, he had longed to see me to tell me how much he loved me. Now that he had finally seen me, he still couldn't tell me what he'd had in his heart for so many years.

"Enkai, I love her, just like I loved Nadia. I just don't know how to show it. I fear that I've lost my child forever," was the statement that Mama Asura said she'd heard him make in his *boma*.

I had come to terms with my father and felt no need to ask for more than he felt he could give. I had decided to accept him with love and without judgment or condemnation.

The rest of the evening was marked with celebrations and feasting. Alex had his first taste of Maasai cuisine, which sent him to the pit-toilet every hour through the rest of the evening. The soothing effect of Pepto-Bismol finally helped him to get some sleep after he'd thrown up and passed-out all the food that he'd eaten that evening.

That night, I sneaked out of the *boma* where we were to be with my mother. It was as though she knew that I was coming—she was sitting on a hide-skin mat on the floor, peaking through the door of her *boma*. She said she felt my presence before I emerged.

"Come in, Mikela," she said.

I sat by my mother who reached out for my hands and held them firmly.

"Thank you, my child. Thank you, Mikela, for coming home. I never thought that I'd ever see you again," she said.

"I'm happy to see you, too, Ma," I responded.

My mother nodded and smiled. "I'm sorry about what happened to Nadia and you. I have spent so many years of my life in agony and grief. I waited seven years after my marriage to your father to conceive Nadia and you. It was devastating to lose Nadia to death twelve years later. When you ran away, and I didn't see you for so many years, I thought that you, too, were dead. During many nights and days, all I could do was cry. No one could comfort me or give me hope for two years until I conceived your brother, Malik. He became my only source of hope to live."

I listened to my mother voice out her pain and anguish through our years of separation.

"Now, I understand what 'cleansing of a woman' can do to young girls. Please understand that I didn't know before. I always thought that it was our tradition that must be passed on from one generation to another. Since Nadia died, many more *entitos* have died in our *enkang* after the cleansing ceremony. Many mothers are still in mourning and pain. No tradition is worth a mother losing her child or a child losing her life.

"Recently, a group of people from the city—I don't really know where they come from—come to visit our *enkang* twice a week and talk to us about stopping this ritual. They show us pictures of young girls that have died or the pain they've gone through for many years after the ritual. Some of them were never able to conceive a child after marriage, while some left their husbands because they could not bear to have them touch them. These people that visit our *enkang* are good people. They bring food and clothes for our children and us. They give us money and offer to pay for our children to get an education. All they are asking us to do is to help convince the men in our village to stop the tradition.

"Your father is very upset about it. He said that those people want to destroy the Maasai tradition. I don't agree with him. He's a man and doesn't understand the pain of a young girl during and after the ritual. The women in our *enkang* have formed a group."

As my mother talked, tears of relief ran down my face. I was filled with excitement about the possibility that the mothers in the *enkang* were now rallying against female circumcision.

"The women have decided that our daughters will no longer be 'cleansed.' Asura, your stepmother, has agreed to stop performing the ritual. She said that she has seen too many *entitos* die in our *enkang*."

They had finally learned the truth—that that aspect of the Maasai tradition needed to be stopped. What a joy it was to me to learn that the work of Aisha's foundation had reached our enkang and perhaps others in the Tanzanian Maasailand, I thought.

"It has been more than six months since any *entito* has been 'cleansed,'" my mother said. "Their fathers have been upset about it, but there's nothing that they can do. We, the women, are the ones that know how to perform the ritual—the men don't. Now that we have refused to do it, no one else can. I think that we are winning the fight. We are planning to spread the good news to other neighboring *enkangs*. I want you to know that your suffering and Nadia's death inspired me to help change a tradition that I once believed in," my mother explained.

Her sincere words were soothing to my spirit and soul. The end of female circumcision, the horrific experience that had killed Nadia, was like a miracle that was unfolding right before my eyes. I placed my head on my mother's chest and sobbed, as I muttered, "Thank you, Ma. Thank you. I forgive you for everything, and I hope you can forgive me, too, for the pain that I have caused you."

"Shhhh…Shhhh…You were only a child, and you did what was best for you. If you had stayed, you would have been married to an old man here. Look at you now, my child. You are educated and have a bright future, and I know that you'll be an inspiration to your little brother, Malik. I thank Enkai for the courage that you had as a little girl and for protecting you all these years. This is not the time to cry anymore; it is a time for jubilation," my mother said, holding me in her arms and rocking me as she had when I was a little girl.

Still sniffing, I wiped away the tears that trickled down my face. A few moments later, I muttered, "Ma, you're going to be a grandmother in nine months. I'm expecting a child."

"Marahaba Enkai!" She exclaimed and held me closer to her heart, caressing my braids.

That night, I slept like a baby in my mother's arms, having finally closed the door on my life of pain, anger, horror, and fear.

CHAPTER 24

❦

A Lasting Friendship

So far, it had been quite an emotional experience—so much pain had been finally released and our spirits purged of any traces of blame. We had come to peaceful terms with the past and were simply grateful to Enkai that no one had died in the past ten years; we all lived to be able to reconcile with one another.

Alex had witnessed all the scenes as they played out; he captured every moment on film and tape. He said he'd never experienced such awesome love and could now better appreciate the saying that even death could not break the powerful bond of true and unconditional love and the expression "blood is thicker than water."

"Indeed, it is the very source of life," he remarked.

The Maasailand had instantly accepted Alex as their new son and welcomed him like a prince in the *enkang*. He said that he felt completely at home and wondered how he could have such a powerful spiritual connection with people whom he'd never met before and who were of a different culture and spoke a language that he didn't understand. Mama Túlélèi told him that he'd been drawn to the Maasailand before he was born, and soon after his birth, he had bonded to me in spirit, though he was not aware of it. I explained to Alex that Mama Túlélèi was known to make deep, spiritual insights that no one else could understand but her. While Alex may not have fully understood her words, he still embraced her love and that of my whole family.

A day after we returned to Nairobi, I managed to find Tulia through her parents' address. It was yet another memorable reunion. Alex finally met Tulia, and her husband Nashilu was just as charming.

"I'm so pleased to meet you, Mikela—I just could not wait to meet you. Tulia never forgot about you, even for one day. She prayed for you daily and always told me that someday, God would bring you back to Nairobi. I guess she was right. Here you are!"

"Yes, Nashilu, Tulia was my best friend and still is," I responded, teary-eyed. "You're very lucky to have Tulia as your wife."

"Well, thank you. Alex is lucky to have you," Nashilu graciously responded.

Alex nodded and smiled, moving closer to hold me in his arms.

"I have always known that I have a very rare gem in Mikela," he said, as he planted a kiss on my forehead.

"And I have you as my handsome and precious prince," I responded.

"Okay! Enough of that, you two love birds," Nashilu said jokingly.

"So Mikela, have you been in contact with Duboef-Duboef in Paris?" Tulia asked.

"Unfortunately, I haven't. But now that I'm here, I meant to ask you if we could visit Les Galeries des Beaux-arts de François Jacques Paquet to see Duboef-Duboef at the City Center," I responded.

"Oh! I forgot to tell you—two years ago, he closed the Nairobi office and went back to Paris. I later heard that he became sick. I never really knew what happened to him."

"I lost contact with Duboef-Duboef after François died," I said. I was deeply disappointed to hear that he was no longer in Nairobi and that I won't see him as I had hoped.

Extra Days of Fun in Nairobi:

Over the next few days, Tulia and Nashilu insisted that they would entertain Alex and me and show us new and exciting Nairobi spots.

Our mornings and afternoons were packed with sightseeing activities at the Nairobi City Center. Some evenings, we watched a movie at the 20th Century Cinema on Mama Ngina Street or a play at the Kenya National Theatre on Muranga Road. Live music was always being played at places like the African Heritage on Banda Street or the Hard Rock Cafe on Mezannine-2.

On the last evening in Nairobi, Tulia and Nashilu invited us to their beautiful mansion, which was tucked away in one of the upscale Nairobi neighborhoods. We had a lavish, eight-course meal of Kenyan and Tanzanian cuisine and drank rather impressive French wines that complimented the tasty and very spicy dinner. Alex faired quite well with the spicy food, having had enough experience sampling my dishes at home.

The next day, as we drove to Jomo Kenyatta International Airport, I stared out of the window of the car replaying the events of the past few days in my mind.

"Marahaba Enkai!" I muttered to myself as the full impact of what had just happened finally began to dawn on me. It was almost unbelievable to me that I had finally made peace with my past after all these years.

I thanked Enkai that through all the years, He had kept my mother, father, stepmothers, and stepbrothers and sisters healthy and safe. Most of all, I thanked Enkai for giving my mother my brother Malik, without whom she would have probably lost her mind.

As the flight took off, gliding into the skies, again I thought to myself, *Ma, I'll see you and Malik soon. This time, you'll be visiting me.*

CHAPTER 25

Final Absolution and Triumph

Back in suburban New York, I could feel the cleansing that had taken place in my spirit. My soul had been purged from the hurt, pain, blame, and bitterness that had lingered for so many years within me. I was free of the emotional burden of living in the past and from the physical burden of my body being maimed at an early age. But I must admit that a little anger and lack of forgiveness still lurked in one dark patch within me—I couldn't release Chege Mathani from my spirit and soul. When I thought of him, I wished that awful things would happen to his life. I still wanted him to pay for what he'd done to me.

It had been a while since Dr. Baker advised me to try to forgive Chege Mathani. Truthfully, I had tried, but somehow, I was unable to do so. I believed that Enkai wanted me to forgive Chege Mathani because he had blessed my life exceedingly and abundantly above and beyond what I could have ever imagined, despite the awful experience with Chege. Why was I holding on to what Enkai had already released me from? Daily, I wondered if I would ever be able to release this very last vestige of pain.

In the meantime, a beautiful and immaculate blessing was on its way. Alex and I were eagerly awaiting our first child—Mikela Nadia Williams—our beautiful Maasai-American baby who was eagerly positioning herself downward in my womb in preparation for her final exit and arrival into our beautiful world. Perhaps her arrival would be my final absolution from Chege Mathani and my triumph over the pain that he had caused me for so many years.

April 1989:

In early April 1989, I was in the Rhode Island hospital where I'd been in labor for almost fourteen hours. Finally, the baby was ready to be delivered.

"Push, Mikela! Just a little bit more. We're almost there," my doctor said.

I was writhing in pain with my teeth clenched and my face drenched in perspiration. My braided hair was in total disarray. Alex stood by my side, his hands clenched in between my fist as he caressed and comforted me. Shortly, he had a chance to peek at what was happening at the other end and saw our baby's little head bulging through the birth canal—a miraculous view, he later claimed.

I let out a loud scream as I attempted a final push, forcing veins to bulge out on my forehead and neck.

"Here we go. She's out," the doctor said, carrying a tiny little angel in his hands after the umbilical cord was quickly snipped.

"You have a beautiful baby girl, Mrs. Williams. Congratulations!" the doctor said.

I felt instant relief and joy, and I started to laugh and cry at the same time. Tears of joy and happiness rolled down my face as Alex hugged and kissed me.

"We have a beautiful baby girl, Alex. Can you believe that? She's all ours, and no one will ever hurt her," I cried.

Equally overwhelmed by emotions, tears of joy trickled down Alex's face.

"Thank you, Mikela, for giving me a beautiful baby girl. Thank you, my love."

A few minutes later, a nurse held our baby, now clean and wrapped neatly in a soft, white sheet.

"Mrs. Williams, would you like to hold your baby girl?"

I nodded, spread out my hands, and took our baby from the nurse.

"She's so beautiful," Alex said.

"Yes, she is, honey," I responded. "Welcome, Mikela Nadia Williams Junior. Welcome to Mom and Dad. Mommy promises you that no one's ever going to hurt you, my angel."

I was at peace with the past and present, hopeful that the future had more blessings for her and our family. As I had hoped, the arrival of Mikela Nadia Williams became my final absolution and triumph from the horror of circumcision and the violence of rape. The emotional scars of my past were no more. Mikela Nadia Williams was my consolation for Nadia—I knew that she'd never experience the horror of female circumcision.

Looking up towards the ceiling of the hospital, not caring who was there and watching, I held up Mikela Nadia Williams and shouted, "Marahaba Enkai! Thank you God!"

April 1990—One Year Later:

One Saturday morning after breakfast, one year after Mikela Nadia was born, I found myself drifting off to sleep in our sunroom, reading a book on gardening. Once more, I found myself in my usual dream world.

I was seated next to Nadia in the lush grassland of the open plains of the Maasailand. We were both adorned with beautiful Maasai necklaces and amulets. It was early, and the glittery rays of the rising sun had occupied the eastern horizon of the Maasaiplains. The air was refreshing as cold, western winds shifted eastward over the plains. Flocking birds seemed to be singing a supersonic rhetoric that rhymed in audible lyrics. Nadia's face was glowing in the daylight, filled with smiles.

"Mikela, let's do the circling game one more time," Nadia said.

The skies swiveled around us as we circled, moving faster and faster until we both seemed to lose our balance and finally slumped to the grass. Then, suddenly, Nadia started to laugh, and I joined her.

"It's been a long journey for you, Mikela, but it's now over. Greater things are still coming your way," Nadia finally said.

When the laughter died out, Nadia vanished.

"Nadia! Nadia! Where are you?" I screamed.

"Mikela look! I'm right here," she said, appearing again for a moment. "But I'm leaving now for a very long time. Everything is fine now, and you're okay, Mikela." Nadia waved, fading quickly into the distance in her ethereal white, flowing gown. Finally, she vanished into thin air.

"Nadia! Nadia! Please come back. I love you," I pleaded.

Alex must have walked into the room at that point and heard me calling for Nadia. He'd just come back from the gas station, where he'd gone to buy the daily newspaper.

"Honey, wake up—you're dreaming again. Here, I have something to show you," he said, gently shaking my shoulders to wake me.

I opened my eyes and let out a gentle sigh.

"Honey, I just picked up today's paper. You won't believe what's on the front page."

"What?" I asked, still drowsy.

He handed me the newspaper, and there was the incredible news.

> The Kenyan Ambassador to the United Nations, Mr. Chege Mathani, tendered his resignation today. This was following an alleged rape accusation by Ms. Aisha Mohammed, a human civil rights activist. She'd known Mr. Mathani for a little over a year. This is following another set of accusations of sexual harassment a few months ago by his secretary, Alice Young. This breaking news has shocked the international community in light of Mr. Chege Mathani's recent nomination, amongst other distinguished candidates, for the position of Secretary General of the United Nations and the high speculation that he was the man for the job.

Suddenly, Tulia's words from many years back rushed into my thoughts.

"Mikela, God will make him pay one day. Believe me, God will make him pay dearly, no matter how many years it takes."

"Yes, Tulia, I knew Enkai would take care of him—I just knew it!" I suddenly exclaimed.

"Honey, you're right. Chege Mathani has finally dug his own grave," Alex echoed.

Little Mikela's cry interrupted the moment. Her voice could be heard through the baby monitor, and Alex quickly said, "I'll get her, honey!"

As he stepped out of the room, I stood up and raised the Saturday paper towards the roof.

"Marahaba Enkai!" My journey of hurt and pain had finally ended.

__The End__

Postscript from the Memoirs:

So, now you, too, know my story. It was for you to see how the challenges that I faced in my life became the stepping-stones of my triumph—how yesterday's pain transformed into tomorrow's strength and became a pillar of hope for others.

Who would have thought that I, Mikela, a simple Maasai entito would become a voice of strength and hope for others? It's the power of Enkai in all of us that fuels our faith to continue even when all odds seem to be stacked against us. It's our faith within us, and the strength we draw from within and others, that pulls us through life's adversities. Mikela is a story of triumph for you to remember always. Marahaba Enkai!

"People grow through experience if they meet life honestly and courageously. This is how character is built."

Eleanor Roosevelt (1884–1962)
United Nations Diplomat, humanitarian, and wife of U.S. President Franklin D. Roosevelt

About the Author

Jacyee Aniagolu was born in Africa and now resides in Laurel, Maryland. She holds a doctorate degree in Microbiology. *Mikela* is her first published fiction work and was inspired by her cultural and medical knowledge of female circumcision, and the human devastation being caused by prostitution and HIV in Africa.

0-595-30677-2